Michael Riley's work of fiction creates suspense from the opening chapter. Not just another "cop story" with a linear rollout of incident after incident, but The Long Last Out is a very methodically written mystery novel. His many years in law-enforcement provide him the insight to bring to life the lives of his characters as he builds the plot. Every detail laid out in each chapter has importance. Pay attention going from page to page as he draws you, the reader, into the story.

Inspector Tom Cooney Jr., (ret.)
Philadelphia Police Department
Police Commander, Police Science Educator,
Published Author

The
Long
Last Out

The Long Last Out

By
Michael E. Riley

LIBERTY HILL PUBLISHING

Liberty Hill Press
2301 Lucien Way #415
Maitland, FL 32751
407.339.4217
www.libertyhillpublishing.com

Printed in the United States of America.

Library of Congress Control Number: 2021901679

Paperback ISBN-13: 978-1-6628-0780-0
Ebook ISBN-13: 978-1-6628-0781-7

Dedicated to my grandchildren Richard, Josephine, and Michael,
they inspired me to keep on writing.

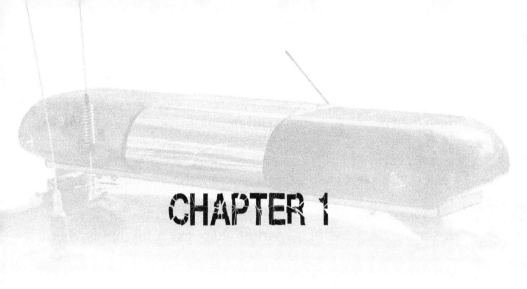

CHAPTER 1

Zurich, Switzerland — 1959

LIKE LEMONS SMOLDERING IN A pit, chlorine tinged the enclosed clammy environment. The acrid taste tinted his tongue and teared his eyes as he barefooted into the immense space. Two hands clenched a fifteen-kilo dumbbell at knee height, and with shuffling steps, he hunched and hurried to his perch. The water rippled at his feet as he gulped air to the brink of hyperventilation. Seconds before stepping off into the murk, he riveted his gaze into the five-meter depth and wished for an abyss.

On a warm summer night, a young janitor glanced up from his task and spotted a ghostly shape at the far side of the darkened indoor pool.

"Sven, someone is in here."

The older cleaner looked up and recognized the intruder.

"Wait, shhh," he warned with an index finger raised to his lips, "move into the darkness — just watch."

They stepped back into the shadows and witnessed the diminutive figure plunge into the deep end of the pool. Sven took notice of the overhead clock.

"Eleven-oh-two," he called out.

"Sven, he will drown."

"Wait."

Like a stone, he sank until his feet rested on the tiled surface. Flat-footed, he stood clutching the weight that secured him in place. As he held his breath, his open eyes fixated on the flickering light fragmenting through the water.

Friends are a waste of time — you must concentrate on your work — you are gifted —you are the best.

The words of his parents replayed again and again in his mind, along with a swirl of chemical compounds, theories, hypotheses, images of bacteria, virus, spirals of molecular shapes all thrashing and squirming for a chance at life, and Isabella.

But, I love her, mother.

There is no time for such things — greatness is your destiny — time is only for your field of study — your body of work, his mother's voice echoed in his mind.

His memory was a kaleidoscope of visions and the sadness he felt while gazing through the windows of his youth, yearning to play with other children. The fluorescence of asylums with the restraints, medications, therapies, and screams, both his and others, shrieked through his soul. The warm water wrapped him and slowed the never-ending loop of noise. Longing to linger in that weepy refuge forever, the fire in his chest fractured the trance. Life won out as he dropped the hand-held anchor, explosively exhaled, and pushed off. Through a boil of bubbles, he rose and punctured the surface, passing from one element into another. He drew in a loud labored breath, swam to the edge, and climbed the ladder. The watery interlude muffled the babel only for a moment.

"Doctor. Five minutes and fifty-two seconds. That is a record!" the janitor announced.

Climbing the ladder, his dripping head tilted in the direction of the voice, squinting he absorbed the words. The corner of his mouth curled as he scrambled to the exit, slid through and was gone.

A quizzical expression spread across the young janitor's face as he turned to Sven.

"Who was that?"

"He is a researcher here at the university; he is brilliant but very withdrawn, a tortured soul."

"Why does he do that?"

"I would imagine — to escape his thoughts."

"Have you ever spoken to him?"

"Except for announcing his time duration underwater, never. Over the years, whenever my wife bakes, I leave portions of 'birnbrot' inside his laboratory."

"You have been in his lab?"

"Yes, but not when he's there. I go in not to invade his space, but perhaps to know him. He possesses nothing but his research, his magical work."

"What kind of magical work? What does he do? Sven, can you show me?"

The older man glowered and cautioned while towering over his young colleague, "You understand he is eccentric, but he is not a carnival freak, and I will not allow anyone to disrespect him."

"I respect you, and I will respect him. I merely wish to learn."

The hulking janitor lowered his head, stooped, and swished his mop over the tiled floor, returning to his duties. The other stood watching him, silently pleading.

Without looking up, he muttered, "Maybe later, when he leaves."

The hours passed, and the workers made their rounds. When they were about to take their lunch, Sven spotted a door close at the end of the long hallway. With a hurried step, he moved towards the exit knowing the doctor finished his work for the night. Through the door glass, Sven recognized the frail figure shuffling down the walkway to a small residential cottage. A wave of the hand brought the young co-worker his way as he turned and faced the lab door. From a substantial key ring, he selected the right one and inserted it into the lock.

"You have a key to his laboratory?"

"I have been working here for twenty years," Sven remarked as the tumbler disengaged, "I have a key to everything."

Without hurry, he swung the door open and emphasized, "Do not touch anything, keep your hands in your pockets, and must I warn you never to speak of this."

"I swear to you, Sven."

Upon entering, they took in the surroundings of a windowless rectangular room measuring six by nine meters. They wandered through a maze of tables containing an assortment of test-tubes, microscopes, culture dishes, and other unknown instruments and equipment. Along a side wall, they marveled upon a glass sculpture of tubes and piping emptying their contents into beakers and jars. A mixture of odors advanced and receded as they moved about the room. The young janitor noticed reflections of light dancing on the walls and ceilings. Curious to determine the source, he scanned to the other side, spotting three long aquariums capped with lights illuminating the contents.

"Sven, what is this?"

"Look, don't touch."

The first contained fish of various shapes and sizes; he stooped and watched their mesmerizing motion. Side-stepping to the second, he stared in when suddenly he let out a small yelp and back-pedaled as a tentacle life form lunged, stopped only by the glass.

"Did he frighten you?" he teased with a chuckle.

"No, when I visited Italy, we would eat these creatures."

Moving to the third tank, the delicate dance of jellyfish delighted him as they sank and rose again. After moments of study, he turned to Sven with a question.

"So, where is his magic work?"

Tight-lipped and with heavy-lidded eyes, the older janitor rubbed his chin for a moment, considering an answer.

"Follow me."

A short walk to the rear of the room brought them to a steel door. Sven reached for the handle and swung it open.

Chapter 1

Overhead bulbs shone from inside, and a humid barnyard stench steamed through the doorway.

"Whew, what's in here?" the young man let out as he turned his head and held his nose.

"See for yourself."

He stepped into the large room, but instead of lab equipment, the space housed wooden stalls, each occupied with many small pot-bellied pigs no larger than a dog. Some were sleeping while others were rooting through the enclosures. Expecting to witness some cryptic creature, he was disappointed.

After walking the entire room and examining all the animals, he faced Sven with palms up and queried, "So, where's the magic?"

The older man stood still in the doorway, his lips curled into a sly grin, and without hurry, he extended his hand to the light switch. To build the drama, he hesitated, then flicked it off. When the lights faded and the young janitor's eyes adjusted, he detected the small, portly animals moving within the darkness, emitting a — *luminous blue glow.*

CHAPTER 2

Philadelphia, Pennsylvania — 1982

L ITTER AND TRASH SPECKLED THE cinder field of
the city playground. The only beauty was a discarded
plastic bag dancing with the wind on that chilly and cheerless
winter afternoon in South Philadelphia. A dirty and dented
police vehicle sat idling, rattling, and belching exhaust at
Fifth Street and Washington Avenue. Parked on the southeast corner of the intersection facing the Southwark high-
rise housing projects was Emergency Patrol Wagon-301.
Two officers occupied the van.

In the passenger seat, a young rookie officer sat ramrod
straight in his out of the box uniform leather coat still shined
and stiff. The garment surrounded him like a tortoiseshell,
and with his thin neck and short haircut, he somewhat
resembled a turtle. Three days prior, he graduated from
the Philadelphia Police Academy, and on that day, Monday,
January 18, 1982, was his first day on patrol.

"Hey kid, we gotta put some meat on your bones," the
older cop cracked from the driver's side, "you need a large
plate of macaroni."

Overwhelmed with the new strange surroundings,
Officer Nick Avner perched on the edge of the seat, bouncing
one knee up and down in no particular rhythm. He sipped

from a Styrofoam cup, not wanting to splash anything on his new uniform.

"Sir, I — I used to be heavier; all that — that running in 'PT' class took the pounds off," he stammered, trying to offer an answer.

"Relax, kid, you shoulda got a couple of donuts with that coffee," the senior cop retorted with a grin as he gave him a side-way glance, "Don't worry, you'll be fat and happy like the rest of us mutts in no time."

Unsure of how to respond, he let out a nervous laugh. Trying to loosen up and careful not to spill the hot drink, he slid back into the seat and took another sip.

"Hey kid, you don't have to call me sir either; you ain't in the academy anymore. The name's Tommy or Tabbs to my friends and associates."

The driver of 301-Wagon Thomas Patrick Tabbozzi, a fifteen-year veteran officer, was twice the age of his new partner. He looked forward to training him and was amused at his anxiety. He liked the young officer's respect, not a wise-guy like some rookies, and sensed from him the impression of being intelligent.

He'll probably be easy to train, he thought to himself, sizing up the recruit.

Tommy was a street-smart cop with the kind of personality where five minutes after you met him, he made you feel like you've known him all your life.

In an attempt to put him at ease, he asked, "Where you from, kid — where'd you go to school?"

"Grew up in Mayfair, went to Holy Ghost."

"Whoa, a preppy. I guess you're a college boy. Huh?

"Yeah, I got a degree in accounting from Temple. I made varsity baseball there too," he revealed, getting more comfortable.

"I played a little football back in the day. The Eagles are my team. My mom would take my sister and me to a lot of the games," Tommy disclosed.

"Your mom took you? What your dad wasn't around? Oh, man, I'm sorry I — I shouldn't have asked," Nick apologized, as he realized he might be out of line.

Tommy sat with his back wedged between the seat and window, studying the rookie, something about him he liked. With a slight grin, he decided to answer.

"No, he was around, and he was a good guy too. I'm a first-generation American. My old man's Italian, and my mom is Irish. They practically met and married as they both stepped off the boat."

"That sounds nice," Avner responded, not knowing what to say.

"Yeah, well, my dad was a chef at a fancy restaurant down-town, and my mom loved football. So, I was raised with a healthy dose of cook, eat, and be merry. It all worked out."

Out of the corner of his eye, Tommy spotted movement. A hunched figure dressed in multiple layers of mismatched clothes shuffled to the side of the truck as the cop turned to face the advancing person.

"Artie, why ain't you up at the shelter? Too cold to be outside today."

"Officer Tabbs, you know how it is; I just had to get out, grab me some fresh air and maybe a little anti-freeze," the man explained, looking up with a toothless grin, "Think you could spot me a couple of bucks?"

"That wine's no good for you, Artie."

"I know, you're right, you're right," he replied while nod-ding and gazing down at his feet.

Tight-lipped and shaking his head, Tommy sized him up. He let out a sigh, reached into his front pants pocket, and pulled out some bills. Peeling off a five-dollar note, he handed it out the window to the forlorn street person.

"God bless you, Officer Tabbs — I really appreciate it." he declared as he snatched the money, turned, and was about to walk away. The cop called him back.

"Artie, wait. You might get a little taste with that," Tommy instructed as he produced another five out the window, "but with this nickel, you're gonna buy some food. You go over to Molly's sandwich shop and have her make you up a hoagie. You understand I'm gonna check later and make sure you did it."

Reluctant to take the money with the new conditions, he swayed back and forth, staring at the cash.

"Okay, Officer Tabbs, I'll do it, I promise," with a grime caked hand, he gripped the bill, lowered his head, turned, and shuffled away.

The rookie sat wide-eyed and silent, watching the interaction play out and all the while thinking back to his academy days, trying to remember a class on that type of scenario. Tommy faced him and detected his questioning expression.

"Listen, kid, street lesson number one. Always treat people decent; you never know when you might need their help."

Nick absorbed the newfound knowledge feeling lucky of his assignment to the veteran officer sensing he would learn many things from him. Tommy shook a cigarette out from the pack resting on the middle console and lit up. While exhaling, he grabbed his cup and gulped a mouthful.

He squinted at the rookie through a haze of smoke and asked, "Hey kid. I ever tell you the horse story?"

CHAPTER 3

WITHIN THE DEPARTMENT, TOMMY HAD made the rounds: uniform assignments, Narcotics Unit, Anti-Crime Team, and back to patrol. He was always able to find the humor in most situations, and the amusing way he told a tale in his South Philly accent made a listener eager to hear more.

"What's the horse story?" Nick asked with a curious grin.

Upon seeing his young partner's interest, he decided to tell him.

After gulping coffee, he started, "I'm working Narcotics Unit up in East Division; we got a search warrant for a house, the guy inside is selling heroin. We head out to the staging area."

Curious, Nick asked, "What happened then?"

"We're calling Radio for a marked unit, you know, for a uniform presence."

Engrossed, Avner sat silent and wide-eyed.

"In the middle of the summer late afternoon, and in the Twenty-Fifth District, ain't no units available. The radio's 'jumpin', the guys are running from one job to another. Hey kid, they don't call it the 'badlands' for nothing."

He chuckled and nodded his head in agreement, unaware of the history behind the badlands.

"Out of nowhere, a mounted cop shows up who heard us on the radio and trotted over from his beat in Hunting Park to back us up.'"

"A mounted cop?"

"Yeah, so down the street we go. We're at the house, we knock on the door, and announce. A voice from inside yells out, 'Come on in, the doors open.' So, in we go, and in the living room is one wiry lookin' dude, black hair slicked back with about ten gold chains around his neck, sitting on a couch smoking a cigarette."

With that thought in mind, Tommy pulled a long drag, and exhaled as he continued.

"Now he ain't upset or nothing. It's like he knew we were coming. We tell him we gotta search the house, and he just smiles and tells us, 'Man, you can check anywhere you want. You ain't gonna find no dope in here.'

"Now, me and my partner eyeball the living room and notice everything is brand new...new deep shag rugs, furniture, wallpaper, TV, stereo, the rest of the neighborhood was a war-zone, but this place was a palace. The guy's either dealing drugs or he's got a great paper route."

Nick chuckled while listening with intense interest as Tommy resumed the story after he flicked his cigarette out the window and took a giant chomp out of his powdered donut. The crumbs and loose sugar snowed down the front of his old and crinkled leather patrol coat, settling into the various cracks and crevices of the thick heavy garment with no effect at all on his train of thought.

"So, the squad all comes back into the living room, and they report the rest of the house is clear and secure. So, I say to this guy, 'where's the dope?' and he starts gettin' real cocky and hollers, 'I told you, man, ain't none in here, you can search anywhere you want!' So I glance at my partner, and right away, we both figured out what happened."

"What happened?"

"We got wired.'"

"Wired — what's that?"

"That's where one of the less than honorable civilian workers at the Round House courtroom gets a glimpse of your warrant and recognizes the location as one of their friendly neighborhood dope dealers. If they drop a dime and warn him, the dealer will slide them a 'note' later on."

"A note?"

"You know, a note, money — a twenty, fifty dollar note, whatever."

"Oh."

"We figure, he cleaned it out, so we decide to mess with this guy a little. I say to him, 'so you're telling us we ain't gonna find no dope, right?' That means you hid it real good. How about we bring an animal in here to sniff around?' He gets super excited like he knows for sure that we ain't gonna find nothing, and he yells out, 'Man, you can bring in any kind of animal you want, ain't gonna find no dope in here.'

"So, I say okay. I turn and whistle out the front door. The mounted cop hears the signal and rides ole Seabiscuit right up the front steps and into the living room. The wiry dude jumps up and stutters, "What the hell is that?"

"I tell him, 'That's our sniffer."

Wide-eyed and mouth agape, Nick hung on every word.

"The mounted cop is swinging the south end of that horse all over the place like he's sniffin' the whole room. The wiry dude is freaking out and yelling, 'What's he doin'? What's he doin'?' I tell him, he's sniffin.'"

Nick was now laughing out loud while Tommy continued.

"All of a sudden, there's creaking and cracking sounds under our feet, and we freak out because in an instant we're all thinking, 'how we gonna explain this to the captain if the horse falls through the floor.' So, we get him out the door and tell the dude he was right; the animal didn't sniff nothing. He's all happy now that we're leaving, and as we're running down the street, he's shouting down to us, 'I told you – that horse wasn't gonna find no dope in this house.'

When we got back to the staging area, we're all laughing our asses off. He mighta beat us that time, but two weeks later, Highway Patrol stops him and finds a half a key of heroin."

Smiling and shaking his head in disbelief, Nick remarked, "No way, you didn't actually bring a horse in the house. Did you?"

Tommy replied with a grin, "Yeah, we did."

In a solemn tone, he added. "Lesson number two, every now and then, try to have a little fun on this job, 'cause you're gonna see a lot of tragedy along the way."

Nick nodded in understanding and pondered the point. The older cop finished the last of his coffee while he glanced at the rookie. He took an instant liking to the kid, and although he was reluctant at first with the assignment of training officer, he was now glad he accepted.

CHAPTER 4

THE LAUGHTER SUBSIDED AS THEY sat back in the old wagon's bucket seats and scanned the area through the cracked and smeared windshield. Nick glanced out of the passenger side and peered down at the concrete sidewalk. The windows in a police vehicle were always open with the heat blasting in the winter.

"Leave the window down, kid. You never know what you might hear," was one of the first things the rookie learned at the beginning of the shift.

It happened over several seconds in real-time, but in the young cop's mind, they passed in slow motion. The concrete sidewalk was mysteriously chipping with sparks of dust rising into the air. The strange phenomenon was progressing closer to the wagon with each blast. Tommy, sitting in the driver's seat, couldn't see it due to the angle, but he heard the popping sounds.

Annoyed, he commented, "Them friggin' kids are throwing firecrackers again."

In an instant, the radio came alive with the alert tones as the dispatcher blared an anxious message.

"In the Third District...Fifth and Washington...report of gunshots...in the Third district...Fifth and Washington... report of gunshots...all units use caution Housing Authority Police on the scene."

The senior officer spotted a Housing Authority cop across Washington Avenue standing under the overhang of the first high rise building waving his arms frantically in the direction of 301-Wagon.

Instinctively, Tommy jammed the gear shift into drive and crushed the gas pedal to the floor. The truck screeched forward from the parking space straight through the intersection across Washington Avenue, narrowly missing cross traffic. When they arrived, the wagon hopped the curb, went airborne, and landed on the small driveway of the high-rise. He slammed on the brakes while turning the wheel hard to the left, causing the wagon's rear end to slide sideways under the building's overhang. In a cloud of smoke and dust, it came to rest about three feet from the wall. He rammed the gear shift up into park, turned off the engine, and pulled the keys.

"Stay right behind me, kid," he shouted as they hopped out of the truck.

At the rear of the vehicle, an older Housing Authority cop yelled, "On the twelfth floor! On the twelfth floor!"

Tommy grilled him. "How do you know?"

Breathless, he replied, "I was across Fifth Street facing the side of the projects — heard the first shot, looked up, seen the rifle barrel sticking out. I saw it was right above the porch with the clothes hanging on the line, in the corner of the building, I counted down twelve in the front."

Constructed from concrete and steel, the high-rise units of the Southwark Housing Projects had a commanding view of the Delaware River and the surrounding area. They were depressing and dingy, with the occupants and visitors eroding the structures over the years. The only products of that crime factory were drugs and violence. Tommy ran to the cab of the wagon, pulled out the microphone, and transmitted.

"Priority...Three-oh-one to Radio...flash information Fifth and Washington...from Housing Police... shots coming from a twelfth floor south side apartment...advise all units to approach the building from the north side only... shots fired at police possibly with a rifle...start Stakeout in...no injuries reported at this time."

In 1964 the City of Philadelphia established the first Special Weapons and Tactics team or "SWAT," and the police department referred to that resource as the Stakeout Unit.

The wail of sirens in the distance was getting closer. The first of the back-up units responded, coming southbound on Fifth Street against the one-way northbound traffic.

Tommy told Nick, "Stay close; we're going in and up, gonna see if we can catch this sucker."

Nick's heart was racing. A few minutes ago, while sitting in the wagon sipping coffee and listening to Tommy's story, a satisfying thought ran through him. *There is no other place I want to be and no other job I want to do.*

Out of nowhere, reality smacked him right in the face. That's when the "universal cop question" popped into his mind.

What the hell am I doing here?

His breathing was quick and shallow, with his eyes darting in all directions. Tommy recognized the signs and clapped his hands in front of his face as he yelled, "Look at me, look at me."

He focused and stared straight into his eyes.

With a reassuring tone, he instructed, "Just do what I tell you and stay close, okay?"

With a nervous nod, Nick replied, "Okay."

They ran into the building, arrived at the open elevator doors, and entered. The rookie turned and, without thinking, tapped twelve. Tommy stepped forward, reached past him, hit eleven, and mentioned, "Just in case he decides to meet us when the doors open."

"Oh yeah."

The elevator stopped, and Tommy ordered, "Un-holster your weapon, keep your finger off the trigger, stay low, we check up and down the hall before we move out. We'll go up to the next floor through the fire escape stairs, and we look before we go in. Understand?"

Nick licked his lips, and with a nervous nod, he answered, "Yes."

The doors opened, they dropped to one knee, and Tommy peered out past his partner into the corridor with Nick emulating the posture on the other side of the door.

Tommy whispered, "Clear."

The rookie focused, making sure the space was unoccupied and responded, "Clear."

They quick-stepped down the dark and grimy passageway to the fire escape door. Checking the stairway, the officers entered and snaked their way through piles of accumulated trash. Arriving at the corner of the hall, the sound of a door opening in the adjoining corridor echoed off the plaster walls. Tommy snuck a quick peek and observed a small individual coming out of an apartment, carrying what appeared to be a rifle and walking away from the officers.

Tommy hurried around the corner and yelled, "Police — stay where you are."

Upon hearing the command, the person dropped the object and started to run. They pursued when halfway down the hallway, Tommy's right shoe came to rest in a substance with the consistency of mud and the fluidity of motor oil, causing his foot to slide forward and up into the air. His two hundred and twenty-five-pound frame landed on his back with the sound of a dead fish slapped on the kitchen counter. Laying there stunned, he glimpsed a dark shadow leaping past him. He tilted his head off the floor, caught sight of his young partner racing down the hall, and pouncing on the slight figure like a cat on a mouse.

"Stop! Stop! Put your hands on the wall! Now! Now!"

Tommy got back on his feet and came up behind the pair yelling along the way, "Cuff him! Cuff him!"

Nick's heart was pounding, and his hands were sweaty as he fumbled for his handcuffs and in a clumsy manner managed to click them on the male's wrists. Tommy searched the suspect and found three .22 LR caliber rounds in his right front pocket. Going back down the hall, he retrieved the object, a .22 caliber old target rifle. Returning; he noticed the young male didn't reach five feet in height. A closer inspection of his face revealed a juvenile not more than twelve years old. The young boy was shaking, almost as much as Nick.

Tommy looked at the youngster, turned to his new partner, and with a grin on his face, declared, "Nice pinch."

The sounds of footsteps and equipment rattling down the hall indicated the arrival of the Stakeout Unit. Tommy yelled out to the arriving officers, "Stakeout, down here, we have one in custody."

He pointed out the apartment where the young male exited as the tactical unit sergeant ordered the district officers to take the suspect down to the wagon until they searched and cleared the scene. They escorted the youngster to the elevator, and after checking the weapon was unloaded, Tommy presented it to Nick, proclaiming, "Here kid, this is your pinch, you carry it out."

The rookie gazed at the rifle like it was the Heisman Trophy, and then with an ear to ear grin, clutched the firearm. On their way down, the Stakeout sergeant informed Radio that a suspect was in custody, and officers recovered a weapon. When they arrived, due to the nature of the call, "shots fired at police," almost every car and wagon from the district responded to the scene. The other cops approached and started calling out, "Yo, Tommy Tabbs. Whatta ya got?"

Like a father whose son just hit his first home run, he replied with pride in his voice, "The rook made the pinch on his own."

After Nick placed the suspect in the back of the wagon, they all gathered around, shook his hand, slapped his back, and cracked jokes.

"Hey kid, a half a shooter is still better than none."

One of the back-up officers' stepped forward, stood between Tommy and Nick, and announced, "Kid, you're going to be Commissioner one day. Just think, your first day on the street, you're working the wagon with Tommy Tabbs, and you make a gun pinch. It don't get no better than that."

CHAPTER 5

NICK, WITH A SLIGHT SMILE, stood rigid, holding the rifle, a little overwhelmed with the attention displayed by the veteran officers on his first day working the street.

Tommy recognized that he was unsure what to do next, "Alright crime fighter, department regulations, you gotta ride in the back with juvenile transports. Gotta put your service revolver upfront. Sit by the doors, make sure he doesn't bounce around in there. I'll check on you through the slider."

The Philadelphia Police Department, in addition to the Radio Patrol Cars, utilized Ford Econoline vans designated as Emergency Patrol Wagons, staffed by two officers at all times.

Nick handed Tommy the firearms, who placed both weapons inside the cab portion. After getting behind the wheel, Tommy quizzed the young suspect through the small opening in the bulkhead, "What's your name? How old are you?"

The youngster answered, "Tyrell Fisher, and I'll be thirteen in June."

Tommy pointed out with a chuckle, "So you're twelve."

His shoulders slumped, he gazed downward, and with a sigh, he responded, "Yeah, I guess so."

With the engine started, he guided the vehicle west on Washington Avenue, advising radio they were in-route to South Detectives with one juvenile suspect. On the trip, the gravity of the situation suddenly hit the boy, and with tears and a trembling chin, he blurted out, "I wasn't shooting at you guys; I – I was trying to hit the playground signboard."

Upon hearing that outburst, Tommy responded, "You telling us you were aiming at the sign on the fence?"

"Yeah, I swear I had it right in my sights. I don't know what happened."

"Don't bullshit us, kid, that was a good twenty-five to thirty yards away, and besides, what makes you think that target shooting anything from the twelfth floor in the city was okay to do?"

At the next red light, Tommy picked up the firearm and inspected the weapon. He detected a bent and damaged front fore-sight, the possible cause for the shots going wide.

"My uncle taught me to shoot on his farm in Jersey, he was a Marine, and he told me the best shot you can take was from the high ground."

"Did he give you the rifle?"

"No, and he's gonna be real mad. He left his gun at my mom's place, so he could take it and get it fixed. He said not to touch it. He didn't leave no bullets, but my friend Donnell found some at his cousin's house, and he showed them to me at the playground."

"Did he give them to you?"

Tyrell explained, "Not exactly, he was just showing them to me, then his mom came around looking for him — and he quick hands them to me and said 'hide these,' then she took Donnell home."

"What happened after that?"

"I went home, and the bullets fit into the gun... so I figured I would target shoot."

"Where's your uncle at now?"

"He's in the navy hospital."

"Where? What's he in there for?"

"He's getting a new wooden leg. His real one got blown off in Viet Nam, and they gotta give him a new one 'cause he wore down the first one they gave him."

Slowing down, he pulled over to the curb and stopped. He put the vehicle in park, got out, went to the back doors, and opened them to address the kid face to face.

"You said he was a Marine, is that right?"

"Yeah, he was a hero in the war, he saved a bunch of soldiers, and he got a medal and everything."

"What's your uncle's name?"

Nick witnessed the exchange in silence and detected Tommy's face turning a pale gray with beads of sweat forming on his brow.

With a nervous feeling, Nick whispered, "Tommy, are you alright?"

"What's your uncle's name?" Tabbozzi asked again in a low, firm voice.

The kid raised his head, stared him straight in the eye, and answered, "Gunnery Sergeant Carl Hutchens... United States Marine Corps."

Upon hearing the name, he stumbled backward. Nick exited and grabbed his arm to steady him as he shouted, "Tommy, what's going on? What's wrong?"

After a minute or two of silence, while staring out into the distance, Tommy disclosed in a hushed tone, "I was one of the guys he saved."

Unsure of what to say, he whispered, "What happened?"

Tight-lipped and with a deadpan voice, he recounted an unforgettable event of his life.

"We were shot up pretty bad in a ditch, losing blood. 'Charley' coming at us, the position getting over-run, down to one magazine, then out of ammo, thought I was dead. Out of nowhere, through the smoke and dust, this giant appears behind us. He's got an M-Sixty and starts spraying the incoming VC. It had to be fifteen-twenty of them. One of them throws a grenade; it lands on the downhill side of him. The shrapnel gets him below his knee; he fires the 'sixty' takin' out the last of them. Right before I pass out, I see he's bleeding. I see him pull out a roll of duct tape from an ammo pouch and watch as he puts a layer around his leg."

22

He paused as the painful scene played out in his memory and then continued.

"I go unconscious, two days later I wake up in a Mash unit, I come to find out that Marine I saw on the battlefield was Gunnery Sergeant Carl Hutchens. It turns out he carried me and another wounded soldier about a half-mile to a rear Evac LZ.

"I never got to thank him; the Army shipped me out to a hospital in Hawaii. We heard stories he was MIA for a while. I lost touch with him, but I found out he was awarded the Silver Star for that day. I didn't know he was from the Philly area."

The youngster, never hearing the full account before, sat unblinking, frozen with awe as he listened to every word spoken. Tommy turned to him and spotted tears of pride streaming down his face. He faced Tommy with his shoulders back and chin held high as he proclaimed, "I told you my uncle was a hero."

Pondering the youngster's words, he replied in a quiet and reverent tone, "He sure is, kid, he sure is."

After a moment of reflection, Tommy snapped out of it, faced Nick, and ordered, "Take the cuffs off him. I gotta call in some favors."

CHAPTER 6

E MERGENCY PATROL WAGON-301 PULLED INTO
the parking lot with the springs squeaking and the
brakes grinding. An old worn-out brick building housed
the 1st Police District and the headquarters of the South
Detective Division. Tommy parked, got out, walked to the
rear doors, and when he opened them, Nick was ready
to step out.

Before the youngster left the wagon, Tabbozzi informed
him, "Okay, kid, this is what we have to do, we gotta take
you up to the detectives, and a Juvenile Aid officer is going
to talk to you."

"Am I goin' to jail? Am I goin' to jail? I ain't never been
locked up before," the youngster cried out.

"Listen, kid; just do what I tell you. If you're telling me the
truth about shooting at the sign, and if Gunnery Sergeant
Hutchens is your uncle, I'm going to try to get you out of this
mess. Do you understand what I'm saying to you?"

The kid was sweating, wringing his hands, and with a
terrified look, he scanned the inside of the truck.

A loud clap from the veteran cop grabbed his attention,
"Kid, look at me."

The slapping sound and the sternness of his voice caused
the youngster to face him.

Low and intense, he repeated the question. "Do you
understand?"

Calming down, he shook his head and answered, "Yes."

Chapter 6

They escorted him up to the Detective Division, and as they entered, they saw sitting at the main desk, an old detective known to all as Larry. He had been with the department so long that his fellow detectives claimed he was the assigned homicide investigator on the Crucifixion. His years of experience included thousands of cases from common thefts to serial killers, so he didn't even glance up from his late afternoon fruit cup snack.

With a monotone voice, he pointed down the hall and instructed, "Put him in room two and give me a memo. JAD is on their way up from the district."

Tommy directed Nick to walk the kid down to the Juvenile Holding room, pat him down, take his belt and shoelaces, and place him in the room.

"Who's the JAD cop tonight?" he asked as he approached Larry sitting behind the desk.

"It's Mullen; he'll be here in a couple of minutes."

Tommy knew him from several past arrests and got the impression that he was an okay guy. Someone he might be able to talk to about the unusual circumstances of the case. He called the Philadelphia Naval Hospital and determined that Gunnery Sergeant Hutchens was a patient, and he would be there for another two days for physical therapy.

Meeting Nick at the front desk, he told Larry they have to take care of something. He asked if he could delay Mullen with the paperwork until they return.

The old-timer retorted, "Whatta youse got a six-pack stashed or something?"

"Come on, Larry, we just gotta do a thing, a half-hour — tops."

With a wave of his hand, he relented, "Okay, okay, I'll hold him off. Bring me back a coffee."

CHAPTER 7

ON THE DRIVE OVER TO the Philadelphia Naval Hospital, Nick watched Tommy gripping and twisting the steering wheel as he mumbled to himself. His eyes were on the road with a pained stare, but his mind was thousands of miles away in a jungle reliving a life and death moment. The main reason for the trip was to confirm the juvenile's story, but there were other things to say to Gunny Hutchens.

They determined he was in room 428, and when they arrived, the door was open. Inside, lying on the bed, was a massive black male with a clean-shaven head and a history of scars on his arms and face. With his left leg missing from the knee down, he was reading the Daily News through a pair of wire-rimmed eyeglasses.

"Gunnery Sergeant Hutchens?" Tommy called into the room.

"Hyo — who wants to know?"

The officers entered the room and asked if he had a nephew who lived in the Southwark Housing.

The Marine barked, "Who, Tyrell? Why? Is he okay?"

"Other than taking some potshots at us with a .22 plinker rifle, yeah, he's doing outstanding."

"I told him do not touch that weapon. Where'd he get the ammo? I didn't leave no shells. Bring him around, so I can properly kick his ass. You probably have to lock me up for murder!" Hutchens yelled out as he tossed the newspaper to the floor.

From his response, they could tell he was genuinely irate. "Take it easy — I'm gonna do all I can to get him out of it."

At that statement, the gunnery sergeant went silent, sat up in bed, and swung his leg over the side. He lowered his head, peered over the reading glasses directly at the unknown officer, and wondered out loud, "Let me get this straight, my nephew takes potshots at you with a rifle, and you gonna get him off. What's wrong with that picture? Why?"

While staring back at him, Tommy declared in a quiet voice, "Because I owe you one, Gunny."

The name tag caught his eye as he studied him up and down, *Tabbozzi.*

After a moment of recollection and reflection, a slight smile came across his face. "Might not be able to lug your sorry grunt ass a half-mile now with all that new meat you put on your bones."

Tommy snapped to attention and saluted the big Marine. "I never got to thank you, Gunny."

Gunnery Sergeant Hutchens returned the salute and commented, "Hey, we don't leave no man behind — even army."

They shook hands and stared into each other's eyes, both re-living that day in the jungle.

Stepping back, he asked, "Tyrell ever been in trouble before?"

"Believe it or not, he's a respectful kid, and I can't figure how he stays that way, living up in that dope tower. His momma, my sister, does all she can. She works hard, lotta hours, ain't always there. Planned on takin' him outta there and live with me on my farm in Jersey, after they set me up with my new leg."

Tommy laid out his plan. "I'm going to reach out to the Reverend and Momma Wilkens over at the First Baptist Church on Twenty-Second Street. You familiar with them? They're certified by the court to take in kids temporarily until a permanent solution is determined."

"Yeah, I know them, they fine people. They kinda steered me to the Marine Corps before when I was running wild on the streets, they helped me," Hutchens revealed.

"I'll have them write a letter to the Juvenile judge to recommend that you're given custody of him when you're released from the hospital," Tommy explained.

"Tabbozzi, tell me straight up. Is Tyrell going to the Youth Study Center? I been there as a kid; that place will turn him bad for sure."

"Not if I can help it," he responded, "I'll call you and keep you updated."

"Thanks, you a good man Tabbozzi," replied Hutchens.

The young rookie officer stood motionless and silent by the doorway, awed by the events of his first day on the street. At that moment, he realized that being a cop was much more than just catching the bad guys and putting them away. The academy didn't teach that dynamic.

Before returning to South Detectives, they picked up a coffee and a couple of donuts to sweeten the deal for Larry. Upon entering the Detective Division, they spotted him in the same location, behind the desk with his feet up intently doing the Daily News crossword puzzle.

"Six letter word for a city in Italy?" the old detective mumbled without looking up from the paper.

"Naples," Nick offered.

"Yeah, hey, thanks, kid. JAD is in the back with your juvey,"

While walking, Nick asked Tommy, "How old is that detective?"

With a chuckle, he responded, "Who, Larry? He's two years older than dirt; they claim he walked a foot beat in front of Ben Franklin's house whenever Ben was in town."

They were laughing as they arrived at the holding room and noticed the JAD officer questioning Tyrell. The Juvenile Aid Officer exited the room, and in the hall, Tommy laid out the details of the arrest.

"You really believe the kid wasn't shooting at you?" Mullen questioned.

Tommy told him about the busted front sights causing the shots to go off target from the signpost. He also mentioned meeting with the juvenile's uncle and talking to the Reverend Wilkins regarding temporary housing.

Standing silent for a moment, he formulated a plan and then answered, "Well, at least he doesn't have a previous record. Okay, process the firearm through the detective division and tell the Ballistics Lab to send me a copy of the report, and as long as it comes back clean, I'll carry the case as adjudicated.

"Thanks, Mullen, I owe you one."

"I'll call Family Court Judge Dyer and request him to sign an order to place the kid with the Reverend and Momma Wilkins temporarily. I'll drive him over after I finish some paperwork," the JAD officer added before they left.

While in-route to Police Headquarters, Tommy lit up a smoke and casually remarked to Nick, "You did a great job today, kid. You didn't freeze up, kept your head, and you had my back when I went down. Now I know I can count on you."

The rookie was surprised and overwhelmed by that comment; he glanced across the cab of the wagon and noticed the cigarette dangling from his new partner's lips while Tommy squinted and peered out to the driver's side mirror.

The thought of his dad popped into his memory as he pictured him sitting in the stands at his Little League games on warm summer days, cheering him on as he rounded the bases.

Wide-eyed and in a wavering voice, he responded, "Thanks, Tommy."

The long day was over, and they arrived back at the 3rd District to report off duty. While heading to the locker room, the older cop turned to the young officer, and with a straight-face, said, "Hey kid, sorry it wasn't real busy today. Maybe it'll pick up tomorrow."

Unsure if he was joking or not, he relaxed when Tommy smiled and patted him on the shoulder.

CHAPTER 8

THE ADRENALINE WAS PUMPING, AND his heart was beating fast as he opened the door to his house at about one-thirty in the morning, and entered quietly, not wanting to wake his mother.

"Nicky, where have you been? I've been worried about you all night. Are you alright?" the voice of his mother called out as he entered the room.

"Mom, what are you doing up? It's late. I'm okay. I'm fine, what a day I had," he answered with a beaming face. He held back telling her about the shooting incident, knowing that would upset her.

His mother was a widow working as a registered nurse for twenty-four years, and his father was an ironworker. Nick was ten years old when a steel cable snapped, sending a two-ton I-beam hurtling to the ground, tragically killing his dad, the biggest fan of his life. There was some insurance money from the accident, but she still had to work to provide. She was protective of him, but not overly. In her nursing career, while working in the Emergency Room at Frankford Hospital, she witnessed firsthand the many tragedies brought in by the Philly Police.

"They assigned me to a wagon with probably the best cop in the department," he stated, trying to ease her worry, which seemed to lower her fear level.

He spared her the details of the shooting and instead exaggerated about getting to put the siren on and going through red lights. As she stood there, hugging her house-coat with one hand veiling her lips, she listened with apprehension. A mother never stops worrying, and although that answer appeared to calm her, she still had a lingering feeling he was sugarcoating his story.

She kissed him on the forehead and said, "You better go to sleep; you have work tomorrow."

"Gonna sit up for a while and unwind a little."

"Goodnight. I love you, Nicky."

"Love you too, Mom, see you in the morning."

Sitting back in the recliner, the excitement of the day turned to thoughts of his father. They were close. He loved baseball, and Nick loved his dad, so he would do everything to excel in the sport. He practiced hard, keeping his dad's words in mind.

Remember, Nicky. Practice might not make you perfect, but it will make you better.

After they laid him to rest, he would ride his bike to the cemetery and spend hours at the graveside perfecting his grounders by throwing a solid rubber ball against the headstone, fielding it into his glove while telling his dad about his day. The memories evaporated, and he felt the pride of his father surrounding him as he drifted off to sleep.

At about nine-thirty a.m., the smell of bacon cooking jarred him from his sleep.

His mother glanced into the living room and said, "Oh, you're awake, come sit, I made you something to eat; you must be starving."

Although he slept in the chair all night as he stood and stretched, he was full of energy and was anxious to get back to work.

"Okay, Mom, gonna wash up, be right down."

When he returned to the kitchen, a plate of eggs, bacon, home fries, and a steaming mug were waiting for him. As he stuffed his face, his mother puttered through the pantry, eventually pouring herself some coffee, and sat across from him.

Watching him eat, she turned her gaze down at her cup, stirred in a spoonful of sugar, and remarked, "You know, Nicholas, while working in the Emergency Room over the years. I treated many patients brought in by the police, from drunks to gunshot victims and everything else in between."

As he shoveled in his breakfast, he chewed and nodded. His mother looked up into his face, and after a slight hesitation, she continued, "so I know a bullshit story when I hear one."

Nick went slack-jawed and silent. He stopped chewing mid-bite as he glanced over at his mother.

"Nicky, be careful out there. You're my whole world."

"I will, Mom."

At two-thirty p.m., the sound of Tabbozzi's booming voice greeted Nick as he stepped into the locker room of the 3rd District. Tommy was buttoning up a blue uniform shirt as he reminisced with another senior officer who answered to the name of "Big Toe," short for "Big Tony." He was about six foot four and weighed over two hundred and seventy pounds, with a given name of Anthony Caruso. He claimed the famous Neapolitan opera singer Enrico Caruso was a relative of his. Audiences would agree that his distant cousin got all the singing talent in that family because whenever "Toe" hit the high notes, it sounded like a duck smacked by the Broad Street subway. Tommy launched into a story of when he and the big cop worked the wagon together.

"Toe you remember we're working 302-Wagon and that call to Einstein, for the '5292' transport?" he asked with a grin on his face.

"Yeah, it was that stevedore that fell into the hold of the ship down on the docks and cracked his melon. Fire Rescue takes him to the hospital; they can't save him, so now he's gotta go to the Medical Examiner, we get the call," Caruso replied.

Without missing a beat, Tommy continued, "So we pull into the driveway and stroll up that steep ER ramp. We walk in there where we see this humongous white male stretched out on a gurney, and he appears croaked, so we figure that must be our guy."

Toe interjected, "Yeah, so we go over to the main desk to pick up the paperwork, and as we're standing there, bull-shitting with the nurse. Outta the corner of our eye, we catch something moving from the general direction of the dead guy."

Building momentum, Tommy added, "When we turn around to see what it was, we watch as this guy, who's lying on the gurney, rolls out the double doors, and is now heading down the ramp."

Most of the squad had heard that particular tale many times before, but they laughed out loud, not because of the story itself, but the way they told it.

Tommy continued. "So now I look at Toe, and he's looking at me, and I swear to God it was like a freakin' Bugs Bunny cartoon. We both head for the exit at the same time, banging into one another, trying to squeeze out the doors. By now, the poor guy is off the ramp and halfway down the block."

A voice in the back of the locker room yelled out, "Yo Tabbs! Was he trying to escape?"

Everyone was now howling with laughter and making comments.

Toe bellowed, "We're running our asses off, and finally, we catch up to the guy just before the intersection. Here what had happened was the brakes on the wheels gave out, and he started rolling. I don't know how the poor guy didn't fall off."

Another heckler shouted, "Hey Toe, we heard you were so outta breath that you laid on the gurney and made the stevedore push you back."

A second voice added, "The last time you ran that hard was 'last call' at Geno's Cheesesteaks."

The overgrown cop was now starting to take the heat as he growled, "Screw you, I'll race you anytime and kick your ass."

With that improbable statement, everyone was jeering harder than ever. The squad continued to mock and goad one another as they rumbled from the room, heading for roll call. Nick was standing with his back against a locker and smiling at the story, but not too much, he knew he was a rookie, and in his mind, he didn't want to show disrespect to the senior officers. When Tommy walked by him, he appeared stiff and out of place.

"Hey, kid relax, they're just breaking balls, besides you're part of the family now. Let's go to work."

Hearing those words, he loosened up but realized he didn't have many people in his own family, only his Mom, himself, a couple of older aunts, and a few cousins, and they never socialized. Nick thought about Tommy's words, and it suddenly registered, *They were like a family, brothers and sisters in blue, all laughing, joking, and arguing with one another, but they would take a bullet for each other.*

On the steps, he met Big Toe, now completely calm, who turned to him and commented, "Nice pinch yesterday, kid. Tabbs said you did real good."

Surprised by the recognition from the hot-headed senior officer, Nick replied, "Thanks," while taking his place in line.

CHAPTER 9

THE ELEVATOR DOORS OPENED, AND as Councilman Ronald Hubbs stepped out and strolled to the ornate office entrance, a memory flashed. Six years ago, during America's Bicentennial observance, he had the good fortune of attending an event held in that office. Only a naïve ward leader at the time, he entered the world of high-finance politics as he was making the rounds glad-handing the movers and shakers. He met Gifford Bennett, the founder, and CEO of Swarthmore Holdings Incorporated, and his political career was sky-rocketed from that night forward. Now, as the leader of the city council, he was at the pinnacle in municipal government, wielding unlimited "juice" throughout the city. Some had said he made a deal with the devil.

Upon entering, a well-dressed middle-aged secretary greeted him, "Councilman Hubbs, Mister Bennet should be finishing his meeting shortly. May I bring you anything while you wait?"

"No, thank you, I'm fine," he replied as he turned and peered out the window down upon one of Philadelphia's most prized possessions.

The Liberty Bell was re-located from Independence Hall during a cold stormy night on January 1, 1976, to the present location, a million-dollar pavilion located on the Sixth Street side of the national park.

That was an exceptional year, he reflected as the inner office door opened, and a red-faced young man exited with his head down, followed by a vile wind of insults.

"Get out of my sight! I am in the profit-making business, not a charity! If you can't uphold your quota, then I suggest you find another occupation! Get out!

"I see he's in an especially sunny mood today," he remarked with a grin to the straight-faced secretary as she announced his presence.

"Mister Bennett, Councilman Hubbs here for the appointment."

While entering the corner office, and even though he had been here many times before, he was always impressed with the view. Although only on the ninth floor of the eighty-eight-year-old building, it had an unobstructed line of sight to America's birthplace and the surrounding historical landmarks.

"Ronald, I'm so happy you could stop by. You're looking well."

"Enough with the snow job, Gifford. What is it you need?"

With a slight scowl forming on his face, the well-groomed man sat back into the plush leather executive chair, folded his arms, and glared at his visitor. A moment passed, and he spoke.

"I can recall times when you needed things."

In a flash, he remembered that Bennett adhered to the "Golden Rule" of those with the gold making the rules. He quietly coughed, adjusted his neck while straightening his tie, and in a sheepish tone, he replied, "Gifford, you know if there's anything I can do for you, just ask. How can I help?"

Continuing to stare, he relaxed his posture, leaned forward onto the desk, lowered his eyes, and casually moved folders from one side to the other. Without looking up, he announced, "I want the contract for the city pension fund as the chief investment broker."

A sudden feeling a warmth came over the politician as he vented his collar with his index finger and responded, "I'm not sure if that's something I can deliver, and besides, why do you want that headache? There is almost eight hundred million in funds you would have to manage, and as you're well aware, the commissions are set at a below-market rate by city ordinance. It's non-negotiable."

"Let's just say I would like to offer my investment expertise to my beloved city, doing my civic duty, so to speak."

Hubbs eyed him with suspicion while attempting to figure out his angle when the fund's asset amount popped into his head.

Eight hundred million. What's he up to? he pondered as he studied the now grinning businessman.

CHAPTER 10

"Slow down, cowboy; the bad guys will wait," Tommy remarked as he watched the rookie methodically inspect the vehicle and prepare the patrol log.

They've encountered various "jobs" and confrontations during the past six months of working together, mostly routine assignments, and several violent incidents. He was learning fast, and Tommy thoroughly enjoyed teaching him.

While sitting in the wagon waiting for another radio assignment, Tommy started a lecture. Nick was eager to work with his training partner every day, not only because of what he taught him about police work, but also the "cop car philosophy," the life lessons, and his humorous nature.

"Yo Nicky, this job is ninety-eight percent boredom, two percent sheer terror, and the other half is bullshit." Tommy pronounced with a grin.

With his full attention, he smiled and nodded, knowing from an accounting perspective; that statement didn't add up, but he was anxious to hear the theory behind it.

On a roll, he continued the lesson, "You got to remember this, the smart man isn't the one who knows all the answers, he's the guy who knows where to find the answers, and always listen to everyone, no matter who it is, whenever possible."

"What do you mean?" Nick responded, knowing more words of wisdom were about to follow.

"I ain't saying you gotta camp out with them, but you gotta pay attention to what they have to say."

Tommy expounded. "Hey kid, most good pinches are made from getting and using information, and you never know where that info can come from."

"Yeah, makes sense."

"You remember that job back in February up in East Division where the bank got robbed, and the security guard got shot?"

"The one where Radio kept putting out the BOLO for the gray Chevy?"

BOLO being an acronym for "be on the look-out" in police jargon.

"Yep, well, I was at court at city hall last week, and we're standing in the hallway waiting to testify, and one of the investigators from East Detectives is there, and he's telling the story of how they caught these guys.

"Yeah, how'd they catch them?"

"A sector car was trying to scoop up a street person in the Twenty-Fourth, it was freezing out, and they wanted to bring him to a shelter. Well, he starts gettin' loud and boisterous about some dude givin' him the 'evil eye.'"

"So, what about it?"

"The cop can't quiet him down, so he asks him about the guy. It turns out he was camped on the sidewalk on Kensington Avenue across from the bank that got held up. He saw the whole thing, and he said the driver was the evil-eyed guy," Tommy explained as he lit up a smoke.

"What, why didn't they shoot the street person? They already shot the guard."

"Hey kid, street people are invisible; they're just another fireplug or a pile of trash to most folks out there. You know how it is; nobody ever sees them."

He nodded, visualized that sad reality of the street, and responded, "Yeah, that's for sure. So, what happened then?"

"So, they take him to East, show him mugshots, and he picks out a suspect. The detectives follow the dollar trail and snatch these guys in West Philly."

"Nice pinch! Yo, what's the deal with the 'evil-eyed' guy?

"One of the doers had one eye pointing to Baltimore and the other pointing to Boston. It turns out; he had a glass eye, case closed."

Nick started laughing, then stopped and asked, "What do you mean 'follow the dollar trail?'"

Tommy gazed over at his young partner and exhaled a cloud of smoke.

"I thought you were a hotshot preppie with an accounting degree. What, they didn't teach you about that?"

Quickly thinking back to his college classes, he tried to remember if he ever learned that concept.

Before he could reply, Tommy elaborated, "They got their informants to see who was throwing money around on the street."

Knowing part two of the lecture was about to occur, Nick got comfortable by squeezing down into the seat and putting his feet up on the dashboard.

"This is one use of the term, but it really means in an investigation when you follow the dollar trail, you try to find out who stands to gain something from the crime."

Nick contemplated, trying to see how it fit into the case, and asked, "So, East Detectives followed the dollar trail to find these guys?"

"Well, along with the identification from the street guy, plus they knew the doers got about ten thousand from the bank, and they had a hunch it was going to burn a hole in their pockets."

"Yeah, I get it."

"Sure enough, these two knuckleheads were spending cash like they hit the lottery."

Tommy finished the lesson. "The point is, Nicky, you gotta listen, always follow the dollar trail to find the real truth, and never ignore your hunches."

Understanding the concepts, Nick nodded while he rubbed his chin between his thumb and forefingers.

"You know, you're gonna to be one hell of a detective one day with your smarts."

Tommy added with a chuckle, "Plus, all the good stuff I teach you."

"Nah, I don't want to be a detective, all that stinking paperwork, I'm happy right here working the wagon."

A flick of his fingers and his cigarette flew out the window. He turned, faced Nick, and with a scowl, he fumed, "What are you talkin' about? Of course, you want to make detective, you're smart, you got a college degree, and besides, you got to use your talents."

"Yeah, but I like working the wagon with you, Tom."

"Hey kid, don't look at me as some kinda pinnacle of success. I didn't have nothing else going for me before I got on the job. Hell, I almost got my dumb ass killed in Viet Nam. If it wasn't for the Gunny, I'd be worm shit, and if I didn't get on the job, I coulda wound up being that street guy up in Kensington. Believe me, Nicky, you're gonna move up, and one day I'll probably be coming to you for a favor."

Nick looked over at him, stunned, wide-eyed, and quiet.

Calming down, Tommy continued in a quieter voice. "Look, it's not I don't want to work the wagon with you. I'm here as long as you want, but trust me, Nicky, things change. I'm just a mutt, but you got too many smarts to be 'working the wagon' for the rest of your career."

The radio snapped the silence, and after Nick acknowledged the call, he stared out the side window watching the street scene go by while he mulled Tommy's words. They conjured a memory of him waiting on the front porch for his dad to come home from work. He would help him off with his muddy boots while recounting his day. With the universal wish of every father in mind, he would smile at his young son and say, "You're a smart boy, Nicky, you can do better than me; always use your talents."

CHAPTER 11

THE ONLY ACTION ON THE street on that mild, clear Sunday morning in February 1983 was the pigeons fluttering between the rooftops and the wires. The party animals from the night before were hung-over and sleeping in, and the regular people were on their way to church or the bakery for the Italian rolls. When 301-Wagon got ready to pull out of headquarters, the wagon crew felt they might be able to have a peaceful morning.

"You want to ride by the deli? We'll grab a couple of pork roll and egg sandwiches. I can pick up a pack of smokes," Tommy suggested.

"I'm in, but hey, Tommy, you gotta quit smoking."

"What are you, my mother?"

The young officer curled his lip and shook his head. Driving the van out of the lot onto Wharton, Tommy made a quick left on Eleventh and headed northbound, carefully avoiding the trolly tracks. The wide street was empty with little activity, and the only people on the sidewalks were the older women scrubbing the stoops.

"Yo, Tommy, spring training is coming up soon. How do you think the *Phillies* will do this year?"

"I think they got a shot, what with Rose hitting and Carlton pitching." Tommy speculated as they arrived at the intersection of Eleventh and Washington, slowing for the stoplight.

Just before the light turned green for the northbound traffic, Tommy noticed three white males in a dark blue mid-sized Dodge making a right from Washington onto southbound Eleventh without using a turn signal. It continued down Eleventh Street, observing the posted speed limit. 301-Wagon proceeded onto Washington Avenue and traveled about twenty feet when, without warning, Tommy turned the steering wheel fast into the on-coming lane hitting the accelerator, which caused the back end of the truck to swerve towards the curb. The van straightened as he steered hard to the right, screeching onto southbound Eleventh Street.

Nick yelled out, "What's up? What's goin' on?"

"Hit the lights; we're gonna stop this car."

At the corner of Eleventh and Annin Streets, they caught up with the Dodge, where it pulled over. Two of the men were sitting in the front of the car, and the third was in the back seat behind the driver.

Before they exited, Tommy instructed his partner, "Watch these guys, un-holster, and hold it beside your leg."

With his service revolver in hand, Tommy approached the driver's side. A stocky male with a shaven head and a full-length beard called out from the rear seat to the approaching officer, "Yo, you can't stop us. We got protection."

"Shut the hell up!" the other passenger yelled back from the front seat.

His heart was racing as Nick proceeded to the passenger side, where he scanned the back seat area through the door window. He spotted a bearded male with a swastika tattoo on his forearm, reaching for a four-inch black revolver next to him.

Instinctively, he shouted, "Gun! Gun! Gun!" as he stepped to the right and brought his service revolver up, pointing it at the occupants.

Tommy backpedaled while bringing his weapon up, aiming into the auto as he screamed at the males with an escalating voice, "Show me your hands! Show me your hands!"

Not complying at first, Tommy cocked the hammer and repeated his orders in a louder voice. With reluctance, the men in the front placed their hands on the dashboard, and the back passenger positioned his on the top of the driver's seat.

"Don't you move!" Tommy screamed while watching the males closely.

Yelling across the roof of the car, he instructed his partner. "Call an assist!"

Nick at once ran to the wagon, grabbed the mike, and transmitted, breaking into radio traffic.

"Emergency... Three-oh-one... give me an assist... Eleventh and Annin...male with a gun inside a vehicle."

Immediately three alert tones sounded, and a message blared, "Attention all units...in the Third District... Eleventh and Annin...assist the officer... police by radio...report of a male with a gun inside a vehicle...three-oh-one is on location... all cars use caution in your response. "

After calling in the 'assist,' Nick returned to the side of the suspect auto covering the occupants with his revolver. The first back-up unit arrived coming north on Eleventh Street and, with squealing brakes, stopped at the front end of the Dodge, blocking any escape route.

Once the officers took up covering positions around the car, Nick jerked open the rear passenger side door, reached in, and retrieved the revolver.

When he opened the front driver's side door, Tommy spotted a silver automatic handgun in the door pocket. Retrieving the firearm, he passed it to one of the backup officers. He hauled the driver out, placed his hands on the roof, patted him down, and cuffed him.

The next one to step out was the front passenger, and as he stood up, Nick observed and confiscated a blue steel revolver from his waistband. After passing it to another officer, he searched and cuffed the male. While focusing on the suspect, Tommy ordered the person in the back seat out of the car; he patted him down without finding a weapon.

Once shackled, he spun him around and demanded, "What do you mean – you got protection?"

A dull look turned to a snarl as he replied, "I don't know nothing about that."

They traded glares for a moment when Tommy pushed him off to a back-up officer and said, "Put him in the wagon."

They searched the interior without finding any additional illegal items; Tommy retrieved the car keys and proceeded to the trunk. In compliance with the legal rule of 'search incident to an arrest,' he opened it. He found a black automatic handgun and a double-barreled sawed-off shotgun, along with a sizable plastic bag containing an off-white crystal powder.

"Holy shit, Tabbs, how the hell did you come up with this one?" bellowed Big Toe, who responded to the call.

"We were making a left, and they were making a right, and when our two vehicles passed ... 'them eyeballs were clickin.'"

They all started to laugh while nodding their heads in understanding. The sergeant ordered the suspects separated, lessening the chance of the males getting their story together. He advised Radio of the manner of transport to South Detectives and requested a Police tow truck for the vehicle.

The partners unloaded and cleared all the confiscated firearms and placed them along with the bag of white crystal powder in the cab of 301-Wagon. They were excited and pumped and were still trying to comprehend the arrest.

As the events of the incident played out in Nick's mind, he turned to his partner and asked, "Yo, Tommy, what did you mean out there when you said 'them eyeballs were clickin"?"

He chuckled and explained, "When I made the left, and they made the right, they saw the wagon, and all three of them kept their heads straight, but their eyes snapped left and up, looking right at me like I was a dog wearing a cowboy hat, I knew something wasn't right with them."

After a slight hesitation, he added with a smirk, "And besides, they didn't use their turn signal."

Nick stared at him for a moment, a smile forming on his face, and with a shake of his head, he said, "Tommy, you are a piece of work. You're like a freakin' bloodhound."

Glimpsing back at him sideways with a sly grin on his face, Tommy put the truck in gear and slowly drove away.

CHAPTER 12

THE TALK AROUND THE DISTRICT was the drug and gun pinch Tabbozzi and Avner made on Sunday morning. The chemical analysis indicated the substance was methamphetamine, weighing a little less than two pounds, which brought the street value to over fifty thousand dollars. South Detectives investigated the guns, and the Ballistics Lab conducted the forensic firearm examination. The wagon partners showed up for work the next day after making the arrest, and while walking into the roll call room, Lieutenant Flores stopped them in the hall.

"Tabbozzi, Avner, those individuals from your car stop were identified as members of the Elmwood biker gang."

"Those guys love to run the guns and the meth. Don't they?" Tommy remarked.

"Not for a long time after their convictions." the supervisor replied with a grin.

"That's for sure," Nick added.

"By the way, Ballistics came back with one of the firearms used in a three-year-old homicide from up in Germantown, and word is from the detectives one of those bikers is going for the murder. You're getting a departmental commendation, and the captain is also referring you guys to the FOP for their award."

Tommy replied, "Thanks, boss, we appreciate it."

He walked into the roll call room with both officers following. As they were approaching the rest of the squad were waiting to assemble, Big Toe pushed one of the younger cops from where he was standing in the front line of the assembly and announced with a considerable flourish:

"Make way, make way. Batman and Robin just entered the building."

Not one for missing a chance to compete in a ball busting session, Tommy quickly retorted, "No, no, gather around the portly one, where my esteemed colleague and I can instruct you mutts on how to properly conduct a felony car stop."

Laughter, along with various comments, were flying about the room. At the desk, the supervisors were smiling, taking in the show. The performance continued for a couple of minutes until the lieutenant turned his head towards the sergeant and, with a slight nod, indicated the fun was over.

Without hesitation, he yelled out, "Okay, you clowns, you gonna play grab-ass all night, or we gonna get some work done? Fall in for roll call."

The laughter subsided as the officers took their respective places in line.

The sergeant read out the assignments. When he got to Tabbozzi and Avner, he mentioned with a grin, "So you made a pinch yesterday. Whatta ya got for me today?"

Tommy retorted loud enough for the squad to hear, "See Nicky, you're only top dog for one day around here; after that, you're just another mutt in the dog pound."

The sergeant ordered, "Dismissed."

As they began the four to twelve tour of duty, they ran from job to job, mostly routine non-emergency calls. During their lunch break, they picked up a couple of hot sausage sandwiches and sodas and ate in the wagon out of service. They parked behind one of the many empty factories out of view. After they scarfed down the food, and while sipping their drinks, they were still riding high from the bust.

Lighting up a cigarette, Tommy was in a jubilant mood as he suggested,

"Yo, Nicky, Why don't you come over to the house for dinner, meet Rosie and my little Sophia."

That was the first time Tommy had talked about his family, and Nick was kind of surprised because he didn't know much about his private life.

"Yeah, it'll be good. Wait a minute; your wife's name is Rosie?"

"Yeah. Why?" said Tommy, looking sideways at him.

"Nah, nothing, I just realized it rhymes, you know Rosie Tabbozzi, it sounds nice."

He smiled and revealed, "Yeah, that's what I thought, when I first heard her name, I said to myself, 'Rosie Tabbozzi, it was meant to be.' I knew right there. I was going to marry her. In one year, we got married, and then later, our little sunshine Sophia was born. Believe me, when I tell you, they are my whole world Nicky, and I swear to God, I would kill anyone who ever tried to hurt them."

Nick studied his partner as he made the remark, and he detected a shadow of darkness come into his eyes. Although knowing that was a common theme among husbands and fathers, he got the feeling Tommy's statement was more of a vow than a bluster.

Tommy turned happy again and with an excited voice said, "Hey, how about Saturday? We're off. I'll call home later. You like Italian food? I'll get her to make her home-made ravioli and 'brajole,' everything made from scratch, even the gravy, wait till you taste it.

"Hey, bring your girlfriend too. She'll love my girls," he added.

"Okay, Tommy, it's a plan."

CHAPTER 13

WHILE THEY WALKED ACROSS THE concrete porch to the well-kept brick twin home on Olney Avenue, Nick and his girlfriend Abby could make out a dog barking from inside the house. About to knock, Tommy's voice boomed through the door as he spoke in a firm voice.

"Quiet, sit," he commanded.

He pulled open the door, greeting them, wearing a white and green "Philadelphia Eagles" football jersey with the number eight on the front and back, blue jeans, and sneakers.

"How you guys doin' this fine day?" he greeted them with a huge smile.

As they entered, Nick answered, "Good, hey Tommy, I want you to meet Abby."

Teasing Abby, Tommy enquired, "Whoa, what's a pretty girl like you doin' with a mutt like this?"

"Just lucky, I guess," she answered with a smile.

"I guess you already heard this guy yapping. This is Chief," Tommy announced as he knelt to hug a well-behaved Australian shepherd, who was happy at his affection and showed it by eagerly licking his face.

"I love this guy. This dog is loyal because he would take a bullet for my family and me."

Nick and Abby briskly petted him as he wagged his tail and rolled over, showing off.

Coming into the living room from the dining room, Tommy's wife held the hand of their shy young daughter.

"Yeah, well, speaking of being lucky—I know I'm am; this is my Rosie and our Sophia."

Rosie moved forward with the little girl in tow. She stopped and hugged the young couple while saying, "It's so nice to finally meet you."

She remarked with a smile as she turned to Nick, "Tommy is always telling me about you and all the jobs you guys handle together."

Tommy cut in, "Yo, Rosie, you're gonna give this guy a big head."

He peered down at his little girl standing to the side.

"Sophia, come over and say hi to Abby and Nick."

The little girl was hesitant at first but then walked towards the guests. She stopped, grabbed her father's leg, and hid behind it.

Tommy stooped down and urged, "Say hello, honey — this is Abby and Nick."

She cupped her hand, holding it up to her father's ear, and whispered loud enough for everyone to hear.

"Daddy, my storybook said, that is Santa's real name."

"What name is that, baby?" Tommy asked.

"Saint Nick!" she replied.

Tommy laughed along with everyone else as he remarked, "Well, this guy ain't no saint, but I guess he could be Uncle Santa."

Without hesitation, Sophia brightened at that idea and bravely approached Nick and Abby, greeting them with a giggle. "Hello, Uncle Santa."

Nick stooped down to eye level with the bright-eyed little girl and produced a gift bag from behind his back, handing it to her while saying, "Hi Sophia, I'm so glad to meet you. I saw your daddy's locker with all the beautiful pictures you drew, so I got you some new crayons and a coloring book."

She was hesitant at first, looking up at her dad. Tommy smiled and nodded with approval as she took the present from Nick.

"Thank you, Uncle Santa." she gushed while looking in the bag.

From that day on, whenever Sophia would see Nick, she would always call him Uncle Santa. He sensed a unique bond with Tommy and his family from that time forward. Sophia calling him 'uncle' felt special because he came from a small family and having no brothers or sisters to provide a niece or nephew.

"Hey Rosie, give Abby the grand tour of the palace. Nicky, come on, I want to show you something," Tommy proposed while leading Nick to the basement doorway.

They plodded down the stairway into a neatly kept room lit well with fluorescent lighting. The walls were cleanly painted, and gray vinyl tile on the floors. Against the far wall were shelves containing six five-gallon glass jugs, each fitted with a device at the neck resembling a miniature "P" trap under a sink. The bottles held liquid in differing shades from pink to dark red. A bulging wood cask rested between chocks, and a spigot was protruding from its flat end. A circular device that resembled an iron vise positioned on top of a wooden bucket with the slats separated from one another was sitting on a workbench to the shelves' right.

Tommy stood there, beaming like he just presented the crown jewels. He reached onto the shelving, took a long-stemmed clear glass, put it under the spigot, and dispensed a burgundy liquid about an inch deep. He swirled the contents of the glass, brought it to his nose, sniffed, handed it to Nick, and instructed, "Check out the friggin' 'boo-kay' on this."

Nick took and inspected the glass with a furrowed brow and asked, "The what?"

"The 'boo-kay, the 'boo-kay,' ya mutt, take a whiff and sip it, its wine, I make my own wine," Tommy barked with annoyance.

Nick swirled the glass, inhaled the vapors, took a small sip swishing it around in his mouth, and swallowed. He gazed up to the ceiling in contemplation, and after a moment, he declared, "I perceive a great depth of flavor and aroma, with a slightly fruity aftertaste. I must say, Thomas, you are a bon vivant and connoisseur of the highest order."

Tommy, with one eyebrow raised and tight-lipped, appeared puzzled as he replied, "I don't understand all that college bullshit, but I do make outstanding friggin' wine."

While Tommy and Nick were sampling the vino, Rosie led Abby through the house, proudly pointing out all the work they had done. Stopping in the kitchen, assorted pots, pans, and cooking utensils were about, and a meal was in the process of being cooked. Rosie pointed out the new cabinets, appliances, and counter-tops.

"We both love to cook, so Tommy put in the new kitchen, and we love it."

"Mommy, can I show Abby my room?"

"Sure, sweetie, let's go."

Sophia took Abby by the hand and led the way up the stairs. The second floor was spacious, neat, and well-kept. Sophia guided her into what could only be described as a little girl wonderland. All pink with a menagerie of stuffed animals and dolls displayed neatly in their place on a small child-sized bed with a small table and chair in the middle of the room. Sophia proudly showed Abby her favorite dolls and drawings, with Abby displaying sincere admiration for the items. The little girl's attention gradually turned to the gift she received; she sat at her table and started to play with the crayons and book. Rosie showed off the new bathroom that Tommy installed with Abby, also showing admiration. They moved down the hall, and Abby noticed, "You have three bedrooms?"

Wrapping her arms around herself with sad eyes staring at the door, Rosie explained as she stopped at the door next to the bathroom. "Yes, our bedroom, Sophia's room, and our son's room."

"You have another baby?" Abby asked with surprise.

As Rosie opened the door to the room, she continued, "He was five years old when he died, Thomas Patrick Tabbozzi Junior."

"Oh my god, Rosie, I'm so sorry."

As she stepped into the room, a wound opened.

"He came home from kindergarten, coughing and feverish. We thought it was just a cold, but after a couple of days, he didn't get any better. We rushed him to Saint Christopher's Hospital; he had developed pneumonia," she added with tears welling in her eyes. "Three days later, he died."

Inside the door, Abby saw a little boy's room decorated with teddy bears, sports pictures, and memorabilia. A small model of a Philly Police car sat on the dresser, and a football rested beside it.

"Tommy and I were devastated; we became terribly depressed. Tommy had so many plans and dreams for our son; he wanted to teach him everything. We didn't know what we were going to do, two years later, God sent us our little Sophia, but I can't have any more children. I had a difficult delivery, my blood pressure bottomed out, and Tommy almost lost us both. The doctors and nurses pulled us through that ordeal, and little by little, sunshine came back into our lives. It was the first time in a long time that we smiled again, she's everything to us, and Tommy is highly protective of us."

Taking hold of her hand, Abby expressed, "I'm so sorry about your son, Rosie,"

"The strangest thing though; I could see Tommy starting to become his old self when he started training Nick. He would come home from work, and he'd say, 'Nick did this, Nick did that, he handled himself good on that arrest, the kid learns quick' — I realize they're only wagon partners, but between you and me, Tommy is proud of Nick. Don't tell them I said anything; you know how men are."

With that, they smiled knowingly and worked their way back to the kitchen. Rosie asked Abby how she and Nick met. Abby told her that she works for a real estate title insurance company, with the main office in center city. Part of her duties was to take many deeds and certificates over to City Hall and file them in the various departments. She described how on one particular day, with her arms loaded with extra bundles of documents, she turned a corner in one of the cavernous hallways.

"A big duffus runs right into me, scattering everything all over the floor," she recalled with a frown. "Well, that duffus turned out to be Nicky, standing there in full uniform with a dumb look on his face; he says to me, 'I'm so sorry! I'm so sorry!' I'm about to cry when I see him gathering up the papers as fast as he can.

"I'm frantic because they were out of order, so he finds a small vacant anteroom with a table down the hallway, and he tells me.

"'In here, I'll help you put them back together.' "It took us about an hour to get them right, and well, the rest is history."

They giggled together at the story as the men entered the kitchen.

"Yo, we gonna goof around all day, or we gonna eat?" Tommy bellowed.

CHAPTER 14

Zurich, Switzerland — 1970

THE WORN-OUT BELL WAS BARELY audible from the phone in the dim, dank utility office on a rainy autumn night. Mouth agape, he arose from a dream. Since his wife died and with the house empty, he had been sleeping at the university more and more. A shaky hand reached for the receiver and lifted it to his ear.

"Hello, Sven, speaking."

"Bring your keys to lab twenty-eight immediately."

He recognized the voice as the Dean of Biological Studies, someone not usually on campus at that time of night.

"On my way, sir."

With a key ring in hand, he shuffled out the door and down the hall. Approaching the lab, he noticed standing behind the administrator were two hulking males dressed in white coats with one carrying a straitjacket, and the other holding a stretcher.

"Sir, they will not need that," pointing to the restraining garment. "You know he is a gentle soul; he will not harm anyone. Please, let me talk to him."

"We haven't heard from him in several days, I fear he is suffering a regressive episode," the dean explained. "Alright, Sven, go in first and check on him."

The elderly janitor unlocked the door, gingerly swung it open, and a stench of biological and chemical odors wafted in the air, but nothing different from the smells of his previous visits to the lab. Treading slowly through the room, he came upon a desk with stacks of various journals and research papers piled high around it. Behind the wall of documents, he found him sprawled in a chair, muttering incomprehensible sounds with wild eyes rolling in his head. Rushing to him, he called out, "Dean, come quickly."

They entered, and the orderlies secured him to the stretcher. They carried him with care out to a waiting ambulance. The administrator and the janitor remained behind and checked the lab making sure no ongoing dangerous experiments were running. While conducting the task, Sven asked, "Dean, why is he like this?"

"He is blessed with extreme intelligence. At the age of ten, tests revealed he possessed an IQ of close to two hundred."

"My God — two hundred!"

"In 1944, at the age of twelve, he wrote a hypothesis which became the basis for the 'Transforming Principle' discovery."

"Ah, yes," the janitor answered and nodded, having no idea what that was.

"He is also cursed with this gift. He rarely sleeps from the never-ending thoughts and ideas that emanate from his mind. These episodes are nature's way of re-aligning his psychological pathways, a safety valve, so to speak."

"He doesn't use the pool as often as he used to, and I've noticed over the years, these episodes seem to occur, more so, when he has no experiments in progress," Sven remarked.

"I believe you're correct; they seem to focus him; however, he does appear to prove the old adage of 'there's a fine line between genius and insanity.'"

CHAPTER 15

South Philadelphia — March 1983

TRAVELING NORTH ON FIFTH STREET, Tommy turned the wagon right to eastbound on South Street.

"See that furniture store over there?" Tommy pointed out on the left side of the street.

"Yeah, what's that?" Nick replied.

"Back when I first got transferred into the district, I got assigned to a steady foot beat right on this block—there was a bad robbery and murder in that store."

"Yeah, you made the pinch?"

"Nah, the hold-up took place the week before, kinda like closing the barn door after the horse gets out," Tommy remarked with a chuckle.

"Eight thugs go in, rob the place, shoot and kill one of the employees, set another one on fire, and tuned-up a bunch of other people in the store; it was real nasty."

"Wow, they got caught?"

"Yeah, detectives scooped them up a little while later. They were part of a gang that was running wild back then."

As they settled into patrol, the radio alert tones broke the silence.

"Attention all units...in the Third District...ten-oh-four Greenwich Street...report of shots fired... a man with a gun...

barricaded person inside the house...Three-eight... Three-oh-one...Three-A-Andy...Sam One-oh-one respond."

Police Radio repeated the call on South Division frequency and "J" band, the city-wide frequency.

"Three-oh-one in-route," Nick replied as he activated the lights and siren while Tommy sped toward the location.

The patrol sergeant, Three A-Andy, answered the call and ordered multiple district units to block designated intersections surrounding the location along with a wagon crew to cover the rear of the house.

Within minutes of the initial radio broadcast, the units were starting to arrive on location. Alert tones again rang out.

"Attention all cars...Ten-oh-four Greenwich...be advised... report of an off duty Three-six-nine inside the location...all cars use caution."

When 301-Wagon arrived, Tommy parked on Tenth Street just north of Greenwich. They exited the vehicle and took up a position at the edge of the house on the northwest corner of Tenth and Greenwich. From that spot, they could observe the front of 1004 Greenwich Street. The white aluminum screen door was dangling off the door frame down a set of brownstone steps. As they were about to work their way across Greenwich Street and down along a corner house facing Tenth Street, an older male came across Tenth Street from the Catholic Church, calling out to Tommy and Nick.

"Officer, officer, I'm the one that called. It sounded like a gunshot."

Tommy pulled him back out of the line of fire and asked him, "What happened? Where were you when you heard the shot?"

"I live in ten-sixty-two. I was taking the dog out and walking up Greenwich to the yard behind the church; I got a little past his house. I saw the screen door broke. There was a lot of yelling and screaming, and it sounded like a gunshot coming from inside the house," he explained.

In a hurried voice, Nick enquired, "You said 'his' house. Do you know who lives there?"

The male replied, "Yeah, he's a cop. John Hallwell, along with his wife and four kids."

Nick transmitted the information to Police Radio.

"Three-oh-one...priority...we have a complainant...be advised the location is a confirmed three-six-nine residence... witness states he heard a loud verbal argument and a possible gunshot... have all units use caution."

"Three A-Andy to Radio... What's the ETA of Stakeout?"

"Sam-one-oh-one, we're two minutes out."

"Three A-Andy to Radio... we'll set up a command post at the parking lot behind the Annunciation Church... Three-Ten will be communications car... have the cars enter off Dickinson... contact Three Command... start the detectives in with a hostage negotiator and a Stakeout supervisor."

"Three-oh-two to Radio...we're on location rear alley behind the house... be advised... yelling and screaming coming from inside."

Tommy and Nick stayed at the corner of Tenth and Greenwich, preventing vehicular and pedestrian traffic from entering Greenwich Street. Nick escorted the complainant over to the command post, where detectives would interview him. Various police units were arriving and checking in with the communication car. The first Stakeout Unit, along with a Stakeout sergeant, arrived, and the sergeant ordered Radio to dispatch an additional Stakeout Unit.

Lieutenant Charlie Flores, Three Command arrived, assumed overall command of the scene, and ordered the Stakeout sergeant to assign a Stakeout officer to the backyard of a corner residence across Greenwich Street from 1004 to cover the front door. The sergeant directed the second officer to work his way to the rear alley behind 1004 and take up a covering position on the back door.

Sam-102 responded and informed Radio they were about three minutes out. A Fire Department Rescue Squad arrived at the command post and two detectives, one being a hostage negotiator. The lieutenant contacted Police Radio by phone, and they informed him that the barricaded person scene was the residence of a Philadelphia Police officer assigned to the 17th District. A grand jury had indicted him in the recent federal police corruption investigation within the district. Because of the indictment, the Police Department suspended him for thirty days with the intent to dismiss.

Once the second Stakeout unit arrived, the Stakeout sergeant directed one of the officers to make his way down Greenwich Street on the south side sidewalk and take up a position in a small alley next to 1004 Greenwich. That position would allow the officer quick access to the front door when necessary. The second officer would escort the police detective hostage negotiator up Greenwich Street along the south sidewalk from Passyunk Avenue. They could take up a cover position on the next-door property steps. When all units were in their assigned places, the hostage negotiator attempted to contact the occupants inside 1004 Greenwich by speaking into the front door with a handheld loudspeaker.

Detective Bill Barren was the assigned hostage negotiator, a well-seasoned detective with seventeen years in the department, nine a detective. Through his unique technique, he had developed a talent for extracting details about a case not typically discovered from witnesses and suspects. Considered an expert in body language, he didn't use intimidation or fear; he had a way of talking to people and reading their demeanor. Due to his propensity for interviews and interrogations, the department selected him to attend the FBI Hostage Negotiator training course. He was one of four trained hostage negotiators in the PPD and was on call twenty-four/seven.

"John, this is Bill Barren from South Detectives, and I'm here to help you. Can you hear me? I can help you resolve this situation. We're here to help you," Barren announced into the handheld bull-horn directed into the front door of 1004 Greenwich Street.

A voice yelled through the slightly opened front door, "Nobody can help me now, I'm done for."

"Is there anyone else with you in there? Is anyone hurt?" Barren implored.

"The wife and kids are in here; nobody's hurt, I'm done for, Bill."

The detective heard a female sobbing inside the house.

"John...please stop this, you're scaring the kids, please stop, we'll be okay."

"John...let the family come out, and then we can talk."

"I don't know what I'm gonna do now, I'm screwed, I'm getting fired, arrested and probably going to jail, I put my family out on the street because of this mess," Hallwell shouted through the door.

"John, you don't want your family to see this. Let them come out. We'll keep them safe. I promise you."

From their location, Tommy and Nick saw and heard the drama unfold. They were unable to offer any other assistance, and they felt helpless, particularly Tommy, who was familiar with Hallwell from the police academy. After about forty minutes of Detective Barren trying to maintain contact with the barricaded officer, Hallwell shouted out the door:

"My family's coming out; they're coming out the back door. Please take care of them."

"I will, John, I promise you," Barren replied.

Detective Barren advised the on-scene commander via a "150" radio, which transmitted over a private tactical channel, that the family will be coming out the rear door of the house. The on-scene commander, in turn, instructed the two wagon crew officers in the back alley to use caution in escorting the family out of the area to Cross Street, the next street over. A Fire Department rescue squad was there for medical evaluation.

On the tactical channel, the Stakeout sergeant advised the Stakeout officer assigned to the rear of the house to cover the family from his position as they exit. The rear door of the house opened, and a hunched, visibly upset woman with her hair askew and a haunted gaze stepped through. Dangling in her arms was a girl of about two years of age, and she was herding three boys who appeared to be three through six years of age, all whimpering and wailing. The officers in the alley heard the oldest boy sobbing and yelling back into the house.

"Daddy, we love you! Daddy! Daddy! We want our daddy!"

The officers, holding back tears, quickly gathered up the children and escorted them through the alley out to Cross Street. They reported to the on-scene commander that a female and four children were at the Rescue Squad on Cross Street. The on-scene commander ordered the officers to stay with the family until relieved.

The commander alerted Detective Barren that the family was out safe, who then called into the house, "John — your family is safe, everything is going to be okay. You can come out now. Just put the gun down and come out. I can help you."

After a few moments of silence inside the house, Hallwell unexpectedly appeared at the front doorway, standing with his left side out the door and his right side still inside the threshold. The "150s" lit up with chatter informing the on-scene commander of his appearance.

Barren, who was approximately ten feet from and somewhat behind Hallwell by the next-door steps, put down the loud-speaker and spoke directly to him, "John — It's me, Bill Barren."

When Hallwell perceived his voice, he turned his head to face the detective but kept his right side inside the doorway. Barren started speaking to him, knowing the Stakeout Officers could take a covering shot from their positions if needed. Stepping sideways, he showed his hands, and calmly began to engage Hallwell, face to face.

"John! We can help. You can come out now."

Hallwell focused on Barren for a moment without emotion, before speaking, "Never wanted to get involved, I'd go to work, do the job, go home, never took a dime before, that wasn't me — then the car went, needed a new roof, the kids got sick, everything hit all at once. They said, 'just gotta look the other way.' Just a steady note for the wagon crew

— came down every month; the money came in handy, I started to depend on it — until it was too late."

While studying, the officer's demeanor Barren appealed to him. "It's never too late. We never know what's around the corner. Let me help you. You can come out now; it's going to be okay."

They were facing each other, with Hallwell standing in the doorway and Barren standing ten feet below on the sidewalk. Detective Barren sensed a change in Hallwell's demeanor; a quiet calmness came over his face and body appearance. Hallwell was staring at Barren when he softly cried out, "Bill, tell my family I love them."

While uttering these words, his right arm was rising inside the doorway. From the detective's perspective, time slowed down, and tunnel vision appeared.

The Smith and Wesson Model Ten, .38-caliber service revolver, four-inch bull barrel, touched Hallwell's right temple on an upward angle, and in a smooth motion, the hammer released. In a flash, the left side of Hallwell's head exploded, spraying blood, skull, and brain matter up and out, and when gravity captured that mass, it rained down onto the detective's face and vest. Hallwell's body stood in place for a second, then dropped onto the damaged screen door and slid down onto the sidewalk, landing at the feet of Detective Bill Barren.

For the officers at the scene, time froze. Still, a combination of training and instinct from the Stakeout officer in the alley next to the house ignited as he bolted towards the doorway, securing the service revolver, and checking for a pulse on the down officer. His chances appeared slim as a Rescue Squad screeched to a stop, immediately attending to and transporting Hallwell to the hospital. At Einstein Hospital, the attending physician pronounced Officer John Hallwell dead on arrival.

When Tommy saw the gunshot, he ran the forty feet and arrived at Detective Barren's side. While covering the distance, he was shaking his head and muttering, "Why? Why?"

He observed Detective Barren blood-drenched and standing there motionless, staring up the steps as if Hallwell was still in the doorway. Tommy could see he was in the early stages of shock as he approached him and gently said, "Bill, it's time to go, Bill."

Taking him by the arm, he guided him back to a waiting Fire-Rescue unit as he thought to himself, *There was more than one casualty here today.*

As was the PPD protocol, the Stakeout Unit entered the house and did a complete search for any other suspects, victims, or weapons. Homicide detectives and the Crime Lab entered the crime scene and performed the processing.

Reassigned to secure the front of the scene, 33-Car positioned in the middle of the one-lane street and blocked all vehicular traffic. From 301-Wagon, Nick took a roll of yellow crime scene tape and strung a line across Greenwich Street, blocking off traffic. The tape would remain in place until the assigned Homicide investigator secured the scene. While sitting in 301-Wagon, Nick noticed that Tommy was agitated and muttering.

Nick asked, "Tom, you alright?"

Tommy, with clenched teeth and a vise grip on the steering wheel, turned to Nick and snarled, "Listen, I ain't saying that Hallwell or any of them guys were right in taking any money, once you start down that road, it ain't easy to stop, 'cause cops are at the bottom of the food chain."

"What do you mean? Bottom of the food chain?" Nick asked in a quiet voice.

"Somebody hands a free cup of coffee to a cop, they call it a 'bribe,'" Tommy explained in an escalating voice. "But you got them scumbag politicians taking money, free trips, free meals, whatever, and that's called a 'campaign donation.'"

"It ain't no 'donation,'" he continued as he brought his fingers up in an air quote gesture. "When some company or group gives a campaign donation. You think they don't want nothing in return. Bullshit, they throw fifty- a hundred grand 'campaign donation' to some sleaze-ball politician, you better believe somebody's gonna come knocking on their door after the election, looking for a big favor, and they'll do it too because they want them 'campaign donations' to keep on comin' in.

"I ain't saying it was right — but a cop takes a few bucks trying to feed his family— and they want to hang him. Hallwell's family is now out on the street, the poor kids have no father, and that whole stinkin' investigation was started by some scum-bag politician trying to turn the heat off himself," as he finished the rant in a scream.

Nick, let him get it out and remained silent. After a moment, Tommy composed himself and, with a stern but quiet voice, cautioned Nick, "Don't you ever take a note; once you're sucked down that sewer, you get shit all over you."

They both quietly stared out the window until Radio broke the silence.

"Three-oh-one...from Homicide...you can resume from your location...the crime scene has been secured."

"Three-oh-one...okay."

Upon the order from radio, Nick exited the wagon, tore down the crime scene tape, balled it up, and brought it back into the vehicle. Tommy put the wagon in gear and guided it slowly away from the intersection.

CHAPTER 16

A COUPLE OF WEEKS PASSED BY, the squad was on the four to midnight shift, and the usual locker room banter was still at a minimum due to the officer's suicide. As Tommy was coming up the stairs and heading into the Roll Call room, Sergeant Rafferty met him.

"Hey Tabbozzi, report to the Captain's office right after roll call."

More out of instinct then guilt, he thought, *What the hell did I do?*

He stood roll call and directly after knocked on the commanding officer's door.

"You want to see me, Cap?" he asked with a little apprehension.

"Tom, come in," the Captain replied. "Tom, I'm aware of Lieutenant Flores informing you of the commendations you and Officer Avner are receiving for the arrest on Eleventh Street. Well, it turns out not only was one of the firearms used in a homicide, but Ballistics also came back with one of the other guns being used in the wounding of a child up in Kensington."

"Wow, I didn't know about the other shooting, Boss."

"That's what I wanted to talk to you about; I have some good news and some bad news, Tom. Besides getting a departmental commendation, and an FOP Citation, you and Avner are getting 'Officer of the month' awards."

Knowing there was more to come, he remarked, "Well, Boss, I've been off the turnip truck long enough to realize you're not telling me the bad news."

"Tom, you're getting transferred to the 17th, and believe me, I'm going to hate to lose you."

"Captain, did I screw up somewhere along the line?"

"No, Tom, you didn't, it's the opposite, and this came from the top."

"What do you mean from the top, sir?"

"Due to the ongoing corruption investigation, every cop presently in the 17th will be transferred out within five days, and they'll be replaced with officers vetted by the Internal Affairs Division and approved by the Police Commissioner. They want top-notch, honest, above reproach, street-smart cops to put that district back in order, and you're one of them."

"Cap, I'm just another mutt working the wagon."

"According to IAD and my estimation, you're an outstanding officer and an honorable man."

Tommy reflected on these words, and after a moment, he asked, "What about Nick, sir, is Nick going too? Yeah, he's still kind of a rookie. With all due respect, captain, I ain't one for calling in favors, but me and Nick made a decent pinch that day, and to be honest with you Cap, I still got more to teach him."

Captain Bowers was silent for a moment staring at his desk phone and tapping with his pen; he then responded, "How do you know he even wants to go to the 17th?"

"Oh, he'll go, I know he will, sir," Tommy answered with confidence.

"Okay, Tom, I'll see what I can do, dismissed."

"Yes, sir, thanks."

As Tommy left the captain's office, he felt strangely upbeat at the news of the transfer. It might have been the new challenges, after all, he didn't mind bouncing around during his career, or maybe he wanted to get a little further

Chapter *16*

away from that Greenwich Street job. At least he would still be in the South Police Division.

Nick was waiting at the wagon parked outside the rear door. Tommy opened the driver's side door and tossed in his briefcase and equipment. He started the engine and prepared to pull off the lot as Nick stared at him with a quizzical expression.

"Well, what was that all about?"

Tommy took his time to answer while adjusting the seat and the outside mirror. After he threw his ticket book onto the dashboard, he turned to Nick, hesitated, and with a grin, he said, "Nicky, I got some good news, and I got some bad news."

CHAPTER 17

THE DOZEN OR SO BLOCKS didn't bother him. He liked to walk. It reminded him of the days from his youth when he would plod the city streets for miles in a day dragging a rattling wagon full of glass. The collection of discarded soda bottles were his main revenue stream back then. On that sunny and crisp fall afternoon, he headed for a meeting with his current source of income. A sense of history filled him as he passed one of the nation's oldest hospitals, which sat across from the four-story brownstone on Pine Street.

"Good afternoon, Councilman Hubbs. I wasn't aware that Mr. Bennett was expecting you," the distinguished butler announced as he opened the ornate front door.

"That's alright, Enrique, I have some important news, and I wanted to surprise him in person. Would you kindly announce me and present my apologies to him for such short notice," Hubbs requested, wanting to observe Bennett's reaction face to face.

"Right this way, sir," the butler replied as he turned and led the visitor up the grand stairway toward a second-floor study.

While the domestic servant tapped lightly and entered, he waited in the hall and read an old framed newspaper article hanging on the wall. The story told of a mine disaster years ago in which twelve miners lost their lives, and destroyed the anthracite coal industry in northeastern Pennsylvania.

The name of the coalmine owner caught his eye, Gifford Bennett III of Philadelphia, as the door opened, and with an outstretched hand, Enrique invited him in.

As he stepped into the room, he offered, "I apologize, Gifford, but I thought you would want to hear the news directly rather than the phone."

With an annoyed look, the businessman glanced up from the document he was studying and demanded, "What is it, Ronald?"

Delaying the news, he commented, "I noticed the framed clipping out there on the way in. Was that your father?"

Looking off towards the hall, he answered, "Yes, I keep it to remind me. He was a buffoon who was more interested in counting his money than watching over his operations. He allowed a dynasty to collapse. I will not make the same mistake."

With one hand in his pocket and half-lidded eyes, the councilman brushed lint from his tie as he declared, "Hmm, interesting. Well, I'm here to inform you that City Council has granted Swarthmore Holdings the contract for the city pension fund."

He stood with a slight smile, waiting for a reaction. Bennett went back to studying the report without comment, and then casually looked up and stated, "How is this a surprise to you, Ronald? You've spread enough of my money around the chambers to guarantee the results."

"I'm still curious as to why you would take on this responsibility for far less commission than you could gain in other areas."

"I told you before, my civic duty."

"I don't buy that, Gifford."

Bennett removed his readers and reclined deep into the high back chair. He sat silent, nibbling on the earpiece tip of his eyeglasses as he studied Hubbs. After a moment of locking gazes, he quietly asked, "What is it you think you know, Ronald?"

"I know you only put your efforts into money-making endeavors. You don't waste time babysitting cumbersome municipal funds for far less profit you could earn elsewhere. I also know there is eight hundred million in the fund at your disposal."

Always one for deducing his options quickly, Bennett realized that leaving Ronald out of his plan would be statistically more detrimental. While sizing him up, he silently considered, *I showed this one what was behind the curtain too many times.*

"Gifford, this doesn't make sense, we're making good money from the real estate scheme, why this, why now?"

His mind calculated Hubbs' negative impact against his usefulness in the new venture. He concluded that the diminutive double-dealing politician would use him as leverage if ever indicted as he proclaimed, "I'm afraid I've let you become too savvy in our relationship." After a pause, he continued, "Alright Ronald, 'in for a penny, in for a pound.'"

CHAPTER 18

A N AFTERNOON SUNBEAM SLICED THROUGH the crystal decanter and lit up the amber liquid. Not taking his eyes off Bennett, Ronald made his way to the tray that held the thirty-year-old scotch. He retrieved the container and poured two glasses. He returned to the desk and placed one down.

"What exactly are you up to, Gifford?"

He regarded the tumbler, reached over and took hold, brought it to his lips, sipped, and swallowed as he studied the swirling liquor in his hand, then turned his gaze up into the politician's face.

"Ronald, the real estate scheme is only one aspect of Swarthmore Holdings' portfolio."

"But it is making money."

"Yes, but not enough. Although the company has numerous shareholders who are content to receive their quarterly statements showing above-average returns, one day, they are going to want to collect the cash."

"I thought the new investors cover this."

"They do — for the time being, but the annuities will start to mature in seven years, and if there's not enough liquidity to begin paying off, we'll be retiring in a federal facility instead of a tropical island," Bennett stated with a sardonic grin sending a message.

Ronald sat upright, mulling the statement, realizing he's in deeper than he realized. After calming himself, he asked, "So, Gifford, how do you plan on addressing the problem?"

He held out his empty glass, indicating for a re-fill. Ronald retrieved the decanter and poured while Bennett explained, "The future of investing will be in identifying and underwriting emerging enterprises," he disclosed before taking another taste.

"What are you talking about?"

"Let's say; one was to discover an idea — a concept so advanced that return dividends of between ten to fifteen times the initial investments could be realized."

"How much initial investment?"

Pulling another gulp, he stared over the tumbler, placed it back on the desk, and answered while rotating the glass, "Thirty million."

"What! That could be over four hundred million in return." Ronald replied with eyes wide, combing fingers through his hair.

"What's the concept?"

"All in due time."

"So, this is why you wanted the pension fund contract — but aren't they going to miss the funds?"

"Ronald, you should have more faith in me. There are many magical ways of covering the withdrawal, and I'll even show them a profit — on paper, of course.

"Yeah, but sooner or later, somebody's going to notice — right?"

"When we receive our return on investment, the fund will be made whole with a healthy dividend. Look at this as a loan."

With narrowed eyes and semi-folded arms, his left index finger tapped his cheek as he mulled the proposal. Several minutes passed, and Hubbs came to a decision.

"I'm in. What part do I play?"

Bennett regarded him with a squinting grin and declared, "Among other things, through your associate Frost, you will acquire the security aspect for the project."

"When do we start?"

"This will take several years to put all the components into place, but all great innovations take time."

"Just curious, Giff, what's my cut of the profits?"

"Thirty percent. I get the greater share."

After a quick calculation, he finished the last of his scotch, and as his grin widened, an absurd thought popped into his head, *That's a whole lot of soda bottles.*

CHAPTER 19

S TANDING THEIR FIRST ROLL CALL in the 17th District, the new squad sergeant assigned Nick and Tommy to Emergency Patrol Wagon- 1701. The 17th, which bordered on the east by Broad Street, the west by the Schuylkill River, the north by South Street, and the south by Moore Street, appeared grittier and possibly more worn out than the 3rd District. In most post-industrial areas, jobs vanished, personal incomes were lost, and law-breaking seeped in.

Mid-summer was the high crime time as the heat and despair drove people to the street. The illegal drug trade was flourishing along with all the other offenses that go with it. Over a year since their transfer, and it felt like they had worked there forever. The first day back on the day work tour, and right out of roll call, the temperature was hot and humid. Multiple calls started coming in for Emergency Patrol Wagon-1701, a Ford Econoline van whose engine protruded into the cab. The air conditioner couldn't over-come the residual motor heat making the truck a rolling pizza oven on a sweltering summer day.

At about two p.m., they received a radio call, "Seventeen-oh-one...take the twenty-two-hundred block of Norfolk...on the highway...hospital case...possible OD...rescue in-route."

Nick retrieved the mike and answered, "Seventeen-oh-one...OK."

He activated the overheads and siren while Tommy accelerated toward the location. They weaved their way through traffic and approached Norfolk. Although designated as a city street, that block was no more than a driveway accessing the small back yards of the houses that face Webster and Christian Streets. Not sure if the truck would fit, he gingerly maneuvered the vehicle into the alleyway riding the miniature sidewalks on both sides of the narrow street. As they moved along, traveling up and down, on and off the curbing, Nick spotted a body sitting against a fence halfway down the block.

"Tommy, right there. See him?"

"Yeah, I see him. I'm going to stop right before him. I don't want to run over his legs."

The vehicle stopped, they leaped out and approached a frail white male lying unconscious, sitting up, and head slumped. He was no more than fifteen years old with foam drooling from his mouth. A belt was cinched around his left arm above the elbow with a bead of blood oozing from a small puncture site in the crook of his arm. On the ground next to him was a hypodermic needle with a tiny droplet of clear liquid at the tip and a reddish-brown coating on the shaft of the instrument. A charred bottomed bottle cap held a damp cotton ball and a small glassine packet containing an off-white powder residue with an identifying red ink stamp on the outside reading "RED DOG" with the head of a dog centered under the two words, were lying next to the needle. Nick felt for a pulse and detected none.

Tommy snatched the microphone and transmitted, "Seventeen-oh-one... priority... what's the ETA on Rescue?"

"Seventeen-oh-one...they're twelve minutes out."

"Resume Rescue...we're going to scoop this "vic" and run... notify Graduate we're coming in with one male about fifteen years...overdose...no pulse...not breathing."

As his partner was transmitting the message, Nick ran to the rear of the wagon, opened the doors, retrieved the wrap-around stretcher, and returned to the prostrate juvenile laying it flat on the ground. Tommy hurried back to the sidewalk and grasped him under his armpits while Nick took hold of his ankles. In one swift motion, they placed the victim on the carrier, secured the straps, and rushed him into the rear of the truck. Nick got in with the male and started chest compressions.

"Hold on, Nicky, it's gonna get bumpy," Tommy yelled through the small sliding door in the steel bulkhead separating the cab from the rear compartment.

The siren blared, and overhead lights flashed as he wove his way to the hospital, which took about seven minutes. The vehicle screeched into the ramp where the medical staff was waiting at the entrance-way, ready to receive the victim with a gurney. Coming to a quick halt, he slammed the gear shift into park, jumped out of the cab, ran to the rear, and opened the doors. With a swift motion, they transferred the young man onto the transporter, and the nurses wheeled him inside.

Their adrenaline was racing, and they were sweating profusely, both their shirts were drenched, and their brows were dripping. They sat on the back ledge of the truck, resting and catching their breaths with Tommy pulling out a cigarette and lighting up. He finished the smoke, and they trudged into the facility where a cold rush of air met them at the door. In the men's room, they cast off their bullet-proof vests, and dabbed the sweat off their soaked T-shirts with paper towels. They were "out of service" and would stay that way until they were able to determine the condition of the male.

They entered the ER and observed the doctors and nurses frantically pumping the male's chest, starting IV lines, and administering oxygen. The doctor in charge called the time of death on the patient twenty-five minutes after his arrival, which affected the officers not so much for the manner of death, for they both had seen numerous overdose fatalities while working the wagon, but that was a kid who hadn't experienced life yet or had the chance to grow up. After gathering information and preparing the "75-48 Incident Report," they made the required notifications by contacting South Detectives and the Medical Examiner's Office. They were silent as they retrieved the stretcher and placed it back in the truck.

In the driver's seat, Tommy gripped the top of the steering wheel, and with his head down, he broke the silence. "Those friggin' dope dealers, that kid got a 'hot-shot.'"

Nick reached into his shirt pocket, pulled out an item, and opened his hand, revealing the empty glassine packet found next to the juvenile with the "Red Dog" markings.

"You know whose junk this is," he stated as Tommy glanced at the item.

"Yeah, that scum sucker at Twentieth and Carpenter," he responded through gritted teeth.

Drug dealers took to marking their packets to market their product through an early form of branding. The practice enabled them to claim that their merchandise was the best or at least better than their competitor's. Chemically both were likely to contain the same amount of opiate in proportion to the "cut" or diluting material. Without quality or quantity control, the mixing process was not precise because those blending the batch would use playing cards, cement trowels, or whatever similar item was handy at the time. With an inexact mix, the possibility existed that a few bags could contain more heroin than dilution material. If a user couldn't handle the extra narcotic in one dose, they received a dosage known as a "hot shot," which could be fatal.

"We have to pay him a visit," Tommy suggested.

A "smack" dealer had laid claim to the area around the intersection of Twentieth and Carpenter Streets. So far, the police weren't able to secure any evidence against him because he wouldn't sell to anyone he didn't know; he posted lookouts on the street. If an officer approached, he had a unique way of disposing of any contraband.

Taking a razor to a tennis ball, he would cut a slit creating an opening like a round change purse. When squeezed, it created a pocket. The tensile pressure of the rubber sphere would hold its shape, and he utilized that little fact of physics to keep his loose packets of heroin in the small void while he was in the act of selling. He would stuff it with enough bags to cover a distribution session. The trick allowed him to throw the contraband container to a co-conspirator when the police approached, so he wasn't in possession when they stopped him.

"What are we going to do about this guy?" Nick questioned.

"He's gonna be tough to snatch, what with that relay system he uses, we're going to have to come up with something creative," Tommy said in response.

"Let's ride by him for a couple of days, sort of rattle his cage for a while, but we're gonna have to get him to make a 'hand to hand' to a cop so we can charge him with felony delivery," Tommy suggested, contemplating a plan.

"He's not gonna sell to an undercover cop, He only deals with people he knows."

"Trust me, we'll think of something."

They drove toward the drug corner, and as they turned on Twentieth Street northbound, several blocks from the intersection, Tommy faced his young partner and instructed him. "Put your hat on."

Nick showed him a puzzled look and responded, "It's friggin' hot out there, Tommy."

"Trust me, just put your hat on."

A sulky glare covered his face as he shook his head and complied. As they approached, multiple people of all shapes and sizes were hovering in the vicinity of a taller male who was pacing back and forth in front of one of the run-down row houses in the 900 block of South Twentieth Street. The individuals sidled up to that person one at a time, and as they drew closer, they reached out hand-to-hand making a quick exchange of money and drugs. They vaporized into the various urban alleys and vacant lots. As 1701-Wagon rolled onto the block, Tommy punched the accelerator, causing a whine of the engine.

In a flash, the customers dispersed like roaches when the lights come on. The seller turned to his left facing north on Twentieth and flung the round yellow object to a waiting male on the front steps of Saint Bart's Church north of Montrose Street. Catching it, he pivoted and hurled it to another posted person at the corner of Twentieth and Christian Streets, where he spun and tossed it as if completing a double play to an unknown person somewhere east of Twentieth on Christian.

In less than thirty seconds, the evidence was now out of the dealer's possession and was at least three blocks away and gone. As Tommy brought 1701-Wagon to a screeching halt in front of the pusher, both officers exited the vehicle, approached him, and physically turned him by the shoulders, placing his hands up against the wall. They patted him down, knowing they weren't going to find any incriminating evidence.

"Hey man, why you hassling me? I ain't doin' nothing," he yelled for all to hear, extolling his innocence.

"Relax, we're just trying to keep you safe. You know there's a lot of bad people around here," Tommy answered.

After about ten minutes of investigation, they got a name, address, and date of birth; Nick relayed the information to Radio checking for wants or warrants. Negative results for the probable false identification provided.

"You have a nice day. Maybe we'll stop by from time to time and say hello," Tommy said as the officers entered the vehicle.

"Yeah, drop by. We'll have a barbecue next time," the male retorted, smiling and chuckling, friendly waving as 1701-Wagon pulled away.

With clenched teeth, Tommy remarked, "I'm going to enjoy slapping the cuffs on that clown,"

"How are we gonna do that? He's got a better assembly line than General Motors,"

"Don't worry, we'll think of something."

For the next five days of day work, the wagon crew stopped the male in the same manner with the same results. Every time Tommy told Nick to wear his hat. With each stop, the dealer became increasingly cocky as he taunted, "Man, you guys are even dumber than you look."

Tommy retorted, "Nah, we just want to be your friend."

It got to the point that when he saw the wagon coming up Twentieth Street, he would casually turn, make the throw, and place the palms of his hands against the wall. As the officers would leave, he mocked them out loud and either waved or threw the finger.

On the first night back of the midnight tour after roll call let out, Tommy stopped Nick as they exited the rear door of the district, telling him to go back in and grab a couple of copies of the "hot sheet," a list of license plate numbers of wanted vehicles. As he turned and went inside, Tommy entered 1701-Wagon, started up, and traveled down Point Breeze Avenue, stopping halfway down the block where he exited the truck, went to his private vehicle, and retrieved a large nylon gym bag. Taking the item to the rear of the wagon, he placed it inside. He got in the cab portion and drove back around to the district's door where Nick was waiting.

"Where'd you go?"

"One of the four to twelve guys thought he might need a jump-start, but he was okay. Come on — hop in. I got a thing I want to do. Hey, by the way, did you ever play baseball?"

"Yeah, you know that I played at Ghost and at Temple. Why?"

"Just curious," he uttered while glancing at the driver's side mirror.

Driving away from the district, Tommy explained to Nick, "Nicky — I'm going to drop you off at Two-one and Montrose, before you go put this old shirt over your uniform and wear this baseball cap, you're going to have to jump out of the truck fast. You're gonna see Father Stan from Saint Bart's standing in the alley, follow him, he's gonna show you where you gotta be."

"What, what the hell are you talking about? What am I supposed to do when I get there?"

"Just do what you gotta do; you'll know what you gotta do when you get there."

With a furrowed brow and palms up, he blurted out, "Where are you gonna be? I don't want to screw up. What am I supposed to do?"

"Listen, you'll figure it out, I got faith in you, kid, I taught you good, sometimes you gotta find things out for yourself, besides I ain't gonna be around forever. Nicky, the next time you see me, you'll know right away what you gotta do."

Puzzled with the plan, he studied his grinning partner and muttered, "Okay."

As Tommy brought the wagon down Twenty-First Street approaching Christian, he declared, "You'll get to where you got to be in less than five minutes, okay, there's Father Stan, let's do this."

The truck slowed, while still moving, Nick got out, shook his head, and mumbled, "Do what?"

At a fast pace, he walked with his head down and met the priest who, without speaking, turned and started walking. Nick followed. They worked their way to the back entrance of the church. In about three minutes, he arrived at a small door to the side and under the church steps. The door was fitted with a push-bar and a small dirty window. The glass provided a clear view south on Twentieth Street past Montrose with a direct line of sight to the dealer. A clearer picture was starting to come into his mind as he took off the old shirt and cap dropping them on the floor.

As he continued his surveillance, coming into sight was an Emergency Patrol Wagon traveling north on Twentieth approaching Carpenter. He started to smile as the vehicle came near, but when it got even closer, he noticed the cab's interior. He could make out Tommy driving, but he wondered who the other cop was sitting in the "recorder" seat wearing a police cap. Time slowed down from that point on. He watched as his partner performed the usual routine of stopping the wagon in front of the dealer, who pivoted, made the throw, and released the orb into space.

Instinctively, Nick punched the push bar crashing through the door. The smell of a summer night hit him; the overhead light was no longer shining down on a grimy South Philly street. He was transported to a baseball field, Connie Mack Stadium, where he spent unforgettable times sitting in the first row of the bleachers with his dad, suited up in his *Phillies* shirt and cap, armed with his glove hoping to catch one.

He would never forget that time he took him to the last game ever played in the old ballyard, October 1, 1970, the *Phillies* against the *Montreal Expos,* where the *Phils* won in ten innings, two to one. It was a bitter-sweet memory. That foul ball went long and fast, ricocheting off the stands on the third-base side. It bounced high straight towards the bleachers — right at him. It was an easy pop-up; he caught plenty on the sandlot. His excitement was high because he knew he had that one. Sensing his dad smiling proudly when at the last second, he took his eye off the ball. It landed in the glove, and before he could squeeze it tight into the webbing, it bounced out, over the rail, onto the field, and into history. He felt crushed watching it drop to the warning track, not so much for himself, but thinking he let his dad down. As he sat there embarrassed and crestfallen, he remembered his father hugging him and saying, *Nicky, that was only a foul, don't worry, I know you'll catch it when it counts.*

Four days later, he lost his dad when a cable snapped on a construction site.

He was no longer a spectator as he burst through the door on the run; his eyes focused as he traversed laterally and backpedaled with the orb soaring through space high and long.

Is it out of here? A sudden worry flashed in his mind.

On the run, he leaped as the sphere entered a downward arc. Sensing the descending object, his left hand stretched to the stars. He felt a sting in the palm of his hand. For an instant, he glanced up, feeling a flicker of his dad's face smiling down from the stands. He clutched and dropped, hitting the ground hard, tucking his shoulder, rolling, coming to his knees, and with a tight grip, he raised his left hand into the air revealing — *the yellow tennis ball.*

Tommy exited the wagon as the suspected pusher assumed the position, and he grabbed him by the scruff of the neck, dropping him to a kneeling position making sure he faced north on Twentieth. The instant he spotted Nick with the evidence, Tommy leaned over, and like a stern talking umpire, he growled into the dealer's ear, "You're o-u-t!"

The young cop moved down the street towards the wagon, squeezing open the incision revealing fifty-three glassine bags packed with white powder and marked with red ink "Red Dog."

Tommy was putting handcuffs on the offender and informing him, "You are under arrest for delivery, possession with intent to deliver, and possession of a controlled substance, and oh yeah, by the way, you throw like a little girl."

They placed the arrested male into the rear of 1701-Wagon, and when Nick opened the cab door, he stopped and blurted out, "What the — !"

When it registered what he was seeing, he started laughing. In the "recorder" seat buckled in was the torso of a mannequin wearing a light blue summer police shirt, a silver toy badge pinned to the chest, and donning Nick's uniform hat. Studying the third wagon partner, Nick shook his head and turned his gaze across the cab, where he beheld

Tommy Tabbs standing outside the open door displaying that ever-familiar grin.

CHAPTER 20

THE PHILADELPHIA POLICE DEPARTMENT REFERRED to the midnight shift as the "Last out" tour of duty. No one knew for sure where the term originated; perhaps from the early 1700's when the town "Night Watchman" manned the small round "Watch Houses." located throughout the old city. When they concluded their night shift, their final responsibility was to lock the Watch House door. If a Watchman neglected to secure the door and the next Watchman found it open, he would ask, "Who was 'last out' the door? They failed to lock it."

Most cops claimed the one good thing about working "Last Out" was when they were driving home in the morning, the rest of the world was going into work, but the way the weather was shaping up that night, it could be a long ride. It was cold for mid-December, and it started to snow. The sky was an amber color created by the ambient city lights reflecting off the clouds, but higher in the heavens, the sky appeared to glow with an ominous green tint.

Tommy arrived at the district about twenty minutes before the beginning of the shift. As he entered the locker room, a voice boomed out from across the room, "Yo Tabbs, you going to the Christmas party?" Big Toe Caruso yelled.

"Not if you plan on singing, I'm not. I still ain't recovered from that song you mangled last year. It was like whenever Cholly's beagle hears a siren, believe me, your cousin Enrico got all the talent," Tommy shot back.

"You wish you could sing like that," Toe volleyed.

"I wish I was a lot more blitzed when I heard it," Tommy retorted.

Sergeant Osborne overheard the ball busting session and stuck his head through the door and yelled, "Yo, yo, yo, we gonna screw around all night, or are we gonna get out there."

The officers scrambled out of the locker room, laughing, goading, and bitching while heading for the roll call room. They lined up in formation as the sergeant ordered, "Dress right dress attention for inspection." The officers came to attention and awaited the formal inspection. The lieutenant and the sergeant proceeded down the line of officers inspecting each for proper equipment and personal appearance. When the review was complete, the sergeant commanded, "At ease, attention to orders." The sergeant called out each officer's name within the squad, with the officers responding "Yo" or "here," or some variation. As they each answered, the sergeant called out their assigned vehicle or foot beat.

"Tabbozzi?"

"Here"

"Seventeen-oh-one is down mechanical, and Avner is on the "Bus Detail" — take out One-seven-eight for tonight."

"Copy that, Sarge," Tommy replied as he welcomed a little change of pace working the sector car. He only got about two hours' sleep that day because his young daughter was excited about Christmas, and he couldn't resist taking her to the mall to see Santa. She was the sunshine of his life.

The sergeant recited the day's orders advising of any wanted persons or vehicles sought by the detectives or other units. Before dismissing the squad, the supervisor addressed the current weather conditions.

"Be careful driving tonight; I don't want to be filling out accident reports with banged-up cars and wagons. I'm not saying to go camping but keep the driving to a minimum."

Sergeant Osborne dismissed the squad, and they proceeded to their assignments with final instructions, "Alright, let's back each other up out there — and be safe."

Tommy grabbed his equipment and walked out the back door, finding 178-Car parked by the curb on Point Breeze Avenue. The snow was starting to come down more intense, and the wind was kicking up, making visibility difficult.

"Yo, Tabbs, maybe the storm will keep 'em quiet tonight," Officer Steve Sullivan commented as he passed Tommy with a black scarf pulled high and his hat riding low on his head against the wind.

"Yeah, it feels slow tonight. I'll catch up with you later. We'll get a coffee."

"Sounds good. I'll pick up a couple and call for you," Steve offered.

With that, both officers proceeded to their vehicles. Tommy arrived at Radio Patrol Car-178, a brand-new blue and white marked unit, where he performed the vehicle pre-patrol inspection and filled out his patrol log. The first box was the date, Saturday, December 20, 1986. He entered the vehicle number, RPC-178, the odometer reading: 74.2 miles, and the first entry "Roll Call 12:00 a.m. — 12:15 a.m."

The snow was falling fast as Tommy drove towards his sector at a slow speed. The night was raw; visibility was low as the headlights reflected off the snowflakes.

Tommy steered with care through narrow streets and decided he would make his way towards the wider avenue to lessen the chance of sliding into a parked car. Radio traffic was slow, with a few calls for auto accidents in the other districts that share the South Police Division frequency making it the kind of night where boredom or reflection could set in. At 12:27 a.m. Radio called 178-Car for a radio assignment,

"One-seven-eight...take Thirtieth and Grays Ferry for a vehicle blocking a driveway of the shopping center."

Tommy grabbed the mike and replied, "One-seven-eight...OK."

He worked his way onto Grays Ferry Avenue, a designated Snow Emergency Route, and found the roadway plowed and salted. New snow was accumulating, but the road condition was better than the smaller side streets. He made his way into the 2900 block, and after making a tour of the parking lot, he didn't notice any blocked driveway. Tommy observed a pickup truck with a snowplow on the front pushing snow to a designated area of the lot. 178-Car approached, and the driver stopped when he noticed the police vehicle. Tommy pulled beside the truck and opened the window.

"Did you call about the car blocking the driveway?" Tommy shouted out through the weather to the driver.

"Yeah, he pulled out about a minute before you showed up. Sorry, I had to bring you out for that, but he wouldn't move when I asked him. I guess he saw you coming and took off," the snowplow driver replied.

"Hey, no problem, stay warm," Tommy said as he pulled away.

Tommy drove the car towards the exit but stopped to fill out his patrol log and a 75-48 Incident Report indicating that the complaint was unfounded. He lit up a cigarette and took in the view. Through the windshield, the flakes were swirling carried by the wind, illuminated by the amber parking lot lights reminding him of the snow globe he had bought for his daughter earlier that day. She spotted it in the display of one of the stores at the mall. She jumped up and down, pointing and begging her dad to buy it for her. After Tommy mentioned that it wasn't Christmas Day yet, he suggested that she ask Santa for it. She turned, gazed up at her dad, and with tears welling in her eyes, softly said, "Daddy, I'll love you forever if I can have it."

Upon seeing her pleading up at him, he melted like "Frosty" at the beach, and after a moment, he reached down and scooped up his little girl into his arms.

"Okay, Sunshine — you got it."

Putting her back down, she took his hand, towing him into the store straight to the snow globe. It had a base of molded plastic in the shape of railroad tracks and a small Santa train encircling the exterior. The glass globe was typical, filled with water and contained an intricate scene of a house with a chimney, a miniature Santa, sleigh, and eight tiny reindeer landing on the roof. A key under the base would wind down, playing "Here Comes Santa Claus." A small switch activated lights in the house and Rudolph's red nose. When shaken, tiny glitter particles swirled about the winter scene creating a world that would dwell forever in a little girl's memory.

CHAPTER 21

A T 12:35 A.M., TOMMY REACHED for the mike and informed Radio that the call was unfounded, and 178-Car was back in service as he began a tour of his sector. After twenty minutes of intense driving, a call came over.

"Seventeen-ten to Radio."

With an immediate response. "Seventeen-ten."

"If one-seven-eight is available, have him meet me at Graduate."

"One-seven-eight meet seventeen-ten at Graduate."

Tommy picked up the mike and answered, "One-seven-eight, OK."

Going easy, he made his way east on South Street and into the hospital lot where he spotted 1710-Car parked in the back row facing out. There was an open space on the driver's side, and he brought 178-Car to a stop side by side. As he put the gearshift into the park position, Officer Steve Sullivan handed a twelve-ounce lidded cup of coffee out the window and over to him.

While taking the hot drink, Tommy declared, "Ah, man, you read my mind. I can use this."

"You want a TastyKake pie? I got a couple," Sullivan offered.

"Nah, I'm good, thanks," Tommy responded as he popped the lid and took a sip. He placed the coffee on the dashboard, shook a cigarette out of the pack, and lit up.

"Yo, how's that new car run?"

"It seems okay, but I didn't get a chance to open it up yet."

"Don't bang it up, or you'll be walking a beat out in 'Forgotten Bottom' for a month."

"Ain't that the truth?"

Forgotten Bottom was a section of the 17th District west of Thirty-Fourth Street. An interstate highway and extensive rail lines separated it from the rest of the district. It sat along the Schuylkill River, and although water didn't surround the area, it had the feeling of being on an island. There were some row-houses, but the section was mostly industrial.

"Hey Tabbs, I'm getting transferred to the Marine Unit."

"No way, who do you know?"

"You remember that job up on Bainbridge Street, the dirtbag that robbed that college coed?"

"The one where she wouldn't give up the money and the doer pistol-whipped her?"

"Yeah, he busted her up pretty bad, concussion, broke her jaw. I pulled up on the scene while he's whacking her. I jump out of the car, he turns and fires a shot right at me, luckily he missed, and I un-holstered as I got out of the car. I tapped him once in the shoulder," Sullivan explained.

"Yeah, that was a helluva shot."

"Yeah, chewed him up a little, but he was okay, went to court, one day trial, he got twenty years. So, after the court case, the victim's father comes up to me in the hallway, wants to thank me for catching this guy, and he asks me is there anywhere special I want to get transferred to in the department?'...so I'm half thinking that this guy's joking, so I say, yeah the Marine Unit. He says, 'Okay,' shakes my hand and walks away. I don't think any more about it."

"So, what makes you think you're goin' there?"

"Lieutenant Doyle from up at the commissioner's office calls me, and he says for me to keep an eye on the teletype that I'm going to the Marine Unit, so I figure the girl's father dropped a dime for me."

"Man, that's unbelievable, her father must have some very heavy drag downtown. Who the hell is this guy?"

"It turns out he's a big-time attorney, Mr. James J. Callahan."

"You talkin' about James J. Callahan from 'Callahan, Latham, and Grimaldi Law Firm'...that guy?"

"He's the one," Sullivan answered.

"Wow. I met him when he was in the District Attorneys' office as a homicide prosecutor. He's a real gentleman. I can believe he went to bat for you. He always liked a cop. He left the DA's office and went into private practice. I heard he's one of the top patent attorneys in the country. He's a classy guy."

"All I know is I get to drive the boats, case closed," Sullivan replied with a chuckle.

"Well, I know you like boating and fishing, the thing is, in that unit, the only fishing you'll be doing is pulling bodies' outta the river in the springtime — Nah, I'm just bustin' 'em — you'll do great, best of luck."

"Thanks, Tabbs, I appreciate it."

Another police car entered the parking lot and approached. The vehicle was 17-B operated by Sergeant Dan Osborne, the west-end supervisor. When the sergeant's car stopped perpendicular to the other two cars, both Tabbozzi and Sullivan grabbed their patrol logs, checked to make sure they were up to date, donned their hats, and exited. As they approached the supervisor, sitting in his car, they saluted one by one and handed him their logs.

"Sarge, how you doin' this fine evening?" Tommy joked as he handed over the paperwork.

"Freakin' peachy. I heard the forecast before hitting the street, supposed to snow all night," he grimly retorted as he signed the document.

Tommy offered, "Ya know Sarge, this is just 'liquid cop,' water-ice style."

"Yeah, it's been slow so far. Let's hope it stays that way," Osborne noted as he took Sullivan's log through the window.

As he handed the signed reports back to the officers, snowflakes were shrouding their hats and shoulders, and he ordered, "You guys better jump back in your cars before you freeze, and listen up: I don't mind you sitting, but spread out, stay on your sectors, and be careful."

"You got it, Sarge."

Sergeant Osborn steered 17-B Car with caution off the lot and headed east. The officers returned to their vehicles, dusting their uniforms before entering.

Tommy stated, "Steveo, thanks for the coffee. I gotta take a leak in the hospital before I head out, I'll catch you later."

As the officers prepared to leave, they felt the cars rocking as a wind gust flew across the lot. Without warning, a loud rumble rolled through the air, and the sky ignited in a sudden burst of light, making the clouds visible, illuminating all buildings and objects on the ground. Startled, Tommy shouted out, "What the hell was that?"

"Wow, that looks like one of those giant oil tanks might have blown up down at the refinery, I'll switch over to 'J' band, see if anything comes over," Sullivan suggested quickly.

EPW-103, a First District Emergency Patrol Wagon, reported.

"One-oh-three to Radio...any reports of explosion or fire at the refinery...we observed a bright flash of light in the sky to the south."

"One-oh-three standby...all units standby."

After approximately two minutes of dead air, Radio announced, "All units South Division...be advised...Twelfth District has confirmed with refinery personnel... no founded report of fire or explosion at this time... repeat...no founded report of any fire or explosion... all units South Division... check your areas for a possible source...KGF587...the time is 1: 38 a.m.

Eager to solve the mystery, Sullivan declared, "I'm gonna roll around see what I can see."

"Okay, be careful," Tommy replied as 1710-Car drove away.

After downing the cup of coffee using the bathroom became urgent as he hustled from his car and made it to the men's room just in time. After taking care of business, he casually left the building without interacting with anyone. He entered 178-Car and cautiously steered out of the driveway, making his way on Nineteenth Street.

He decided to head back to the shopping center, and if need be, set up camp. With the street staying plowed, except for occasionally clearing off the front and rear windshields, that would be a relatively central location for future calls. While driving to his destination, he was feeling tired, and with the headlights reflecting off the snowflakes, he had to catch himself from nodding off. When he arrived at Grays Ferry Avenue, and as he passed under a train trestle approaching Washington, he noticed the stone wall enclosing a lot next to the elevated railroad tracks. He spotted a small shadowy figure through the gloom. Squinting as he peered through the fog of falling white powder, he caught sight of a wet and shivering dog sitting on the lot barely inside the open gate.

"What's this little guy doing out here on a night like this?" Tommy muttered aloud.

He stopped the car before the entrance and directed the side spot-light on the animal who stared back at the beam, then turned and wandered into the darkness.

"I gotta get this little guy inside," he mumbled as he pulled into the dark enclosed space to a point where he could see one shipping container positioned against the concrete railroad embankment. He noticed it was about twenty feet long, and the open doors were facing the gate entrance. As he swept the interior with the spotlight, he discovered it was empty. He maneuvered the light around the perimeter of the enclosed grounds trying to locate the dog.

Where the hell did he go? he wondered to himself.

Noticing another entryway on the northwest corner of the stone wall, he got out of the car and trudged towards it where he found a wide locked iron gate, and at the bottom was enough space for a dog to fit. Shining his flashlight through the sides, he caught sight of the wet animal trotting away on a paved driveway leading to the riverbank.

"Crap, ain't no way of helping him now, I guess he knows what he's doing," Tommy commented out loud.

While walking back to the patrol car, he turned his attention to the empty container. As he brushed off his coat, he pondered, *Hmm — enough room for a police car to fit in out of the weather.*

With the decision made, he thought to himself, *Yeah, here's the spot, clean off the windshield, stay dry, fifty feet from the road — jackpot.*

As he prepared to finesse the car into its new shelter from the storm, Radio called out,

"One-seven-eight...two-three and Oakford...disabled auto blocking the highway."

"Crap," Tommy grumbled as he reached for the mike.

"One-seven-eight...okay."

He U-turned within the lot, exiting through the gate and crossed Grays Ferry, going onto Washington Avenue heading eastbound. While navigating down the pot-holed roadway, the sky for a split-second jolted the night into day, followed by a loud rumble. He skidded to a stop, slammed the gearshift into park, opened the door, and stood on his left leg peering up into the storm.

"What the hell's goin' on?" he yelled into the darkness.

Completing a 360-degree survey, he was even more baffled. He re-entered the car, pulled the door closed, and continued to the assignment. During the trip, Radio received multiple reports of a flash and explosive sound. Radio informed the units that the area was experiencing a unique atmospheric condition with a projected forecast of ten inches of snow or more accompanied by high winds.

"All units use extreme caution in your driving."

RPC-178 approached Twenty-Third and made a right. The snow in the roadway was getting deep with ruts forming from previous vehicles making a path. Although impressed with how well the new 178-Car was handling, he still used caution. As he approached the 1200 block of south Twenty-Third Street, he observed three males pushing a dark auto stuck in the road before the intersection. They were telling the driver to "rock it." The car gained traction, made a sharp right-hand turn onto Oakford Street, and fishtailed into an open parking space opening up the roadway. The men were laughing and high-fiving one another, and all were agreeing that "rockin' it" got the job done.

Tommy pulled up beside them, leaned over, lowered the passenger window, smiled, and yelled out, "Chuck Berry would be proud of you guys."

"Chuck Berry, whatta you mean, Chuck Berry?

"Cause you was 'a-rockin' and a-rollin' with that car."

The young men started howling and proudly declared, "Oh yeah, oh yeah, rockin' and a-rollin', dat's right, dat's right."

"You guys stay warm."

One of the males yelled out, "Oh yeah, we gonna get a little taste later, stay nice and toasty."

"I hear ya, have a good one," Tommy replied as he readied to pull away from the intersection.

Before he moved the vehicle, one of the men inquired, "Yo, yo, officer, what's with all the fireworks tonight?"

"Hell if I know, might be the Martians landing," Tommy joked with a grin.

The males started laughing and high-fiving again, and as Tommy was pulling away, they yelled back, "Tell them guys to stay in their own hood."

Tommy waved his hand out the window as he drove down Twenty-Third Street.

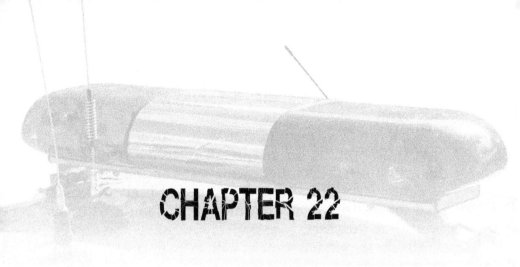

CHAPTER 22

A T 2:33 A. M., TOMMY reached for the mike, "one-seven-eight... back."

"One-seven-eight ...okay," Radio responded.

Driving along Twenty-Third Street and wanting to go back to the previously discovered "hole," his stomach started to growl as he realized he hadn't eaten since late afternoon. He decided to head over to the Broad Street diner, the only place open at that hour. He chuckled while thinking, *That place has never been closed. If nuclear war broke out, it would still be in business serving SOS to the mutants.*

"A few of them already patronize the place," he mumbled with a grin.

Tommy drove extra slow as he worked his way through the canyons of row houses in the western end of the district, taking extra care with the new car. The drive took about twenty minutes, far longer than usual. Once he informed Radio of his lunch break, he entered shortly before three a.m.

Whew, that was an adventure. A good meal, then back to the hole, he thought while taking a seat at the counter.

For a Friday night, it was unusually slow because of the weather.

"Hey, Helen, how you doin'? You catch a little break tonight?" Tommy greeted the elderly waitress while placing his wet hat on the next stool over.

"Yeah, Tommy, only a dinner tonight, no 'dinner and show' all the usual clowns couldn't make it in," Helen retorted.

"I'll take it, who needs the grief anyway," Tommy replied with a grin.

"What can I get you, hon? You want coffee?"

Without waiting for a reply, she placed a stained and chipped cup on the counter, swinging an ancient coffee pot over the receptacle, and pouring the hot brew in a practiced motion performed an unknown amount of times throughout the years.

"I'll take the western omelet with extra crispy home fries and a side of scrapple," Tommy ordered.

"You got it, hon. Hey, how's that cutie little girl of yours doing? Is she getting excited about Christmas?" she asked while writing up the order.

"Oh yeah, took her to see Santa today," Tommy beamed with pride.

"You're a lucky man, Tommy Tabbs," she commented with a smile while passing the check into the kitchen window with a fluid motion.

"Ain't that the truth," Tommy answered, reflectively staring down at the steaming coffee.

When his order arrived, he took his time enjoying the respite from the street. He swallowed the last bite and sipped the remnants of his cup. Helen came by asking if he wanted anything else while calculating the tab and tearing it from the pad, somehow knowing he had enough to eat.

As she placed the check in front of him, he answered while reaching for it, "Nah, I'm good, thanks, Helen."

The total was five dollars and fifty cents. He reached into his pocket, pulling out six one-dollar bills, and laid them on the counter.

"I'll bring your change."

She took the money and check and walked to the register. Thinking of a tip, Tommy pulled out his wallet and discovered he only had a twenty-dollar bill. He considered asking for change but stopped, and after a moment, he decided to leave it for her. Christmas was days away, and besides, he had always felt a special kinship for people who had to work the midnight shift and deal with the public, cop or not.

Returning with the change, and as she went to hand him the coins, Tommy declared, "I'm going on the four to twelve and day shift for a couple of weeks, so if I don't see you have a Merry Christmas."

As he handed her the bill, her face passed in an instant between surprise and joy, not just from the gladness of getting a nice tip, but the feeling that someone recognized her as a person and not just another fixture in the diner.

"Thank you, Tommy," she responded as she gazed from the gift to his face.

"God bless you — you and your family have a Merry Christmas," she professed as he left.

He checked the dashboard clock upon returning to the police car. The time was 3:38 a.m., and although he went past the twenty-minute allotment, he knew Radio would unofficially allow a reasonable extension as long as the shift wasn't busy. Before pulling out on northbound Broad Street, he cleaned the accumulated snow off the front and back windshields.

At Washington Avenue, the left-turn arrow turned green, and out of the corner of his eye, he spotted a red vehicle coming eastbound on Washington, attempting to stop for the red light. The horn sounded, and the car skidded right through the intersection at Broad Street. Tommy brought 178-Car to a stop and watched the show. Luck was with the operator because that intersection was at the juncture of two uniquely wide city streets. The vehicle skidded in a 360-degree turn coming to a perfect rest against the curb on the southeast side of Washington Avenue. Snow swirled around the car, temporarily obscuring it from view. Tommy hit the dome lights and carefully pulled in behind the stopped vehicle directing the spotlight on the interior. He got out and approached the driver's side as the operator was rolling down the window. Tommy noticed a middle-aged male dressed in a work uniform who didn't appear to be under the influence.

Tommy shouted jokingly through the wind, "I'm gonna score you at a 9.8 for that one."

"Holy crap, I thought I was gonna wind up wrapped around that light pole. I didn't realize how slick it was," the driver blurted out.

"Where are you coming from at this hour?" Tommy inquired as he was having difficulty holding on to his hat from blowing down the street.

"I just got outta work at the electric company dispatch center in West Philly. With the storm, we're getting slammed, worked sixteen hours before I got relieved," he yelled.

"Do you have your PECO ID?"

He showed him the card. Tommy inspected it and enquired, "Okay, be careful. You got far to go?"

"No, about six blocks. Thanks, officer, you stay safe too."

The driver started to roll the window up as Tommy turned and leaned into the wind holding his hat tight. When he returned to the police vehicle, he was relieved that the operator was not hurt, and the guy wasn't a drunk driver. Too tired that night for paperwork, he decided to forgo the incident report on the car stop. He figured no harm-no foul while turning the vehicle around heading westbound across Broad Street.

CHAPTER 23

ON WASHINGTON AVENUE, TOMMY HIT one of the countless potholes, and the vehicle bottomed out. "Crap gotta be more careful," he said out loud.

Washington Avenue was a cratered street that served as the main artery feeding the multiple factories, the majority of which were abandoned. The storm was visually turning the urban roadway into a country lane, but the wear and tear hazards were still there. Tommy had to navigate around those potential landmines from memory.

In about thirty minutes, he arrived back at Washington and Grays Ferry, stopping twice to clear the windshield and wipers of snow and ice. Crossing Grays Ferry, he drove through the stone wall opening, where he stopped and focused the spotlight into the shipping container making sure the car would fit. After assessing the dimensions, he shut off the light, put the gear into park, got out, cleaned off the roof and glass, re-entered, and backed in.

Once inside, he turned off the headlights, killed the engine, and opened the window. From that vantage point, there was an uninterrupted line of sight to the intersection through the open gate.

He shifted his weight around in the seat, got comfortable, and smiled as he thought to himself, *Oh yeah — snug as a bug.*

He turned on the interior light, picked up his Patrol Log, and wrote down various checks of buildings on the sector with the entry of "4:15 AM to 4:30 AM...Washington and

Grays Ferry...check the food warehouse." A property directly in his line of sight from his lair. Tommy was warm and content, happy to be out of the wind. After shutting the light, he reached inside his leather coat into his shirt pocket and retrieved a pack of Kools. He shook one out while pushing in the lighter. When it popped, he held it to the tip of the cigarette and inhaled. As he sat there smoking, his thoughts wandered to his wife and young daughter.

He was glad that it was the final day of the "Last Out" tour, and he would be home with his family soon. They had plans to go out for dinner, but the weather might change that. He didn't mind if they had to stay home. He loved being with them, often thinking to himself, *How did a mutt like me get so lucky?*

Taking a long last drag, he flicked the butt out the window and into the snow onto the lot surface. A feeling of peace and contentment surrounded him as he watched the flakes flutter chaotically in the storm. A fog gradually enveloped his view. It seemed to drift into the enclosure as he glanced down at the dashboard clock.

4:28 a.m.

A dream of his family carried him off to sleep.

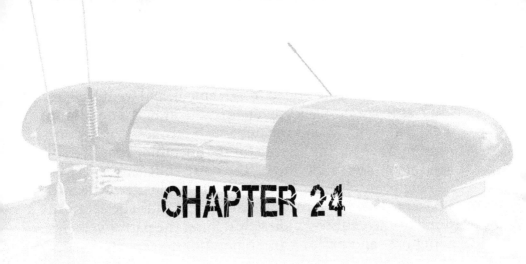

CHAPTER 24

OVERWHELMED GUTTERS WERE CAUSING A cascade of water to splatter to the sidewalks below. At 7:45 a.m., the weather was clear, the temperature was climbing fast, and the smell of sunshine was in the air. The morning was heating up so rapidly the snow was turning from stark white to gray from the meltwater escaping.

Sergeant Osborne, the late end supervisor, guided 17-B Car westbound on Federal Street, making a slow left-hand turn onto Point Breeze Avenue. A city firehouse on the corner was triangular shaped and situated on the north side of the 17th Police District headquarters. The police building's front entrance was on Twentieth Street with the rear door on Point Breeze Avenue, used as the primary entrance for police personnel, suspects, and prisoners. The sergeant entered into a small hallway and saw the day work "inside crew" and corporal in the Operations Room at their desks preparing for the shift.

"Yo Sarge, that was one bizarre storm you guys had last night," a desk officer commented when he entered the room.

"I heard the weather forecast on the way in; they said it could go up into the seventies today. It's a real freak show out there," the corporal added.

"Yeah, the snow's melting fast, and that was the slowest Friday night I can ever remember in this district," the sergeant replied. "I'm not complaining, hey, I'll take 'em every night like that except hold the storm."

They all smiled, nodded in agreement, and went back to work as Sergeant Osborne opened the drawer containing the schedule book and various squad business paperwork. Wanting to check the line-up for the upcoming tour of duty, he grabbed the "Pull Sheet," the daily shift roster. While making some changes, he glanced at the clock, which read 8:03 a.m. The day shift was holding roll call. The sergeant stood at the counter widow, watching the patrol vehicles going past and parking in preparation to report off duty. The officers started to gather at the rear of the building, awaiting their relief.

"What the hell was all that lightning and thunder last night? It was snowin'. It can't do that," Big Toe bellowed.

"Yeah, it can sometimes happen, "Steve Sullivan pointed out.

"What are you? 'Wally Kinan the Weather Man,'" Toe responded sarcastically.

"When a warm front meets a cold front, it can do that," Sullivan continued.

"Oh yeah, what is it when my foot meets your ass?"

"Hey Toe, I'm just trying to educate you."

That statement ignited a volley of comments from surrounding officers within earshot.

"Yo, Steveo, they only let you work about thirty years on this job. You ain't got enough time to educate this guy."

Toe took the heat and barked with his usual, "Hey, screw all you assholes, what do you guys know anyway?"

The everyday chatter continued between the other officers, not engaging in the banter. Their conversations ranged from bitching about the weather, the chances of the Eagles making the playoffs to what they were going to do on their days off. At 8:08 a.m., the day shift broke from roll call and started to exit the rear door. At first sight of their relief, the Three Squad members entered, one by one, and stopped at the window with Sergeant Osborne standing on the other side of the glass.

Centered in the partition was a circular speaking vent where they announced their badge numbers while they saluted and reported off duty. A tray below allowed the officers to slide in their Patrol Logs and any reports or tickets from the shift. Big Toe Caruso approached. "Twenty-eight-thirty-two reporting off."

The officer saluted as the sergeant returned the salute while checking off their badges against the squad Pull Sheet and collected their reports from the tray. The last officer reported off, and Osborne gathered up all the paperwork and placed it on the corporal's desk. He was relieved that the shift was over. He had worked too many during his career and casually commented to the corporal, "I'm getting too old for this crap."

About to put away the roster, he noticed that he hadn't checked off Tabbozzi's badge number. Turning and glancing back at the window, he wondered, *Did he report off, or did I miss marking him off?*

He decided to check out back for the patrol car. When he exited the building, the day tour officers were heading towards their vehicles.

"Hey, any of you guys seen One-seven-eight out here?" he yelled.

They shook their heads or verbally replied, "No."

A younger officer was walking down the sidewalk from the firehouse and said, "I checked on Twentieth. It's not there. I'm working that car today, Sarge."

"Alright, thanks. I'll call for Tabbozzi on the air."

Back in the Operations Room, he retrieved a hand-held portable unit from the charger and spoke into the microphone.

"Seventeen-B."

Radio responded, "Seventeen-B."

"Seventeen-B...see if you can raise one-seven-eight."

"Radio to one-seven-eight."

No answer.

"Radio to one-seven-eight."

No answer.

"Radio to one-seven-eight."

Still, no answer.

"KGF587, the time is 8:28 AM... Radio to seventeen-B... no response from one-seven-eight."

"Seventeen-B...okay."

The sergeant commented with a scowled face, "Where the hell is he? I want to go home," as he returned the radio to the charger.

Upon entering the Operations Room, Sergeant Rafferty from the day shift spotted Sergeant Osborne.

"Dan, what are you still doing here? I figured you'd be on the road by now?" Rafferty asked.

"Tabbozzi didn't report off yet. I tried to raise him on the air, no answer," Osborne stated.

"Why don't you take off? I'll get my guys to check his sector; he probably zonked-out somewhere and overslept. I'll chew him out when he comes in."

"Thanks, Ed, I'm beat, I appreciate it. I'll deal with him when we come back on Tuesday for blowin' the radio call."

Sergeant Osborne left the Operations Room when Sergeant Rafferty ordered the corporal to dial Police Radio and instruct 1703-Wagon to contact headquarters by phone. A few minutes passed when the hand-held unit on the Corporal's desk announces,

"Seventeen-oh-three...contact headquarters by phone."

"Seventeen-oh-three...okay."

In five minutes, the phone rang. The corporal answered and handed it to the sergeant.

"Yeah, listen, Marty, do me a favor and check around "F" sector, check out some of the holes, see if you can spot One-seven-eight. Tabbozzi didn't report off," Rafferty ordered.

"That ain't like him," Marty answered with concern in his voice.

"I know. Hey, first time for everything, I guess."

"We'll let you know, Sarge."

At 8:50 a.m.1703-Wagon started checking the shopping center parking lots, playgrounds, and church lots, and then continued to the side streets in the industrial section where the more obvious holes are located. The air temperature rose quickly, and the snow was fast turning to slush making it easier to maneuver the wagon through the less-traveled areas. The tension rose in the searching officers as they both scanned back and forth on each new street or parking lot they surveyed without finding the car. At 9:35 a.m., 17-B called for 1703-Wagon's location for a meet.

"Seventeen-oh-three...we're at Three-five and Wharton."

"Seventeen-B... await my arrival."

"Seventeen-oh-three... okay."

At 9:42 a.m., 17-B-Car pulled up to the driver's side window of 1703-Wagon.

"Sarge, we were up and down most of the streets where the usual holes are, so far nothing," Officer Martin Kaminski informed the supervisor.

"Damn, where the hell is this guy?" The sergeant wondered.

"He mighta got out to check a building, and with all that snow, he coulda slipped and got hurt," Kaminski offered.

"Yeah, but where's the car?" the sergeant pondered out loud.

"With that storm last night, I can't imagine he went any-place where the car could get stuck. He would most likely stay near the plowed streets. Alright, you guys keep looking. I'm going back to the district and confer with the lieutenant. If you spot him, call on the air immediately."

"Okay, Sarge, we're on it."

On the drive back to the 17th District, Sergeant Rafferty called Radio and requested 17- Command to meet him at headquarters. At 10:12 a.m., as Sergeant Rafferty pulled 17-B into the small side lot next to the building, he noticed 17-DC, the lieutenant's vehicle, parked in the designated space. Upon entering the Operations Room, Lieutenant Benjamin Haywood met him at the door and directed him into the roll call room.

"Lieutenant, Seventeen-oh-three is looking at all the possible spots he could have pulled into. I wanted to use 'Oh-three' because Kaminski is working it. You know him, send him out to hunt for something he usually finds it. I figured when they do find him, and God forbid he's hurt, I got two cops with him right away. So far nothing, I told them to keep looking," Sergeant Rafferty reported.

"Okay, Ed, but it's been over two hours. I'm notifying the captain. Order the corporal to contact South Detectives and start them in; I don't want to put it out over the air just yet. I want all cars and wagons to call headquarters; advise them over the phone to do a sub-sector search first to ensure all the streets are checked."

The corporal entered the room.

"Excuse me, Lieutenant. Tabbozzi's wife is on the phone. She got worried he hasn't come home yet."

The lieutenant and the sergeant anxiously glanced at each other. After a moment, the lieutenant ordered, "Corporal, tell her he's still on the street, and he may be delayed for a while. We'll have him call her as soon as possible. Then contact South Detectives."

CHAPTER 25

LIEUTENANT HAYWOOD NERVOUSLY DIALED THE number of Captain Arthur Weber. A call to the boss with bad news was always dicey, but especially so on a Saturday, his regular day off. When he was not working and wasn't at the district or available on the air, the squad lieutenants were the de facto commanding officers of the districts. An expectation of them was to make command decisions in his place. A missing officer was critical, and although he was confident with his orders so far, it was now time to notify the captain.

A woman's voice answered the other end of the phone, "Hello."

"Yes, ma'am, this is Lieutenant Haywood of the Seventeenth District calling for Captain Weber."

After several minutes, "Captain Weber speaking."

"Captain, Ben Haywood, there's a situation you need to be aware of."

The lieutenant outlined the facts. After contemplating, Weber responded, "Okay, Ben, I'm going to make my notifications, and I'm on my way in, establish a command post in the roll call room, start a scene log. Nice call on not putting anything out over the air. At some point, we might have to broadcast a BOLO citywide, and the press will go nuts. I don't want his wife to see anything on the news before we talk to her. I'll be in as soon as possible."

"Yes, sir, I'll make the preparations until you arrive," Haywood responded before hanging up and heading to the Operations Room.

Weber's first call was to the South Division Commanding Officer, Inspector John Donovan. He presented a summary of the details, and after a moment of silence, the divisional commander responded,

"We are now past three hours from reporting off time," Donovan stated, "this is serious in more ways than one. Before we send out a BOLO, I will notify the chain of command to the top so the news media doesn't catch them with their pants down. So, Art, I'm telling you now, if we find him asleep behind some factory — I will have his ass — do you understand?"

"Inspector, I do understand your position, but sir, this is way out of the pattern for this officer. He's a decorated cop, highly respected by everyone, and as you're aware, sir, he was vetted by IAD before being transferred into the Seventeenth," Weber proclaimed.

After a moment of silence, Inspector Donovan declared, "Okay, Art, respond in and get the ball rolling. I'll make the calls up the ladder, whatever you need, and Art —."

"Sir?"

"Find him!"

"Yes, sir."

At noon the commanding officer arrived at the 17th District.

"Corporal, where's the lieutenant?"

"He's in the roll-call room captain, and the detectives are also here."

Upon entering the room, he met Lieutenant Haywood, who saluted and started briefing him on the details of the investigation so far.

"Boss, the detectives are here. They're starting to compile all the Radio Logs, Patrol Logs, 48's, and tickets from Last Out. We're providing them with a roster of Three squad for phone interviews. As the cars and wagons call in with the streets they've searched, I'm having the corporal mark up a district map. I've taken the liberty of reaching out to the Marine and Aviation Units advising them of a possible order requesting their deployment."

"Okay, Ben, contact Detective Headquarters, request a female detective to be transported to the Tabbozzi residence by Highway Patrol ASAP. I want her to stay with the family until further notice. When we get the word, she's at the house and informed the wife I want a city-wide BOLO put out. Coordinate with the detective lieutenant for all press releases to go through Detective Headquarters. Call Radio and order supervisors from the Marine Unit, Aviation Unit, and Highway Patrol to the command post. And Ben, have the corporal activate the phone jacks and hook-up the extra lines in here."

They set up tables in the Roll Call room, the largest area within the district building, as officers and investigators scrambled to start a major investigation.

Upon his arrival at South Detective Division, Detective Al Fleming was first up on the "wheel," the system devised to allocate assignments. The first case went to the first name on the list. The supervisor would not issue another job until the wheel revolved around back to his name. The number of detectives working and the workload determined the rotational speed. After his supervisor advised him of the case and designated him as the assigned investigator, he was getting a sinking feeling he would be off the wheel for an extended period.

The Philadelphia Police Department directive stated as the assigned investigator on a crime scene or criminal complaint, he had total control of the investigation, but that was no ordinary case. He would work the job as a Missing Person with extenuating circumstances because the police vehicle was also missing. With all the bosses showing up, he would tread lightly; however, he was the "assigned" until told otherwise.

When he arrived at the 17th, he first met with the captain.

"Sir, as in any Missing Person case, we always check in the house first. I suggest we search the district building top to bottom, and I'd like to examine Tabbozzi's locker and personal auto," Fleming requested.

Weber considered Fleming for a moment and then ordered the lieutenant to assign two officers to carry out the request. He turned back to the Fleming and stated, "Al, I realize you know what you're doing, so keep doing your job, but make sure you record your moves on the log."

"Thanks, Cap. I'll keep you informed."

The detective realized he was dealing with an administrator familiar with the directive and wasn't afraid to delegate. Although he believed strongly, they wouldn't find the missing officer in the building; he instructed the officers to scour the building from basement to roof.

The corporal escorted Fleming to the locker room and keyed open Tabbozzi's lock. When opened, they found pictures of his wife and little girl along with scribbled drawings displayed proudly, finding nothing out of the ordinary nor any evidence Tabbozzi was depressed or wanted to run off somewhere. All indications were the occupant of that locker was a happy man. The investigator found and took a set of keys from the top shelf.

"Corp, can you run Tom Tabbozzi's name through DMV to find his car on the parking lot."

"I figured you'd want it. I ran it earlier, the print out is upstairs, and we located the car down the street on Point Breeze."

"Hey, thanks, Jim, I appreciate it."

They searched the personal vehicle, and again they found nothing to explain the cause of Tabbozzi not reporting off duty on time. Both officers returned to the Command Post.

The log officer advised the search of the 17th District building was negative, and the Highway Patrol team transporting the female detective was at the Tabbozzi residence and presently informing the officer's wife.

Fleming approached Weber, informed him of the results of the searches, and requested, "Captain — at this time I suggest we put out the city-wide BOLO along with ordering a Marine Unit response to the Schuylkill River and the Aviation Unit to start a search on "F" sector first."

"Marine and Aviation supervisors are on their way here, and their equipment is on the water, and in the air. Until something changes, we can coordinate their searches from here. Oh, also, stay sharp; a Night Command Chief Inspector is on his way here too," Weber informed him.

"Thanks, Cap, I'll contact Radio."

He called the Radio Room supervisor in charge. He instructed him to broadcast a city-wide BOLO for Radio Patrol Car-178 last seen being operated by Officer Thomas Tabbozzi, badge number 4431, assigned to the 17th Police District. If either vehicle or officer was sighted, contact Police Radio immediately.

Aware that the BOLO would trigger calls from the press because the media outlets monitor all Radio transmissions. He typed out a "white paper" outlining the incident's particulars and summarized the actions taken so far. He faxed the information to Detective Headquarters for use in all future inquiries.

CHAPTER 26

DETECTIVES WITH LOOSE TIES, ROLLED-UP sleeves, and papers in hand were moving from table to table. Others with cigarettes dangling from their lips were operating the phones and scribbling notes at 1:30 p.m., five and a half hours since the end of the tour for the Last Out squad. The investigator utilized the pull sheet to ascertain who worked the shift. When coming to Avner's name, it indicated his assignment to the Bus Detail and not present in the district last night. The detective was about to skip calling him when the officer recording the Scene Log advised that Avner and Tabbozzi were regular partners on 1701-Wagon.

Fleming overheard the exchange and ordered, "Call him first."

Nick was at home, sipping coffee, when the phone rang. "Hello"

"Is this Officer Nick Avner of the Seventeenth District?"

"Yeah, who's calling?"

"Detective Jim Lenzi from South Detectives; I'm calling about Officer Tom Tabbozzi."

Nick stood up and shouted, "Tommy, what happened? Is he alright?"

Lenzi advised, "He never reported off duty this morning."

"What do you mean? Is he in the hospital or something?"

"No, Officer Tabbozzi is missing along with One-seven-eight car."

116

Lenzi calmed him down, provided a summary of the case up to that point, and inquired, "Nick, I hate to ask, but did he seem depressed the last time you worked with him or say anything that would indicate he would just take off?"

"No, no freakin' way. Tommy was always up, always joking around; he has a nice family too. Ah hell, does Rosie know about this?"

"Yeah, she's aware, a female detective is staying with the family, and a Highway team is watching the house."

"Listen, I'm coming in," Nick declared as he rushed to hang up the phone.

Fleming had ordered the communication tapes pulled and a timeline of assignments for all cars and wagons from Last Out to be prepared.

Detective Lenzi reached Officer Steve Sullivan, and after Lenzi informed him of the situation, he explained the meeting with Tabbozzi at Graduate Hospital.

Sullivan added, "Yeah, after the sergeant signed our logs, he left. Tommy said he had to take a leak, we were about to leave when the sky lit up, and we heard a loud explosion. We thought it was down at the oil refinery, but it was just thunder and lightning."

"Did he appear to be despondent or anything out of the ordinary when you were talking to him?" Lenzi asked.

"Other than looking a little tired, no way, he was his usual Tommy Tabbs."

"So, is this the last time you saw him all night?"

"Yeah, I left first; we didn't roll too much except for assignments because of the storm. The night was slow. I only responded to one call, that unfounded assist officer at Broad and South."

"Okay, Steve. Call us if you think of anything else."

"Hey, I'm on my way in," Sullivan remarked as he hung up the phone.

Although the investigators contacted the majority of Three Squad personnel, they kept trying until they interviewed everyone. The special unit commanders and Chief

Inspector Kenneth Breevac arrived at the Command Post and reported into the Scene Log.

The assigned investigator and the supervisors conferred at a large map to formulate a search plan.

"I suggest we do an aerial survey of "F" sector immediately and a visual inspection of the all river embankments on the Schuylkill bordering the Seventeenth at this time," Fleming proposed. He followed up with a question to the Marine Unit, "Do we have sonar capabilities on the boats?"

Lieutenant Jack Snellings reported, "No, we'll request assistance from the Coast Guard for that. I'll reach out to them right away. Also, be advised with all the snowmelt today, we may not be able to put divers in the water until possibly tomorrow. The current is running too fast."

After agreeing to a strategy, they relayed instructions to the vessels and aircraft via a dedicated frequency giving the team real-time results. Although being relieved by the on-coming squad, Corporal Jim Hansen reported completing the one squad sub-sector search. The department geographically divided each sector into four separate zones for search purposes and other administrative functions.

Captain Weber commanded, "Jim, notify them to start in on two squad sub-sectors, make sure they hit all the streets, if the cars miss any due to calls, the wagons will follow up. And Corporal, aren't you off duty now?"

"Yeah, boss, but I'll stick around as long as you need me."

"Thanks, Jim, I appreciate that we can use you," Weber replied with his stomach-churning as the gravity of the situation hit him.

Overcome with a sudden feeling of dread, the captain wanted to increase the intensity of the search, "Chief, I'd like to request sub-sector searches ordered city-wide at this time."

Breevac agreed and issued the order.

It was about 2:15 p.m. when Nick entered the 17th District, followed by other squad members. Lieutenant Haywood ushered them into the locker room for an updated briefing. They proposed taking their personal vehicles out on the street to hunt for their brother officer. The lieutenant directed them to ride two to a car, and each group would carry a hand-held radio.

"Stay in sight of one another. I don't want to be looking for another missing cop," Haywood mandated.

Nick and Big Toe paired up with Toe declaring he would drive.

"We'll take my car. Ain't no way I'm gonna be able to fit in that go-cart you got," Toe said while walking to an older Cadillac parked in the lot, which was more boat than a car.

Nick didn't care; he grabbed a radio before leaving the building and hurried to Toe's auto, anxious to get out on the street and start searching.

They concentrated on the industrial sections along the river; first, places such as rear loading docks, driveways, access roads leading up to the rail tracks, any possible site where an auto could fit. The temperature during the day had risen to seventy-two degrees and melted most of the snow from the previous night's storm. They used caution in any unpaved spots because of muddy conditions.

The Marine and Aviation units were reporting in the locales of their initial survey. A U.S. Coast Guard vessel was on the way to meet with the city craft to coordinate a sonar sweep of locations where a car could enter the water. There was precedent for that scenario from a prior case with another officer in the late seventies who became despondent and drove his police vehicle into the Schuylkill River, committing suicide. Police Divers recovered both the body and vehicle at that time.

The department painted large Radio Patrol Car vehicle identification numerals in black on the roof of all marked units allowing Aviation officers to spot and identify the vehicle from the air. Police helicopter pilots would focus on three numbers until the case was closed... *178.*

CHAPTER 27

WORRIED AND ANXIOUS AS EACH hour passed, Nick and Toe, with their heads pivoting from side to side, scanned down alleys and up side streets noticing every little thing. They decided to check out a section named Forgotten Bottom because Toe was familiar with the neighborhood from his time working at the shoe factory, at Thirty-Sixth and Reed Streets, before becoming an officer. The area was mostly industrial and commercial, with some residential housing bordered to the east by railroad tracks and woods bordering to the west along the Schuylkill River. While cruising, they called in the blocks and sections searched to the Command Post. The sun was setting with the darkness creeping in as Toe retrieved an oversized spotlight from the trunk. It was going on ten hours since reporting off time, and all kinds of scenarios were going through Nick's mind.

"Hey Toe, you worked with Tommy a lot longer than I did. You don't think he did something to himself? Like you know?"

"What the hell you talkin' about, bump himself off, no freakin' way, better chance somebody else woulda bumped him off first."

"What are you talking about? What? You think he had enemies?"

"No, I don't mean that. Tommy always treated every-body decent, even the knuckle-heads. I'm just saying he just wouldn't do that."

After a few moments of contemplation, Nick posed a question, "Hey, wait a minute. Tommy is a straight shooter, but what if he found out some information about, say, some dirty people. You know those guys don't play, they could make the car and everything disappear."

"What, you mean the mob? Yeah, they got some psychos working for them, but the mob bosses know you don't mess with a cop, it would bring too much heat back on them, and besides, you gotta relax, we're gonna find him."

"Yeah, but what if, for whatever reason, it was one of them. How would they disappear a car?"

Contemplating the question, Toe replied, "I guess all kinds of ways. Dump it in the river, pull it into a garage or building, strip it down, or somehow move it down to the auto crushing yard in Southwest Philly."

After digesting the answer, Nick declared, "Hey Toe, find a phone, and then let's take a ride."

Nick called and explained his theory to Detective Fleming. After listening to his idea, Fleming advised they've already considered that possibility. They had Twelfth District units in-route along with the Police Bus for a foot-search of the facility. He also reported that all railroad companies running through Philadelphia were checking any empty rail cars and all areas near their tracks, along with statewide 'BOLOs' being put out in Pennsylvania, New Jersey, and Delaware. Nick was relieved to find out the investigators were consid-ering all possibilities but still decided to check it out.

They made their way back to Twenty-Fifth Street, turning south, and when they arrived at Passyunk Avenue, they made a right and went west. Passyunk Avenue took them over the Schuylkill River into a heavily industrial section of the city. A forest of enormous oil and chemical storage tanks crowded the area along with blank-walled warehouses storing a myriad of material and goods. That section of the city also contained scrap metal facilities and acres of auto junkyards, one with the capability of turning a vehicle into an unrecognizable block of steel, rubber, and plastic. Arriving at the location, Nick was both discouraged and optimistic about discovering a padlock on the entrance.

"Yo, on the sign, closed on Saturday and Sunday," Nick noted as he read a placard posted on the fence.

"That don't mean nothing. The guy running this place is a little shady. He got popped awhile back for doin' some guys a favor by getting rid of their cars for the insurance money. They bring them in, and he sends them through the crusher. They get paid, and he gets paid — believe me, he wasn't doin' that during normal business hours," Toe explained.

Disheartened, Nick asked, "So this place could have taken in a car last night or today on the sly?"

"Yeah, if he owed somebody a favor, especially if it was the wrong kind of people, hard to tell, kid," Toe woefully answered.

Diverting their attention to the secured front chain-link gate of the property, they noticed a Twelfth District patrol car, a wagon, and a supervisor pull in with their dome lights on. Nick and Toe approached the officers with their badges and identified themselves. Sergeant Al Larson, 12A-Andy, advised them that other Twelfth District units were bringing the manager from his residence to the property, and the Police Bus was about ten minutes out.

An unmarked police vehicle pulled in occupied by two detectives from the Major Crime Unit. The scene was rapidly becoming more active with the arrival of another patrol car and 1200-Wagon, which contained the manager, Lester Collins, known to his friends and associates as Crunchy. No one was sure if people tagged him with the nickname before entering the auto salvage business or a result of his chosen occupation.

A tall, slim, straggle haired male wearing greasy overalls and a welder's cap stepped from the wagon. "You guys can't go in there without a warrant," he protested through missing teeth.

"You got something you're hiding? Did you accept any vehicles last night or today? You make us secure a warrant, and we're going to be finding VIN numbers, and whatever else, and if anything pops, I think you're bright enough to know what's going to happen," Major Crimes Detective Chuck Warner informed Crunchy.

"What is it you guys are looking for?"

"A marked police vehicle."

"A police car! What the hell are you talking about? You guys lost one of your cop cars, and you think I have it. This place ain't been open since Friday afternoon, and I'm the only one with keys, so if the only thing you're looking for is a police car, be my guest," Crunchy confidently answered while digging a sizable keyring out of the deep side pocket of his greasy overalls.

As he started walking towards the entrance, he abruptly stopped, gestured the detective for a private conversation, and asked in a low voice.

"Detective, you say you guys are only going to be looking for a police car, right?" He enquired with trepidation.

Warner hesitated, answering back in a whisper, "That's right, Crunchy — this time."

While turning the key in the lock with reluctance, the Police Bus arrived with fifty officers to perform a walk-through search. Nick and Toe witnessed the exchange, and both concluded that a substantial probability existed that 178-Car was not there. Deciding enough personnel were on the scene to run down the lead, they elected to return to the 17th District and continue their search. Upon their return, they continued riding relentlessly through the streets, occasionally stopping with Nick getting out on foot and shining the spotlight into alleys, lots, and vacant industrial buildings.

At the edge of Forgotten Bottom, they walked the banks of the Schuylkill River as the Marine Unit vessel bounced their light beam off the ripples over the water, and the Police helicopter showered down a shaft of light onto vast swaths of territory. The Aviation officers could see the marked police vehicles as they searched the grids of the sectors, their spotlights moving back and forth, slicing through the darkness. They felt that time passed slowly during the long night, but when Toe checked his watch, the time read 7:08 a.m.

"Nicky, I'm beat. We gotta go into headquarters. I need a little break. Sorry kid, I ain't been asleep since about eleven yesterday morning," Toe implored with an exhausted voice.

Although Nick didn't want to abandon the search, the constant influx of adrenaline from optimistic expectations on every turn of a corner to the disappointment of empty spaces took a toll on him. After agreeing to return to headquarters, and while on their way back, Toe indicated that although he was tired, he realized he was hungry and wanted to stop for a pork roll and egg sandwich at Lou's, a little deli that opened early at Twenty-Fifth and Kimball. Nick wasn't hungry, nor did he care if Toe diverted to eat, so he agreed to the plan.

They were traveling northbound on Grays Ferry Avenue when they approached Washington and stopped for the red light. As they sat, Nick glanced through the road salt smeared window of the Caddy" across Grays Ferry Avenue, where observed a lot with a fifteen-foot stone wall surrounding the property. In the middle of the wall was a massive solid iron sliding gate blocking the entrance secured with a rusted industrial padlock. Before the light turned green, Nick enquired, "Toe, what's that lot across the street with the stone wall?"

"Used to be a factory building, they knocked it down a while ago, but they left like fifteen feet of the outside walls in place, kinda like a fort around the lot. I remember seeing shipping containers in there from time to time."

"I wonder what's in there now. Pull up on the sidewalk. I'm gonna try to climb on top of the wall and take a look," Nick proposed with a shot of energy.

Toe steered the car over and onto the sidewalk alongside the wall. Nick got out and grabbed a foothold and handhold onto the stones of the barrier, but he was unable to secure a firm grip.

"Nicky, climb up on the hood — that'll get you to the top," Toe suggested while pointing to the front of the Caddy.

Although near dawn, the sun hadn't risen yet, so Toe handed him up the spotlight. Nick shined the light around the interior of the triangular-shaped lot following the linear footage of the border.

"What do you see?"

"Nothing yet... looks like an empty lot... I'm gonna jump down and check it out."

"How you gonna get out?"

"Bolts and hinges on the inside of the gate. I can climb up."

"Okay, be careful."

On the northernmost part of the lot, he noticed a twenty-foot-high concrete wall, the foundation abutment of the abandoned rail line resting above, and another closed gate in the northwest corner. Once on the ground, he started walking the wall's perimeter sweeping the light across the land. The floor was composed of larger, tightly compacted crushed stones and was relatively level. Nick didn't observe any tracks or markings on the surface. At about twenty-five feet from the concrete abutment wall, something caught his eye. As he moved toward it, he detected a medium brown substance along with some orange-brown material.

While kneeling and shining the light onto the object, he pulled out a pocket knife, and with the point of the blade, he moved the substance for a better view. A closer inspection revealed the remains of a crushed cigarette butt, saturated and broken apart. He could not determine the brand, and speculated someone could have flicked it down from the railroad tracks above or over the wall.

He continued to survey the lot for several more minutes. It seemed like nothing had been in the enclosure recently, and with the gates locked, a vehicle couldn't enter. Climbing up and over the gate, he dismounted, re-entered the car, and Toe drove away, stopping for a quick sandwich before heading inside.

When they entered, the room was buzzing, and the smell of tobacco and stale coffee hit them immediately. Numerous detectives dressed in suit coats, or shirt-sleeved, ties loosened were either talking on the phones or typing reports. White shirted Special Units supervisors monitored their radios for any updates from their units, and the captain was in his office conferring with a Night Command Chief Inspector.

Nick and Toe learned the Mayor and the Police Commissioner responded with the Mayor issuing an order making all city resources available to the search effort. A Fire Department Battalion Chief stopped in and advised the captain that Engine Company 24, the firehouse next door, would provide cots, coffee, and hot meals from their kitchen to all the officers.

The Police Department and the Fire Department historically had a healthy rivalry like two scrapping brothers; however, whenever one of their ranks went down, they were always there to back each other up.

The news media responded in force, and numerous tips were coming into the hotlines with the detectives following up on every piece of information. Three Squad officers straggled into the district weary and worried from a night of fruitless searching, every possible scenario going through their minds as they slumped into any available seating. Unable to find their brother officer, they were exhausted, frustrated, and discouraged.

Officer Thomas P. Tabbozzi, Badge #4431, was then missing for twenty-four hours.

CHAPTER 28

N EWS TRUCKS FROM THE LOCAL television stations were swarming the neighborhood. Shortly after the initial broadcast of the "BOLO" in the morning, reporters attempted to enter the building. By the afternoon, national media agencies were on the scene, which was becoming chaotic and interfering with the investigation. The police blocked all streets surrounding the district headquarters and set up a press area across from the front doors where Captain Weber conducted the first news conference.

Based on radio tapes, the investigators determined the calls assigned to 178-Car, and when and where Officer Tabbozzi went out to lunch, the diner at Broad and Ellsworth Streets. On the only two assignments dispatched to 178-Car, the call taker had recorded the names and phone numbers of the complainants. Detectives made contact and interviewed them.

Detective Jim Lenzi tracked down the midnight waitress from the diner, a Mrs. Helen Murkowski, who lived five blocks from the restaurant in a little well-kept row home. At about 4:30 p.m. on Saturday when Detective Lenzi arrived at her residence. He knocked on the aluminum storm door, and after several minutes an elderly female cautiously opened the inner door until the security chain stopped its swing.

"Yes, can I help you?" she enquired, considering the man with a slight sense of fear.

"Yes, ma'am, I'm Detective James Lenzi with South Detective Division, and I'd like to ask you a few questions if I can," he responded while holding up his badge and identification card.

"What's this about?"

"It regards Officer Thomas Tabbozzi from the Seventeenth District."

"Tommy? What happened to Tommy?" she implored as she hurriedly disengaged the chain, opened the door wide, and invited him in.

Lenzi stepped inside, telling her that he didn't report off duty at eight a.m., and a search was underway to find him.

"Do you remember him coming into the diner last night at any time?"

"Why yes, he came in about three in the morning. It wasn't very busy for a Friday night. He had a western omelet, home fries extra crispy, a side of scrapple, and a coffee. He stayed for about thirty to thirty-five minutes."

"Does he eat lunch there often?"

"When he's on the midnights, he comes in about four nights out of the shift, plus he always stopped in when he was in the Third District."

"So, you've known him for a while? Did he seem upset or anything out of the ordinary when you last spoke with him?"

"No, Tommy was always pleasant, always treated everybody with respect, he seemed happy."

"Did you talk about anything?"

"Yes, I asked him about his little girl, and he beamed right up when he told me he took her to see Santa."

"Did you notice anyone else in the place at the time, watching him or following him out when he left?"

"No, because of the storm, there was hardly a soul in there, and I watched him go out the door by himself."

"Okay. Can you think of anything else?"

"Yes, he gave me a twenty-dollar tip for a five-dollar and fifty cent tab, wished me a Merry Christmas, and then walked out the door. Oh my God, I hope everything will be alright with him. He's such a nice man, will you find him?"

"We're going to try our best, ma'am."

As he handed her his business card, he mentioned, "If you think of anything, please call me right away."

Lenzi returned to the Command Post, where he learned about information received from the tip line. A "PECO" Electric Company employee heard the news report and called in. He told the investigator that at about 3:40 to 3:45 a.m., while driving home from work, his car spun out at Broad and Washington right in front of a police car. Although he couldn't provide a good physical description of the officer, he was able to make out the car number as "178." When the vehicle left, it made a U-turn and went westbound on Washington Avenue.

Before finally going home, Detective Fleming conducted a meeting with the scene commander and other detectives to update and review all the facts they had gathered up to that point.

At thirty-six hours missing, officers throughout the city had visually scanned every sector in an effort to locate the missing officer and patrol car. The air search started on "F" sector, moving outward, up and down the river. The Coast Guard detected three sonar anomalies in the riverbed, and the Marine Unit deployed Police Divers to the locations. Hopes were bittersweet when they discovered vehicles disposed of many years ago and not associated with the case.

The ground, air, and water searches did not find one clue into the disappearance. The FBI and the Pennsylvania State Police sent investigators to the Command Post to form a joint task force.

At forty-eight hours missing, 8:00 a.m. on Monday, Captain Art Weber ordered all Three Squad members to go home and get some rest. They were still required to report for duty on Tuesday afternoon at four p.m. There were protests, but they sullenly realized they virtually searched the entire police division. They were tired and morose, but they reluctantly shuffled out the door and went home. The Detective Bureau ordered the 'Command Post' secured at noon on the twenty-third of December as the case turned into what appeared to be a long-term investigation.

On Tuesday, December 23, 1986, at about 3:35 p.m. Three Squad reported for duty and were grim as they conversed with one another quietly about the latest information and the course of action that had taken place. They were all wary of offering up any personal theories, not wanting to appear to have given up hope.

They filed haggardly into the Roll Call room. The squad lined up in two rows facing the sergeant and lieutenant. Just before the command of dress-right-dress, Big Toe left his customary position in the second row and walked to the front of the assembly, where he halted and faced Officer Vincent Lopez, the shortest member of the squad. Toe's action immediately redirected everyone's attention to him. Standing there, he stared down into the eyes of Lopez, who was baffled, not knowing what that oversized hothead wanted of him. As Toe stared more intently at him, his face turned into a scowl, and the thought struck Lopez that he should possibly move, which he did.

Toe lowered his head and stared solemnly at the floor. After a moment, he produced a roll of duct tape from his jacket pocket and kneeled where he tore about a one-foot piece off, and carefully stuck it to the scuffed vinyl tiles. He ripped a second piece and attached it diagonally over the first, creating an "X." He rose to his feet, took a step back, and stood at attention, looking at the "X." Both supervisors and officers were transfixed on the mark. Without taking his eyes from the floor, Toe proclaimed, "This is Tommy's spot, and it will always be his spot, and nobody stands here until Tabbs comes home."

There was a moment of silence, and then with heavy steps, Toe returned to his place in line. The Commanding Officer ordered City Maintenance to paint a permanent "X" replacing the tape.

The sergeant re-assigned Nick to a solo sector car from that time forward, and the department didn't replace Radio Patrol Car-178 with the 17th District staffing one less patrol vehicle. Shifts came and went. Time crept by, with days and weeks rolling into months since Tommy went missing.

On one of his twice-weekly visits, approximately six months after the disappearance, Nick stopped by to check in on Rosie and Sophia. While the little girl was watching "TV" in the living room Rosie and he were having coffee in the kitchen. After pouring the cups, she sat facing him and anxiously announced, "Nicky, I have something to tell you about Tommy."

"What? What is it, Rosie?" he ceased stirring his cup, and with a snap of his head, he looked up at her.

"Nicky, about a week before — before that night, Tommy had gone to the doctors for an annual physical. They did a complete work-up on him; I was always after him to stop smoking and to lose a little weight."

"Yeah, but he was in pretty good shape, except for the cigarettes. I tried to get him to quit, but you know him; he's a hard-head."

Starting to shake and tearing up, Rosie crumbled, "I got a call from the doctor about two weeks after — after he went missing.

With tears streaming down her face, she continued, "Nicky, they found cancer, lung cancer, stage three. I didn't want to tell you because I hoped Tommy would come home, and we could face this together."

Bursting into a hysterical bawl, she blurted out. "He probably killed himself. He didn't want us to see him go through that ordeal."

She put her head down into her arms and sobbed. He reached out and hugged her, stunned by the revelation. While holding her, his mind went over the words she said, and he asked, "Wait, Rosie, you said the doctor didn't speak to you until two weeks after Tommy disappeared. Right? So how could he know? Did he say he told Tommy?"

"Well, no, I'm — I'm not sure, I just thought he had," she answered, raising her face to meet his.

"Rosie, call him now. We have to know for sure if Tommy knew about this."

Rosie retrieved her phone book and dialed the doctor. She explained the situation to him, and he replied, "No, Mrs. Tabbozzi, I was unable to contact your husband. When I viewed the news reports, well, I wanted to tell you because I thought it could be pertinent to the police investigation, and you're listed as his 'medical contact.' I'm very sorry for your troubles, Mrs. Tabbozzi."

Rosie relayed the doctor's information to Nick, who left the house more perplexed than before.

CHAPTER 29

THE LOUD METALLIC THUMP ECHOED outside the room and down the basement hall. The squad members backed away from Big Toe as he took out his frustration on the steel locker.

"How the hell could somebody just vanish into thin air?" he roared, asking no one in particular as he leaned against the metal door held up by two huge fists.

Eight months had passed since the disappearance, and everyone was going through the motions in the performance of their duties, but ever searching for Tom Tabbozzi and 178-Car. The daily ball-busting sessions had ceased, and the storytelling was a thing of the past. They were discouraged, frustrated, and baffled. Every day brought unanswered questions of how an on-duty officer, along with a marked police vehicle, could have disappeared without a trace.

Especially affected was Nick, who was not only suffering the loss of a brother cop but his friend and mentor. He was deteriorating, and out of frustration, he started drinking heavily. After shift and days off, he drunkenly drifted along the streets, alleys, and riverbanks of the 17th. Helplessly hoping the next turn of the corner would uncover a clue. As he stumbled on these wanderings, he recalled the adventures and lessons learned while working with Tommy, but now it was just another dead-end job. His demeanor and work habits were slipping to the point of carelessness as he became shoddy in his appearance and negligent in his duties.

"Avner, your firearm is not loaded," Lieutenant Foster exclaimed as he stopped in front of Nick during Roll Call inspection.

He turned to Sergeant Osborne and commanded, "Sergeant, take this officer out of the assembly and instruct him on the proper procedure of loading and unloading the issued service revolver."

"Yes, sir. Avner, fall out to the rear, now!" Osborne ordered.

The other squad members, although standing at attention, were visibly peeved. Re-holstering, he marched to the back of the room, along with the fuming supervisor. When they arrived, Osborne pulled him into an ante-room, got right into his face, and began to chew him out.

"What are you thinking? You know better than that. Do you realize you put yourself and the rest of the squad in danger? You have to keep your head in the game. How in the hell did you not load your service revolver?"

"Sarge, I'm sorry. I was going to clean it, I unloaded, — left it in the locker, running late for Roll Call, forgot to re-load."

"There's no excuse, and button-up that shirt pocket, straighten out that gun belt. What's goin' on with you?"

After a moment, the sergeant calmed himself, shook his head while scanning the floor, then looked up into his face. "Nick, I know you're hurting, we're all hurting, but you've got to stay focused. You don't want to get somebody injured out there, now load up, and fall back in line."

Embarrassed, he answered, "Yes sir," as he loaded and re-joined the group.

At the briefing, the sergeant assigned him to 179-Car, and as he headed out on patrol, the radio was active. In the first four hours, he was running from job to job along with the rest of the squad, when unexpectedly, the wind kicked up, and the clouds moved in. A heavy August rain pounded down on the grimy landscape, causing steam to rise from the blacktop. Thunder and lightning accompanied the downpour, and with the volume of water cascading, the roadways appeared glass-like and clean. The storm caused the calls to slow down. Police referred to that phenomenon as "liquid cop," so Nick decided to take advantage of the lull, pick up some food, and eat lunch in the vehicle.

He stopped in front of a little sandwich shop at Twenty-Fifth and Kimball Streets. A place that Tommy loved, not just for the sandwiches but because of the people who owned the business. Once when explaining to Nick their background, he would say, "Nicky, they don't make people like this anymore. The lady that owns the place is 'one of a kind,' don't ever forget to stop in from time to time, and check up on her," adding with a chuckle, "not that she needs it."

The shop was an end of the row building with the entrance diagonal on the corner and the owner's apartment on the second floor. Mrs. Anna Moretti, known to everyone in the neighborhood as Nonie, was an elderly but sturdy Italian widow who owned and operated Lou's Deli for the past thirty years.

After marrying in Italy, Lou and Nonie immigrated to the United States. When World War II broke out, although not a U.S. citizen, he joined the U.S. Army, fought honorably, and at times, acted as an interpreter; once discharged, he returned home, worked nights at the food distribution center. During the day, he would push a wooden cart selling produce down the streets and alleys. They saved their money. In the early 1950s, they purchased the property at Twenty-Fifth and Kimball Streets, and an American dream began.

The store provided basic groceries plus hot and cold sandwiches prepared behind a small deli case on the side-wall next to the cash register. Over the years, the community started down sliding. Derelict and dilapidated properties were popping up within the blocks with more rental households than homeowners. Lou took pride in his property and business right up until the day a drug addict strung out and broke decided to try to rob the deli with a "Saturday Night Special." As a hardworking man who built the shop from nothing, he wouldn't tolerate anyone trying to steal from him, so he took direct action.

"Get outta here...ya bum," he commanded as he took the robber by the scruff of his neck and the seat of his pants and physically threw him out the front door onto the sidewalk.

The addict turned, pointed the gun at Lou, and fired one .22 caliber round into his lower chest. The projectile entered his body between two ribs and didn't exit. Instead, it hit bone, ricocheted, and tore apart his aorta, killing the man and another American dream in an instant.

Neighbors called 911, who broadcasted a description, and a 17th District wagon crew stopped a suspect on a pathway leading up to the railroad tracks running over Twenty-Fifth Street. The suspect, who had numerous arrests for drug possession, burglary, and theft, was not bright enough or coherent enough to dump the gun. The cheap, barely operable .22 caliber was a dead-on match to the bullet recovered from Lou's lifeless body.

It had been ten years since the tragedy occurred, and Mrs. Anna Moretti grieved over the loss of her Lou but decided to run the store by herself. Astute enough to realize the neighborhood was declining, she decided to acquire protection for herself. At a gun shop and pistol range on Spring Garden Street, she purchased a Smith and Wesson .357 Magnum four-inch revolver. While taking a training class, she showed amazing ability in handling the firearm. She carried the handgun holstered under a butcher's apron.

Several years later, one evening, about an hour before closing, two suspicious males entered the premises going to the rear soda case. One stayed in the back and called up to her, asking how much for a quart bottle, re-directing her attention as the other turned towards Nonie and approached the register. He lifted his shirt, exposing the butt of a handgun, and began pulling it as he moved forward.

What the two males weren't aware of was that she had reached into the apron and un-holstered her firearm when they first entered. The individual approaching the register had the barrel cleared from his belt and started to point it at her, but she produced the .357 faster and squeezed the trigger, striking him in the center of his chest, leaving an astonished expression on his death mask. The second person drew a pistol and fired with the shot going high and hitting the wall to her right. After recovering from the recoil, she pointed at him, fired once with the bullet catching him on the left side of his face, and instantly relieved him of his jaw and the right posterior portion of his head.

Multiple 911 calls came into Police Radio for a report of gunshots inside the store. When the first units arrived, the metallic smell of blood and gunpowder met them at the door, and they found the two males prostrate on the floor of the shop in ever-expanding pools of red liquid. She had re-holstered and was cleaning the glass of the deli case as if nothing happened.

The first statement she made to the officers was, "Ma-dawn! Madonna Mia! They got stuff all over my potato chip rack."

The Homicide Unit investigated and determined it was a justifiable shooting. Upon completion of the mandatory testing, the Ballistics Lab returned Nonie's Smith and Wesson .357 Magnum to her, and she has carried it ever since.

As the young officer stepped inside, a couple of kids were leaving, carrying sodas, but no other customers were there. Behind the counter, Nonie was "running a rag" cleaning. Her face brightened when she glanced up and saw him.

"Officer Nicky, how ya doin' tonight?"

Her face became solemn as she blessed herself and proclaimed, "I pray for Officer Tomas every day that he should come home."

"I know, Nonie. We're all praying," he replied with his head down and blank stare.

Trying in her way to change the subject, she asked, "Hey Officer Nicky, whenna ya gonna marry that pretty girl ya tell me about?"

"One of these days, Nonie, one of these days," he answered, smiling.

After a moment, he added, "You know something, Tommy loved stopping by here, he always wanted to check on you, make sure you were okay, he told me about your husband and everything, so if you ever need anything, you call me right away."

As she stood behind the counter with a motherly smile staring at him, listening to his words, she reflected momentarily and softly offered, "Officer Tomas teach-a-you good, you be careful when you work, you remember what he teach you, okay?"

"Okay, I will."

After a moment of silence, she said with a smile, "I make-a-you a nice sang-wich... whatever you want."

Nick ordered a Lou's Special, a provolone cheesesteak with peppers, onions, and egg on a perfectly baked South Philly roll. With a South Philly roll, the taste was unique, but the preponderance of its essence laid within the distinctive texture. Possessing the right amount of crust enclosing the soft inner dough, and when sliced, it cradled the stuffing like a shell, not messy. Dependable. It didn't crumble like so many imitations. It was authentic, just like Lou and Nonie.

CHAPTER 30

THE SOUND OF SNICKERING CAUSED Sergeant Osborne to turn from his paperwork, where he observed Nick stooping over and gathering up the contents of his briefcase while squad members passed by him. As he monitored his actions, the supervisor detected him staggering and slurring his words. In recent weeks the disappearance was making him progressively discouraged and frustrated. He was missing work, calling out, and when he did show up, he was hungover and useless.

Before leaving the room, the sergeant called him over to the side, leaned in close to his face, perceived a slight odor of alcohol, and inquired, "Avner, you been drinking today?

"No, Sarge. I'm just a little tired; I didn't sleep too well last night."

"How did you come into work this morning?" After asking the question, he hoped he wasn't going to create a problem.

"I got a ride in with Lopez, we take turns, and it was his turn."

A little relieved but still concerned, he stepped back and inspected the young officer. After a moment of consideration, he stated, "You have two choices here, you can go off sick and take a cab home, or if you refuse, I'll have to confiscate your service revolver and send you down to the Police Surgeon for a medical evaluation."

They stood there for a few minutes staring at one another, and then he dolefully answered, "Alright Sarge, I'll take the taxi home."

Nick changed, left his firearm in the locker, and went home. That was the last day of the day shift, so in his mind, it allowed him three days to stay drunk.

When he arrived, the house was empty; his mother was working a twelve-hour shift at the hospital and wouldn't be home until after eight p.m. The weather turned dreary with misty rain, and the house was dark as he sat on the couch, filling and draining glasses of whiskey. Alone with his demons, he passed out around five o'clock. As his mother entered the house, she spotted the discarded liquor bottles with her son sprawled out and unconscious. Twenty-eight years as a registered nurse wouldn't allow her to sit by and not take any action.

She set off into the kitchen, started a pot of coffee, then to the freezer, and pulled out every ice cube, placing them into a bucket. At the spigot, she filled it with cold water and retrieved multiple towels, carrying the items into the living room. Carefully she hoisted the pail and, with one smooth motion, poured it directly onto her son's head. The shock of the water startled him from a molten dream like a bolt of electricity. In an instant, he sprang to his feet, stumbling, unable to focus, trying to comprehend what was happening.

"What the hell are you doing?" he yelled out as he staggered into a lamp, knocking it to the floor.

In a calm voice, she answered, "I want to ask you the same thing."

As he stumbled to his feet, trying to maintain balance, he screamed, "Leave me alone, I don't want to talk about it."

His mother grabbed him by the shoulders, pushed him down into an armchair, picked up a towel, and dried his face and hair. He quieted down, and with his head bowed, he didn't resist. She noticed tears welling in his eyes.

"When Dad died, it was hard on me; I missed waiting for him on the porch when he got home from work. I miss all the Phillies games we saw together, I miss him every day, but even as young as I was, I could understand accidents happen, and sometimes people die, and I moved on," he expressed in a low voice.

"Then I got to work with Tommy. He was like a father or an older brother to me. He taught me about the job and life. Not knowing what happened to him, and with him missing is almost worse than if he got killed in the line of duty."

Breaking down, unable to speak, his mother consoled him and let him vent. After a while, she offered, "Nicholas, things are going to be difficult. You learned many things from both of them. Your Dad taught you to study hard and play baseball, and Tommy showed you how to do the job and stay safe on the street. Now you're going to have to step up, use what you learned, and move on. Neither one of them would want you to be like this."

With a throbbing head, he sat holding it in his hands, watching the floor spin. Eventually, she suggested, "Come on, take some aspirins, have some coffee, and I'll make you something to eat."

"Okay, Mom," he whispered while slowly rising and following her to the kitchen.

The first night back to work was the Last Out tour. He made it a point to show up early and sober, double-checking his equipment and uniform, ensuring everything was in order.

"How ya doin', kid?" Big Toe Caruso said, passing Nick in the hall.

"I'm good, Toe, feeling better."

"Nicky, I'll call for you later; I want to talk to you."

"About what?"

"Out on the street, kid," he declared with finality.

The first half of the shift was average with the usual amount of calls. At about three-thirty a.m., the jobs tapered off, and a request for a meet came over the radio.

"One-seven-six, if one-seven-nine is available, have him meet me at Taney and Catherine."

"One-seven-nine...Taney & Catherine...meet One-seven-six."

"One-seven-nine...okay."

The location was the Old Naval Home, an abandoned facility the site of the first United States Naval School before the academy in Annapolis, Maryland. He pulled up to the driver's window of 176-Car.

Nick looked over, and Toe started in, "Listen, if I ever see you make a car stop the way you did down on Thirty-Fourth Street last week, I'm gonna kick your ass. You don't ever stand fully in front of the driver's window, especially with someone sitting in the back seat. What the hell is wrong with you? Tabbs taught you better than that."

"Hey, if you don't want to do the job anymore, then quit, you got that fancy accounting degree, go push a pencil instead of a police car, you won't get hurt doin' that."

He stared at Toe, not sure how to answer.

Toe simmered down and continued, "Look, this is how it is. Shit happens in life, people live, and people die. One day they're here, the next day they ain't. It is what it is. The only thing we can do is keep on livin'. Nicky, I think you're a good cop, but you gotta get it together."

After a moment of embarrassment, he mumbled, "Sorry, Toe, I guess I've been a little screwed up lately."

"It's okay, kid, just keep your head in the game. Alright?"

"Here, have a coffee, take a donut too," Toe instructed as he passed a cup with the wrapped pastry on the lid out the window handing it over.

"Is that all you wanted to tell me?" Nick prodded.

"Relax, kid, have a little snack first."

After they ate and sipped down the coffee, Toe turned and, with a concerned expression on his face, told him.

"Yo, don't ever repeat what I'm going to tell you to anyone, understand?"

Nick apprehensively replied, "Yeah, Toe, what is it? What do you want to tell me?"

"Yeah, well, you know I live down in the Fourth District, my whole family and all my paesan are from down there. Well, I got this cousin; he's a little mobbed up. Now don't get me wrong, he ain't no 'made guy,' he's what you'd call an 'associate,'"

"Yeah...What about it?"

"So, I run into him, and I ask him to do me a favor."

"What kind of favor?"

"I asked him to check around with his goombahs to see if anybody had any kind of beef with Tommy."

"What makes you think he's going to do that?"

"Because I did him a favor. I run into him at a family function. He's pissed like he wants to whack somebody, so I calm him down, and I push him to tell me the story."

"Why'd he want to do that? What happened?"

"Here, his daughter, fifteen years old, runs away from home with this guy like twenty years older than her. He's lookin' to find him, and I figure he's gonna like chop him up and put him through a meat grinder. I quiet him down and tell him he doesn't need a murder rap following him around, so I tell him, let me look for her, I'll bring her back."

"So why would you do that, I mean, he's with the mob, and you're a cop?"

"Hey, it's still family, and besides, he'll owe me one."

"So, what happened?"

"It took me about a month, but I finally track the guy down to one of those big old single houses up in Chestnut Hill. I sit on the place, and I spot all kinds of young girls going in, staying overnight, and hanging around the house."

"What'd you do then?"

"So, I touch base with one of my old buddies who works in Sex Crimes. I tell him what I got. Here this asshole I'm looking at has a record of doing this shit in the past, he's got these girls like hypnotized, he's like one of them 'Chen-gollies,' you know."

"Svengali?"

"Yeah, what I say? Well, anyway, they do a raid, I go in with them, and I made a deal with my buddy that I could take my cousin's daughter outta there, like not have her be involved in the case. So, I walk her out, put her in my car, and I go up to this crud, and here he's some kind of college professor, and he's mouthing off and shit like that. So I tell him that he should shut up and thank us cause we probably just saved his life."

"So, what happens when you take her back home?"

"So, on the way back, I'm talking to the kid, I'm trying to find out what made her run off with that guy, and she gives me the story that a least he listens to her problems, and he pays attention to her, and all that stuff. So I ask her did he hurt her in any way or like assault her, she tells me no, he just let her stay in the house, some of the other girls did that but not her."

"Man, that was lucky she wasn't assaulted. What happened then?"

"So, she doesn't want to go back home because her father doesn't care about her, he doesn't come to any of her school things or nothing, so I promise her that I'll talk to her father about that."

"Yo Toe, you're a regular social worker."

"Yeah, yeah, yeah. So I take her home, I talk to the cousin, I tell him, yo, you were goin' to whack this guy for your daughter. Ain't it just easier to pay attention to her and take an interest, instead of choppin' a guy up? So, he's so glad that she's home safe that he swears to me, he's gonna do the right thing."

"So far, all I hear is you doing him a favor."

"I'm gettin' to that. So, like I say, he's all happy, and he says to me — 'Ant-knee — even though you're a cop, you're a stand-up guy, I owe you a one. 'So, I say funny; you should mention that.

"So, I ask him, could he find out if there's any word on the street about Tommy or if anyone heard any theories as to what happened, anything, if he could just keep his eyes open and drop a dime to me. I tell him I figure he can't give anybody up, but at this point, we're just looking for, you know — 'closing.'"

"Closure?"

"Yeah — closure."

CHAPTER 31

S HE SLID HER LEGS INTO the car; he shut the door and came around to the driver's side, pausing at the trunk to allow a vehicle to pass. While standing there, a warm spring breeze washed over him, along with a deep sense that a new phase of his life had started.

Over the last six months, he made significant changes, deciding to take what Tommy had taught him and do his best. He was learning to love the job again; things improved in both work and his personal life. In March 1988, Nick proposed to Abby, and she happily accepted. They decided to visit Rosie and Sophia to announce their engagement, although he thought subconsciously asking permission. A year and a half since the disappearance and in the back of their minds, they wondered if it was too soon. They were not sure how she would react.

On the ride over, they discussed the impact of the mystery on Rosie and Sophia.

"I don't know how she can hold up, first losing their little boy, then her husband," Abby commented without thinking.

"What do you mean, their little boy?" He glanced over with raised eyebrows.

"Oh, I shouldn't have told you that. She didn't want me to tell you," she tried to explain.

"Well, it wasn't that she didn't want you to know about their son."

"What do you mean? What was it then?"

"Well, she told me that they had a five-year-old little boy, but he died of pneumonia.

"They had a son who died?" He never told me that."

"She told me that Tommy loved having a son and had so many hopes and dreams for him. They were both devastated and depressed, then Sophia came along, and they gradually came out of their depressions. Of course, he became overly protective of them, but they were getting happy again, and she said that Tommy began to really come out of his depression when..."

"When what?"

"Well, when he started training you, she said that he was actually proud of you. I guess he looked at you like a son or something."

They were quiet for the rest of the ride as he contemplated the revelation with mixed emotions of both contentment and sadness.

They rang the doorbell and heard a growling bark from inside the house. A female voice called the dog off and commanded him to sit as the door opens.

"Abby, Nicky, come in. It's so nice you could stop by." Rosie smiled and hugged them as they stepped in.

"Uncle Santa, Aunt Abby, I can't wait to show you my new drawings," Sophia gushed with excitement as she dashed in from the kitchen.

"Sophia, hey honey, you look so pretty. What did you draw for us?" Abby said.

Nick reached down and scooped her up into his arms as she clutched him tightly around his neck.

"I missed you," he said, realizing he may have a daughter of his own in a few years.

He put her down and revealed, "I have something for you."

He opened the front door, reached out onto the porch, brought in a rectangular carton, and handed it to her.

"Nicky, what are you doing? You're going to spoil her." Rosie admonished as he handed her the gift.

"Hey, I'm Uncle Santa. I gotta bring her presents?"

Smiling with joy, she opened the box to discover a disassembled painting easel and several new brushes.

"Thank you, Uncle Santa, I love it, and I love you."

"We love you too, Sophia."

After he assembled the present, they went to the kitchen for coffee and cakes.

They sat; he smiled at Abby, then turned to Rosie and announced, "Rosie — Abby, and I have something to tell you."

"What? What is it?" she said, smiling, looking at both of them with an inkling of what it might be.

"We're engaged and getting married."

"Ah, I'm so happy for you, and so would Tommy. I'm sure he would."

Thinking back to all the funny things he would do and say, she sat there dreaming of the past as she reminisced, "He loved life, he was so contented with his little world, he enjoyed going to work, and then come home to us. On Sundays, on the day shift, I would cook a big meal and have it ready for him; we'd sit and eat and talk and laugh. He would tell me that one day when he retired, we would move down the shore. Sophia always loved the beach. He would spend hours with her building sandcastles. Oh, Nicky, I miss him so much, and I only wish he could be here for your wedding."

Sitting there, listening to her yearn for her husband, Nick swore to himself to uncover what happened to Tommy.

CHAPTER 32

O N FRIDAY, APRIL 8, 1988, he returned to work for the four p.m. to midnight shift, and as usual, the night was hectic with radio calls. The sector cars and wagons were handling multiple jobs throughout the district. At eleven-ten p.m., the alert tones rang out again for about the twentieth time.

"In the 17th District... Two-Two and South... Lonnie's Bar... Hold-up in progress...point of gun...no further information at this time... One-seven-six... One-seven-nine... Seventeen-oh-three... Seventeen-B... Sam-101...respond."

The assigned units acknowledged the job, hit the lights and sirens, and responded.

"One-seven-six... I'm a block out... I'll take the front," Officer Lopez reported on the air.

"One-seven-six...OK," Radio replied.

Nick answered the call and accelerated 179-Car north on Grays Ferry, approaching the right turn onto South Street. Within three blocks of the scene, he cut the lights and sirens. Getting close to Twenty-Second Street, he spotted 176-Car parked just before the front entrance of the bar with the driver's door open, but he couldn't locate Officer Lopez. Nick stopped 179-Car directly behind the other unit, and as he stepped from the vehicle, his ears rang, hearing the loud report of gunshots from inside. He dashed low to stay under the side window of the business, un-holstering as he moved.

Hugging the north side wall of the building, he progressed toward the corner entrance, peripherally he perceived another responding unit coming eastbound on South Street. He heard the distinctive squealing brakes from yet another unit on Twenty-Second Street. When he got to the door, he took a sideways glance, spotted Lopez firing his gun towards the back of the darkened interior, and saw him drop his weapon, grab his stomach, and collapse. Rampant heartbeats caused his chest to rebound off the inside of Nick's bullet-proof vest, and he was sweating to the point of losing the grip on his service revolver. Taking a deep breath, he pointed the firearm into the doorway, duck walking at floor level, he fired two quick shots toward the back of the taproom.

Down on his stomach, he crawled towards Lopez, grabbing hold of his bloody gun belt, and started to drag him back to the entrance. Back-up officers fired through the door to provide cover. He sensed the whiz of bullets passing over his head and smelled the combination of stale beer and gunpowder in the air as he tumbled the wounded officer through the doorway. The air was full of screams, but he perceived the sounds in slow motion and a vacuum. His body jolted with a sudden spasm from a sharp burning pain in his right calf muscle and an immediate slush mouth sensation, with the taste of copper. Rolling Lopez to safety, other officers drug them both out of the line of fire. Lying face up and dazed on the sidewalk, he recognized a familiar Stakeout Officer as he entered the scene, pointing a shotgun into the darkness.

No stranger to that type of scenario, Police Officer Walter "Butch" Warrington had responded to countless violent incidents involving firearms and shootings while assigned to the Stakeout Unit for the past twelve years. With two officers down, he took decisive action and entered the active shooting scene. Crossing the threshold of the door, he discharged the shotgun, rapidly pumping and ejecting the spent "pumpkin ball" shell, racking a double-aught buck round from the tube onto the lifter and into the chamber. He fired precisely with one goal in mind, to neutralize the threat. His partner followed behind, covering his rear. After spending four rounds, the back-up Stakeout cop shouted into the radio, "Suspects down! Suspects down!"

The report of two officers down and wounded initiated multiple "assist officer" calls. A bullet struck Lopez below his vest and lodged in the lower left stomach area, which was gushing blood as brother-officers bundled him into 912-Car with a 17th District officer cradling him and applying pressure to the wound.

Radio advised the hospital of two incoming wounded officers. Lopez arrived first, and the vehicle came to a screeching stop. Medical staff snatched him from the car onto a gurney and prepped him as they rolled.

They hurried Nick into 174-Car with a 17th District officer driving and another in the rear seat, struggling to keep him conscious. Arriving barely awake, and because of his leg wound, they hauled him out of the vehicle, and with his arms wrapped around the necks of two fellow officers, they ran him into the Emergency Room. At the examination section, immediately, nurses removed his gun belt, placing it on a tray. Nick's service revolver was not in the holster because it dropped at the scene during the haze of the shoot-out,

A nurse was cutting up his right trouser to expose the limb wound, and another was cleaning blood from a jagged hole on the left side of his face. Two doctors examined his injuries while the nurses cleaned them. He faintly registered the prick of an IV needle as saline, antibiotics, and pain relievers started to flow through his veins.

"Officer, it initially appears you are one lucky person," one of the physicians pronounced. "The wound in your leg is an in and out, not hitting anything vital. The real luck is in your facial area... in — out... bullet fragment — ricochet... two-inch scar on face... leg wound ...stitches."

Between the combination of adrenaline, shock, and the pain meds, he was fading in and out, catching snippets of what the doctor was saying.

Lopez endured seven hours of surgery where they removed a bullet that pierced his lower abdomen, tore through his gut, and lodged next to his lumbar spine. They repaired the intestines and stopped the major bleeding before placing him in a medically induced coma. His survival chances were marginal due to potential blood infections setting in, and if he did survive, his prospects of walking again were slim.

The medical facility was alive with activity with numerous police personnel. All the top brass were there from the commissioner on down the chain of command, and the mayor was in-route. Patrol units were bringing in family members of the wounded officers. The department held a news conference outside the Emergency Room with Lieutenant Frank McClendon, the designated spokesperson, conducting the event and answering the reporters' questions. All the local media outlets gathered, and they granted the incident complete coverage. WVPI News Station Anchor Dan Hastings reported during a special bulletin.

"Two Philadelphia Police Officers sustained gunshot wounds after responding to a hold-up inside a bar at Twenty-Second and South Streets at approximately 11:15 p.m. Officers transported the two Seventeenth District officers to Graduate Hospital, where one officer is presently in surgery for a gunshot wound to the abdomen in critical condition. Doctors are treating the second officer for two wounds. Preliminary reports are that his injuries are not life-threatening. It is reported that two unidentified suspects were shot and killed inside the crime scene after exchanging gunfire with members of the Police Stakeout Unit."

Nick was unsure where he was. He awakened from a deep sleep and felt a bandage taped to the left side of his face. His right leg, from the knee to the ankle, was throbbing. At first, he was having trouble focusing his vision, but once it cleared, he could make out the anxious but grateful face of his mother, standing at his bedside, tenderly holding his left hand. He turned his head and noticed his fiancé Abby York, displaying a similar expression.

"Nicky, Nicky, I was so worried. I don't know what I would have done if I lost you. I love you, Nicky," his mother expressed as she embraced him, trembling and weeping.

Abby burst into tears as she approached him, leaning in holding his hand to her face as she blurted out, "Nicky, I can't believe this happened. I was so scared when they told me; I didn't know what to think. Thank God you're going to be okay."

The picture of the shooting re-focused in his mind, and he asked, "Vinnie, how's Vinnie?"

In a solemn tone, Abby responded, "He's finally out of surgery, but he's in critical condition."

Still trying to comprehend the events, he stared blankly at the ceiling as his mother and fiancé sobbed. A nurse entered the room, checked his vital signs, adjusted some IVs, and informed him that there was a lot of brass waiting to visit him. She inquired if he would be willing to speak with them. He glanced at both his mother and Abby; they nodded with approval, and he agreed to allow them into the room.

"Nicky, you know they're calling you a hero. You saved Vince's life," Abby gushed. He said nothing, just stared into space, worried about his brother officer, but glad to be alive.

Captain Art Weber, the Commanding Officer, was the first to enter, greeting Mrs. Avner and Abby and then approached the bed.

"Nick, we're so thankful you're going to be okay. The whole squad is out there in support. The Police Commissioner and the Mayor would like to stop in if you're feeling up to it."

"Yes, sir — I don't mind."

"I'll bring them in."

The Police Commissioner entered and momentarily after Mayor Samuel T. Attwood, a physically imposing man of six-foot-four inches, stepped into the room. Although never serving as a police officer, his father was on the job for thirty-three years. Along the way, the Mayor had to play the political games, but he held great respect and a soft spot for the Police Department.

Ever the politician, he proclaimed bombastically, "Mrs. Avner, Miss York, it instills in me immense gladness that one of our 'sons of the city' is recovering in such capable hands. Officer Avner, I can't begin to tell you how proud we are of you."

Turning to each person in the room and staring into their eyes, one by one, and with deep concern in his voice, he continued.

"We are all praying for Officer Lopez's speedy recovery, but from the information I was given, he wouldn't be this far along if it hadn't been for you and your brave actions. You are an apex example of the dedication to duty that you and all your fellow officers display daily, and the city thanks you."

He tried to respond, but the Mayor continued, "Commissioner, upon completion of the investigation, I want the highest departmental honor bestowed on Officer Avner."

"Yes, sir, Your Honor," the commissioner responded.

"I don't want to disturb your rest any longer, so I will beg your leave," the Mayor said.

Nick weakly responded, "Thank you, Your Honor."

"Get well, son," the mayor expressed as he left the room.

Commissioner John Keyser stood there patiently smiling, waiting for the door to shut entirely, and once closed, he declared, "He means well as do all of us if you need anything, just ask. By the way, Nick, I'll be announcing the detectives' test in two weeks, and I expect to find your name on the applications. Just something to think about. Well, I won't bother you any longer, get some rest, and get strong."

With that, he saluted the young wounded officer, shook his hand, and left the room.

###

Three days after the shooting, the doctor discharged Nick to heal at home. Highway Patrol Officer Charlie Spurgeon and his partner, Officer John Pike, were in Nick's room, escorting him home. His leg wound and hospital regulations dictated he would exit the facility in a wheelchair.

A nurse entered his room with his medical instructions and a set of crutches. "Officer Avner, I understand your mother is a nurse. Have her change the bandage daily, and have her check for infection."

"I will. Thanks for everything."

By the way, I thought you would like to know, Officer Lopez is out of the coma, he's still unable to speak because of the intubation tubes, but he can communicate with the doctors through eye and facial inflections."

"He's going to make it?" Nick asked, hopefully.

"Still touch and go, but this is a good sign."

From the wheelchair, he looked up at the two Highway officers and implored, "Guys, you've got to take me to his room before we leave."

"Hey Nick, you got it." Officer Spurgeon answered.

Once the elevator doors opened on the fifth floor, they observed a packed hallway of relatives and friends, along with brother and sister officers. Officer Pike wheeled him to the entrance of room 508. When the family became aware of Nick's presence, they became very emotional and surrounded his wheelchair.

Vincent Lopez was a first-generation American, the first person born from his family on American soil. His parents escaped the communist dystopia of Cuba, risking their lives to get to America. They had relatives living in Philadelphia so, they decided to move there and start their new life. The father was so excited when he realized the significance of Philadelphia; he would expound to his family. "We are going from the 'grave of freedom' to the 'birthplace of liberty.'

His son, Vincent, wanted to be a police officer since he was a child. Watching all the cop shows on television and studying hard in the parochial schools he attended.

Parochial schools seemed to teach the prep courses for the city civil service exams. When Vince Lopez was nineteen years old, he took the test, entered, and graduated from the Police Academy. His parents were so proud of him, like he won a Nobel Prize.

The family gathered around Nick. The mother bowed down, took his hand, and started kissing it, speaking rapidly to him while blessing herself numerous times.

Que Dios te bendiga para siempre. Gracias por salvar a mi hijo. Eres un héroe entre los héroes

The father gently pulled her back. A young teenage girl, Vince's sister, spoke and translated, "My mother said, 'May God bless you forever, thank you for saving my son. You are a hero among heroes.'"

Emotionally overwhelmed, he softly asked, "How is Vince?"

"He's out of the coma. The doctors said, 'Thank God he is very strong.' We haven't been allowed to see him yet, they're cautious of infections, but we will be here until we can," the sister explained.

"When you're permitted to talk to him, will you please tell him I stopped by?"

The sister translated Nick's message to the family and the mother exclaimed, *Sí, sí, le diremos que estuvo aquí para él. Nunca olvidaremos lo que hizo por nuestra familia. Nicholas Dios lo bendiga.*

The sister translated, "Yes, yes, we will tell him that you were here for him. We will never forget what you did for our family, Nicholas, and God bless you."

Honored but worried, he left, with the Highway officers escorting him to the parked Highway Patrol vehicle, H-39.

CHAPTER 33

THE WARM SPRING BREEZE SWEPT across his face through the open window as he breathed in deep, feeling grateful to be alive. The Highway team brought Nick home to the house he shared with his widowed mother at 4008 Teesdale Street. It was the last one on the end of the block of connected dwellings, prevalent throughout the city, a little row house with a small open porch and a shared driveway on the side. They could have moved over the years, but they felt comfortable in the home, and his dad's life insurance policy paid off the mortgage. The commercial thoroughfare of Frankford Avenue, with its stores and offices which ran through the Mayfair section of the city, was about fifty feet from the front door.

He peered out of the vehicle as they approached the street, thinking of the times he experienced growing up in the neighborhood. Visions of him roaming the "avenue," checking out the shop windows, and afternoons at the Mayfair Theater popped into his mind. One of his favorite memories was of the Mayfair Diner, two blocks from his house. After his dad died, when his mother worked the night shift, she would leave him money for food. He'd walk to the restaurant and order a meatloaf dinner, ice tea, and a slice of apple pie with vanilla ice cream.

H-39 made the turn onto Teesdale Street, and Nick was surprised that most of the porches were full of neighbors. The car rolled steadily down the block while they clapped and cheered. The kids were holding up handmade signs welcoming him home. A security detailed Fifteenth District officer was waiting as they arrived at the house. The Highway vehicle came to a stop, he exited, and as he stood on the sidewalk, braced by his crutches, he heard a resounding ovation from the crowd of well-wishers, making him feel appreciative but self-conscious as he smiled and waved.

After several minutes he slowly climbed the four lower concrete steps to the house, across a small walkway and up to five more steps, across the little porch, and into the front door, waving to all before entering. Inside, his mother, Abby, various white-shirted and blue-shirted uniformed officers, and coming from the other side of the room was little Sophia Tabbozzi with Rosie behind her.

With tears in her eyes, she ran to Nick and hugged him as he stooped to meet her, and she said. "Uncle Santa, I'm so happy you're okay. We prayed for you in school. Mommy said you're a hero."

"Sophia. I'm so glad you're here to welcome me home," Nick responded sincerely.

His mother and Abby both embraced him, with Rosie Tabbozzi approaching as she kissed him on the cheek and hugged him. She bawled, "Nicky, thank God you're alright; I couldn't take losing two of you. Tommy would be so proud of you."

She turned away, sobbing with a police sergeant helping her to a chair and consoling her. The dining room table was full of food, dropped off by neighbors and friends of the family. The well-wishers left after about three hours when they recognized Nick was tired.

He went to his room and finally dropped off to sleep. In the middle of the night, he tossed and turned from the smell of gunpowder, snippets of him on the wet and sticky bar floor, and a vision of Lopez coated in blood. He bolted up-right from the flashes of gunshots over his head, gasping for breath, soaked in sweat, not yet realizing it was just a dream. He clicked on the small night-stand light and calmed down, wondering how many more nights would these sights and sounds haunt him. When he came down in the morning, both his mother and Abby were in the kitchen.

"Oh, you're up, sit, let me get you some coffee. How are you feeling?" his mother said as she hovered around him.

Surprised, Nick asked, "Abby, what are you doing here so early?"

"I wanted to stop by and see you before I went into work."

"I'm glad, but won't you be late?"

"I called and told them I'd be late, and my boss saw the news and told me to take the day off."

"Great, we'll hang out if you like."

Nick's mother sensed they should be together by themselves, and she gave them privacy as she busied herself in the kitchen. Abby listened intently to Nick as he answered her questions about the shooting.

"Were you scared?"

"Not in the bar. It happened so fast. It hit me when they put me into the car, and I started shaking."

"When I found out you were wounded, I almost fainted. I thought I lost you," she said as she teared up, holding him tight.

They stayed together most of the day with Abby waiting on him, getting him his medications, food, and drink, and making him comfortable as they continued to talk.

"Will you quit the department now?"

"I'm not quitting, Abs, I'm going to 'rehab' and get back on the job — and I'm taking the detectives test."

"Nicky, I'm so afraid for you to go back. What if something worse happens?"

"Abby, it wasn't my time to go, and besides, something's telling me I have more things left to do — and I know one of them is to find out what happened to Tommy."

###

When the department announced the detective test, Nick applied, securing all the necessary reading material. He recorded all the pertinent study information onto cassette tapes to listen to them, repeatedly, while rehabbing, pounding the facts into his head.

In the months ahead, Rosie kept in touch with him, concerned about his recovery. After telling her he was running again, she suggested that he take Chief with him.

"Rosie, you and Sophia need him for protection."

"We're moving in with my brother, his wife, and children. He has a large home in Somerton, and I won't be able to take the dog with us."

"But what about your home? You and Tommy loved it."

"Without Tommy, it's just a house, and I can't take care of it by myself anymore, and I can't walk the dog properly, you know how those Aussies love to run, and besides, Sophia will have her cousins to play with."

The memories of them enjoying their lives together in their home saddened him as he thought about how Tommy's disappearance transformed so many lives, even Chief's. Nick agreed to take the dog, thinking it would somehow be like Tommy being there beside him, just like in the wagon.

The vanishing was never off his mind. At times he placed Chief in the car, drove to the 17th District, and ran by the river through the deserted industrial sections and along the abandoned railroad tracks. The dog loved to run and listened to all of Nick's commands.

One day while jogging north on the elevated rails over Twenty-Fifth Street, they crossed Grays Ferry Avenue heading for the river. Chief suddenly stopped, then paced back and forth, barking, and growling down into a triangular-shaped enclosure with a stone wall. Nick was slightly ahead of him, and he was surprised at the behavior as he turned and approached the dog, who continued to bark.

"What is it, boy? What do you see?

He gazed down, attempting to locate the source of the dog's attention. Noticing both gates were closed, and the

160

yard was vacant, recalling the patch of ground from the night Tommy went missing. He calmed the growling animal, and as he re-attached the leash, he stared at the vacant land for several minutes, then turned and walked away.

"Nothing down there, boy... just another empty lot."

CHAPTER 34

THE SOUND OF METAL CLANGING at the front door caused him to look up from his book. He spotted a large letter size manila envelope dropped to the floor through the mail slot. After retrieving and opening the item, it revealed information from the City of Philadelphia Pension Board. The documents inside outlined the requirements to apply for a "Regulation 32" pension for a city employee injured in the line of duty and deemed physically unfit for full duty.

One of the items was a financial statement detailing the assets and expenditures of the city pension fund. It listed the names of the board members and the board's Chief Financial Advisor, Swarthmore Holdings. The name was familiar, but he couldn't place it. After reading for several minutes, he threw the entire packet in the trash. Not wanting a disability pension, he intended to return to full duty.

###

Nick's life had turned a corner, and he wanted to share it with Abby. He picked her up for a dinner date at the Chart House, an upscale establishment whose specialty was seafood. The restaurant was prominently located on the Delaware River on the south end of Penn's Landing. The area started as a landfill in 1976, intending to be the focal point for tourism in Philadelphia.

On that balmy July night in 1988, as Nick pulled the car into the parking lot extending out into the river, he and Abby saw the four sailing masts of the "Moshulu," an old windjammer, now a floating restaurant. The ship moored against the concrete bulkhead at the edge of the complex, and the water views beyond, gave the location a "down the shore" atmosphere.

Her long dark hair and deep blue eyes shined in the candlelight while he gazed and listened to her. He reflected on his ordeal and recovery and how grateful he was to be with her. The times they shared flashed in his mind, the way they met at City Hall, the dates they had, the first time he introduced her to Tommy and Rosie, and how proud he was to call her his girl. He couldn't believe he was sitting there, alive in that place with that beautiful girl. Tommy's words popped into his head of how he was one "lucky mutt" to have Rosie and Sophia. Nick realized what he meant. Their dinner came, and while enjoying it, they laughed and joked as he teased with the lobster claws. Leisurely finishing their meal, they shared a quiet conversation over coffee.

On the drive home, Abby asked if he was still having any pain from his wounds.

"Sometimes, I get sharp pains in my right jaw. The doc said it was probably a bullet fragment hitting a facial nerve."

"You know, Abbs, I'm not going to let anything stop me from getting back to full duty."

"I know, although I'm frightened, I'll always be there for you."

Continuing to talk, he told her about the Pension Fund documents he received, and out of curiosity, he asked her if she's ever heard of a company called Swarthmore Holdings.

She answered immediately, "Yes, don't you remember the day we met at City Hall when you knocked all the papers out of my hands?"

"What do you mean?" Nick replied puzzled.

"When you helped me put them all back in order, you asked me how somebody could buy all that property for one dollar, like Swarthmore Holdings," she explained.

As he visualized it, the picture suddenly became clear. "Yeah, I remember now. That's where I saw the name before. So how can they buy all that property for one dollar?"

"They weren't buying. They were selling."

"So, here's a company selling properties for one dollar, and now I find out they're investing our pension money. Shrewd," Nick remarked mockingly.

"They're hedge fund investors utilizing REIT's, 'Real Estate Investment Trusts.'"

"Well, it's been a while since I studied accounting. I'll have to brush up on that concept one day."

CHAPTER 35

O N A WARM SATURDAY MORNING in September 1988, Nick sat for the detectives' exam. He carefully marked the last answer box with the number two pencil, glanced at the wall clock, and noticed that three hours had passed. Not wanting to second guess himself, he handed it in without double-checking. Outside, other officers who finished the test earlier were standing, smoking, and asking one another what answers they gave on various questions.

"What did you have for number 28?" one officer asked, with another answering, "That was 'C.'"

They each tried to gauge how well they performed. Some were satisfied, others were discouraged, but nothing was official until the city posted the list.

###

Things were moving fast in Nick's life now. He had just completed the detectives' promotional test, and he had his appointment with the Police Surgeon, clearing the way to return to work.

He made it a point to visit Vince Lopez at the hospital, bringing him books and magazines. On his latest trip, he was surprised to see him out of bed and sitting in a chair. Several members of his family were there attending to his needs.

"Yo Nicky, check this out. I'm up and about. I told you all those sit-ups I used to do would pay off."

Expecting him to be bed-ridden for a long time, he turned to Vince's older brother, who was about six inches taller than the wounded officer, with a questioning expression. He shrugged and remarked, "Hey, for a half-pint, he's strong as a bull, God bless him."

He faced Lopez and declared, "Vinnie, you are something else, man."

Vince reached out for Nick's hand, holding it tight in both hands. With a low voice, he professed, "Nicky, I wouldn't even be here if it wasn't for you, thanks, brother."

"Listen, if I had been first on the scene, you would've been pulling my ass outta there.

"Well, I'll never forget what you did."

"Hey, the only thing you gotta do now is to get healthy, so you can go home and be with your family."

"Nicky, they sewed me up pretty good... I'm coming back on the job."

He glanced at Vince's brother with a puzzled look. The brother, with palms turned up and a tilt of his head, stated, "We learned a long time ago, when Vinnie gets an idea in his mind, he usually does what he says."

He turned back to a determined grin on his friend's face. While shaking his head, he smiled and declared, "I believe you will."

On the second Saturday in October, Nick Avner and Abigail York were married at Saint Matthew's Parrish in Mayfair. The weather was damp, and the skies were cloudy, but the church was bright and cozy as little Sophia Tabbozzi took her cue from the organist and slowly moved with measured paces, gracefully spreading petals along the way. The family and guest trained their gazes on Abigail, dressed in a delicately embroidered gown and veil, as she glided down the aisle on the arm of her father.

Tommy would have been the best man, but without him, Nick asked the only other person who knew him better than himself to stand in, Anthony "Big Toe" Caruso. The hulking man stood next to the groom in a bulging rented tuxedo, and with his slicked-down hair, he bore a strong resemblance to "Lurch" from the *Addams Family*.

As Sophia approached the altar, she gazed up at Nick with an adoring smile; looking back at her, he smiled and winked. Proudly, she performed her duties and stepped to the side, allowing the bride to take her place at the altar.

The Cottage Green hall on Ashton Road was the reception site serving a formal dinner to a relatively small gathering of about sixty people.

"Except for Aunt Abby, you were the prettiest girl at the wedding today, Sophia," Nick remarked as they danced with her standing on his shoes and holding his hands.

Rosie sat at a table with her head slightly tilted, smiling and sniffling while she studied the dancing couple, dreaming of things that should have been.

In January 1989, the Police Surgeon examined Nick and found him fit, signed the required certificate, and reinstated him to full duty. He would report to the district on the Last Out tour the following night. On his first night back to work, the second anniversary of the disappearance had just passed. He arrived early, entering the locker room, and heard the bellowing voice of Big Toe towards the back, recounting an adventure he and Tommy had years ago while working the wagon together.

"So, it's about four in the morning, Radio sends us to a disturbance house call down in the Fourth, 'cause they didn't have any wagons available, so we ain't never been there before. So, I'm driving, and before we get there, Tommy puts his sunglasses on and says to me, 'play along.' It turns out. The place is a house full of winos, raisin' hell, gettin' loud.

"So, we stop, he gets out with his nightstick and starts tapping it on the ground, you know like he's a blind guy. So, I catch on, and I go around and take his elbow, and you know, guide him up the steps, and I'm tellin' him 'okay... three more and you're at the front door.'"

At that juncture, the rest of the squad, most of which didn't work with Tommy, somehow knew the best was yet to come, so the excitement was building as they called out, "What he do then?"

Toe continued with great relish, "So he's in the door, and he's like feeling around with the stick and his hand, and he's got his head up like he's looking at something on the ceiling and moving his head back and forth like Stevie Wonder."

Everyone was listening to every word with anticipation.

"So now he's starting to bump into things like the end table, a lamp, and all the drunks in the house calm right down and are like fascinated by him, one of them asks me... 'What's wrong with him?'

"I point to my eyes and whisper, 'He's blind. Didn't you see the news, the police now got to hire the handicapped people,' and then another drunk says 'Yeah, I think I seen that on the TV'...and now they're all like 'Wow...that's wild, man'...so then one asks, 'Yo, how's he shoot his gun?'

"And I says...' He just points it, and I aim him, a little to the right, a little to the left', and they're all... 'Yeah...yeah... that sounds right'...so we mess around with them for a little while, and I says to them, 'Hey, you guys got to chill out for the night, okay?' So they agree to quiet down, and we start leaving, doing the routine all the way back to the wagon."

At that time, the audience was now laughing loudly, banging on lockers, and making various comments.

"So they're all out on the porch watching us when we reach the curb, I walk Tommy around to the driver's side, and he gets in, so now they're going ape-shit on the stoop, 'Yo, he's gonna drive the truck.' So he starts it up, puts it in gear, and pulls off, swerving side to side right on down the street. We're looking back in the rearview mirrors, and they're goin' nuts back at the house, yelling, 'He's drivin' the truck...the blind policeman is drivin' the truck'...we ride off into the sunset...laughing our balls off."

The officers were now howling with laughter and commenting, "You guys were crazy as hell."

Standing behind a row of lockers while listening to the story, he was smiling but melancholy. His friend was gone, but at the same time, he liked hearing the old stories about him. As he came around the corner, they noticed him and all abruptly quieted down while staring. Toe sheepishly mumbled, "Sorry, Nicky."

He glared at them straight-faced for a moment, gradually warmed into a smile, and replied, "I worked with both those guys, and you're right. They were crazy as hell."

The bulky cop stepped forward, grabbing him into a bear hug as the squad gathered around, shaking his hand and back-slapping, all welcoming him home.

"Welcome back, Nicky. We missed you."

A few months passed, and on a four to twelve shift, after roll call dismissal, Lieutenant Foster called Nick aside.

"I was talking to my guy from up at the FOP earlier, he tells me the detectives list is out, and I wanted to be the first to congratulate you. You came out at number two." He revealed while shaking his hand.

The news surprised him; he didn't expect the posting for another couple of months.

"Thanks, LT. I can't believe they posted it already."

"Word is the department wants to make thirty right off the bat.

"I gotta call my wife."

"Well, what are you waiting for? Hit the phone."

CHAPTER 36

D URING THE DAY SHIFT, NICK was on patrol in 179-Car when a radio call came over the air.

"One-seven-nine...take headquarters."

"One-seven-nine...OK."

He wondered what they wanted inside as he entered the Operations Room in the 17th. The corporal took notice and stated, "Yo, Nick, we got a call from Lieutenant Doyle up at the Commissioner's Office. He wants you there right away. I'll hold you out 'headquarters assignment' in-route to the 'PAB.' Who'd you piss off?"

With that comment, the other officers in the room started in with the usual ball-busting knowing he was not going up there to get his ass chewed out.

While exiting the district and getting into 179-Car, he pondered why the commissioner was calling him up to his office. He drove out and worked his way through South Philly out onto Broad Street while going north; he approached City Hall. The majestic 'urban fortress' sat directly in the middle of Broad Street. The morning sun highlighted the limestone, granite, and marble facade of the largest municipal building in the country. Although he had been inside for numerous court appearances, he had never really studied the exterior. Driving around the massive structure, he glanced up at the clock tower and spotted "William Penn" looking down on his domain. He wondered how many lives were changed with both positive and negative outcomes behind the walls of that historic building.

At Eighth and Race Streets, the site of the Police Administration Building, the main headquarters of the Philadelphia Police Department, he turned into the parking lot. The 'PAB,' also known as the Roundhouse, built in the early sixties, got its name from its unique handcuff shape. The outside walls and everything in it was round, from the exit signs to the elevators.

He found a parking space along the curb and pulled in. An older officer designated to the 'PAB' security walked by, and as Nick stepped out of the patrol car, he asked, "You gonna be awhile?"

"I'm not sure... I got called up to the Commissioner's Office."

The cop spotted Nick's name tag and remarked, "Officer Avner, that's okay, leave it there. Hey, that was one helluva job you did down there on South Street. Take your time, and don't worry about the car."

"Thanks, I appreciate it," he replied, surprised at his new notoriety.

Lieutenant Doyle, the administrative lieutenant, met him at the Police Commissioner's outer office.

"Officer Avner, come in. The commissioner will see you momentarily."

"Yes, sir, thank you."

The lieutenant picked up the phone and made a short call. After a few moments, there was a buzz, and Nick strode into the Commissioner's office. Entering, he saluted, and announced, "Officer Avner, reporting as ordered, sir."

The commissioner returned the salute and reached out, shaking his hand.

"Nick, I'm glad to see you back on full duty. Please take a seat."

"Thank you, sir."

"As you're aware, when an officer is wounded in the line of duty as a result of a shooting incident, he or she is awarded his choice of assignment within his present rank."

"Yes, sir."

"Well, we have an unusual circumstance with you. Confidentially, I'm going to issue orders very shortly, promoting thirty officers to detective. With your position at number two on the list, I will allow you to pick your assignment within the Detective Bureau. So if you want to think it over, you can call Lieutenant Doyle with your decision."

"Well, sir, since it was posted, I've been thinking about it, and if it's alright with you, I can give you my answer now."

"Okay, Nick, what is it?"

"Sir, Major Crimes, and Commissioner, I realize this may be stretching it, but if at all possible, I have one other request."

"Go ahead, let me hear it."

"Well, sir, I found out that Detective Fleming is retiring at the end of the month, and he's the 'assigned investigator' on Officer Tabbozzi's disappearance.

"Well, sir, you know I have a personal interest with the investigation, being that Tom and I worked the wagon together since my first day on the street."

He hesitated and then continued.

"If my appointment to Major Crimes is approved... I would respectfully request to be named the 'assigned investigator' on the case."

He studied him for several minutes and asked, "How can you be sure that you'll be able to handle it, impartially?"

"Commissioner, for his family's sake, I'll do my best to find an answer as to what happened to Tommy."

After contemplating for several minutes, he then spoke, "Okay, let me think about it. Keep an eye on the teletype, thank you for coming in, dismissed."

"Thank you, sir." As he saluted, turned and left the office.

In two days, the department issued an official statement, announcing the promotion of thirty officers to the rank of Police Detective. In two weeks, they would hold the promotional ceremony at the Civic Center in West Philadelphia. On the day after the promotions, Nick learned of his transfer to the Major Crimes Unit, where he would report for duty in two days. Upon his arrival, the Commanding Officer of Major Crimes, Captain Edward Lacey, appointed him as the "assigned investigator" on the Officer Thomas Tabbozzi missing person case.

"Detective Avner, welcome to Major Crimes," he declared as he shook Nick's hand.

"Upon completion of your training period, I want you to reach out to Detective Fleming at South Detectives, where he'll brief you on all aspects of the investigation, and you'll take possession of the case file," Lacey instructed.

"Once you're up to speed on the details of the case, you'll coordinate and liaison with the Task Force FBI Special Agent, and I'll want a weekly "75-51" outlining all updates."

"Yes, sir," Nick eagerly answered.

He was anxious to start, and after completing the training a week later, he called Detective Fleming and set up a meeting.

CHAPTER 37

Larry, the veteran detective, appeared like he should have been sitting on a park bench feeding pigeons; instead, he was behind the South Detectives' operations desk when Nick arrived. The old-timer glanced up from the pile of Investigative Reports he was filing. His ever-present ancient coffee mug was teetering on a stack of paperwork.

"Yo kid, I remember your first day on the street. Now, your first day as a real 'crime fighter.'"

He gingerly stood to shake his hand.

Nick smiled and responded, "Thanks, Larry, I figured you'd be retired by now."

"I ain't goin' nowhere. They're gonna have to drag me out kickin' and screamin'. Hey, I heard you got 'assigned' on your partner's case."

"Yeah, I'm gonna give it my best shot; I gotta find some answers."

"I remember when I handled a missing cop investigation back in '59."

"What? What are you saying there was another case like Tommy's?" Nick asked, stunned by the revelation.

"Yeah. It was August 1, 1959, almost eleven p.m.; Officer Joe Reese was an hour late making a 'pull' at the 'call box.' The desk sergeant got worried, so he sent other cops out to look for him. They couldn't find him anywhere; he just disappeared." Larry explained.

"What? What do you mean, he disappeared?"

"Well, at first, we couldn't figure out where he was. Nobody knew what happened. It was dark out, the four to twelve shift. All the cops in the district were looking for him. Then we start getting calls about a foul odor in the area of Fifth and Clearfield. One of the sector cars drove over there and called in that he found the entire intersection had caved-in.

"What do you mean? The street caved-in?"

"Yeah, it was a hole in the ground, probably went down about forty-fifty feet. The trolley tracks stayed in place, but all the cobblestones went in on both sides. It musta' been leaking for a long time because it created a void the size of a barn.

"From the weight of the stones crashing down, it opened up the waste sewer, which stunk up the neighborhood, and the storm drain, which was originally an old creek — Gunners Run. They bricked it into a channel and buried it many years before.

"Well, we searched everywhere. We were thinking at the time; he mighta' got injured while on his foot beat like he mighta' been laying hurt up in an alley or someplace." Larry recalled, with a faraway gaze in his eyes.

"Did you find him?"

"We couldn't locate him anywhere in the neighborhood. We searched the cave-in but couldn't see any sign of him, and that storm channel was pushing a lot of water and running fast. The Water Department said about 15,000 gallons a minute."

Nick absorbed every word as Larry continued.

"We didn't want to believe he might be in that waterway, we kept searching, hoping maybe he just got on a trolley car and went somewhere. We were wishing for anything other than that storm sewer."

"Where did you search?"

"We scoured the city, and finally, on Saturday, August 8, 1959, we found him under the intersection of Richmond and East Somerset Streets, in the storm channel, two blocks away from being swept into the Delaware River and possibly out to the open sea. This was over two miles from Fifth and Clearfield, where he went in. A WWII vet, he made it back alive from a nightmare war, he gets 'on the job,' only to end up like that — God rest his soul."

"Larry, this is unbelievable."

"I was the assigned investigator on that job. I mighta' slept five hours over those seven days, yeah, he wasn't my partner, but he was a brother officer. It was real personal to every cop in the city at that time."

Standing speechless, never knowing about the story, he stared at Larry, unsure of what to say.

"Listen, Nick, I know what you're going through, searching for Tommy, so if you need a second opinion on something, call me kid, I'll be here."

He was awestruck at the amount of investigative knowledge the older detective accumulated over the years and the events he had witnessed.

"Larry, I appreciate telling me about that case, and believe me, I will be coming to you for advice."

Nick walked toward the back office with a newfound respect for a man, who up until that moment, was just another character in South Detectives.

Detective Al Fleming was in the five squad room, used by Divisional Detectives who were off the wheel, no longer assigned day to day cases, but conducted long term investigations within the division. He was assembling files. After twenty-eight years on the job, he was retiring, deciding to take his pension, and was lining up a second career as an insurance fraud investigator. Nick tapped lightly on the open door while saying, "Al, how you doin'? Getting ready to do some fishing?"

He turned and greeted him, "Yeah, I wish, but I might be going from the frying pan into the fire. Hey, congratulations on your promotion. I was glad to hear they made you the 'assigned' on Tommy's case. I have the entire file packed up for you."

"You gotta couple of minutes to go over it with me?"

"Yeah, sure."

The files filled four boxes, so Detective Fleming presented a summary.

"We had unlimited cooperation from the Feds, the State Police, and out-of-state departments," Flanders explained.

"They didn't turn up any leads?"

"Nothing credible, we searched rail cars, truck trailers, even container ships."

"How about any tips, even far-fetched ones from psychics, or whoever?"

"A case like that brings everybody out of the woodwork, yeah; we had various information and suggestions from many sources. We investigated anything that came in. Nothing panned out. Nick, we had access to all databases. I put a phone list in here for all agency contacts, so if you need anything from them, just reach out, and if you need anything from me, call me anytime."

As he loaded the boxes onto a small hand-truck and as he was about to leave the office, he expressed, "Thanks, Al, I appreciate all you've done on the investigation."

They shook hands, and Nick left. When he finished loading up the trunk, he stood back, rubbed his forehead, and stared at the files, now realizing he was officially the custodian of the last day of his wagon partner's life.

###

Nick's office contained a desk, a phone, and two file cabinets. After wheeling the case boxes, he started to set up shop. Pulling out the numerous folders, he felt overwhelmed with the new responsibility, not knowing where to start. He concentrated and decided to begin at the beginning. He took a couple of days to peruse the details, to acquire a basic working knowledge of all the particulars before coordinating with the other agencies, especially the FBI.

At midweek, Nick called Special Agent Michele Bohonik, the FBI Agent assigned to the case, meeting with her in the Federal Building at Seventh and Arch Streets.

"Detective Avner, welcome to the FBI. Have you fully recovered from your wounds?" S/A Bohonik asked cheerfully.

"Yes, I have, thanks for asking," Nick replied, realizing he was not in the locker room, bantering with his squad. He recognized he would have to draw more on his college background and become more analytical and refined in his demeanor.

"How about the other wound? Has the healing process started with that yet?" S/A Bohonik asked dryly.

Slightly perplexed, but somehow knowing what she meant, he replied, "What other wound?"

"Detective Avner, we're aware you and Officer Tabbozzi were wagon partners, and we realize you're very close to this case. We want to be sure your personal bias doesn't interfere in the investigation," she answered directly.

As she asked the question, she was drawing on her eleven years with the FBI, numerous investigations, and a psychology degree to elicit the right answer.

A spark of anger rose in him, but he composed himself and declared, "I worked with Tom Tabbozzi for almost five years on the wagon. He trained me on everything about police work from my first day on the job. We made multiple arrests, receiving many commendations. Tommy was not what one would call a formally educated man, but he held a PhD. in street smarts, and he taught me everything he knew. So believe me when I tell you, I'll use all the cop knowledge I gained, along with my formal education and one other factor — hope to conduct the best investigation I can. I owe it to him."

S/A Bohonik stared at him straight-faced for a moment, studying his demeanor, and then a smile appeared as she asked, "How do you take your coffee?"

At the meeting, S/A Bohonik summarized their investigation, which mostly mirrored the city's, and provided copies of a list of "tips" the Bureau received. He inquired if the FBI formulated a theory about what happened to Tommy. She became quiet for a moment and then revealed.

"After untold hours of investigation, thousands of unfounded leads, no physical evidence, and no direct witnesses, I can honestly say we have no idea how or why Officer Tabbozzi disappeared."

Nick thanked her for her input and honesty and assured her he would share any information he received.

Back at the unit, he decided to continue to study the case file, concentrating on the search maps. At about two p.m., the phone rang.

"Major Crimes, Detective Avner."

"Whoa, Detective Avner, I'm impressed," the caller on the other end said.

Nick recognized the voice and answered, "Yo, Toe. How you doin'?"

"Good, good, listen, Nicky, I gotta talk to you."

"Yeah, sure, you anywhere near my office, stop by."

"You kiddin' me? Them 'staffies' make me nervous. No, we'll grab a plate of mussels up on Fifth Street. You know the spot by West Ashdale up in Olney. We'll meet, okay?"

"Yeah, I'm in. Give me about forty-five minutes."

A little hole in the wall, the restaurant had been there for years. The place was somewhat worn out, but the food was the best-kept secret around. Tommy introduced him. They served a plate of steamed mussels with home-made red gravy, and the portion contained about two dozen, piled high, fresh, and perfectly cooked with just the right amount of garlic. A half a loaf of Italian bread on the side came with it for sopping. Toe was already sitting at a table, getting ready to order his second round of mussels, when he spotted Nick. He turned to the waitress and remarked, "Hey hon, make it two plates. My buddy is here."

Toe stood, shook Nick's hand, then gave him a bear hug, and commented, "Check you out — suit and tie. I like it. Yo, you better put a bib on. This could get messy."

"You mean the mussels or what you have to tell me?" Nick remarked with a smile.

"Cute, sit down, we'll eat, then we'll talk."

They enjoyed their meal, and while drinking their coffee, Toe started to speak.

"Nicky, you remember way back when I told you about my cousin, you know the one I did a favor for?"

"The time you got his daughter back when she ran off?"

"Yeah, that's right. He kept his word, and he reaches out to me and tells me that a guy who knows a guy works at a shipping container leasing company, and he says like a couple of months before Tommy goes missing, these two guys come in and want to buy a twenty-foot container."

"What's so unusual about that?"

"Well, my cousin's guy says, because companies just usually lease the containers and pay a per diem rate. If a company does buy any, it's always in bulk, like a hundred at a shot."

"So did this guy sell them any?"

"My cousin was a little hesitant to tell me. I guess it kinda goes against his nature to talk to a cop, but he owed me. It sounds like the guy did sell them one. He says they don't have serial numbers like a motor vehicle; they got what's called ISO numbers, which identifies who owns the container."

"So how does he think he's going to get away with selling somebody else's container? Doesn't he figure sooner or later the real owner is gonna find out?"

"I don't think he sweats it, there are so many containers, coming and going, and the ISO numbers are only painted on."

180

"Does he sell a lot of them?"

"Not so much the containers, but anything else he can steal from inside them, he's got a 'seal fabricator,' so he can pop the bonded seal, open it up, take a few items, and then re-seal the lock. He mighta' sold them some guns too, my cousin kinda' indicated that all kinds of stuff might 'fall out' of the containers from time to time, and this guy likes to make a buck."

"How's he know which ones to open?"

"Well, it's like this, if a box has guns in it, like Smith and Wesson, they ain't gonna ship under their own name, they use a code, and supposedly he got his hands on the master code list, which ain't legal, by the way."

"Did he give you where this guy works? Where's the container company located?"

"He wouldn't give it up out-right, all he would say it was in South Philly, and he said we couldn't miss it, so I do a little digging, and the only one down there is the Packer Avenue Marine Terminal."

"So if they only sell in bulk, and this guy sold them one, he got the right price, he got greased pretty good. Right?"

"No doubt, my cousin won't give up his name, but he did say the guy ran the yard."

"I'm thinking, we'll put a little sting together, flush him out, and then we can talk to him," Nick replied while contemplating.

With a broad grin, Toe retorted, "Well, you know, Nicky, you are a big hot-shot detective now."

CHAPTER 38

WHILE DRIVING BACK TO HIS office, Nick felt upbeat and concluded that was the first possible lead, not in the case file. He formulated a plan to interview the manager of the container company. Based on Toe's information concerning him selling stolen guns, Nick reached out to Special Agent Bob Clermont from the ATF, the Bureau of Alcohol, Tobacco, Firearms, and informed him of the details. He agreed to meet at the Major Crimes Unit.

"I appreciate you stopping by. Let me tell you what I have." Nick said, welcoming him into his office.

Starting right in with the particulars, he stated, "My source tells me this person of interest probably sold some guns to two individuals that may be of interest in my investigation."

"Can you tell me where he got the firearms?" the ATF agent asked.

"Sounds like, from inside the containers. He's got the 'master shipping code' so he knows which boxes to open."

"How's he do that? They're all locked with a bonded seal."

"Yeah, well, this guy covered all his bases. He also possesses an illegal 'fabricator' so he can gain access, do his thing, put on a new seal, and nobody can tell the difference."

"I wonder if it's the same guy whose name came up in one of our wiretaps."

"Can you tell me his name?"

"Yeah, a Frank Millburn, he's the dock manager."

"Bingo, my source says that the guy I'm looking for runs the yard. Agent Clermont, all I'm asking is after you guys make the arrest, I get to interview him?"

"No problem, if we snatch him the way I plan, he's going to want to talk to you, and he's for sure going to want to talk to me."

"Whatta' you got in mind?"

"We're going to ship him a little piece of cheese. We'll set up a container with a false front at the doors, stack boxes of firearms, non-operable of course, all the way to the roof about four feet deep, place ballast in the rest of the box, use one of the firearm companies' shippers code — on board in Boston and offload in Philly."

"You think he'll go for it?"

"With what we have on him and what you just told me, he'll go for it like a duck to water.

\#\#\#

After the ATF agent left and based on Larry's recitation of the case of the missing police officer from 1959, he scanned the chronology of the case file. He determined the investigators looked into that angle. After completing the review, he felt a small sense of relief, thinking back to the results of Larry's case.

The case files included the City-wide radio logs, listing every call dispatched or received from each district the night of December 20, 1986. He went through these documents, and a couple of things caught his eye. There were two "assist officer with a report of an officer shot" calls in the proximity of the 17th District. Officers responded to both dispatches, investigated, and declared them unfounded.

Knowing Tommy would always respond to an "assist officer" call, he verified on that night he did not. 178-Car received no other radio assignments for the remainder of the shift.

"This was when he went missing and why we didn't find out until 'reporting off' time," he mumbled. "But how, and why?"

CHAPTER 39

I N MID-NOVEMBER, NICK GOT A call.
  "Major Crimes, Detective Avner."
  "Detective, Bob Clermont from ATF; I'm wondering if you can stop by our office, I can update you on the investigation.
  "I'll be right over."
  As he traveled the four blocks over the oldest streets in the city, he wondered what new information had been uncovered and if it might help his case. Upon entering the Philadelphia Field Office of Alcohol, Tobacco, and Firearms, Agent Clermont greeted him, and they walked into a conference room. A woman in her thirties with blue-tinged spiked hair, a nose ring, and several studs protruding from her ear lobes was sitting in one of the chairs. Numerous tattoos covered both her arms and were visible from a sleeveless tank top.
  When first seeing her, Nick thought she was a suspect; detecting no handcuffs, he became slightly concerned when she stood, and he spotted a Glock 9mm handgun in a holster attached to her belt.
  "Detective Avner, this is Agent Amy Hampton. She's one of our undercover operatives on the case," Clermont said, introducing the two.
  Breathing a sigh of relief, he quickly stepped forward, extending his hand, not realizing he was staring at the tattoos on her arms.

"Tattoos aren't real, but they're not easy to take off either," she explained with a smile.

Embarrassed, he stammered, "I'm sorry, I guess I just wasn't expecting — um —my world is all uniforms, and I'm thinking you were a suspect."

"Hey, good; you didn't make her for a cop, did you?" Clermont asked.

"No way."

"Well, neither did our boy down at Packer Avenue."

"Agent Hampton is one of our best undercover operatives; hard to imagine she's just a regular soccer mom, off duty," he added.

Everyone sat, and they proceeded to brief Nick on the case.

"So, we staked out the guy you told us about, and we found his drinking spot," he explained.

"Yeah, and I was able to secure a bartending job there. We got friendly, and Millburn sold me a handgun." Hampton said.

"Her cover story is, her boyfriend is with a biker gang down in Virginia, and he's looking to lay his hands on some MAC-10's," Clermont added.

"A week later, I bought another gun from him and reminded him of the MAC's," she remarked.

"So, how's he going to come up with those kinds of firearms?" Nick inquired.

Clermont replied with a smile, "Two days ago, the bait container arrived at the Terminal, coded on the manifest as Ingram Military Armament, and loaded with them."

"You think he'll open the box and grab a couple?"

Hampton interjected, "He came into the bar last night, he was all excited, and tells me he scored some MAC-10's. Then he asks me 'how many do I want.'"

"Told him I wanted five, and he told me two hundred apiece."

"Did he go for it?"

I charmed him down to eight-fifty total, and he agreed," she replied, smiling.

"We'll set up a surveillance team on the Walt Whitman Bridge, we already scoped the terminal out, and we got lucky with a direct line of sight to the front of our bait box, so we'll be able to see him do his thing. We're going to let him open the doors, take the guns out, and deliver them to Amy. We'll scoop him up outside the bar, and we'll take her too, to keep the cover intact. Wait 'til you hear the mouth on this one when we cuff her. She really plays it up."

"Who says I'm playing?" she commented with a grin.

After laughing, they outlined the plans. The ATF would make the arrest; Nick would accompany them along with Philly Stakeout as a backup. Clermont advised once they executed the apprehension and processed him, Nick could talk to him.

The next night the operation went off without a hitch. The surveillance team videotaped the suspect opening the container, taking out the firearms, using the illegal 'seal' device, re-sealing the doors, and then delivering the items to the undercover agent. They made the arrest without incident, except when they 'arrested' Hampton; she was true to form, hurling enough threats and profanities to make a longshoreman blush. A Philly wagon transported the suspect to the ATF Field office for processing.

The investigators positively identified the suspect as Frank Milburn, the terminal manager, and he resided in Cherry Hill, New Jersey. They photographed and fingerprinted him and discovered he had a minor prior record. The arresting agents completed the process at about two a.m. That was his first significant arrest, and he was looking at substantial prison time if convicted. Milburn wasn't a stupid person, so he was waiting for the right opportunity to cooperate. Clermont and Nick sat across from him in an interview room, and the Philly detective started in with the interrogation.

"You're aware of the federal charges that are being lodged against you, but I'm here on a different matter. There's reason to believe, back in November-December 1986, you sold a twenty-foot container and some guns to two individuals. Do you remember the incident?"

"Whoa, what are you trying to do? Put another charge on me. I don't know nothing about nothing," Milburn responded.

Clermont interjected, "Listen, Frank, we have enough on you to send you away for about forty years. We don't need another one, so from this point forward, you can only help yourself, so think really hard."

Sitting and mulling over the words, he looked back and forth between the two officers and finally responded, "No charges on that incident?"

"No charges, with the right answers." the ATF agent stated.

"Okay, okay, yeah, these two goons come in and ask about buying one twenty-foot container, I tell them I can't sell one box, but if they want a hundred, we can talk. They didn't have a sense of humor."

"When exactly was this?" Nick asked.

While thinking over the question, his eyes scanned the ceiling, then he recalled, "It was the end of October in '86, yeah, I remember it was around Halloween."

"What happened then?"

"Well anyway, they pull out a wad of cash and start peeling off 'Franklins.' The one guy says, 'tell me when to stop' ...you know when I was happy with the amount. So, it got up to three grand, and I figured I better not push my luck, so I said 'stop,' and we made a deal. They wanted the ISO numbers painted over, so I threw in a new paint job for the whole box."

"What color?" Nick prodded.

"Gray, they wanted gray."

"What about the guns?" Clermont grilled.

"Yeah, I had two *Berretta 92FS* and two silencers, I figured these guys might be interested, and we made a deal for another two thousand."

Nick continued, "How did they take the container away?"

"I had the box painted overnight, and they come back the next night and picked it up. Crazy thing, they back in with this double tandem pickup truck with a hitch. They open the back drop-down gate and slide out this rig. It was light, mighta been made out of aluminum, like a bed frame with wheels. They pull out a customized jack, put these hooks into the corner 'lift slots' on the container, raise the box, glide in this 'dolly type rig,' attach it to the hitch, slap on a trailer license plate, brake lights on the back, plug em in, and away they go."

"Which way did they leave?"

"When they pulled out of the terminal, turned right, went north on Delaware Avenue, and that's the last time I ever saw them."

"What these guys look like?"

"Huge, six-four–six-five, white, military look about them, close-cut hair, no smiles, not a lot of talkin', all business, wearing those wrap-around sunglasses, scary dudes," Millburn added with trepidation.

"Anything else you can remember about them, any scars, any other physical features?"

He pondered the question, obviously trying to recall, when he suddenly disclosed, "Yeah, one thing, on one of the guy's right hand, you know on the back of his hand, he had a tattoo of a 'bulldog' and the words — ' Semper Fi' — I guess he used to be a Marine or something."

He started to run down the information on the container guys. The main clue was the Marine Corps tattoo on the back of the right hand. Nick's thoughts wandered back to his first day on the street and meeting Gunnery Sergeant Carl Hutchens. He wondered if he was still alive, so he decided to take a trip to the Philadelphia Naval Hospital, where he could ascertain Gunny's address in Buena, New Jersey, on the outskirts of Vineland.

He started out driving down to Gunny's farm the next day, working his way south on I-95 and over the battleship gray structure of the Walt Whitman Bridge. Crossing the river on the Pennsylvania side, while looking down, he caught sight of the Packer Avenue Marine Terminal.

An hour and fifteen minutes later, he entered a farm driveway. He passed through about two hundred yards of pine trees. Those woods were part of the "Pine Barrens," a vast natural forest throughout South Jersey, the alleged victim burial site of various mob hits, and the home to the "Jersey Devil," a creature allegedly sighted by many people throughout the years. The driveway eventually came to a clearing, an apparent farm field of about twenty-five acres, winter-barren, and muddy.

A well-kept small ranch house with a red two-story barn to the rear sat in the center of the farmland. Rolling across the gravel to the end of the drive, he stopped the vehicle and got out. On that cold and misty February afternoon, the stench hit him right away. A heavy farm aroma of damp earth, manure, and the same odor he smelled when he drove past the slaughterhouse on Aramingo Avenue back in Philly. He figured the smell must have bothered him more because he was a city boy all his life. He took a few steps towards the house when he heard a deep voice coming from the left rear.

"Can I help you with something?" the voice said with a suspicious tone, from behind a tree.

"Gunny, it's Nick Avner, Tom Tabbozzi's old partner. I met you at the Philly Naval Hospital," announcing loudly, hoping he was at the right address.

"You look like you put some meat on your bones and like you been through some trouble along the way too."

Turning towards the voice, he spotted and recognized the man he met years before standing on two legs, one human, one made of wood, stepping into sight. Although older and grayer, he was still huge and appeared healthy. They met midway and shook hands. Nick asked how he was doing and how Tyrell made out. The old Marine explained that he got his young nephew away from the city, and he brought him up the right way, down on the farm.

190

"That boy turned out good. You guys went to bat for him. Believe me. I never forgot that."

"Gunny, you heard about Tommy, I'm working the case, and I got a lead you might be able to help me with."

"What do you need?"

Nick told him about the male with the tattoo on his right hand who purchased the container and asked if he ever ran into any Marines with such a marking.

He rubbed his chin whiskers with his left hand while gazing at the ground, and with a slight motion, shook his head then posed a question, "This be a white guy about six foot four — real intense?"

"Yeah, that's sounds about right."

"I might know who he is, I knew lots of guys with tattoos, but only one I can remember with a 'tat' on the back of his hand. He felt it necessary to advertise."

"Where'd you know him from, Gunny?"

"He was in the platoon in Nam. He was a freak. Now listen, killing the enemy in battle is one thing. You got to do what you got to do, but this animal enjoyed the slaughter. He got a kick out of it."

"What do you mean, Gunny? What did he do?"

"He thought he was some kind of engineering genius, 'cause for him takin' out the enemy with military-issued ordnance wasn't sporting enough for him. He would make up all kinds of gadgets and traps, like trappin' a bear or something."

"What would he do with those things?"

"He'd catch one of them VC, then sneak in, up-close and personal, and do 'em with a knife, gut 'em. Like I said, he was a real freak. Me and him did not see eye to eye, 'cause I told him if any of our guys ever get caught up in one of his traps, me and him was gonna dance."

Nick detected a distant look in Gunny's eyes as he inquired. "You got a name?"

"Conrad Grimes, affectionately known as Slimes, and if you want to piss him off, call him Connie. The dirt-bag shoulda been in Leavenworth, and he ain't no fan of me either. You ever cross his path, be real careful. He's evil. What, you think he's in the Philly area, and he might have something to do with Tabbozzi?"

"Sounds like this mighta been him down at the Packer Avenue Terminal — but I'm not sure if he had anything to do with Tommy. Do you believe he could do jobs for the mob?"

"Maybe, there was some talk he was doing some money collectin' work, awhile back, and I know first-hand, he's a killer,"

They stood quiet for a moment when Nick broke the silence. "You have a nice place here, Gunny."

"Let me show you my prize passel of hogs," Gunny announced with pride as he directed him toward the rear of the barn.

When they approached, he spotted a sturdy fenced-in pen, with an entrance leading into the side of an outbuilding. The enclosure housed about thirty portly sized swine, white-skinned with a rose-colored tint.

"These here are called Chester Whites...'cause they originated in Chester, Pennsylvania," Gunny declared proudly.

"What do you feed them?"

"I feed mine cereal grain, I buy up a lot of day-old donuts at the bakery to fatten them up, and though, I don't particularly like to do it, every now and then — garbage.

"But you know, Avner, hogs will eat most anything, they'll devour meat, bone, gristle, anything, and they'll keep on eatin' — right on down to the shadow."

He stood there admiring the animals for as long as he could, but the acrid stink started to overwhelm him. Not wanting to disrespect Gunny, he put his hankie to his face feigning a running nose. Gunny spotted his discomfort, and with a chuckle, he remarked, "A couple of days sloppin' in the pen, and you won't even notice that fragrance."

"Sorry, Gunny, they are fine-looking hogs, though."

Shaking hands with the young detective, Gunny declared, "You gotta be going now. You got a job to do."

192

"Thanks for your help, Gunny; I'm glad I got to see you again."

Just before Nick got into the car, he called over to him, "Avner, you be careful, you hear."

CHAPTER 40

AFTER SLAMMING THE DRAWER, HE stood with his head hung low as his hands clutched the top side of the file cabinet. Six months of trying to locate Conrad Grimes proved a dead end. It was like that person ceased to exist. His last know whereabouts was from an arrest stemming from a bar fight in New York City. The victim didn't show for the hearing, they dropped the charges, and that's where the trail ended. Not sure how to proceed, a hunch struck him, and Tommy's words came to mind, "Follow the dollar trail."

He grabbed for the phone and dialed a number. Officer Peter Farrell, the police department representative to the City of Philadelphia Pension Board, answered, "Pension Board, Pete Farrell."

"Hi Pete, this is Nick Avner, from Major Crimes."

"Yo, Nick, how you doin'? I remember talking with you after you got wounded. How are you feeling? Okay?"

"Yeah, I'm good, thanks. I was wondering if you have a couple of minutes to talk?"

He told him he was running down all aspects of Tommy's disappearance case, no matter how absurd they might be.

"I don't like to think this way, but I'm lookin' at all angles."

"I understand. How can I help you?"

"Well, what if Tommy committed suicide and made it look like something else. I'm checking to determine what the Pension Fund rules would be on such a hypothetical premise?"

"Why would he do that?"

"Let's say, he found out he was — like terminally ill, and he wanted his wife and daughter taken care of."

"Wow, I never thought of that." After thinking for a moment, Pete continued. "The rule would be after seven years missing; the family would petition the courts, and have him declared dead, at which time they could apply to the Pension Board for payments. Once the court issues the declaration, they would also receive his life insurance and pension money."

Nick continued to ask questions along those lines, and when it seemed as if he was satisfied, he said, "Pete, thanks for your time, you know, as the 'assigned,' I have to run down all possibilities."

"I understand. Any time you need anything, call me," Pete offered.

Before hanging up, Nick asked, "By the way, how's the Pension Fund doing, we makin' money?"

"Oh yeah, for the past seven years, ever since Swarthmore Holdings took over as our contracted 'investment firm,' we've been makin' a lot of money," Pete advised proudly.

"Hey, if any extra is lying around, send it my way. I can use it," Nick joked with a chuckle.

"All on paper, Nick, all on paper," he declared.

One night while eating dinner with Abby, he brought up the day they met at City Hall. They smiled at the memory, and he asked her if she remembered him asking her about the name on the papers, Swarthmore Holdings.

She recalled and asked, "What about them."

He explained the investigation and told her he was trying to gather as much information he could about the company.

"I sure would like to take a look at their books," he mentioned casually.

After a moment of thought, Abby replied, "We don't have their financial records, but my company handles all the settlements on their real estate transactions."

"So, you would have records of any properties they bought and sold?"

"Yes, and any property they re-financed, also."

"Abby, do you think you could put together a list of these transactions?"

"Why? What are you looking for?"

"To be honest, I don't know, just a hunch."

Abby brought home the documents, and over the next several weeks, Nick studied them, detecting several unusual items. Swarthmore Holdings would purchase the properties for a low amount, record them at City Hall for one dollar, and then re-finance them for a much higher value through a Redstone Savings and Loan. He made a mental note to investigate both these companies further.

CHAPTER 41

T HE OCCASIONAL BARK FROM CHIEF at the blinking lights was the only noise in an otherwise quiet holiday celebration for Abby and Nick on Christmas Day 1990. Four years had passed since the disappearance, and that time of year brought painful memories. They invited Rosie and Sophia over for dinner, not sure they would show up.

"Your decorations are beautiful," she remarked while stepping through the door with Sophia in tow, trying to be cheerful, not wanting to dampen the spirit.

"Sophia, come and see what Santa left for you." Abby gushed while fussing over the child.

Pale-faced with sunken eyes, she shuffled to the tree, showing a slight smile. Nick and Abby exchanged glances, both worried about the little girl's appearance. Attributing her demeanor to the sadness for her father, they tried to cheer her up by showering her with gifts.

"Thank you, Uncle Santa and Aunt Abby, for all the presents," Sophia expressed, responding to all the attention.

"I hope Santa brought you what you asked for; with me being Uncle Santa, I kinda help him out, but he's the guy that brings the toys," Nick explained, hoping for a brighter smile from her.

"I ask him for the same thing every Christmas, but I never get my wish," she blurted out, bursting into tears.

Rosie wrapped her in a hug, and after a moment, the little girl turned, stared Nick directly in the eyes, and begged, "Uncle Santa, can you bring my daddy home?"

He knelt on one knee, took hold of her small hand, and replied, "Honey, I promise you, I'll never stop trying if you'll promise me that you'll never stop hoping."

As she reached out and hugged him, she professed, "I promise."

CHAPTER 42

AFTER ARRIVING BACK TO HIS office from a hearing on a partly cloudy Monday morning in March 1991, he found a message from Detective Mark Benaducci with the Erie Police Department. Grabbing a cup a coffee, he spilled some on his tie.

"Damn, this is brand new," he mumbled as he wiped the spill and read the note. "Erie PD — wonder what they want?

Dialing the phone, he reached their Major Crimes Unit.

"Benaducci, can I help you?"

"Yes, this is Detective Nick Avner, Philly Major Crimes, returning your call."

"Detective Avner, thanks for getting back to me. The reason I called is a little unusual. We have an unidentified male that a patrol unit found by some railroad tracks, semi-conscious and delirious. We transported him to the hospital, and he's in and out of consciousness."

"How can I help you?"

"Well, the strange part is, like I say, he's in and out, but when he comes to, he's rambling out words, more like babble, seems like a foreign language."

"What's he saying?"

"Something like — *policst toddygrada* — which when you hear it, it sounds like he's saying 'police' and then some kind of name starting with the letter 'T,' with some other indecipherable words. We have the flyer on your missing officer, and we noticed his name started with a 'T.' Hey, this may be nothing, but I figured I better give you a call."

Bolting upright in his chair, with a spark of hope, thinking they might have found Tommy, he quickly asked, "What's this guy look like?

"He's a white male, about five foot five, thin build, late fifties, gray hair. Benaducci answered.

Nick's heart sunk, knowing that was nowhere near Tommy's description.

"After we found him, we took him to the hospital for medical evaluation; physically, he had some scrapes and contusions in the facial area, and various body bruising. He also had some ligature marks on his wrist and ankles, no major injuries, but the doctors believe he's suffering from some type of mental shock. We had to 'Three-oh-two' him for a 'psych' evaluation. He's now in the Erie County Psychiatric Hospital."

Section 302 of the Pennsylvania Mental Health Procedures Act provides for an involuntary commitment of a person who are a danger to themselves or others due to a mental illness.

"Detective, I'd like to come out and attempt to interview this guy."

"Well, like I said, he's in and out at this time, but you're more than welcome to come on out and try."

Nick thanked him and hung up. Standing with his heart pounding, he considered the call. He was excited and leery at the same time as Nick rubbed the scar on his face figuring out his next move. The drive to Erie would take about seven hours, and he wondered if the trip was worth it, yet that was the first "tip" of that nature to come in.

A thought flashed in his mind, remembering something Tommy told him years ago, *Always listen to people — you gotta listen — you never know what they might tell you.*

That memory convinced him he should make the journey and at least check it out. He informed Lieutenant Dave Tricoste of MCU about the call from Erie PD.

"Okay, let's run this lead down. I want two detectives interviewing this guy so take Chuck with you. You can use Dan Nine-oh-eight to drive out. Oh, yeah, save the receipts."

Meeting up with Detective Chuck Warner in his office, he explained the game plan. He was an experienced investigator being with the Bureau for more than ten years, handling hundreds of cases. With seven years on the job, Nick was a veteran cop, but he was only a detective for eight months. He was relieved knowing Chuck was along to make sure he didn't miss anything. After stopping home to pack a bag, they finally made their way west on the turnpike at about two-thirty p.m.

"Did you bring any photos of Tommy?" Chuck inquired.

"Yeah, I have departmental copies in uniform and a couple of him in street clothes. I got them from Rosie, and I had them enlarged at the Photo Lab."

"Good, hey, this may be nothing. It could be some guy who saw Tommy's picture on the TV, but we'll check out how he reacts when we show him the photos. Did Erie PD identify him?"

"No, not yet, they still have him as an 'unidentified male.'"

The trip was long and tedious, with several traffic delays. They ran into a short rainstorm as they were approaching Pittsburgh, and Chuck was dozing. He woke, yawned, and stretched.

"Yo, next rest-stop, how about we pull in. I gotta take a leak, and we can get a couple of coffees," Warner suggested.

"Yeah, sure, no problem, hey, by the way, if you were trying to catch a little beauty rest, it didn't work." Nick joked with a grin.

"Yo, Avner, that bullet to the face didn't improve your looks any, but with a mug like yours, nothing could help," Warner rebounded.

They both started laughing, remembering back to the ball-busting sessions with the squad. He was glad to see his new partner possessed a cop sense of humor and realized he would learn a few things from him. The smile left his face as he posed a question.

"Hey Chuck, let me ask you. What's your theory as to what happened to Tommy?"

He turned in his seat and stared past him as he contemplated the right answer. After scratching the stubble on his face, he responded, "Listen, Nick, I know you and Tommy were partners on the wagon for years, and believe me, we should never lose hope, but I got to be honest with you, I think he got hit by the mob."

"What makes you say that?" he asked as he glanced across the seat.

"Look, killing a cop is one thing, but I worked in the Organized Crime Unit for a while, and from all them 'wiretaps' we used to do on these mafia guys, it was one thing to 'whack' a guy, but with these guys, it was also — 'we gotta send 'em a message' when they had a guy clipped."

"A message. What kind of message are they sending with that?"

"You know we find a body stuffed in the trunk, and the guy's tongue is cut out, well the message was he was a rat, an informer, so the one thing why I think it was a mob hit is because the car is gone too. I think the message was, 'not only will we clip a cop, but we'll take his patrol car — because we own the department.'"

"What are you saying? Tommy worked for some mobster, and somehow he screwed up and got himself whacked?"

"No, no way, he wasn't working for the mob, but I do think a boss might be, and from the message they sent, it's got to be a heavyweight like a commissioner, a deputy 'commish' or higher, like a city councilman."

"So a 'boss' is getting a note and Tommy gets whacked, I don't get it."

"Listen, my theory is some top dog might be grabbing a large 'note,' and for whatever reason, he didn't want to play nice anymore, or the 'boss' tried to tell them he was calling the shots, and they sent this message, 'no, we're pulling the strings, and you'll do the dancing.'"

"So why, Tommy?"

"I don't think they were after Tommy specifically. Any cop and an RPC would've sent the same message; I think he was in the wrong place at the wrong time."

Looking back out the windshield, Nick considered the theory. They arrived in Erie at about ten p.m. and found their way to the Erie Police Department headquarters at 626 State Street. Arriving, they located a diagonal parking space next to the town square across from the municipal building. Once inside, they asked for Detective Benaducci.

"He should be out in about ten minutes; he's finishing up an interview. Do you fellas want coffee or anything?" the desk officer asked.

"No, thanks, we had some a little while ago; we'll wait over here for him."

In the lobby, they noticed memorial pictures of two Erie police officers killed in the line of duty. While waiting for the detective, they paid their respects.

CHAPTER 43

THE METAL DOOR CRASHED OPEN and caught the waiting detective's attention. A burly tattooed male was bolting towards the exit, followed by a uniformed officer. In an instant, Nick reacted by sticking out his leg and tripping the fleeing individual. The cop, along with the Philadelphia detectives, subdued and cuffed him. A tall thin Erie detective approached as they yanked him to his feet.

"You must be the guys from Philly. Sorry about that, he's with one of our local biker gangs, and he didn't like the accommodations we were giving him."

"Hey, no problem, we had a little party with a biker gang awhile back." Nick declared with a smile.

"Detective Avner, nice to meet you, Mark Benaducci,"

"Mark, I'm Nick, this is Chuck Warner, thanks for calling; we appreciate it."

"Well, like I said, this guy may be nothing; I hate to bring you out here for nothing."

"That's okay; we're running down any possible leads."

"Come on back. I've got copies of our report for you. I also have a photo and prints," Benaducci stated as he ushered the Philly detectives back into the office area.

"Were you guys able to identify him?" Warner inquired.

"Nothing yet. We ran his prints, nothing came back on him, but he is without a doubt different. Although the clothes he was wearing were messy, they are what you might call more expensive than the average street person. He doesn't appear to be your run-of-the-mill urban camper, but he is suffering from some sort of delirium or dementia. The only physical injuries were the ligature marks on his wrists and ankles."

"What do you make of them?" Nick asked.

"It appears he was restrained with a rope or some type of cordage, his hands possibly secured behind him. From the angle of the bruising on his ankles, it appears like some kind of weight might have been attached to the bindings. He somehow broke free of the restraints and got away from whoever tied him up," the detective explained. "

It's a good thing he wasn't out here in the winter; we'd have to thaw him out first to talk to him," Benaducci added with a chuckle.

Once in the office, he produced the copies of the report and asked about the disappearance. Nick explained the background he had with Tommy and the circumstance surrounding the vanishing and summarized the investigation.

As he recounted the details, the Erie detective listened to every word. When finished, he professed, "This is an unbelievable case. When we first received the "flyer" and the "NCIC" alert, we couldn't imagine an officer and his patrol car going missing in a large city like Philly. I can't imagine what you're going through as his wagon partner. Whatever our department can do, just ask."

"Thanks, Mark, we appreciate it," Nick replied.

Directing them towards a rear exit of the building, he said. "Let's go. I know you're anxious to check this guy out."

Benaducci led them to the lot and a parked, unmarked police vehicle. After ten minutes of driving, they arrived at Second and Cherry Streets, the location of the Erie County Psychiatric Hospital. The red brick early modern institutional architect style reminded Nick of a small-scale version of Byberry State Hospital located at the end of the Roosevelt Boulevard in Northeast Philadelphia. As the vehicle stopped at the main gate, a security officer stepped from the booth, recognizing Benaducci he greeted him. "Mark, how's it going?"

"Good, Jack, I have two Philly detectives with me tonight."

"Okay, you know the drill, if you would leave your firearms in the lockboxes and sign in at our office."

They complied with the procedures, and a guard buzzed them into the secure area of the facility. As the door opened, the smell hit them, a combination of bleach, anti-septic, bodily odors, and despair. Escorted to the third floor by security, they entered room 308 and observed a white male in his late-fifties, gray hair, and stubble face lying on the bed. Leather straps restrained his wrists to the rails. The male had his eyes shut, and he was moaning. One moment he was whispering and the next shouting out indecipherable words. A psychiatric physician was standing in the room, reviewing the charts. The detectives identified themselves, and Nick asked the doctor, "Is he coherent enough to talk to?"

"He's been like this since he was brought in."

Chuck laid the case folder down on a table in the room and pulled out the photos of Tommy to present to the unidentified male. The Philly detectives approached the bedside, and with a loud voice, Nick spoke, "Mister, mister. Can you hear me?"

He placed the pictures in front of the male's face. His eyes rolled in his head as he squirmed from side to side, tugging at the restraints doing battle with unknown demons. After a few minutes of attempting to communicate, Chuck came in close to the side of his face and clapped loudly. The sharp sound got the patient's attention, and he stopped squirming and opened his eyes wide, staring straight at the images. His eyes wandered across the pictures from the center to the four corners digesting every square inch for several minutes. He then whispered in what sounded like a mixture of a foreign language and babble.

Polleest toddy-grad... nezz hoose schi...aecken.

He repeatedly uttered the phrase while staring at the images of Tommy. They attempted to question him, but the male was unresponsive, only repeating the unknown phrase until he tired, fell back to his pillow, shut his eyes, and descended into a restless sleep.

"Has he said anything else since he's been here?" Nick queried.

"Just babel, but this is the first time he's repeated anything multiple times."

"What could that mean?"

"It could signify nothing, but it could indicate that the photos are a catalyst or a stimulator of repressed memory."

Chuck asked Nick and Mark out into the hallway and suggested, "Look, I don't think we're going to get anywhere with him tonight. Why don't we take another run at him tomorrow."

They all agreed, and as they were leaving, Chuck stated, "I'll meet you at the elevator. I just want to ask the doctor one thing."

After about five minutes, they met up in the hall, went down to the office, retrieved their firearms, and left the hospital.

While pulling out of the parking lot, Nick asked Mark, "Is there anywhere close by we can get a room until tomorrow?"

"Yeah, no problem, we got you set up at the Holiday Inn. One of our retired cops is the night manager there," Mark replied and then suggested. "Hey, you guys hungry? I got a great spot for a burger and a couple of beers."

Realizing they haven't eaten since late morning, Chuck announced, "We're in."

"We'll stop by headquarters and pick up your car, and then you can follow me over."

Within ten minutes, they were back in D-908 and following Mark to the location, a corner bar about three blocks past the hotel. Parking the vehicles, they entered and noticed several off duty police officers arriving to have a few after their three to eleven shift. Benaducci introduced the Philly detectives to the owner, an older woman who reminded Nick of 'Nonie' from Lou's store, back at Twenty-Fifth and

Kimball. The Erie cops went out of their way to make the Philly detectives feel welcome. Nick put money up, saying to the bartender, "A round for everyone."

The off-duty Erie cops protested, "You're our guests — put your money away."

Chuck whispered to Nick. "Well, we can't insult these guys."

As they ate and drank, they gladly answered the many questions the Erie cops had about the case. Nick told them about Tommy training him from his first day on the street and how they worked the wagon together up until the time he went missing.

He recounted the stories about the pinches they made while partners, the unforgettable way he introduced him to his winemaking hobby, and the way he would tell a story in the locker room. They were engrossed in the recital, laughing at the humorous escapades about a brother officer from the other side of the Commonwealth, who vanished into thin air over four years ago. They proposed a toast to Tommy Tabbs, and by the end of the night, everyone in the place felt like they knew Tommy all their lives. He still had that effect on people.

The next morning all three detectives met back in the hospital room. The same doctor was there at the door, holding a folder, and revealed as they approached, "I have the items you requested, detective."

Chuck stepped forward, took the binder, and said, "Thanks Doc, can we go in?"

"You may proceed."

Nick glanced at his partner inquisitively, not knowing what was on his mind when Chuck turned to him and said, "Give me the photos."

Handing him the file, Chuck put it on the table. He arranged Tommy's photos into an assortment of pictures of objects, animals, and anonymous people. He told Nick to hold them in front of the patient's face, still restrained and squirming with his eyes shut, but less so than the previous night. Chuck clapped his hands, causing him to open his eyes, where they focused on the images Nick was holding. The first was a dog, no response, the second was a car, and he said nothing, the third picture was of Tommy in uniform, he muttered, *Polleest toddy-grad... nezz hoose schi...aecken.*

They continued the process until they depleted the stack of pictures, and on every one of Tommy's photo, he mumbled, *Polleest toddy-grad... nezz hoose schi...aecken.*

The detectives determined that the words seem the same every time. Abruptly the male shut his eyes and rambled numerous other indecipherable words, both yelling and whispering.

Chuck turned to the doctor, looking for an answer. "Well, Doc, what do you think?"

He took a moment, contemplating an explanation, and finally spoke, "I would say after observing his reaction to the photos of your missing officer, this could very well be stimuli into a repressed memory."

Nick was curious. "What is that, Doc?"

"They are recollections that have been unconsciously blocked due to the memory being associated with a high level of stress or trauma. Some psychologists believe these painful thoughts can exert an influence on an individual's behavior, which could undermine that person's mental state. This is because even though repressed, it's still an intact memory."

"Doctor, do you think we'll be able to obtain any further information from him at this time?" Nick inquired.

"No, I don't, but this new data will give us a basis to proceed with treatment and lead to his possible identification. I hope that these repressed memories are not so traumatic as to send him into a catatonic state where he could become unresponsive to therapy."

"How long can you keep him here, doc?" Chuck inquired.

"By way of a 'Three-oh-two Hearing', we can hold him indefinitely without anyone taking responsibility for him, or until he's deemed psychologically adequate to be on his own."

Before leaving, Nick made a request. "Mark, if you could do us a favor if he becomes coherent and they might release him. Could you contact me right away?"

"No problem, I'll keep tabs with the 'Doc,' I'll call you with any news."

They shook hands, and departed heading back to Route 79 south and eventually home. While driving, Nick glanced at his partner and commented, "With all the gibberish this guy was saying, I wish we would have brought a tape recorder."

Chuck reached into his jacket pocket and pulled out an object. "Forty bucks —Radio Shack."

Looking from Chuck's hand to his face, Nick spotted that ever-familiar grin.

CHAPTER 44

T HE DETECTIVES RETURNED TO PHILLY, and they were exhausted from the long trip. They agreed to meet in the morning and brief the lieutenant. The next day, between munching a bagel and gulping his coffee Nick finished the report and headed to the boss's office.

Over the next two weeks, between other investigations, Nick listened to the tape recordings and documented the words spoken. When he finished, he studied the list. Most of the terms seemed indecipherable, but there appeared to be a repeating pattern. Chuck was passing by the office, and Nick called out to him. "Yo, Chuck, you got a minute?"

"Yeah, what do you need?"

"Check this out; see if you can make anything of it."

He took the list, and with squinted eyes and head tilted back, he studied it at arm's length.

"Yo, pal, you might want to think about getting glasses — or a longer arm," Nick cracked.

Chuck raised his eyes, stared with a scowl, and replied, "What are you, an eye doctor, all of a sudden?"

Nick held his hands up, chest high, palms out, "Alright, alright, I just didn't want you to hurt yourself," he commented with a slight grin.

With a peeved look, Chuck went back to reading. After several minutes of study, he suggested, "To be honest with you, most of these words are bizarre; nothing makes sense. You oughta take this to Professor Woodward, out at

Pennypacker. He's a 'linguistic expert — we used him in the past. He might be able to do something with this; I'll give him a call and tell him you're stopping by."

###

The pedestrians were leaning into the breeze, bracing against the March winds as they staggered across Market Street. Crossing the intersections, Nick gripped the wheel of D-908 tight as he felt the car sway with each blast of air whistling through the urban canyons. After passing over the Schuylkill River on the Market Street Bridge, he worked his way through West Philadelphia and down to Pennypacker University. Locating the building, he parked and entered, dodging a crowd of students all bearing books, hurrying back and forth between classes. Within minutes, he was in the Department of Linguistics, where he met Professor John Woodward.

"Detective, come in. How can I help you?"

Nick handed him a copy of the list, outlining the context in which the unknown male had used the words.

"I'm particularly interested in the second word; do you think it could be a person's name, a surname?"

The professor sat at his cluttered desk, lighting a pipe as he studied the paper, and after ten minutes of scrutiny, he announced, "I do perceive some words which at the outset may have meanings; however, I would like to study this further and deliver my findings to you."

"That would be great. Thanks, Professor; I'll wait to hear from you," Nick remarked as he presented a business card, shook his hand, and left.

###

In the office on Monday morning, while pouring a coffee, he thought about the case and what Chuck had said during the trip. He wondered about the possibility that Tommy had been in the wrong place at the wrong time, and the mob had killed him. Stumped on how to proceed, Tommy's words came to mind, *A smart man doesn't know all the answers; he knows where to find them.*

The first name that popped into his head was Larry.

Yeah, Larry's been around so long, he knows where all the skeletons are buried, he mumbled to himself. *He might be able to point me in the right direction.*

A call to South Detectives revealed that Larry would be in at two-thirty p.m., so at two-forty, Nick arrived. As he walked in, he saw the familiar bald head and short, slim frame of the old detective sitting behind the operations desk, eating a cut-up apple.

"Yo, pal, what are you trying to do, get healthy, or something?" Nick remarked as he stepped up to the desk.

"Hey kid, how ya doin? Yeah, my doc says I gotta eat more fruit. What are you up to?" the elderly detective said as he stood up smiling.

"Hey, Larr, I need your advice on something."

The old-timer held up his index finger as he stuck his head into the lieutenant's office, "Hold on, kid, hey 'Loo' I'm goin out for a coffee, you want something?"

He answered no; they left and proceeded to a little diner on Passyunk Avenue. Once sitting in a booth, they ordered, and Larry asked, "What's on your mind, Nicky?"

Nick informed Larry about Erie and Chuck's theory on Tommy's disappearance and asked him for his thoughts and advice. Larry stirred his coffee contemplating, drawing on his years of experience, and finally responded, "Chuck may not be wrong with that theory, but to 'hit' a cop and take the car to send a message takes either two things, no brains, or air tight dirt on someone."

"What do you mean, what kind of dirt?"

"Well, you're too young to remember, but back in the day, they say that the mob had all kinds of pictures of J. Edgar Hoover wearin' dresses and stuff. It might have been true because he never would publicly recognize the existence of organized crime, it sure did seem like they owned him."

Larry stared out the window and continued, "But to do that to a cop, I don't know. Now I may be wrong, 'cause I believe that a few of the politicians down at city hall would steal a hot stove, but you gotta figure it this way, to do that, they have to be paying someone off with serious money, in return for a huge favor."

"Paying them off for what?"

"Well, let's figure this out. Has anything changed for the worse crime wise in the city? Any more bookies? More drugs? Now I realize we have a crap-load on the street, but any drastic upswing. I don't think so. More hookers? In my mind, it don't add up, I ain't saying you don't stop looking at this angle, but to me, it don't add up."

Nick studied the old detective, digesting the explanation.

Larry, looking back, declared, "Nicky give me a little time, I'll put feelers out and see what I can dig up, and I'll let you know if I come up with anything."

"Thanks, Larr."

"Yo, Nicky, you think apple pie counts as a fruit?" Larry inquired with a grin while shoveling in a considerable chunk.

Nick just shook his head and smiled.

A flock of pigeons fluttered over Florist Street, startled by the train crossing the Ben Franklin Bridge as Nick stepped out of D-908 at MCU headquarters on that April morning. He didn't expect too much activity in the office that day. Practically the whole unit attended a retirement party the night before, and he knew there would be call-outs and hang-overs. The ones that did show up would be walking on eggshells and nursing headaches.

"Lenny, how you doin' this fine day?" Nick bellowed to a co-worker sitting at a desk with his hair askew and his head in his hands.

The ailing detective slowly peeked through his fingers with bulging bloodshot eyes and pleaded in a whisper, "For the love of God, Nicky, please not so loud."

Nick smiled and wanted to bust his chops further, but took pity on him and quietly offered, "I'll grab you some coffee and a couple of aspirins."

After retrieving the remedies, he started to review his notes, when an hour and a half later, his phone rang. Professor Woodward from Pennypacker University was on the other end, advising him that he completed the linguistics analysis. In forty-five minutes, Nick was in his office, where he introduced him to Professor Klingman and handed him the report.

While he reviewed the information, Woodward explained, "Although at first, it appears to be the ramblings of a psychotic individual, my analysis shows it could be linked to a foreign language."

"What language?"

"Possibly German, with a Swiss accent."

"Were you able to translate it?"

The professor pointed out on the list and explained, "The second word is somewhat unclear, but I listed numerous possibilities. These words are probable for the German words, 'Polizist — nach hause schicken,' with a possible translation of, 'Police or policeman — send or sent home.'"

Nick read the findings, and after a moment, he asked, "Do you think these words could be related to the officer's disappearance?"

"It may also mean nothing. I recall the incident being highly reported and televised at the time, with news outlets from all over the world covering the case. It could very well be the ramblings of an extremely psychologically disturbed individual, who, for whatever reason, is very empathetic towards the officer and his disappearance."

Nick was crestfallen as he stared at the list and shook his head.

"However, there is one possible derivative that I found for the second word of the phrase."

With a spark of hope, he looked up and asked, "What do you think it could be, Professor?"

"Possibly, the word could be *Tardigrade*. The name *Tardigrada* was given in 1777 by the Italian biologist Lazzaro Spallanzani."

"Tardigrade? What does it mean?"

"Professor Klingman is with the university Microbiology Department. I want him to explain the meaning."

The micro-biologist proceeded. "Yes, most definitely, you see a Tardigrade is a microscopic animal. A species of water-dwelling, eight-legged, segmented micro-animals, the Tardigrade, or water bear, or at times referred to as the moss piglet, are no bigger than one millimeter in length."

Intrigued, Nick asked, "A millimeter. What makes this animal so unique?"

"They are recognized as nature's greatest survivor. These creatures appear to be positively indestructible. Some Tardigrades can endure being frozen to -359°Farenheit. They can also be boiled, exposed to extreme pressures, and have even been found to survive a nuclear explosion."

"How's that even possible? What do you mean? They can't be killed?"

"It is virtually impossible to kill a Tardigrade, it can be frozen, boiled, crushed, bathed in radiation, deprived of food and water for years, and it will wiggle back to life. Their DNA is protected by a protein called 'dsup,' and their cells by a sugar solution, called 'trehalose.'"

"DNA. I've read some articles about that in college, but could you tell me more about it?"

Professor Klingman proceeded to explain, "DNA stands for 'deoxyribonucleic acid.' The Swiss physician Friedrich Miescher, in 1869, was the first researcher to isolate nucleic acid. That is the genetic material that determines the makeup of all living cells and many viruses."

"What does it do, professor?"

"The molecular compound consists of two long strands of nucleotide linked together in a double helix, a structure resembling a ladder twisted into a spiral. In layman's terms, DNA is a code and the blueprint for a living entity, human DNA is unique like fingerprints, no two are alike, except possibly in the occurrence of twins."

"Fingerprints? Can it be used to identify a person?

"It has been utilized in England quite recently. In a case where two young girls were raped and murdered several years apart. DNA analysis led to the suspect's arrest in 1987."

"How does that work?"

"Genetic material is recovered from a crime scene and compared to a sample from a suspect. If they match, it could put the suspect at the scene of the crime."

Nick stood there, with half-folded arms pinching his chin, digesting the information, and wondering how he might be able to use the new procedure.

"Detective Avner, do you have any indication who the person is that uttered these words?" Professor Klingman inquired.

"He's still unidentified; we have no idea. Why do you ask?" Nick responded.

"Because use of the word Tardigrade is not considered to be in the general lexicon of the average person. Someone using or knowing the term Tardigrade would most likely be associated with the study of biology or specifically micro-biology."

He rubbed the scar on his face, contemplating his next move, and then replied,

"Professors, Thanks for your help. Would the university library have any reference material on these subjects?"

"They will have a relatively good selection," Klingman advised.

On his way out of the building, he stopped at the library, where he identified himself and photocopied articles and books relating to DNA and Tardigrades. When he arrived back at Major Crimes' headquarters, he felt upbeat although not sure how it could fit into the case, just that it was a new lead, not there before.

CHAPTER 45

L UNCHTIME IN EARLY MAY, AND Chuck Warner stuck his head into Nick's office. "Yo, you wanna grab some pizza?"

Nick responded, "Sounds good. I'm in."

They retrieved their coats, a set of vehicle keys and headed out the door. As the car pulled out of the lot under the Ben Franklin Bridge onto Florist Street, Police Radio called, "Dan nine-oh-eight, return to headquarters immediately."

They looked at one another as Chuck reached for the mike, "Dan nine-oh-eight, okay."

"What the hell is this all about?" Nick wondered.

They made their way back to 319 Race Street; Lieutenant Tricoste met them at the door.

"Your guy in Erie...he woke up."

Nick ran up the steps into his office and grabbed for the telephone. He dialed the direct phone number for Detective Mark Benaducci at the Erie Police Department. After a few rings, a voice answered. "Detective Benaducci."

"Mark, Nick Avner. What have you got?"

"Nick, this guy woke up, and he's talking."

"What's he saying? Anything about Tommy?"

"No, he's just answering general questions. When we show him Tommy's picture, he just turns his head away and stares. The docs placed him on some type of medication. I think they said 'L-dopa,' or something like that. It got him out of his semi-comatose state. Listen, maybe you want to come back out here."

"For sure, we'll grab a flight and be there as soon as we can. Thanks, brother."

"You got it; I'll meet you when you land."

Chuck and the lieutenant were standing in the office overhearing the call, and when he hung up, Tricoste ordered, "What are you waiting for — mount up."

They were able to book a flight from Philly International into Erie, departing at 4:30 p.m., allowing them time to drive to their homes and pack a bag.

They caught their flight and landed without incident. At the terminal, Benaducci met them, directing them out to his parked vehicle.

"Hey Mark, I can't believe the guy woke up," Nick stated excitedly.

"Yeah, the docs tried different medications; I guess they found the right one. He's coherent and speaks with a strong accent, but you can make out what he's saying. He appears to be a gentle person, but it could be the drugs he's on."

Mark worked the police vehicle out of the airport parking lot onto semi-flooded streets. Heavy rain was falling, and a cold wind was blowing off the Great Lakes, making the trip hazardous.

After thirty-five minutes of hard-driving, they arrived at the Erie County Psychiatric Hospital. When they entered room 308, the same doctor was there as before. In the bed, sitting up, was the same white male, late-fifties, gray hair combed straight back, with a silver beard, wearing wire frame spectacles. He had the meal tray cart across his lap and was drinking from a porcelain teacup. As the detectives entered the room, he turned his head towards them and smiled.

"Can I offer you, gentlemen, some tea; I would imagine you are quite chilled with this weather."

Chuck stepped forward and replied, "Yes, that would be nice. It is cold out there."

Extending his hand, he made the introductions, "My name is Chuck, this is Mark and Nick. May I have the honor of knowing your name?"

He accepted the detective's hand, shook it, and slowly responded, "In due time, I suppose."

The patient's manner of speaking conveyed the impression of being educated and refined. Sensing that, Chuck requested, "Can we sit and visit with you for a while?"

"Yes, I would enjoy that immensely."

The detectives proceeded to interview the patient being especially careful not to upset him into silence.

Nick started with general questions. "Do you know where you are?"

"I would say no doubt in a psychiatric facility; I'm quite familiar with them."

"Can you tell me what city you are presently in?"

"I was informed — Erie, Pennsylvania."

"Are you aware of how you got here?"

"I remember a long trip, but traveling by rail always takes longer. Don't you agree?"

"You came in by train? Do you recall from where?"

"Somewhere from on the other side of the mountains."

"Do you know how you got those marks on your wrists and ankles?"

He fixated on the bruises, staring with a labored expression conjuring a memory, and after a moment divulged, "I'm an excellent swimmer. I once held a record for holding my breath underwater."

"We weren't aware of that. From where? In school?"

With a vacant stare and indistinguishable sounds, he appeared to be drifting into a memory and said nothing.

Chuck, sensing he may be regressing, remarked, "Hey, where's that tea you promised?"

His mood brightened as he turned his gaze up, and responded, "Yes, of course, I'm a dreadful host."

The patient rang for the nurse and ordered for the group. After the beverage arrived, Nick attempted to engage the man in a casual conversation rather than direct questions.

He started with, "I had a fascinating discussion with an associate of mine a while back regarding the durability of the Tardigrade. I was awed at the immense abilities of such a minute creature."

At the mention of that topic, he perked up and dispensed a lengthy dissertation about the animal. He spoke in a tone that suggested there could be no doubt of his expertise on the subject, and he was taking considerable joy in his recital. Upon completion, he asked Nick who he had the conversation with regarding the Tardigrade.

"Professor Klingman."

"Ah yes, Klingman, I'm well-aware of his work, but he wanders on occasions in the rosebushes, so to speak, " He said with arms folded and a satisfied smile.

They sat quietly for about five minutes, and then he professed, "Gentlemen, I want to thank you for your kindness of spending time with me, but you must excuse me. I'm becoming quite tired."

Nick replied, "It's been our pleasure, but one thing before we go, maybe you could return the kindness, and perhaps assist us in locating our friend."

"I will do what I can."

Chuck produced the picture of Tommy and placed it on the meal tray in front of him. Still, with a contented smile on his face, he slowly lowered his eyes and focused. After a moment, his face darkened, and he turned away.

The doctor stepped forward, fearing the male's condition could become impaired, and stated, "Gentlemen, that will be all for the evening."

They left the room and conferred in the hallway with all agreeing he was, without a doubt, some type of college professor or researcher in the field of microbiology. He appeared to possess exceptional intelligence, with a gentle way about him, and he became conflicted when confronted with Tommy's photo.

"I got a gut feeling this guy is tied to Tommy in some way," Chuck contended.

"Yeah, but how?" Nick responded.

"Well, one thing, he knows Klingman — let's see if Klingman recognizes him," Chuck suggested.

Mark provided them with a recent picture of the unidentified person while he was conscious.

They stayed at a Holiday Inn, arose at four-thirty a.m. to catch an early flight back to Philly with Mark meeting them at the hotel and driving them to the airport.

During the ride, Nick laid out their next step to Detective Benaducci, "When we get back, I'm going to apply to have this guy declared a material witness. When I get the court order, we'll set it up for the U. S. Marshalls to transport him to Philly."

"Let me know what you need. When the time comes, we'll coordinate with the Feds. Hey guys, best of luck." Benaducci offered.

"Thanks, Mark. I'll keep you updated."

When they arrived at their headquarters, in the early afternoon, Nick started an affidavit of probable cause. After review, Lieutenant Tricoste ordered, "Okay, run this over to the DA's office for their approval before we coordinate with the Feds."

Nick made another trip to Pennypacker University to interview Professor Klingman. He brought along the photo and the report, which documented the specific words of the interview.

After studying the material, Klingman opined, "I don't recognize the person's picture, however from the transcript, the obvious detailed knowledge, and his recitation on the subject of Tardigrades, I'm convinced that his scholastic philosophy is in the field of microbiology."

"As you can see, he's familiar with your findings." Nick pointed out.

"Somehow, I feel I've heard his words before," he reflected as he ruffled through a massive stack of papers on his desk.

In a pile towards the corner of the room, he retrieved a manuscript.

"Here's what I was looking for," he announced as he opened the thick document. "The theory was written by a highly-regarded molecular biologist from Switzerland by the name of Doctor Hans Wolfgang Mauer. His gene theories are incredibly advanced but unproven, undoubtedly due to their complexity and the fact that research facilities lack the resources to test the hypothesis.

"What degrees does he hold?"

"What I recall, he holds a doctorate of medicine, in addition to dual PhDs in microbiology and genetics. He's immensely gifted; however, I recall he's been plagued with psychological issues all his life."

"Do you know where he studied or did his research?"

"I believe the last known place was the Swiss Federal Institute of Technology in Zurich, but that was well over six or seven years ago. He seemed to have vanished, no theories published since then, nothing, perhaps he was permanently institutionalized."

Wanting to get more information on the person, Nick asked, "Professor, where could I find other theories of his?"

"You might try Province University's Genomic Library. They house a vast amount of theory manuscripts for research purposes."

The detective recorded the interview in his notebook as he continued.

"Would you have any idea why he would show up in the United States? Could he conceivably be working for some government agency?"

"I think that would be highly unlikely; I don't think any facility would gamble on him due to his psychosis. He could be a security risk," the professor speculated.

Nick hurried back to his office, armed with the new information. Recalling the male's reaction to Tommy's photo and the recent information, he believed he could be one step closer to the person's identity. He felt optimistic as he entered Major Crimes' headquarters. After conferring with his supervisor, Nick contacted Special Agent Bohonik of the FBI and updated her. She advised him the FBI attaché at the American Embassy in Bern, Switzerland, would conduct a background investigation on Doctor Hans Wolfgang Mauer.

Over the next three weeks, Nick prepared and secured the Material Witness order authorizing the unidentified male's transfer to Philadelphia. Selected for the designated facility was Friends Hospital, the nation's oldest private psychiatric sanatorium. The site dated back to 1813, when the Quakers established the institution known as "The Asylum for the Relief of Persons Deprived of the Use of Their Reason." Once the court issued the material witness and "302" mental health commitment orders, Nick arranged for the U. S. Marshalls Office to transport the stranger from Erie to Philadelphia.

Nick decided to check out the Province University source, and once in the car, he drove four blocks down Race Street and up onto the entrance ramp of I-95. In an hour, he arrived at Province University and stepped into the Goodwell Library. A massive building housing thousands of printed works, reference materials, and many rare books. Within those walls was the Genomics Library, which collected and maintained numerous theory manuscripts from all over the world used as reference sources in the field of microbiology. He approached the check-in desk and identified himself. After explaining his purpose, the young student worker produced a clipboard from a drawer.

"We don't get many outsiders using this library, mostly grad students," she said as she placed it on the counter and reached for a ringing telephone.

While she spoke on the phone, Nick signed in on the next vacant line of the old and yellowed paper towards the bottom of the page. Glancing at the names on the sign-in sheet, one of them caught his eye, Gifford Bennett. He noted the date of November 1983 while he directed his stare across the room. He thought, *That was over seven years ago.*

He re-read it to double-check as the young lady hung up the phone and addressed him. "Is there any manuscript, in particular, you're looking for?"

Deep in thought, he hesitated in answering. Finally, he inquired, "How would a person research a theory paper?"

"The documents are kept on 'microfiche,' and are cross cataloged according to the subject matter and the scientist who authored the manuscript."

Nick pointed to Bennett's name on the sheet and asked, "Would you be able to tell me what this person was looking at?"

The young clerk studied the name, and spotting the date; she answered, "No, I'm sorry that was well before we kept records for hard-copy requests."

He clenched his lips and slightly shook his head as he muttered under his breath, *Damn.*

"Could you help me locate any theories or manuscripts written by a Doctor Hans Wolfgang Mauer?"

"Let's see what we have on him," she said as she led him to a nearby machine. The student worker entered the name and was able to retrieve multiple files under his name.

"Wow, it appears he published more than two hundred papers in the field of microbiology and genetics," and as she studied the index, she added, "This is unusual."

"What is?

"Well, there are no co-authors listed, which means he conceived and documented the theories by himself, and it appears he hasn't published since January of 1985."

While scanning the list of Mauer's hypothesis, the vast amount and the complexity of the titles overwhelmed him.

After absorbing the new information, he turned to the student and inquired, "Could you provide me with a copy of all the titles of his published theories and a photo-copy of the sign-in sheet?"

Confused, she turned her gaze from the machine to Nick, and then replied, "It may take a while, but sure.

CHAPTER 46

B Y MID-JUNE, THE INVESTIGATION WAS starting to move forward as the FBI identified the person of interest as Doctor Hans Wolfgang Mauer. Nick attended a meeting with the FBI to go over the dossier.

"Detective Avner, come in." Special Agent Bohonik said from inside the conference room.

After entering and sitting, he asked, "What did you learn about this guy?"

"We were able to do a comprehensive background investigation and came up with some interesting details."

"What do you have?"

"He's been identified as Doctor Hans Wolfgang Mauer, 59 years old, born in 1932, in Zurich, Switzerland, the only son of a neuro-surgeon mother and a renowned chemist father. At the age of ten, he was tested, and he scored close to two hundred IQ."

"Two hundred IQ! He's smarter than Einstein."

"He holds three doctorates. One in medicine, a Ph.D. in microbiology, and a Ph.D. in genetics from Lund University in Sweden and the Swiss Federal Institute of Technology Zurich."

"Three doctorates, my God. How could one person accomplish so much?"

"Well, he possesses an eidetic memory and superior intelligence. Also, from what our investigation revealed, the only thing he's ever done since childhood was studying. He had no friends, only sporadic work associates, and he never socialized.

"Is there any indication he may be working for the government or a private company here in the U.S.?"

"No, nothing. We were able to trace him to his last known whereabouts in London in November of '85 and then lost track of him."

"Was he doing research work there at the time?"

"Actually, he was committed to Maudsley Hospital, a British psychiatric facility in south London. He's been in and out of mental health facilities since his teenage years. He's been plagued with psychotic episodes throughout his life, but there was nothing to indicate he was ever violent or suicidal."

After sitting in the conference room and digesting the information, he then commented, "Although he's a brilliant man, I kind of feel sorry for him. When I interviewed him, his personality seemed like a gentle person lost in the world."

A week later, the U. S. Marshall's Office physically transported the male from Erie, Pennsylvania, to Philadelphia. On the day of his arrival, he waited in Mauer's room at the Greystone facility. Although no direct evidence linking the doctor to Tommy's disappearance was evident, a gut feeling made him anxious to talk to him again.

The room was on the top floor of the three-story, two-hundred-year-old manor house serving as the residential unit built solidly from the stones bearing its name. The grounds were meticulous and peaceful, and the room was modern, spacious, and decorated with tasteful furniture. He scattered several medical and scientific books throughout the place in the hope of making it more comfortable for Mauer, putting him at ease, and creating a more conducive setting to answer questions.

While sitting and studying the FBI background file, the door opened, and two U.S. Marshalls escorted a handcuffed man inside. The male was short, about 5'5", and frail. He appeared tired and possibly confused as Nick arose from the chair and approached.

"Doctor Mauer, hello, I'm Nick Avner. We met some time ago in Erie. Do you remember me?"

The disoriented person stared with a blank expression as the Marshalls released him from the handcuffs and restraining belt. Free of the restraints, his face brightened as he recognized the detective.

"Why yes, I do recall, we had a wonderful conversation regarding our mighty little friend the Tardigrade."

"That's right, Doctor, I'm glad you remember me," Nick replied while he shook his hand and gently guided him towards a chair.

"You no doubt had a tiring trip, but I wanted to be here to welcome you when you arrived."

"So nice of you, you are very kind."

Sensing he was tired and not wanting to trigger a regressive episode, Nick suggested, "Doctor, I want you to settle in and get some rest. If it would be agreeable with you, I'd like to visit in the days to come and talk. Would that be all right?"

"Why yes, that would be delightful. I look forward to conversing with you again," he answered, obviously tired.

Over the next five months, Nick visited Mauer as much as possible, and he was starting to develop a rapport able to learn more things about him. One unique aspect was the only thing coming close to a hobby for the doctor was knitting. He created complex patterns to visualize the three-dimensional configuration and structures of various molecules. He never completed a blanket or gloves, or any other usual knitted goods; his finished objects were strands of intricately interwoven shapes, inter-twined through assorted colored hollow beads. Nick was amazed at how he could hold an in-depth conversation while assembling the elaborate items and make notes into a leather-bound journal labeled "Formeln Verarbeiten."

Gauging from his cheerful demeanor, Mauer enjoyed the visits, so Nick started to press him for more information about himself.

"Doctor, I've seen your FBI background report, but I was wondering if you could tell me more about yourself?"

"What do you want to know?"

"Can you tell me why you were here in the United States?"

He remained silent, lowered his head, and looked away. Nick pressed him, deciding to use the leads he gathered so far.

"Doctor, do you know a person by the name of Gifford Bennett?"

He slowly shook his head while gazing at his folded hands. Nick studied his demeanor and then asked, "How about a Conrad Grimes?"

The doctor answered the same way while Nick watched his reaction and noticed he started to mumble and sway his head. Not wanting him to have a regressive episode, he called for the nurse who entered and administered his prescribed medications. The meds eventually took effect and made him more alert and coherent. On his subsequent visits, the doctor would ask Nick for the current date. After telling him the month, day, and year, he questioned him, "Why do you ask?"

Mauer hesitated, then with a slight grin, he proclaimed, "Christmas is getting closer."

Larry called Nick in July and suggested they meet and grab a bite at the Reading Terminal, a former railroad station now an enormous market place. In half an hour, they entered the Twelfth Street entrance. At Carmen's, a famous sandwich stand inside the building, they ordered a couple of roast pork, provolone cheese with broccoli rabe sandwiches, and slid into a booth.

While sitting, Larry disclosed, "I think I got something. Sorry I didn't call you sooner, but my source did a lot of digging and came up with the one guy who might be capable of doing what we talked about"

"Yeah, what is it?"

He scanned the room and then whispered, "You heard of Councilman Ronald Hubbs? He's been down there a long time."

Nick responded, "You mean the head of City Council?"

"Yeah, that's the one. Well, the word is, he's a power-hungry little bastard who likes to make a buck."

"Wow, a dirty ruthless politician, who coulda guessed."

"Yeah, my informant not only told me what he does, but also what makes him tick."

"Yeah. How?"

"The reason why he's like the way he is goes back to when he was a kid."

"Why? What happened back then?"

"He grew up in Fishtown in the fifties and sixties. The family didn't have any money. He would collect and redeem empty soda bottles to put a couple of bucks in his pocket, plus he was a runt, he'd always be gettin' the crap kicked out of him by the neighborhood tough guys, but then one day he got lucky."

"What do you mean? How?"

"He's standing on the corner one day with his soda bottle wagon, and he spots a little kid break loose from his mother's hand. He's about to step off the curb right into the front end of a car, so Hubbs reaches out and pulls him back just in time."

"Sounds like the kid got lucky."

"Yeah, but it turns out he's the younger brother of the main thug in Fishtown, one Mickey Frost, who, from time to time, tuned Ronald up just for kicks."

"What happened then?"

"So the kid's mother is so grateful, she orders her older son to quit kicking Ronald's ass and to keep an eye on him instead."

"So, Hubbs gets a bodyguard."

"Oh yeah, so now he's got some street respect, what with Frost standing behind him. He likes the power, so he gravitates towards politics, small stuff at first, block captain, committeeman, right on up to where he is now."

"What became of this guy, Frost?"

"Ronald takes care of him, gets him into "L and I" as a zoning inspector, and my source says he's Ronald's bag-man and enforcer."

"So, they're making money together."

"Word is he's also been hooked up with a big financial character from downtown who's been bankrolling his campaigns."

"Who is he?"

"Guy by the name of Gifford Bennett, the CEO of an investment firm, Swarthmore something or other."

"Swarthmore Holdings?"

"Yeah, could be. Why? Whatta you got?"

"Swarthmore Holdings is the investment firm that handles all the city pension fund accounts."

Leaning forward and hanging his head, Larry responded, "Ah crap, I knew I shoulda' retired by now."

"So he's got major money backin' him now." Larry continued, "Hubbs will do anybody a favor, for the right price, but he's vindictive too."

"What do you mean–how?"

"When he was a kid, his mother tried to start a tab with a local grocer, a guy named 'Lippo.' So not only does Lippo not run the tab, he embarrasses her in front of the neighbors and Ronald."

"What did he do, tell Frost to pay him a visit?"

"Not right away, but he never forgot. So, years later, when he's in the city council, he finds out Lippo is rehabbing the grocery into a restaurant, and he took out big loans to do it, but he starts doin' the work before getting the permits."

"So then Frost stops by. Right?"

"You got it. By the time they got done with him, he had his house and store foreclosed on, and he found himself in

Episcopal Hospital with a major stroke — only lasted about three months before he croaked."

"Wow, don't screw with Ronald — right?" As Nick said, that a memory flashed in his mind.

"Larry, you remember when me and Tommy got transferred to the Seventeenth because of the corruption scandal? Did you ever hear how the investigation got started with the Feds?"

"I heard they had an informant, but no one knew for sure who. Why?"

"You recall the Greenwich Street job when Hallwell shot himself."

"Yeah, what about it?"

"Well, after the shooting, we're in the wagon, and Tommy goes into this rant about politicians and campaign donations and how the whole thing was started by a scumbag politician who wanted to turn the heat off himself."

They stared at one another as they both contemplated the scenario. After a moment, Nick spoke, "You think Tommy knew something about Hubbs, and maybe he somehow made him disappear?"

Larry gazed out the window, turned back, peered over the rim of his eyeglasses, and responded, "Personally, I don't think Ronald has the balls, and Frost doesn't possess the brains to pull off something like that, but I guess anything's possible."

CHAPTER 47

NICK TRIED TO OUTRACE THE downpour from his car to his front door on a rainy, chilly fall afternoon in late September while arriving home from work. Abby was waiting as he stepped onto the porch with tears in her eyes.

"What's wrong? Are you okay?" as he took her by the shoulders.

"Nicky, Rosie called, they took Sophia to the Pediatric Hospital," she gushed.

"What happened? Is she hurt?"

"She's sick; they don't know what it is."

"Grab your coat. We're going down there," he stated as he put the key into the door lock.

When they arrived at the hospital, they determined Sophia was in room 208 and rushed up the stairs where Rosie met them outside in the hall. At the sight of them, she became frantic, crumbling into their arms. They attempted to console her and asked questions.

"Rosie, what happened? What's wrong with her?" Nick asked.

"Over the summer, she was always tired and didn't want to do much. She lost her appetite, she complained of headaches and her joints hurting. I took her to the pediatrician, who at first said she probably had the flu."

"Did he give her a prescription?"

"No, not really, she wasn't getting any better. So, I called him again, and he told me to take her to the hospital right away. The hospital is running tests, oh my God — what could it be?" she cried out as she shattered, "Oh my God, first Tommy, now Sophia sick. What am I going to do?"

Abby hugged her as Nick consoled her. "Everything is going to be alright, Rosie. Let's wait for the results. It's going to be alright."

They walked her to a waiting room to support and stay with her through the night.

In the morning, Nick called his headquarters. Chuck Warner answered the phone, and he told him about the situation with Sophia.

"Do they have any test results?"

"Not yet. We're expecting something sometime today."

"Did you sleep?"

"No, nothing. I wanted to make sure she isn't here by herself. We're gonna stay with her until we know what's going on."

"Hey, don't you worry, I guarantee she ain't going to be alone. Hang tight. I'll catch up with you later."

Chuck hung up, called John McCarthy, the president of the Fraternal Order of Police, Lodge 5, and informed him of the circumstances regarding Tom Tabbozzi's young daughter. After telling everyone in Major Crimes, he grabbed a set of car keys and headed out the door. On the drive out to the hospital, the thoughts of the sick child filled his mind. When he arrived on the second floor, he met with Nick, Abby, and Rosie in the waiting area lounge.

"Rosie, is there any word?" Chuck asked.

While wringing her hands, she numbly replied with a pained stare, "No, nothing yet."

"Everything's going to be okay," Chuck reassured her, "we're all going to be here for Sophia and you until she's better."

Abby, with her arms around her shoulders, gently guided her into a chair.

Chuck and Nick stepped into the hall to talk when they heard the elevator doors open. A group of uniformed and plain-clothes officers entered the hallway and walked towards them.

Nick spotted the gathering and did a double-take as he inquired, "What's all this? Where'd they come from?"

"I told you she wouldn't go through this alone. I called the FOP, and just about every cop in the city will be here one way or another," Chuck explained.

When Rosie looked up and noticed the group, her hands formed a steeple, and she pressed them to her lips, grateful the department hadn't forgotten Tommy and his family. It was early evening as they sat slumped, weary, and worn out with grief when Nick first noticed the attending pediatric physician and signaled Abby. She gently reached for Rosie's hand and held it, who looked up into Abby's face and sensed a foreboding moment.

The physician approached, and she stood to face him as he quietly revealed, "Mrs. Tabbozzi — we've concluded the test on Sophia."

Her pleading eyes focused on him, and sensing the worst; she cried out, "Oh my God. What is it?"

"Mrs. Tabbozzi, we've detected a rapid rise in her white blood cells," the doctor started to explain.

"What does this mean? What's wrong with her?" Rosie demanded.

"The abnormal lymphoblast, or white blood cells, are growing at an advanced rate, and replacing the normal cells in the bone marrow, preventing the production of healthy blood cells."

While wringing her hands and her eyes searching his face, she cried out, "What are you saying, she has leukemia?"

"Acute lymphoblastic leukemia, I'm very sorry, we want to start treatment immediately."

Stunned by the doctor's words, Rosie stumbled backward, and her legs buckled as she collapsed. Nick and Abby surrounded her, reached out, and grabbed her arms, catching her before she dropped to the floor.

The doctor ordered the nurse to administer a mild sedative. The couple was heartbroken for her and Sophia. Upon learning the diagnosis, the officers in the hall became tight-lipped, shook their heads, and glanced at the floor or one another with dire expressions.

The medical team administered chemotherapy throughout the fall, and at times Sophia appeared to be responding to the treatments, but then she would relapse.

The week after Thanksgiving, the medical team decided to start radiation therapy and bone marrow transplants. Nick and Abby visited Sophia as often as possible. Rosie was there around the clock sleeping in a chair until the Pennypacker University Police arraigned for her to use one of the small apartments, usually reserved for visiting professors. There was a rotation of both the city and university police officers in the hallway if she needed anything, providing escorts and transportation between the hospital and the apartment. No one forgot Tommy Tabbs or his family.

Nick still tried to stop in and talk to Doctor Mauer, but his commitment to support Rosie and Sophia and his work schedule prevented him from seeing him as much as before. On his next visit, Mauer asked, "Nicholas, I've noticed your visits are becoming fewer. Have I done anything to offend you?"

"No, Doctor, I'd like to stop by more often, but the daughter of a close friend of mine is ill, very ill, and she's in the hospital."

"What is the diagnosis?" he inquired with a grim tone.

"Acute lymphoblastic leukemia."

"Who is this friend you speak of — if I may ask?"

About to answer, he hesitated, and then turned to his briefcase, reached in and retrieved Tommy's photo, and said, "My friend, Tom Tabbozzi."

The doctor glanced down, stared, and said nothing. He continued to gaze with a vacant look on his face, and after several minutes, the detective placed the image into the briefcase. As he pivoted back to face him, he was trance-like, still staring at the same space where the print occupied. Nick became concerned and yelled, "Doctor — Doctor Mauer."

Calling his name, he clapped his hands in front of his face with no reaction. He rushed to the door and called out to the nurse. The attending psychiatric physician entered the room, and while Nick explained the actions leading up to Mauer's condition, he shined a light into his eyes, checked his pulse, and snapped his fingers in his face.

"What happened to him, doctor?"

"I can only say, the conversation you had with him could have triggered a repressed memory inducing a catatonic reaction."

"Will this be permanent?"

"I can't say until we conduct further testing, I don't know, at this time."

Nick left Greystone, got into his car, and sat behind the wheel. Frustrated at the dead-end leads on Tommy's case, his worry about Sophia, and his time away from Abby, his mind began to race. Tired and burned out, he had a lingering migraine headache for the last week, and now he may have lost the most promising lead yet.

"Balls!"

Frustration was boiling over as he screamed and alternated between punching the car's ceiling and banging the steering wheel with the palms of his hands. The rage ran its course, and he eventually calmed himself. As his composure returned, he suddenly realized where he was and wondered if anyone saw his outburst, thinking he could go from being a visitor to becoming a patient.

CHAPTER 48

CHUCK STOPPED IN THE OFFICE to say hello and catch up on each other's cases. Nick informed him about the latest incident with Mauer.

"Yo, Nicky, the L-T put me on a new city-fed task force."

"Yeah, how's that going?"

After looking over his shoulder and out into the hallway, he turned and said, "Hey, between you and me, we're looking into possible embezzlement from the city pension fund. It looks like someone's skimming."

"Really! How much money we talkin' about?" Nick asked with a quiet surprise.

Chuck replied, almost with a whisper, "Millions."

"Chuck, did these two names ever pop up — Ronald Hubbs or Gifford Bennett?"

Chuck walked over and shut the door, returned, sat, and faced Nick.

"Here's the story — I started doing a background investigation on Bennett, Chuck whispered.

"Is he involved in the skim? What did you find out about him?"

"He could be, for one thing, he's rich, and his personal wealth is estimated at ten million."

"Ten million! So why's he gotta embezzle?"

"I don't know. It doesn't make sense."

"What's he like personally?"

"I did some digging and found out he has a colorful family history."

"Like what?

"Well, he comes from a real well-to-do heritage; their money goes back like four generations. The great grandfather started as a coal miner in Wales. He works his way up to owning like about ten mines, sells out, moves to America, and starts buying up anthracite mines around Scranton/ Wilkes Barre area. His son and grandson take over the business on down to the present Gifford Chadwyck Bennett the fourth.

"My dad's family were from Pittston; they all worked as coal-miners up there for a long time. They probably dug some coal for that clan somewhere along the line. So this guy got his money from the old man?"

"Not exactly — turns out the mine owners were greedy, raking in the dough, until one day it bit them in the ass."

"What do you mean?"

"Well, these owners were really nasty, they kept pushing the miners to produce more and more coal, and they didn't care how it was done. So, one day in 1959, tryin' to get out the daily quota, they dug up under the Susquehanna River, and the shaft roof caved in."

"Hey, I remember that the 'Knox Mine Disaster,' my dad told me that story, said one of his cousins was killed in that pit."

"Yeah, besides killing like twelve miners, the cave-in destroyed the mining industry in the northern anthracite fields, and at that time, our boy Bennett the fourth was about to graduate from Barton School of Economics at Pennypacker. He finds out the family went bankrupt from the disaster, and they find the old man swinging from the railing in the grand staircase at the estate up in Chestnut Hill."

"How did he take that?"

"Not too bad actually, him and the old man didn't get along too well. He was probably more upset he didn't leave him any money."

"So where'd the cash come from to start out in business?"

"Grandma left him a townhouse on Pine Street and put a few bucks in his pocket.

"How'd you come up with all that info?"

"Hey, Nick, you'd be surprised what you can learn in the library."

"Speaking of libraries, guess whose name I found on a sign-in sheet at Province's Genomics Library from seven years ago?"

"Who?"

"Gifford — Bennett," Nick replied with a slight grin.

The detectives stared at one another, both fitting puzzle pieces together in their minds.

CHAPTER 49

DECEMBER 1, 1991, AND THE five-year mark of Tommy's disappearance was fast approaching. The Fraternal Order of Police held the memorial service on the anniversary date of the vanishing, Friday, December 20, 1991, at seven p.m. at the Cathedral Basilica of Saints Peter and Paul. All department members able to attend were there, as well as city dignitaries, family, and friends. Rosie stayed by Sophia's side.

In 1986, worldwide news outlets and wire services responded when the department first disclosed the case to the public. Because of the unusual circumstances, where both the officer and the patrol car went missing, the press covered the story extensively after the initial report. On past anniversary dates, the media would broadcast repeat stories and mini-documentaries across the country and worldwide regarding the unusual case.

The Philadelphia Police Department commanders wisely anticipated a massive media response to the memorial service. A press staging area was set aside in the park, directly across from the Cathedral entrance. Traffic Division blocked all traffic in the surrounding streets. Due to the anticipated size of the crowd, the planners decided that the Archbishop would hold a short prayer ceremony, followed by speakers, the last one being Nick.

On the night of the memorial, although in their hearts, the officers sensed that after five years, the likelihood of finding Tommy was slim to none; the theme of the evening was 'hope.' The Archbishop's prayer was from the Bible parable of the *Prodigal Son*, but unlike the slacker in the story, Tommy was more like the brother who worked hard and did the right thing, so somehow the sermon didn't fit.

The turn-out was huge, with a sea of officers wearing formal blouse coats and shined Sam Browne duty belts lined up down the Parkway, all the way to City Hall. While waiting in line to enter the Cathedral, officers offered possible answers to the disappearance.

"I heard he's in the 'Witness Protection Program,'" remarked a young uniformed cop repeating one of the many rumors.

"Where did you hear that? Nobody knows what happened," replied another.

A detective overhearing the conversation interrupted, "Listen, his little girl is sick. I worked with Tabbs, and I know for sure, no matter what program he might be in, he would find a way to be at that hospital with her if he could.

During the service, mostly officers who personally knew Tommy made the speeches. Some were humorous, some sad, all melancholy, but with the central theme of not losing hope. Nick was the final speaker. He looked up from his memories, slowly rose from his seat, and fastened the coat button on his blue pinstripe suit.

You can do this, he thought to himself, trying to maintain his composure.

Abby squeezed his hand before he stepped forward out of the pew. His years of experience and reputation had produced in him a command presence as he moved across the altar toward the ornate stone podium. Once reaching the top, every person in the building focused on him.

While staring out onto the crowd, he struggled back tears, but after a moment, he straightened up and spoke loud and clear. "Tom Tabbozzi is my friend — my best friend," he paused then continued, "You notice I said 'is' not 'was' because even though Tommy is missing, he's still here with us. He's with each one of us. Every time we think of him, he's here. Every locker room story we tell about him, every radio call we answer, he's with us. Every distant siren wailing late in the night, Tommy is riding along with that cop."

After wiping tears from his eyes with the back of his hand, he continued, "I'm not here to tell you why he's missing. I don't know why; I just don't know. I'm here to tell you how he lived. He was bigger than life, he loved his family, and he enjoyed 'cooking, eating, and being merry.' You could count on him, he would always have your back any time you needed it, and five minutes after you met him, he made you feel like you've known him all your life. He just had that way about him." The crowd smiled and nodded in agreement. Nick took a moment to reflect and gather his thoughts.

"My dad died when I was ten, and without any brothers or sisters, I kind of had to figure things out for myself."

As he slowed his speech, he scanned the audience and continued, "I met Tommy on my first day out of the academy, and he taught me everything about the 'job,' and things about life. He was one of the smartest guys I ever knew, and I always looked forward to his 'wagon lectures' and his unique 'street philosophy.'" Members of the audience smiled and nodded, remembering their encounters with Tommy.

After a momentary pause, Nick finished, "At this point in my life and as I stand here today, there are three things I'm sure of: Tom Tabbozzi is my best friend, I can't tell you why he went missing, and I vow never to stop searching for him."

Standing at the pulpit, he bowed his head, turned, and walked back to his seat.

CHAPTER 50

WHITE NOISE, STATIC BUZZING IN his ears, his eyes blinked open, looking down, he sluggishly focused onto greenish-blue illuminated shapes. His vision was clearing; he became more alert and realized the garbled din was coming from the radio speakers. Fumbling for the volume control, he turned it counter-clockwise, lowering the sound. He was now more awake and discerned it was the dashboard clock, which read 4:38 a.m. He sat up straight, stretched, and yawned. Now more alert, his mind took an assessment of his physical body.

Man, did I need that nap. I feel great, not bad for only ten minutes, he mumbled to himself.

He adjusted the unit, turning the control louder, quieter, switching frequencies.

"Crap, all static," he uttered while he reached for the microphone and depressed the button attempting to transmit: nothing, only interference.

"Friggin' radio," he mumbled while concluding that the device had malfunctioned.

He decided to go into the district and sign out a hand-held unit. Turning the ignition and putting the gear shift into drive, he pulled forward onto the lot. The damp frigid air hit him immediately through the open driver's side window. Abruptly stopping, he scanned the vicinity seeing fog and a slight mist.

"Where the hell did all the snow go?" he wondered out loud.

246

Ramming the gear-shift up into park, he stepped out of the car and into the darkness, shivering as the cold cut right through him. The sky was glowing from the ambient city lights reflecting off the clouds. He felt the damp air on his face and sensed the world was quiet, just like the poem said, "Not a creature was stirring."

After several minutes of confusion, he sat back into the vehicle, rubbed his chin between his fingers and thumb. He slipped the gearshift and gradually pulled out through the gate onto Grays Ferry Avenue. Reaching into his leather coat, he retrieved a pack of cigarettes; he shook one out and depressed the lighter down by the ash-tray. Upon popping, he lit up, took a drag, exhaled, and with a contorted expression on his face, he flicked the cigarette out of the car.

"Man, they're friggin stale. I just bought them tonight," he mumbled while spitting out the window.

He inhaled the cold, damp air deeply, and when he exhaled, he sensed the persistent hacking and pain in his lungs he had felt for a while was gone.

Wow, this weather must have cleared up my cough, he thought.

"Must be something in the smog," he muttered with a chuckle.

The streets of South Philly were empty, and the visibility was terrible with the fog reflecting off the headlight beams. Upon reaching Twentieth Street, he made a left and proceeded to the twelve hundred block. A few feet before the main entrance of the 17th Police District, he spotted an open parking space. After pulling in, he exited and opened the double glass doors. When he entered the building, he stopped before proceeding down a long corridor leading to the Roll Call room. The hallway was somehow dingier than usual, lit by one flickering fluorescent light giving off an eerie ambiance.

His eyes adjusted to the fluttering glow as he moved at a slow pace when something caught his eye, and he glanced up at a framed photo of an unknown officer. His eyes lowered to a bronze plaque below the picture, which stated

'Killed in the Line of Duty" and indicated the name, a street location, and 'Date of Death' July 10, 1989. He noticed another encased image a couple of feet down the hall; he approached it and read the engravings. It revealed the same format, 'Killed in the Line of Duty,' the name, a location, and Date of Death, April 12, 1987. Now becoming more mystified, the sight of a third memorial came into view. He side-stepped turned his gaze up and stared at a picture of himself. He scanned the plaque, which read, Police Officer Thomas P. Tabbozzi #4431,'Missing in Action', Location: Unknown, Date: December 20, 1986.

Known throughout the years as a practical joker, he had been the instigator and recipient of many pranks. As he stared up at the memorial, his first thought was, *the guys got me on this one,* but something in his heart felt the prank wasn't that funny.

With his head shaking, he walked towards the operation room, where a Police and Fire Federal Credit Union calendar hanging on the wall caught his attention. His eyes came to rest on the month, which read December. He detected someone crossed out all the days up to and including the twenty-fourth. While reading the year "1991," he started to grin and shook his head as he mumbled out loud, "These assholes got me this time."

Although his brain was processing these images as a practical-joke, he didn't like it. He didn't mind them using his photo and hanging it up as a joke, but the other two plaques didn't sit right with him. While standing there studying the calendar, he heard a latch click behind him. To the side of the assembly room, the bathroom door swung opened, and a hulking uniformed cop stepped out, who was looking down and securing his duty gun-belt.

"Yo Toe, what did you eat for lunch? A small goat? You musta put on twenty pounds since roll call."

Upon hearing those words, Big Toe glanced up from his belt buckle, looking in the direction of the voice. He squinted at the source, and then his eyelids retracted as he recognized the person as someone he knew from over five years ago. Not believing what he was seeing, he blessed himself and blurted out, "Jesus, Mary, and Joseph — T-t-t-Tommy — am I dead?"

"No, but you do look like crap."

The color left the huge officer's face as he stumbled back and flopped onto a bench against the wall.

"Are you the mutt that put those pictures and phony calendar up in the hall?"

A young cop entered the roll call room from the hallway. Not recognizing the strange officer, he turned to Toe and announced, "Hey Toe, there's an old 'blue and white' sector car parked at the curb."

"Well, what color is your police car — kid?" Tommy asked with a grin.

While facing the unknown officer, he scanned him up and down and answered with a puzzled expression on his face, "White — all white."

Toe was trying to catch his breath while he stared with disbelief at the sight of his prior partner and implored, "Tommy, where have you been?"

"Yo, I took a ten-minute nap. What? I blow a radio call, and you gotta put my picture on the wall 'missing in action.' Funny, real funny."

Toe told the young officer to get the sergeant. Tommy walked towards the distressed cop and called out, "Hey kid. You better call rescue; Toe's not looking too good."

"Tommy, is that really you? I missed you, brother," he proclaimed in disbelief.

"Yo Toe, what's up with you? You been hittin' that 'dago red' again?"

CHAPTER 51

T HE DOOR TO THE OPERATIONS Room swung open, and Sergeant Marty Kaminski entered the room and spotted the back of an unknown uniformed officer standing over Big Toe. Taking a few steps in, he stopped when the officer turned to face him. He recognized him instantly. Startled, he stared with intensity.

"Oh my God —how —!" he whispered, becoming over-whelmed with confusion and a slight sense of fear. Although surprised, he was the consummate professional, so he decided to take direct action and control of the situation until he could figure out what was going on.

"Tommy, could I talk to you in the Captain's office for a minute?"

Instantly recognizing Kaminski, he remarked, "Marty, When the hell did you make sergeant? I thought you were still working in One Squad."

"Yeah, you probably missed the teletype orders," Kaminski replied, thinking quickly.

"Yo, Marty, if I blew a couple of radio calls, I ain't gonna bitch. I admit I did zonk out for about ten minutes," Tommy explained as he entered the captain's office.

Before following him in, the sergeant turned to the cor-poral, who had trailed in behind him into the room, and whispered, "Call the lieutenant; tell him to take headquar-ters immediately."

"Hey Sarge, a blue and white RPC is parked out front," he advised.

"Guard it as a crime scene, bring the tarps up from the basement, and cover it up from view. Put two cops on the door, and he doesn't come out of there until we can figure this out. Start a 'crime scene log,' and call rescue for Toe — he's not looking good."

"Okay, Sarge," he responded and proceeded to carry out the orders.

The lieutenant arrived at the district within five minutes, entering the Operations Room from the Point Breeze Avenue entrance. The corporal met him at the door and excitedly briefed him by telling him the sergeant was with the officer in the captain's office.

"Who is this guy?" The lieutenant questioned with an annoyed tone.

With a little hesitation in his voice, he answered, "Tom Tabbozzi."

"Are you drinking in here? What the hell are you talking about? If you guys are screwing around, I'm gonna kick some asses. Is the sergeant in on this? Because this is not funny," he fumed.

"Lieutenant, I swear this is not a joke. There's a 'blue and white' RPC parked out front."

With an annoyed look, he ordered, "Show me."

They exited the Operations Room, stepped into the hallway, and out onto Twentieth Street to a vehicle covered with blue tarps, parked against the curb. The lieutenant approached, raised the cover, and observed three digits painted on the side front quarter panel, "178." He pulled out his handkerchief and opened the driver's side door, peered in, and scanned the odometer mileage, which read 79.8 miles. He shut the door, turned to the corporal, and ordered, "No one touches this vehicle, call 'Night Command,' and request a 'Bus Detail' response. Jimmy, use the phone, tell them no lights or sirens, and don't put anything out over the air. You understand?"

"Yes, sir, I'll take care of it right away."

The squad commander came back into the district, went to the captain's office, knocked gently on the door, and opened it. In the room was Sergeant Kaminski standing and looking down at Tom Tabbozzi. Lieutenant Paul Dunphy never met Tommy but recognized him from his photographs. He said nothing but stood and listened.

"I ain't gonna lie to you. I did doze off, but I swear it was only for ten minutes," he explained while glancing between the two men.

With confusion in his voice, he raised a question, "Yo, Marty, what's up? I saw you about three days ago, when I was reporting off, you were working 1703-Wagon. How the hell did you make sergeant that quick?"

"It was a special promotion, real fast, they said they needed me back here in the Seventeenth," Kaminski answered with a bluff.

Glancing at him sideways, he was not sure if he believed him.

"Where did you take a nap at, Tommy?" Kaminski inquired in a calm voice.

"On the lot, right at Grays Ferry and Washington."

"You just pulled in and fell asleep?"

"Well, no, I backed into a twenty-foot shipping container; you know to get out of the weather, and hey, by the way. Where the hell did all that snow go? There had to be eight inches on the ground before I nodded off, then I wake up ten minutes later, no snow, only fog. What the hell happened?" he rambled excitedly while pushing his hair back with both hands, getting a sense that something was not right.

The night of the disappearance flashed back to the sergeant, and not wanting to upset the reappearing officer, he thought quick and answered, "We had some crazy weather tonight, Tommy. It rained hard for about ten minutes, washed away all the snow. It must have happened when you were napping.

CHAPTER 52

T HE LIEUTENANT LEFT THE OFFICE, went into the Operations Room, and called the captain's home number. The phone connected, and after six rings, a sleepy male voice answered, "Hello."

"Hello, Captain McClendon, this is Lieutenant Dunphy."

"Paul, do you realize what time it is on Christmas morning?"

"Captain, sorry to wake you, you're going to want to hear this."

"What is it?"

"Officer Thomas Tabbozzi is sitting in your office."

"Paul, did you start knocking back the eggnog already? What are you doing?"

"Captain — Captain — he's here, and RPC-178 is parked out front of the district!"

The commander sat up, more alert now, realizing that was not a prank or a crazed subordinate who decided to call him on Christmas morning.

"I'll be right in, good job, and Paul, sorry for that drinking crack, I apologize."

"I'll brief you when you arrive, boss."

Before leaving, McClendon called the Inspector of South Police Division, waking him with the news.

"Frank, before you go in, contact Detective Headquarters, have them reach out to Detective Avner of Major Crimes. He was his old wagon partner before he went missing and is the assigned investigator on the case."

"Yes, sir — I'll make the call."

It was about 5:02 a.m. when loud rings roused Nick and Abby from a dead sleep. She heard it first, and with the phone on his side of the bed, she nudged her husband to answer.

"Ah, man, who's calling this early?" He groggily mumbled as he reached for the receiver.

"Hello," he whispered.

"Detective Avner, this is Detective Headquarters."

"Yeah — what do you need?"

"Detective, you have to respond to the Seventeenth District, ASAP."

"Why? What's going on down there?" he yawned into the speaker while rubbing his eyes.

"This is coming from Inspector John Donovan; he's ordering your presence immediately. He didn't say why. He ordered that you respond lights and siren."

Nick awakened and bolted upright, wondering why he would receive such a call on Christmas morning.

"Alright, I'm on my way."

Abby, listening, rolled over and asked, "What's that all about?"

"Not sure, but it sounds serious. I hope I'm not too long. I want to spend the day with you."

Nick quickly dressed, grabbed his badge, snub nose revolver, and headed out the door. He had been taking D-908 home, and as he worked his way over Cottman Avenue, the neighborhood was quiet and still. The sunrise was about an hour and a half away, but through the cold morning mist, he glimpsed the holiday decorations on the row houses. He was thinking about all the kids starting to wake on their most exciting day of the year, anxious to rip into their gifts, and he wondered what present was waiting for him at the 17th.

When he reached I-95, with lights and sirens activated, he headed south, and the traffic was light; he surmised the other cars contained late-night holiday revelers traveling home or critical employees commuting into work on just another day. He approached Point Breeze Avenue, where he noticed about fifty uniform officers posted around the building with the Police Bus idling in the small municipal lot across from the district. With a space against the curb open, he parked, got out, walked past a Fire Department Rescue Squad vehicle parked on the sidewalk with the EMT's inside, securing a patient. A large figure was lying on the stretcher wearing an oxygen mask on his face, and just before the doors closed, Toe spotted him and yelled out, "Nicky, it's him! Nicky, it's him!"

A uniform officer stopped him as he approached the rear door to the 17th District. Showing his badge and ID card, he inquired, "What did he say?"

With a shrug, he recorded his name on the log and declared, "Okay, detective, you can go in."

Upon entering, he observed the Operations Room was a beehive of activity. Captain McClendon met him at the door and directed him into a small anteroom off the entryway. Upon turning to Nick, he explained, "Detective, the reason you were called down here is we thought he should be in the company of people who worked with him."

The vagueness of the orders was confusing Nick, as well as becoming agitated when he finally requested, "Captain, with all due respect, what are we talking about?"

McClendon stared him straight in the eyes and replied in a grave tone, "Officer Thomas Tabbozzi is in my office now, and RPC-178 is parked by the front door."

Nick stumbled backward; his legs buckled as tunnel vision appeared, and he labored for a breath. He couldn't grasp the words as a flood of emotions swept over him from surprise and disbelief to a slight sense of relief.

Nick was having trouble speaking.

"How? When? How"

The captain grabbed him by the shoulders, steadying him.

"Detective, you are the assigned investigator, and this case is not yet concluded. Keep it together. Do you understand?"

Although Tommy had returned, his professional instincts kicked in as he realized the investigation was far from over.

Still, in a daze, he muttered, "Yes, sir."

"All we got out of him is that he thinks he pulled onto a lot and took a ten-minute nap. He's not aware that the ten-minute nap was five years and five days."

"What do you want me to do, Captain?"

"I'm ordering the Police Surgeon to respond to the district, rather than take him to a hospital right away. I don't want the media to turn this into a shit show. So far, we've been doing things off the air, but eventually, they're going to find out, and that's why I have the Bus Detail around the building. Detective, you're going to have to ease him back into the reality of the situation. If you can, try to secure his service revolver, no telling what he might do when the gravity of the truth hits him."

Nick straightened up, indicated he understood, and proceeded to carry out his duties. On the way, he spotted a copy of the latest Philadelphia Inquirer, the Christmas edition, on the counter. Grabbing the newspaper, he turned to the corporal and requested, "Corp, could you do me a favor, and turn the thermostat up high in the captain's office, leave it for about ten minutes, and then back it down to normal."

The corporal considered him with a puzzled expression and replied, "You got it."

CHAPTER 53

NICK PROCEEDED TO THE CAPTAIN'S office, not sure what to expect. He couldn't believe his old wagon partner was in the room. While knocking lightly, he opened the door and saw Sergeant Kaminski standing behind the desk, speaking to a uniformed individual sitting on the other side. Stepping into the room, he closed the door and turned back towards the two men. The seated figure swiveled and faced him. Nick almost fainted as he felt the blood rush from his head. Here was the man, who for the last five years, himself and police agencies from all over the world had been searching to find.

"Yo, Nicky, what the frig you doin' here? I thought you had the 'Bus Detail' tonight. Hey, you better sit down. You ain't lookin' too good. What — were all you guys drinking or something?"

Nick's mind was having trouble comprehending what he was seeing. There was a man, who should be forty-nine years old, but he appeared the same as he remembered him, the night before he disappeared, five years and five days ago. With no idea how he went missing, and how nor why he came back, he realized Tommy was not yet aware of these bizarre circumstances. He would have to psychologically treat him delicately and knew he would have to draw on the experience and knowledge gained while interviewing Doctor Mauer for many months.

"Yeah, Tommy, they got short-handed down here, so they sent me back to the district," Nick replied, trying to buy some time and devise a plan for telling him he disappeared over five years ago.

"When did you roll into the district?"

"Just a little while ago."

"Well, suit up; we'll take the wagon out."

"The truck is still down mechanical, Tommy," Sergeant Kaminski stated.

"Man, it's hot in here," Tommy remarked as he wiped some sweat from his brow, pulled off his clip-on tie, and unbuttoned his collar.

"Well, take the leather off," Nick suggested, knowing he would first need to take off the 'Sam Browne' strap and gun-belt.

"Yeah, Tommy, make yourself comfortable. You still owe me a memo for blowin' that radio call," the sergeant suggested.

As he took off the gun rig and leather patrol coat, the sergeant reached out and grabbed the items while casually commenting, "Here give them to me, I'll put 'em in the Operations Room. Pick 'em up when you bring me the memo."

"Okay," as he handed over the service revolver, "Yo Marty, crap, you only been a boss for three days, and already you're bustin' chops," he mentioned, wondering why he was making a big deal out of 'blowing' one radio call.

"Hey, Tommy, I'm new in the rank. You know how it is, when you're new, you gotta go by the book for a while. Don't worry. I got your back. I ain't gonna hurt you over this. I just need the paperwork," Kaminski responded with a smile.

"Thanks, Marty, and hey Sarge, congratulations on your promotion, even though that's the fastest I ever seen."

As the sergeant was leaving the office, he glanced sideways at Nick and replied, "Thanks, Tommy."

Nick stood there in amazement, staring at his friend, not sure if he was real or if he was still asleep and dreaming.

Tommy sensed the stares, and questioned, "Why you eyeballin' me? Wow, all you guys sure been acting goofy tonight. What the hell is goin' on?"

The detective glanced away. When the sound of the phone ringing snapped the tension, he swiftly scooped up the receiver. On the other end was Captain McClendon, who advised him the Police Surgeon arrived, and an examination of the returned officer was going to become necessary. He inquired if he's broached the subject of the disappearance. Nick answered, "No — but shortly."

The captain laid out a quick briefing as to what was going to happen from that point on. They hung up; he turned to Tommy and declared, "Tom — we gotta talk."

Sensing something was not right, Tommy's mind started to race, as multiple questions ran through his mind.

Where did all that snow go?" Why are all those memorial photos and plaques on the wall in the hallway?" Why did that calendar say December 25, 1991?" Why is Marty Kaminski a sergeant in our squad? He didn't hold roll call tonight, Sergeant Osborne did, and the lieutenant — yeah, and it was a 'formal roll call' too.

Sensing Tommy was becoming panic-stricken as his eyes darted with anxiety in every direction, Nick remembered back to his first day on the job, just a rookie frozen with fear. He smacked his hands together directly in front of Tommy's face and yelled, "Look at me, look at me. Everything is going to be okay; you're back with us now."

He flinched at the sound of the clap and focused on Nick's face searching for an answer. His eyes scoured every inch when he zeroed in onto a spot on his cheek.

"What the hell is that scar on your face? When did you get that? You didn't have it last night when we worked together."

Nick grabbed him by the shoulders and realized that physical act confirmed his friend was, in fact, real as he revealed, "Tommy, listen to me — I was wounded in a shoot-out three and half years ago.

Like in a feverish dream, Tommy started to sweat profusely as he shook his head, refusing to accept the words.

"Can't be — we were working 301-Wagon — we weren't in no shoot-out. What the hell are you talkin' about?" he rambled as he searched his memory.

"Tommy — today is December 25, 1991 — and you've been missing for over five years! We've been looking for you all this time! You left without a trace. Do you hear me, Tommy?"

His eyes narrowed, and his thoughts were rambling while he continued to shake his head back and forth. Nick took the newspaper, unfolded it, and presented the front page to him. He lowered his gaze, focused, and read the date.

Nick quietly revealed, "I made detective, and I've been the assigned investigator on your disappearance case for the last three years."

Tommy's eyes slowly raised from the paper gazing back at him, realizing the face he was looking at was no longer that of his young wagon partner.

"How — how can this be?"

"Tommy, think. What do you remember?"

"I — I stood 'roll call,' went out on the street. It was snowing real hard. Met Sullivan at the hospital for coffee. The Sarge signed our logs, had two unfounded calls, and ate lunch at the diner. Found a 'hole,' took a ten-minute nap, woke up, the radio not working, came into the district — what do you mean five years and five days. I don't understand — I gotta go home! Rosie, Sophia, I gotta go home!" he yelled out, as panic set in.

Upon hearing the commotion, Captain McClendon opened the door allowing the Police Surgeon and a Fire Department Rescue Squad crew to examine him. Tommy went silent, slumping back into the chair, with a vacant expression in his eyes.

"He could be going into shock," the doctor stated as he began the examination.

CHAPTER 54

CHIEF INSPECTOR BREEVAC, FROM NIGHT Command, arrived at the 17th District. The captain briefed him and ordered a Stakeout team and a Highway Patrol unit dispatched to the district. The chief notified the Police Commissioner, who devised a plan to transport Tommy to a secure room in the hospital at Pennypacker University.

At the end of the call, the Commissioner issued his orders. "Chief, I want four officers, consisting of a Highway team, and a Stakeout Unit, with him from this point forward. I do not want him out of our sight until we get to the bottom of this, do you understand?"

"Yes, sir, I understand Commissioner, as you know, Officer Tabbozzi's daughter is in the Pediatric Hospital, and once he's made aware of her condition, he'll want to be with her."

"Chief, when he's been medically evaluated, and we do need this evaluation for evidentiary purposes when that is completed, he's to be escorted to his wife and daughter. So far as I can tell, the news media has not picked up on this yet, so as soon as he leaves the district, resume the Bus Detail, inform — no order, all officers that are aware of his return, to refrain from making it public knowledge, at least until we can control the environment with the media."

"Yes, sir. May I ask? Is there anyone outside the department that's officially privy to this development?"

261

"I have not made any call upstairs yet, but I know we don't have too much time. When he gets to the hospital, and you determine he's in a controlled environment, contact me immediately."

Secured on a stretcher and wrapped in a blanket to conceal his identity, the EMTs placed Tommy in the back of the Rescue Squad. They transported him to Pennypacker University Hospital. The escorting units and the squad made a smooth and quiet run without lights or sirens.

A medical team was standing by when they arrived, and they rushed to examine Tommy utilizing X-rays, CAT-scans, MRI technology, and drawing blood for testing.

Tom Tabbozzi was never what one might call athletic; however, he was strong. Probably his best physical shape was when he got out of basic military training and the police academy. Through the years, he put on weight, considered normal, but he was not overweight for his height. He smoked cigarettes since high school and was the cause for a constant cough, which developed in recent years before his disappearance.

The initial examination showed Tommy did not lose weight, his muscles appeared toned, and the preliminary impression indicated he was in excellent health. Although he was in a daze during the exam, he was cooperative.

Nick stayed with him throughout the testing and prepared to tell him about Sophia. With the Highway officers standing by, he faced him and revealed the bad news.

"Tom, we're going to take you to Rosie and Sophia now, but before we do, I need to tell you something."

With his head down, hearing these words, he turned his gaze upward and stared with a blank expression into Nick's face.

"We're going to take you to the Pediatric Hospital." with a hesitation in his voice, he continued, "Sophia is ill."

Tommy didn't comprehend the revelation at first, obviously overwhelmed with the unbelievable nightmare of the circumstances. His mind was reeling.

"She can't be; I was just with her yesterday, at the mall, I bought her the snow globe — she can't be — my Sophia, no, my little Sophia, no, she can't be sick. Nicky! What are you telling me?"

He screamed as the words sunk in, and he stood and appeared to want to run from the room and destroy anyone who caused his nightmare. Officers Spurgeon and Pike stepped forward, and as most Highway Patrol officers, they were imposing. Grabbing him by the arms, they restrained him until he calmed down. Nick attempted to quiet him by saying, "Tommy, listen to me, Rosie and Sophia need you now. Do you hear me? They missed you, Tommy — they need you."

The rage ran its course as he quieted; he focused on Nick, and with a low and intense voice, stated, "Nicky — you gotta find out who did this to me."

With a shadow of darkness in his eyes, he declared, "So I can — kill them."

CHAPTER 55

THE OUTBURST FROM TOMMY BROUGHT the attending physician into the room, where he checked his vital signs and administered a mild sedative. The Highway team guarded him, allowing Nick to make a quick call to Detective Chuck Warner's house and tell him what was occurring.

"Chuck, it's Nick."

"Hey, why are you calling this early? Merry Christmas, by the way."

"Listen; go out to Philly Pediatrics right away."

"Did something happen to Sophia?"

"No, she's still the same, but I need to tell you something. You better sit down."

"What — what is it?"

"Chuck," with a hesitation in his voice, "Tommy is back. He walked into the Seventeenth at about four-forty-five this morning."

After a momentary silence, he responded, "Nick, don't screw around, that ain't funny. What are you doin?"

"Chuck, you gotta' go out there and tell Rosie, we have him at Pennypacker Hospital now. Go down there, break it to her, and then we'll bring him over."

The seriousness of Nick's voice made him realize he was not joking; he stood and, with urgency, declared, "I'm on my way."

Detective Warner quickly got to his car, making his way to West Philly. His mind was racing as he remembered how he wrote Tommy off as a victim of a mob hit, and a slight feeling of self-consciousness for losing hope came over him. Once at the hospital, he raced to the nearest phone and called Nick, advising him of his arrival. He took the elevator to the fifth floor, ICU Unit, where the officers standing vigil met him.

"Chuck, what's going on? Why are you running?" one of the cops asked.

"Where's Rosie?"

"She's in the room with Sophia."

He hurried to the room, looking through the glass; he tapped lightly, getting her attention. When she turned, he waved for her to come out to the hall. Once outside the room, he reached out, held her hands, and directed her to a chair. He was hesitant, not knowing what to say.

"Rosie, come sit with me for a minute," he whispered as he eased her towards the waiting area. As she stood, he motioned to the other officers to come down the hall to him.

"I have something to tell you, something you've been praying for — for a long time."

With a wide-eyed stare, and without an inkling of what he was about to tell her, she appealed, "What — what is it?"

With a slight reassuring smile on his face, he finally announced, "Rosie, Tommy came back, we have him, he's okay."

Unblinking, she mimicked his grin, searching his face trying to comprehend the words.

"Rosie, we're going to bring him to you and Sophia now."

With a sudden grasp of that revelation, her legs crumbled, and she slumped back towards the chair. The officers' rushed to her side and caught hold of her before she hit the floor as she let out, "Tommy! Tommy's back! Oh, my God — Tommy's back!"

The officers stood by and supported her, and when they heard the news, they gaped at one another with puzzled expressions. Minutes passed, and the ding of the elevator rang out as it approached the fifth floor. The signal light illuminated, and the doors opened. First out was Nick, who stepped sideways and gestured with an outstretched hand. A figure dressed in dark clothes, wearing a hooded sweatshirt, stepped through the opening with head down and turned right, facing Rosie. She got to her feet and squinted intently, not able to make out the face. The person moved with slow, deliberate paces down the hall until he stopped a foot away from her. He reached up and pulled the hood back away from his face. She gazed fearfully at first, and then, recognizing him, the sun broke through the clouds as she felt the warmth. Their eyes locked, one recalling the other from just eight hours before, and one remembering the other from five years and five days ago. A dam of emotions breached as they clutched one another, never wanting to let go. Rosie broke down and called out, "Tommy, Tommy — we missed you so much."

He held her face in his hands as he kissed her, and though, in his mind, it was only eight hours since he last saw her, he missed her just as much. After several minutes of embrace, He gazed into his wife's eyes and asked with a doleful look, "Rosie — Sophia?"

She sobbed and cried out, "Oh, Tommy, our little girl is very sick."

He scanned above her head, trying to locate his daughter's room, wanting to go to her.

"Where is she, Rosie?"

She took him by the hand to ICU room 508. When he peered through the window of the door. He could see his little "sunshine" older, but with the same beautiful face, lying unconscious in the hospital bed with tubes and monitors everywhere. A glass Christmas snow globe was resting on the bedside table. In Tommy's mind, the same one that was purchased less than twenty-four hours ago. He stood staring in disbelief, and with a sudden force, dropped to his knees and hysterically wailed while pounding his fists into the concrete hospital floor. His heart was broken, they tried to console him, but the rage took over as he yelled out,

"I want them, Nicky! Whoever did this to my family and me, I want them!"

He replied while trying to reassure him, "Tommy, I promise you I'll find out what happened."

Then with fury and hate clouding his thoughts, he lashed out at his friend, and with vile in his voice, he shouted, "What the hell are you gonna do? What makes you think you're gonna find out anything? You're nothing but a rookie."

Understanding the anger, Nick let him vent, unable to comprehend the nightmare he was experiencing.

CHAPTER 56

PHIL KARBE SAT IN THE empty newsroom nursing a slight hangover from a holiday celebration the night before. While the young reporter cursed his lowly status for having to be in the office on Christmas morning, the phone rang, shattering the silence sending a bolt of pain into his right temple. He scooped up the receiver in a quick motion. On the other end was a confidential source he had developed in his short career.

"Phil? This is Hector."

"Hector, what's up? Why are you calling?"

"Had to work. Hey, listen, I saw something you might want to know about."

"What have you got?"

"A bunch of cops, Highway Patrol, Stakeout, and a whole lot of brass. They bring someone into the hospital."

"Who? Who was it?"

"Hard to tell — shrouded in a blanket — looks like some kind of VIP."

"What were they doing?"

"They hustled this person into different departments — X-ray — MRI — like they were doin' a rush physical."

"Are they still in there?"

"Stayed like about an hour and a half, then the craziest thing — the cop show comes out of the hospital pushing the hoodie-wearing dude in a wheelchair."

"Where'd they go?"

"This is real nuts — they go over to Philly Pediatrics."

"Thanks, Hector. I'll catch up with you later."

The reporter became curious, he was not aware of any VIP visiting the city, and he pondered, *Who, if they became ill, would rate that kind of police protection? And why would they bring that person over to a children's hospital?*

He began to check into the information by reviewing current news articles and didn't find any extraordinary stories; No VIPs reported in the city recently, nothing unusual, just typical holiday features. A review of past headlines revealed an article about a recent event from five days prior. The headline read:

HUGE TURN-OUT FOR MISSING OFFICER AT THE CATHEDRAL.

He started reading further into the story and landed on a curious part.

"The missing officer's young daughter is reported seriously ill and being treated at The Philadelphia Pediatric Hospital."

The reporter put the paper down on his desk and stared across the room, rubbing his chin stubble with his fingers. After several minutes, he rose, grabbed his coat, and ran out the door. When he arrived at the hospital, uniformed police officers stopped him as he attempted to gain entry, where he started hurling questions at them.

"Is Officer Tabbozzi in the building? Where was he found? What are you hiding?"

They kept him back and did not respond to his inquiry. The department couldn't hold Officer Tabbozzi's return unrevealed for much longer. Too many eyes have already seen him. Chief Inspector Breevac contacted the Police Commissioner by phone and advised him of the incident with the reporter.

"Commissioner, I'm afraid the media is now aware of our situation."

After a moment of thought, he issued orders. "Alright, Chief, tell them we will hold an official news conference at eleven a.m., but tell them I'll hold it at the Police Administration Building. I want to provide Officer Tabbozzi and his family as much privacy as possible."

"Yes, sir."

In the next couple of hours, the department prepared as Police Headquarters came alive with activity. As word got out to all the major media outlets, they ramped up their staff in anticipation of that unusual event on Christmas morning. At 11:00 a.m. at the Cherry Street parking lot of the Police Administration Building, Philadelphia Police Commissioner John Keyser, took to the podium. Because of the unusual date and time, various rumors circulated, with many reporters turning out for the event.

The Commissioner held out his hands, palms down, gesturing for the crowd to quiet. Once they were silent, he proceeded, "At approximately four-forty-five a.m., this date, Officer Thomas P. Tabbozzi badge number forty-four-thirty-one, entered the Seventeenth Police District headquarters, located at 1201 South Twentieth Street. Radio Patrol Car-178 was subsequently discovered parked against the curb on Twentieth Street, in front of the district building. The Police Surgeon examined Officer Tabbozzi and ordered his transport to the Hospital at Pennypacker University. After a series of medical and evidentiary assessments, the detail escorted him to the Philadelphia Pediatric Hospital to reunite him with his wife and ill child. The investigation into his disappearance is ongoing. We would request, because of the extraordinary nature of the case, you respect the officer and his family's privacy."

At the end of the statement, the reporters hurled a volley of questions. He answered one at a time and only with the stated facts. He didn't answer anything regarding speculation of how he went missing or how he came back, concluding with, "The investigation is still active and ongoing."

The media went wild, interrupting scheduled holiday programs. Talking heads, usually off on Christmas, hurried back to their respective studios to be the face of the story for

270

their news organizations. Agencies from around the world converged on Philadelphia, attempting to cover every angle of the event. Previously televised documentaries regarding the occurrence were re-shown, with various authorities presenting numerous theories on the case.

CHAPTER 57

NICK STAYED AT TOMMY'S SIDE for the next couple of days, primarily to help ease him back into reality but also trying to glean any clues to his disappearance. Hoping to jog his memory, he showed him some news coverage on TV. Tommy stared in wonder at the images, unable to comprehend that he was the center of so much attention. His recollections of December 20, 1986, and the previous day were vivid. He listed everything he could remember in the twenty-four hours leading up to him backing into the shipping container. He recalled details that Rosie didn't, but when he described them, her memories came back. Small items: the dress she was wearing that day, the little song that Sophia sang, and how Chief howled along with her. The picture she drew for Tommy to thank him for the snow globe. Little things, he remembered them like they happened yesterday, for in his mind they did.

Nick received a message to contact the Police Surgeon immediately. He located a phone and dialed. The Chief Police Surgeon for the City of Philadelphia, Doctor Edwin S. Kuebler, answered.

"Doctor Kuebler speaking."

"Yes, sir, this is Detective Avner from Major Crimes. I was instructed to call you."

"Yes, detective, I have some amazing information directly related to your case."

"What is it, Doctor?"

"As part of our assessment of Officer Tabbozzi, we acquired his medical records from his family physician. You may not be aware, but before his disappearance, he was diagnosed with stage three lung cancer and diabetes."

"Yes, I knew about it. His wife had informed me of those conditions after he went missing."

"Well, the results are in, and I can't explain how or why, but Officer Tabbozzi is cured of those afflictions. In fact, he's clear of all illnesses, he's in tremendous physical shape, as though all his physiological systems had a re-set."

Stunned by that news, he was speechless. Finally, he managed to speak.

"Doctor, this may sound like a strange question, but are we sure this is actually Thomas Tabbozzi?"

"Detective, we gathered all available documentation, private, military, everything we could locate. He was wounded in the Viet Nam war and carried shrapnel in his body. Our X-rays, when compared to the previous, still show the metal with an identical unique shape and in the same positions within the body. Yes, detective, this is the same person, one Thomas P. Tabbozzi, whatever happened to him was a miracle, and I only wish we could find one for his daughter."

Contemplating the new information, Nick got back to work in earnest, now possessing tangible clues. Sitting in his office, he went over the case file and concentrated on the night of' the occurrence. He wanted to review all the statements in particular. The investigation revealed that Steve Sullivan was the last police officer to talk with Tommy before he vanished. In an attempt to take a closer look at the details, Nick decided to review his statement. After reading the report, nothing new stood out. The only thought he had was when Officer Sullivan mentioned Mr. James J. Callahan. Nick recalled how, after the shooting, he donated that special wheelchair Lopez needed for his recovery, and the gift card he sent to him for dinner at Bookbinders.

He's a real gentleman and a classy guy, Nick thought to himself.

###

The next day he made the trip to the Police Garage, located on Adams Avenue at the Roosevelt Boulevard, across from the Friends Hospital facility.

The Tow Squad transported the missing vehicle to one of the smaller Police Garages for a forensic evaluation. Secured, in the rear corner of the large building was a cage-type area, fitted with assorted tool cabinets and a hydraulic lift. RPC-178 was up in the air. A technician wearing dark blue overalls with an embroidered "POLICE — CRIME LAB" identification patch across the garment's back was inspecting the under-carriage with a hand-held ultraviolet light. Officer Samantha Richmond was the department's first female Forensic Specialist. Known throughout the department as 'Sami,' she was a dedicated trace evidence professional.

"Sami, what have you got so far?"

Not looking away from her examination, she stated, "I've collected some swab specimens from several areas on the car and ran them through a spectrographic analysis to get a better idea of what we could be looking at, and I came up with several points of interest. In the left front wheel well, I took samples of the accumulated road dirt and found traces of Halothane."

"What is that?"

"Halothane is made commercially under the name of Fluothane; it's a general anesthetic in vapor form."

"An anesthetic — under the car? He wondered. "What are the other things you found?"

"While examining for fingerprints, I did come up with multiple prints on or in the vehicle. However, most of them I identified and eliminated as other officers from the Seventeenth District or Police Garage employees who did maintenance work. There is one print, or let's say a partial unidentifiable smudge of a possible palm impression, found on the roof over the driver's side door."

"Why is that interesting if it can't be identified?"

"Well, it's more about the substance deposited than the hand-print. We tested and detected a trace sample of microalga scenedesmus rubescens. Before you ask, that's a micro-algae used for various products, one being skin-care, and these samples indicate a higher quality product. Some commodities sell for one hundred and fifty dollars for a four-ounce bottle. It's not just for vanity purposes. This is also effective for disorders such as eczema and psoriasis. The one interesting factor about this trace evidence, although Officer Tabbozzi was gone for five years, someone placed the substance there over the last week, or so, it's relatively fresh."

"How about the car itself, was it damaged or altered in any way?"

"So far, it appears to be in pristine condition. Not tampered with or mechanically altered in any way. We also tested for any type of radiation exposure — negative results."

She finished on the undercarriage and lowered the vehicle back to the ground level. Nick conducted a visual inspection, careful not to touch anything. He examined both the interior and exterior for about twenty minutes, and while leaving, he remarked, "Thanks Sami, when can I expect your report?"

"I'll have it completed by the end of the week."

Before returning to his office, Nick stopped in to see Doctor Mauer. When he arrived at the suite, he heard classical music playing inside the room.

"Doc," he called in and tapped lightly on the ajar door.

"Nicholas, so nice to see you," greeting him in an upbeat mood attributed to his present studies.

"Good to see you, too, Doc." He found him writing copious formulas and mathematical equations on a whiteboard.

After some small talk, Nick made it a point to observe the doctor's reaction before he revealed, "Have you seen the news? My friend returned after five years gone."

Mauer turned away with his hands stuffed in his pockets, squinted, then inquired, "How is his health? I wish him well."

"His physical state is excellent. His previous illnesses are gone. That part of his nightmare is a miracle. However, his daughter remains very ill and in a coma. He's with her now."

When Nick mentioned the miraculous cure, he noticed a slight smile take shape on the doctor's face. When he commented on the daughter's illness, he became morose, sat, and slumped in the chair, staring at the floor. Watching his response for several minutes and not wanting to trigger a regressive episode, he suggested. "Doctor, I haven't eaten yet. Would you like to join me? We could go out, sit, and enjoy a cooked meal."

Mauer sat with his head in his hands, said nothing, and then suddenly looked up and asked, "We can go out?"

Although he was a Material Witness, Nick got permission from the attending psychiatric physician, and through the door, they went. He was excited to be getting out and away from the hospital as they slid into D-908 and left.

"We're going to a favorite place of mine. I ate there growing up. The place brings back some fond memories. The food's not fancy, but it's good."

"That would be delightful, Nicholas. I am immensely looking forward to it."

Nick maneuvered D-908 out of the parking lot, and in fifteen minutes, he reached the intersection of Frankford and Cottman Avenues. He drove north on Frankford to the 7300 block, where a classic 1950s style diner stood with an 'art deco' design, all stainless steel and glass shining in the mid-afternoon sun. The Mayfair Diner, constructed in 1932, served millions since it first opened for business. They parked and walked into the sparkling structure through the double glass doors. The hostess showed them to a window booth with a view of the Avenue. The interior consisted of a long counter with stools, and along the windows were booths, with freestanding tables and chairs, placed comfortably in the center. The waitresses were friendly and hard-working, most employed there for many years. Once handed menus, Doctor Mauer asked, "What do you recommend, Nicholas?"

"I always get the 'meatloaf dinner,' ice tea, and for dessert, apple pie with vanilla ice cream."

"On your recommendation, I'll have the same."

They placed their orders, and while waiting with the hopes of Doctor Mauer opening up and disclosing more information, Nick started to reveal the story of his life. He related how he lived a couple of blocks from there, and when his widowed mother had to work an evening shift, he would walk there and eat a meal. He recounted his school years, baseball, how his dad died, how he met his wife, and then about the police department.

Explaining how he came to know Tommy during his first day on the street, he described his personality and family. He divulged the death of Tabbozzi's young son and the devastation that would result if Sophia died. Also, he told him about the effect of the disappearance on everyone in the department and gave an account of the shooting incident and the wounds he received. As their meals arrived, he carried on with the details of his life as they ate.

The doctor listened intently, absorbing every word, and after the story ended, he gazed out the window, watching the people, and the traffic, studying the scene. When they finished, Nick paid the bill, they left, and he toured the streets of his youth, pointing out to Mauer the landmarks of his life.

Upon their return to Greystone, he escorted him in, and before he left, the doctor declared, "Nicholas, I can't begin to tell you what today has meant to me. You have shown me great kindness in sharing your life story with me. Forgive me; I have never really experienced a human relationship before, a friendship if you will. My parents were overbearing; it was always about school, the 'field of study, the research.'"

He dropped his eyes and drooped his shoulders. "The only connection that came close to fellowship was a kindly janitor from my university many years ago. Since the time they found me wandering alone 'out of my mind' in Erie, you always showed me compassion. I will never forget that, Nicholas."

Nick was surprised at that personal revelation but could tell he was sincere. A feeling of sympathy rose in him for the lonely yet brilliant man as he softly replied, "You look tired, Doctor. Why don't you rest, and I'll stop in again soon."

He shuffled to a recliner easing down, and said, "I will always remember this day, Nicholas."

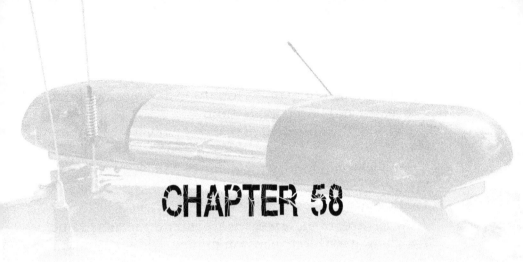

CHAPTER 58

THE NEXT WEEK, WHILE ENTERING headquarters, Nick spotted Detective Chuck Warner in the hall.

"Yo, what have you been up to?" Nick asked.

"A lot of things are happenin'."

Once inside the office, Nick pumped for details, "What's goin' on? Something good?"

"We got this guy, works down the Municipal Services Building in License and Inspection, goes by the name of Mickey Frost, we've been looking at him for a while. We got him shaking down contractors, small businesses all over the city. The guy's been doing this for a while, but the amount of money he's been making, he's not stuffin' his own pockets, he's sending most up the ladder."

"Let me guess who, Councilman Ronald Hubbs."

Chuck glanced at him sideways. "How'd you know?"

"I got people who tell me things."

"Well, maybe you ought to be tellin' me the story."

"My source tells me, for sure, Frost is the bag man for Hubbs," Nick disclosed.

"What else you got?"

"Hubbs is financed by a money guy — that financier you told me about, Bennett."

"Yeah, we had a feeling about that," Chuck revealed.

"Here's something you might not be aware of, Bennett runs a Real Estate Investment Trust, and through Swarthmore Holdings, he buys the properties and re-finances them through the same company, a Redstone Savings and Loan. Nick revealed and posed a question.

"Guess who the president of that company is – on paper?"

"Who?"

"A fine Fishtown boy by the name of Michael Frost."

"Mickey?"

"That's a fact, Jack."

"Wow, all three of these weasels are runnin' the same game."

"Yeah, along with our pension money. Did you find out any more on Bennett?"

"Well, here's one for you. I interviewed the CEO of Swarthmore Holdings yesterday in his office."

Chuck went on to explain that he wanted to see the person up-close. He called him and asked if he could come by and consult with him on a financial investigation.

"Yeah, I wanted to eyeball him, so, bullshitted him, I told him we're working on a case involving a local company suspected of fraud. So, I tell him, being he's one of the top economic advisers in the city, with his firm handling the pension fund, and all. I ask him if I could stop by his office for his advice."

"No way. He went for that story?"

"He was a little reluctant at first, but I 'schmoozed' him and told him, you know, like how he's so respected in the financial sector, and all that crap, so after a minute or two, he huffs and says to me, 'Okay — stop by.'"

"So, what happened?"

"So, I go to the office, real ritzy, nice view, I go in, and he's behind this enormous desk, all high-class furniture. He's like signing some papers. He doesn't even look up. With his index finger, he motions to me to sit down. So, I do, and after a while, he stops writing and looks up at me like I was a bug crawling on the couch. I start into my bullshit story, he thinks it over and gives me some answers, and this goes on for about ten minutes. Then he kinda is giving me a hint that 'time's up' cause he's looking at a gold Rolex watch laying on his desk."

"He had a Rolex on the desk?"

"Yeah, sitting there in front of him."

"What happened then?"

"So, I said, 'can I leave my business card,' and he mumbles, 'yeah, sure, why not.' Well, it turns out I don't have any with me, so I ask, 'can I write my number down?' He's getting impatient, and he pushes over a blank piece of paper and hands me the pen he was writing with. I jot it down, slide the paper over and give him back the pen, and he tells me, 'keep it, you need it more than I do,' so I smile, clip it into my notebook, and leave."

"What's the Rolex doin' on his desk — why isn't he wearing it?"

"Looked like he had a rash on his wrist, 'cause he was scratching the whole time we're talking."

"What, wait a minute, he was scratching his wrist? You still have the pen?"

"Yeah, it's still in my notebook?"

"Chuck, do you use any high-end lotions or creams?"

Chuck glowered and declared, "What — you pulling my chain? Yeah, 'Ben-Gay,' four bucks a tube, swanky enough for you?"

"No, I mean, did you touch the pen any time since yesterday?"

"No, I left it in my briefcase. Why?"

Nick reached into his lower desk drawer and retrieved a six-inch 'evidence envelope.'

"Chuck, this might be something. The Crime Lab detected a high-end skincare cream on the roof of 178. Let's bag the pen. I'll type out a Property Report and Seizure Analysis. Being you retrieved it, would you do me a favor, continue with the chain of evidence, and take it down to the Chem Lab for analysis?"

With his chin down and peering over the rims of his eyeglasses, Chuck hesitated and then asked, "You got a theory on the case – don't you?"

###

Nick stood, and from the top file cabinet drawer, he produced a manila folder. Returning to the desk, he sat and opened it.

He focused on the other detective and declared, "Chuck, I did a lot of digging, and I think I know what happened to Tommy — and with what you just told me about the pen, I might have the proof."

While raising his eyebrows, Warner slid his chair closer and stated, "Yeah, well, I gotta hear this."

"Well, for sure, Tommy didn't go through some time warp or get beamed up by the Martians — no; this was about one thing and one thing only."

"What's that?"

"This was all about the gold."

"What do you mean?"

"I believe Tommy was kidnapped, and an experiment was conducted on him for money."

"How did you come up with that idea?"

"After we became aware of Mauer and the Tardigrade. Professor Klingman pointed me to Province University, and I found all of Mauer's published theories."

"So, what about them?"

"I located over two hundred titles, and they were way over my head, but one word caught my eye, and I uncovered its meaning."

"Yeah, what was the word?"

"Cryptobiosis."

"What the hell is that?"

Nick hesitated, and with a sly grin forming, he answered, "Suspended animation."

Chuck sat with his mouth agape. After a moment, he shook his head and exclaimed, "You're friggin nuts. You've been watching too much 'Star Trek.' They can't do that — can they?"

"Listen, all the pieces fit. This is one of Mauer's theories published in 1980, and he falls off the radar in '85.

"You think Mauer was in on this? He doesn't seem the greedy type."

"No, he doesn't, but they couldn't do it without him."

"What else you got?"

"Bennett's name shows up on a sign-in sheet at Province back in '83 looking at genomics hypothesis of this nature. I got Councilman Hubbs pushing through an ordinance awarding the pension fund contract to Bennett in '84, so that gives him access to millions to finance the experiment."

"Okay, but there ain't no way these guys personally snatched Tommy."

"That's where Grimes comes in — we got him buying a shipping container two months before the disappearance. I figure he was the muscle and the security component of the project."

Chuck scratched the back of his head as he stared across the room, and after digesting the theory, he posed a question.

"Alright, but how were they gonna make money from all this?"

"I'm not sure, but I'm guessing the first thing they had to do was prove the experiment could work."

"Well, Tommy is back with us — so I guess it worked," Chuck stated, and added, "Nicky, that all sounds good, but what's your next move?"

Nick studied the contents of the folder and disclosed, "I'm going to have to go after Mauer."

CHAPTER 59

NICK STOOD JUST INSIDE THE room, with his back to the closed door. He watched Tommy and Rosie sitting quietly on both sides of Sophia's hospital bed, each holding one of her hands, staring intensely. He was physically tired; his mind choked with dread and fear as he felt hope slipping away.

The rhythmic beeps from the vital sign monitor and the low steady "whoosh" from the lung ventilator were the only sounds in the room.

Sophia laid upon the bed, frail and fragile, part little girl, part machine. The mechanical component was keeping her alive. Standing and watching, Nick's heart was breaking; he couldn't imagine what thoughts his two heartsick friends were thinking. The hours went by with no change in Sophia's condition or her parent's demeanor. He heard a light tap at the door. When he cracked it open, the detail officer was standing close, and in a whisper, he said, "Detective, a call for you."

Silently leaving the room, he gently closed the door behind him, walked to the phone, and answered, "Detective Avner."

"Nicholas, you must come here straight away. I must speak to you."

"Doctor Mauer, this is not a good time. I'm at the Pediatric Hospital with my friend and his family."

"I implore you. You must come here; we must talk."

Sophia's condition seemed hopeless, Nick didn't want to leave his friend's side, and if he was right with his case theory, the doctor was part of the disappearance and a potential criminal. Mauer kept pleading with him to come to the Greystone facility, and as the detective was about to tell him no emphatically, Tommy's words came to mind, *Listen to people; you never know what they might tell you.*

He thought it over and decided that would be an opportunity to confront him with his suspicions about his involvement.

"Okay, I'll be there in an hour."

He stood motionless, not wanting to leave Tommy, Rosie, and Sophia, but he knew he had to. As he was ready to depart, the attending pediatric physician walked down the hall, about to enter Sophia's room. When Nick spotted him, he approached and said, "Doctor, I understand you can't say, but is there any indication that her condition may improve."

He looked at Nick woefully, dropped his stare to the floor, and solemnly shook his head side to side as he quietly replied, "A week, possibly two."

The doctor turned and left. Standing still and stunned, he gradually turned and walked to the elevator. Arriving at Greystone, he went to the room and knocked.

"Come in, please," was the enthusiastic response.

When he entered the room, he instantly noticed multiple whiteboards throughout the suite. On a desk were numerous notebooks and journals, piled high. Mauer was standing with his hair askew, wearing a short sleeve hospital shirt.

"Nicholas, Nicholas, come in, come in, please," he gushed while waving his hand inward.

"What is all this, Doctor?" Nick inquired, looking around the room.

"Nicholas, please sit. We must talk."

"You're right, Doc — we do have to talk," the investigator stated with a coldness in his voice.

Mauer detecting his abruptness, became quiet and implored, "Nicholas, what's wrong? Why do you speak to me this way? I thought we had become friends."

"Friends? How can we be friends when you hurt someone close to me?"

The doctor backed away and stumbled into a chair as he shook his head and began to mumble.

"Don't go playing that regressive act either. You know what you did. You used my friend as a lab rat on your experiment for what — money," Nick fumed.

"No — no — no — you don't understand I did not want to perform the process on him."

"Well, you did, and you know that you did," Nick bluffed, inwardly surprised at his admission.

The doctor turned his gaze towards him, and with glazed eyes, he disclosed, "You are correct, I did conduct an experiment on your friend — but not for money."

"Not for money — than for what?"

"To keep him alive."

"What do you mean — keep him alive?"

Mauer hunched back into the chair where he removed his eyeglasses, rubbed the bridge of his nose, and stared at the floor in thought. He spoke in a quiet tone and revealed, "Over seven years ago, I was recruited by a venture capitalist to develop a process to prove one of my hypotheses."

"Cryptobiosis?" The detective interjected.

Surprised, Mauer looked up, and with squinted eyes, he answered, "Yes, cryptobiosis."

The two men studied one another for a moment when Nick finally demanded, "Why, Tommy?"

"Nicholas, I must explain, I had no indication the test subject would be a human. They told me it would be a primate, of course, but I envisioned a chimpanzee or a gorilla, not a human. I would have rejected it outright if I had known."

"So why didn't you refuse when you found out it was going to be Tommy?"

"I protested profusely, I adamantly refused, but that — that creature in charge of security informed me that I would carry out the process on the officer, or he would kill us both. I didn't so much care about myself, but I couldn't let this innocent man die, so I proceeded.

"The security guy — he had a tattoo on the back of his hand?"

Surprised at the question, Mauer queried, "Yes — how did you know?"

"I know more than you think, doctor."

Over the years, Nick had taken many statements from suspects and had developed an instinct to detect fabricated stories from those individuals. After listening to the doctor and observing his demeanor, his gut told him that he was truthful.

The only sound was the classical music playing softly on the radio as Nick walked to the window while rubbing the back of his neck. A thought struck him as he turned and posed a question, "Doctor, you were found in Erie back in March, and Tommy didn't return until December — why didn't you tell us back then? We could have rescued him."

"Because the parameters for the proof of concept was for five years. If your friend was located beforehand, they would have killed him."

"Then why weren't you there for the full five years?"

"They decided to dispose of me."

"Why?"

"I suppose they viewed me as unstable — I started conversing with myself. I had no one to chat with because no conscious human with the intelligence level above the Tardigrade occupied the lab.One night that animal bound me hand and feet and threw me in a river."

"You somehow survived and made your way to Erie," Nick remarked while imagining the scene.

Mauer leaned forward in the chair, faced him, and confided, "You are no doubt in possession of my FBI dossier, so you are well aware of my background, but I swear to you I have awakened."

"What do you mean, doctor?"

"When we had our lunch together, and you revealed your life experiences with me, I have never realized or considered another person's life from a friend's perspective."

"Why not?"

"Because I had no friends, the only one that came close was a kindly janitor from my university many years ago. Nicholas, I have made magnificent scientific discoveries in my lifetime, but I have never had a friend."

"Why are you telling me all this, Doctor?" he asked with a curious tone.

"You have shown me how important friends are in life's journey."

The detective studied him, and a feeling of sympathy rose in him. He realized how true his statement was while he posed his next question.

"What was the venture capitalist's intention, once the experiment turned out successful?"

"They would secure a patent for the process, which is very costly to reproduce and market. I would say in the area of twenty-five to thirty million. I suspect that they would sell it to a large multi-national organization for a set sum. I would say a corporation would pay possibly a half a billion dollars for the 'process,' once they have determined it is genuine."

"A half a billion dollars!" Nick blurted and posed a question, "Yeah, but they wouldn't just take their word for it, won't they want some kind of proof that it actually works?"

"That's correct, it's referred to as proof of concept, and Nicholas, your dear friend Officer Tomas, is the proof of concept."

"What exactly would they need to file a patent?"

"My formula, which is documented in the notes and journals that were left behind in the lab, before they attempted to kill me."

"Is that all they would need?"

"They would also need to have another researcher in the field of genetics and micro-biology to claim to be the inventor of the 'process,' due to the fact, they think I am dead."

"How soon would the corporation file for a patent?"

"It could take a month or two. They would be required by their board of directors to perform 'due diligence' to ensure the process is proven before dispersing funds.

"However, once they own the rights, it will be worth billions. I would imagine they already have enlisted a top researcher, to take my place, as the 'inventor'...possibly Tolbert or Schick."

"How is all this even possible? Before I investigated the case, I had never even heard of genetics or DNA. The research seems to be in its infancy. How is it even conceivable that you were able to crack the code?"

"I am not one to extol my abilities, but I came to realize at a very young age that I was bestowed a gift. Other persons throughout human history were also endowed with gifts from the universe, people such as Archimedes, Galileo, Albert Einstein, Nikola Tesla, these great men were all considered, ahead of their times, but they provided the world with amazing discoveries."

Astonished, Nick listened intently then came to the realization; he was in the presence of scientific greatness.

"I must ask, what is the present condition of Officer Tomas's young daughter?"

"She probably has a week, maybe two," he revealed sullenly with a bowed head.

Doctor Mauer stared at Nick for a moment and then said, "Nicholas, I think of you as my friend. Do you consider me the same?"

He thought about his explanation of the events from the last five years, and after a moment, his gut told him to say, "Yes, doctor, I do consider you a friend."

"Nicholas, as a friend, I'm asking you to trust me," Mauer said as he picked up one of the knitting needles and proceeded to puncture his left arm between the bicep and bone, up under the short sleeve shirt.

Nick, not expecting that, yelled, "Doc, what the hell are you doing?"

"Wait, trust me," he replied, verbally holding him away.

He was working the needle in a circular motion as if picking for something. In less than ten seconds, he dropped the instrument to the floor, and with his right index finger and thumb, he pulled a small item from his arm and placed the bloody object in the palm of his left hand.

Nick gazed down and observed what appeared to be a 'crack vial,' containing a brownish liquid. He had seen hundreds of those empty containers in his career, littering the streets of some regions of Philadelphia, but that minute canister contained an unknown substance.

Fascinated, he excitedly asked, "What is it?"

Doctor Mauer took the item to a counter area, opened a bottle of rubbing alcohol, poured some in a cup, and dropped the object into it.

"Nicholas, this, my friend, is a by-product of the process. When I originally theorized the hypothesis, my calculations indicated that it was possible, but not until you informed me of Officer Tomas's healing did I realize that my projections were correct."

"Doctor, are you saying you've discovered a cure for all diseases?"

"No, not entirely, you see when Officer Tomas went through the process, his DNA was genetically re-combined with the Tardigrade, and one of their traits upon re-emerging from the cryptobiotic state is to purge itself of any physiological defects."

"So, what, Tommy can never get sick again? What's he going to live forever?"

"No, I'm afraid not. Yes, the process gave him a second chance, but he is a living organism, and all biological entities will eventually die. This is not a vaccination against disease or illness. When he was awakened, his DNA started to re-acclimate, but he could lead a long healthy life."

"Well, then what's in the vial, doctor?"

"My hypothesis was correct regarding the genetic clearing, and my theory also indicated it would be effective down to the second generation of the test subject. In the capsule is the original recombinant DNA. I concealed it in my arm while in the lab."

"Doctor Mauer, I'm not sure I understand you. What does all this mean?"

"It means, my dear friend Nicholas, you must transport me and this little package of life to the Pediatric Hospital."

CHAPTER 60

THE BUILDING WAS AS CLEAN as a hog barn could be. Every tool and piece of equipment, hard-used, but dirt-free, hung neatly from a pegboard on the walls. The many years spent in the United States Marine Corps produced certain customs and routines, one of which was to be "squared away" in all he did in life. That was his mantra and the values he taught to his young nephew. He raised the boy to be strong, both physically and intellectually. His protégé, who was away at a military school camp, learned well, high-lighted with his appointment into the United States Naval Academy.

Gunny was finishing cleaning up the last of the day's tools, standing at a workbench with his back towards the door. A reflection of movement in the farm tractor's window glass, parked by the wall, caught his eye.

He turned and faced a figure lurking inside the doorway.

Gunny stated with disgust, "Thought I smelled something foul in this hog barn."

The male standing there was about six foot four, closed cropped hair, deep-set eyes, wearing dark clothing.

"Well, if it ain't old, "Slimes. What you doin' in this neck of the woods? We already got plenty of snakes down here."

"Wanted to pay you a little visit, Gunny, and take care of some unfinished business before I retire."

"Retire? I know you ain't getting' no Marine Corps pension. So, what you gonna live on? The Corps had the good sense to throw out a scum like you."

"Yeah, well, I got me a big payday comin'."

"Yeah, what you got robbin' on your resume now? Besides guttin' people?"

"You musta heard about the cop. He got himself missing, and then he comes back."

"What are you sayin'? You did that with one of them Viet Nam 'man-traps' of yours?"

In a twitchy manner and a nervous laugh Grimes revealed,"Yeah, he was easy prey, but we had to wait for the right weather. Them cops are suckers for stray dogs and lost kids. I used a dog to bait him, 'cause they're easier to train."

"Do tell."

"Once I got him in the box, I owned him, knocked him out with the gas, sealed it up, and moved him down the rails with my special rig. When we got him in the lab, the lunatic doctor starts bitching about experimenting on him."

"Experimentin'? What're you talkin' about?"

"He didn't want to do it at first, said he ain't gonna do no experiment on humans, well I set him straight — told him he's gonna do it or him and the cop are gonna get gutted."

"Who you talkin' about?"

"The crazy doctor, he stayed with him day and night after he put him to sleep. We were gonna roll him back five years to the day, but the weather didn't cooperate, had to wait for the right night."

"Why'd you bring him back? Ain't your style, Slimes; you usually catch 'em, then kill 'em."

"I would have, if that experiment didn't work, I would have sliced him up, but he had to return, so the 'money boys' would have their proof.

"Well, they got what they need now, and I'm walking away with a million. Plus, as a bonus, I got rid of the doctor, tied him up, weighed him down, and dumped him in the river, so I could watch him drown."

'Why'd you take the car? Didn't it slow you down with your little game?"

"The 'money-boys' came up with that idea. The car kept the whole thing in the news for five years so that they could keep an eye on the show from a distance. They wanted the guinea pig to be some kind of public official. They didn't care who, as long as it wasn't some slob nobody would miss."

"So why you tellin' me all this? No — no wait, I get what you're doin'. You braggin', you just had to tell somebody. Right? Just like in 'Nam, well, what makes you think I ain't gonna' tell somebody else — Connie?"

"Like I said, Gunny, I'm here to take care of some unfinished business."

Conrad Grimes, also known as 'Slimes,' reached behind his back, and from beneath his jacket, he pulled out an eighteen inch 'Kukri' or 'Gurkha Blade.' That formidable weapon had a curved razor-sharp edge, and a trained handler could dismember a human limb with one stroke.

"Whatcha' got? A new toy?" Gunny commented as the glint of the shined steel flashed in his eyes.

"This is the only knife in the world I would bring to a gunfight, and in sixty seconds, I'm gonna show you why," he declared with a sardonic grin.

Grimes held the huge instrument in his right hand with the cutting edge up, swinging the blade in a figure-eight pattern, and moving towards Gunny. With a lunge, he reached out with the weapon, attempting to slice him. On the second lunge, the one-legged Marine was able to parry and duck his thrust. As they moved around the dirt floor in that deadly dance, he continued to avoid fatal contact.

Anger and frustration were building in Grimes at Gunny's ability to evade his assault. In a rage, he rushed forward, causing his prey to back away. The one-legged Marine's prosthesis slipped from under him, and he plunged to the ground next to a barn support pillar. Grimes recognizing his chance, moved in swiftly for the kill bringing the curved sword-like weapon down and up. The blade descended as

Gunny raised his artificial leg to block the blitz. The razor edge struck the limb about two inches above the ankle, severing it in two. The blow caused Grimes to topple off balance for a split-second, allowing Gunny to kick out with his right leg, sending the attacker back to the center of the barn.

Recovering, he turned, and with a snarl, faced the downed Marine. He glared into his eyes as a slight smile formed on Grimes' face, knowing the "kill" was coming. As he was about to step towards his prey, he spotted Gunny glancing up to the ceiling. With a questioning look, he followed his eyes up until he focused on what appeared to be a large farm implement, straight above him.

The last thing Conrad 'Slimes' Grimes heard before a half-ton manure spreader crushed his skull was the rapid 'click-a-ty-clack' release sound of a metal ratchet and a chain pulley. Letting out a long breath of relief, Gunny pulled himself up onto his leg. Stooping and reaching out, he retrieved the severed bottom portion of his prosthetic. He hopped over to the workbench, and with several feet of duct tape, he repaired the damage.

Four days later, on a sunny afternoon, a Vineland Police cruiser entered the dusty driveway and drove to the buildings. Police Officer Dombrowski was the officer assigned to the unit. He noticed Gunny standing by the hog pen fence as he stopped the vehicle, shut the engine, and exited.

"How you doin' today, Gunny?" he called out as he approached.

"Doin' fine this wonderful day, Officer Sam, how you been?"

"Can't complain. I stopped by to see if you may have spotted any strangers in the area. We found a vehicle abandoned out on Route 55, comes up stolen out of Philly."

"Can't say that I have, and the dog's been pretty quiet too, 'course he ain't as young as he used to be," Gunny replied with a smile.

"Yeah, well, we're checking with the farmers down this way. They probably dumped it and hot-footed it out of the vicinity," the officer mentioned, indicating he wasn't looking too vigorously for the occupant of the stolen car.

"Well, thanks, Gunny. I don't want to take up any more of your time. By the way, your hogs are lookin' real healthy."

"Yeah, they just fat, dumb, and happy."

"What do you feed them?"

With a subtle grin, Gunny replied, "Mostly grain, day-old donuts to fatten 'em up, and though, I don't particularly like to do it — every now and then — *garbage*."

CHAPTER 61

THE OFFICE APPOINTED WITH OLD rich hardwood, built-in bookshelves had an ornate 'grandfather' clock, ticking the time in a corner. An oversized antique desk was the opulent room's focal point, located on the second floor of his Pine Street townhouse. The house had the smell of old money.

City Councilman Ronald Hubbs entered the residential office of Gifford Bennett and sat in a chair facing him as he said with a smile, "Well, he's safely back, we kept the event in the news for five years, it's over. Now when do we get paid?"

"Ronald, as you are well aware, when we started on the venture, payment would occur after and only after, a progression of due diligence phases by the corporation."

"Well, what are they waiting for?Hubbs impatiently asked while sitting on the edge of the chair. "We've completed everything on our end."

"They will not consider settlement until the process formula is delivered and reviewed, the videotapes of the test subject in the suspended animation state are examined, and through their covert sources, a review of the subject's medical assessment. Only when they are satisfied with irrefutable 'proof of concept' will they pay. I realize patience is not one of your strong suits, especially when money is involved, but you must persevere."

"Giff, I am patient; however, I'm not quite sure how much patience the FBI will possess if they ever find out about the borrowed capital from the pension fund."

"Ronald put your mind at ease. The fund is solvent and showing a profit from our Real Estate Investment Trust."

"Sure, on paper."

"If the FBI were to conduct an investigation, it would take them many months to wade through the maze of financial documents. By that time, the corporation will have completed their verification, we will be paid the agreed-upon sum of four hundred and fifty million, and the retirement trusts will be made whole. Grimes and his colleagues will be compensated, and I'm not sure what you plan to do with your portion of the proceeds, but I will be well on my way to a non-extradition paradise."

"You're pretty sure of yourself, Gifford."

"I am not one of your common shakedown associates, such as that Mickey Frost individual. By the way, did he complete the delivery of those tapes? My biggest fear is he's the only weak link in our plan."

"He'll be okay. He does whatever I tell him to do, he knows I call the shots, and he's known since we were kids together."

"Although Grimes is repugnant, he is efficient. He already disposed of the lab equipment and the container. Besides Ronald, if the authorities ever find the body of our esteemed scientist, and if they're able to tie him and us to the lab, an FBI embezzlement investigation will be the least of our worries."

"I still don't understand why we had to dispose of the doctor."

"You will recall, although he was a genius, he was unstable, and besides, he suffered from one other major defect that could have brought down the whole scheme."

"What was that — Gifford?"

"A flaw that can be deadly in the business world and as you well know, also in the political world — *ethics*."

CHAPTER 62

THE DRIVE FROM THE GREYSTONE facility to hospital was frantic due to the route taken and the traffic of the day, even with the lights and sirens. During the drive, Doctor Mauer was excited because he would get the chance to save the life of a little girl, and he was again going to do what he loved, science. Nick explained to him that they'd first have to present their plan to Tommy and Rosie. They were eager to make the miracle happen as they entered the building on a sprint and finally arrived on the fifth floor. Stepping off the elevator and into the hall, Nick met with the detail officer standing with the Highway Patrol team and the Stakeout Unit officers. Nick approached the officer and said, "Smitty, where are they?"

"They're still in the room, and I think something is happening. A doctor and a couple of nurses just rushed in there about five minutes ago."

The pair shared a worried look. Nick secured the conference room's use down the hall and had the officer escort Doctor Mauer there. Nick went to the door of Sophia's room, opened it slightly, and looked in. The doctor and the nurses were attending to her, administering various drugs intravenously to make her comfortable. She was still unconscious; Tommy and Rosie were both sobbing beside her. Nick waited until the medical staff left the room, and then he approached Tommy and said in a low voice, "Tommy, I

299

have to talk to you, it's about Sophia. I have someone with me who can help her."

Tommy looked up, not comprehending, through the grief.

"Please come down the hall with me. I'll explain it there."

Tommy was trance-like as Nick escorted him out of the room and down into the conference room. The two Highway officers followed. When they arrived inside the room, DoctorMauer was sitting at the conference table, writing copious notes into a tablet. He looked up when Tommy entered the room with a flicker of pride on his face. Here was the finest academic and scientific achievement of his life, standing in front of him, living, and breathing, but with a heart full of anguish. Tommy glanced at the doctor and then looked over at Nick with an expression of confusion.

"Tommy, this is Doctor Hans Wolfgang Mauer, and he can help Sophia," Nick said.

"What do you mean? He can help, Sophia?" Tommy asked with a confused look.

"Tommy, Doctor Mauer is the world's leading researcher in the field of DNA and microbiology, and he has a process that will help Sophia."

"What the hell you talkin' about? Who is this guy? I'm not letting any quack near my daughter."

Tommy became agitated and angry and said in a loud voice, "Nicky, what kind of goofy games are you playing here? What's wrong with you?"

Nick tried to calm him down and explain, but he was becoming more and more agitated. Finally, Doctor Mauer stood and revealed in a firm voice, "Officer Tomas, I am the reason you came back."

Upon hearing that statement, Tommy turned quiet, looked directly at Doctor Mauer, and asked, "What do you mean, you're the reason I came back?"

Doctor Mauer proceeded to tell Tommy the details of the disappearance and his involvement in it. He further explained how he concealed a quantity of the recombinant

DNA molecules, and he expounded on how that will save Sophia's life.

Tommy stood there listening, as in a trance with glazed-over eyes. He was silent for several minutes when the doctor finished his account of his role in the situation. Tommy only heard the part where the doctor admitted to being the reason for his return. He became enraged and swiftly lunged, across the long conference table, sliding diagonally on his stomach until he tumbled onto Doctor Mauer, grabbing him by the neck, and raising him off his feet, screaming,

"I'm gonna kill you! You took me away from my family for five years, my baby's dying, my baby's dying, I'm gonna kill you!"

Upon seeing the outburst, Nick and all the officers in the room immediately rushed and grabbed him. It took six of them to loosen his grip on the doctor, attempting to get him under control. His strength was enormous, not from the 'process,' but from the anger and rage inside. As the six officers, all over six-feet, attempted to bring him under control, they got him to his feet, but he continued to grapple them off. The detail officer was about to call an "Assist Officer" over the radio when a loud booming voice rang out.

"TABBOZZI...STAND DOWN!"

Everyone, including Tommy, immediately turned towards the doorway and the direction of the voice. The door was open, but the bright hallway lights were not visible due to an enormous figure of a person occupying the entire space of the entry. The individual took one step forward, and both Nick and Tommy immediately recognized him as Gunnery Sergeant Carl Hutchens. He came to the hospital to support Tommy and Rosie in their time of grief, and while in the hallway, he overheard Doctor Mauer's explanation. He stepped to the table, and with a scowled look on his face, he stared directly at Tommy. Everyone in the room was fixated on the massive man. Gunnery Sergeant Hutchens finally said, "Tabbozzi, did you trust me in Viet Nam to get you out of that mess I found you in?"

Tommy went quiet; he looked down at the floor, thinking the question over. After a moment, he looked up at Gunny and said, in a clear, calm voice, "Yes — yes, I did, Gunny."

Gunny looked back at him and asked, in the same manner, "Well then, are you gonna trust me now?

"Yes, Gunny, I'm gonna trust you."

"Well then, don't ask me how I know, just believe me, this man did everything he could to keep you alive for those five years." the Marine said as he pointed to Doctor Mauer.

Tommy slowly turned his head, looked at Mauer, then back to Gunny. After several minutes of contemplation, he faced the doctor and pleaded, in a contrite voice, "Please, help my little girl."

CHAPTER 63

TOMMY LEFT THE ROOM, SLUMPED over and shuffling, with the enormity of all the new revelations beating him down. He wasn't having much faith in that new promise of hope, as Gunny helped him back to Sophia's room,

Nick stayed in the conference room with Doctor Mauer, checking him for any injuries from Tommy's charge. The assault slightly disheveled him, causing minor bruising, but he was okay. He explained to him, what he just witnessed, was not the real Tommy.

"Nicolaus, I completely understand. How would anyone react if they had awakened from one nightmare into another?"

Mauer sat back down, his mind racing, planning the upcoming process when he stated, "One crucial required instrument would be the 'hyperbolic chamber.'"

Nick gave him a wary, sideways glance, and remarked, "Doc, we may need to rent one of those, because mine is in the shop, getting the tires rotated."

He faced him and replied in a grave tone, "No, my friend — this is a highly specialized piece of equipment. It is my own design and invention."

With that statement, he blurted out, "Oh no, Nicolaus, the device will not be at the hospital nor anywhere in America."

"What about the DNA? Why do you need the chamber?"

"It creates an external environmental stimulus. The Tardigrade DNA does not protect itself unless it's necessary.

It will only react to the surrounding environment. The chamber is essential to initiate the 'tun.'"

He then became despondent, started mumbling and shaking his head back and forth. Nick seeing he was having a possible psychological set-back, tried to keep him coherent by asking a question, "Doctor Mauer, look at me. Is that the only thing that can be used, is anything similar, something that can be adapted?"

He stared at the floor with sad eyes and replied, "No, it is one of a kind, manufactured to exact specifications I had formulated to perform the 'process.'"

Nick stood scratching the back of his head as he cast his eyes out the window for several minutes; he then turned and asked, "So, without the machine, you can't help Sophia?"

"I'm afraid without the same apparatus, which I utilized with Officer Tomas, I would be unable to begin the process."

"Wait a minute, Doc. Were you aware if they were bringing you to Philadelphia?"

"I did not know where they were taking me or the lab's location."

"Did you get a sense of your whereabouts? Do you think they transported Tommy a long way to the lab?"

"The one detail I can say about Officer Tomas is when they opened the container, in my medical opinion, he appeared recently rendered unconscious."

"How did you travel to the United States?" Nick quizzed.

"Once discharged from the Maudsley Psychiatric facility, the emissary met me, and we took a prolonged flight in a private jet from London to an unknown airfield.

"Do you know where you landed?"

"No, the only thing I can say is moments before landing, the aircraft banked where I observed a coastline and a small city of brightly lit buildings, very shortly after we touched down."

Atlantic City Airport? he thought to himself.

"What happened after you came to the terminal? Did you catch a glimpse of any signs indicating the name of the airport?

"No, that security person came on the plane, where he obstructed my vision with a hood before entering a limousine."

"How long were you in the limo?"

"The car ride took over two hours, with numerous stops along the way, probably due to highway traffic. When we reached the destination, they drove directly into the laboratory building. The night I left London, I gazed up at the sky, and I didn't lay eyes on the heavens again until my night in the river."

"What do you remember about the night, Doctor? How did you get through such an ordeal?"

"On that night, I monitored Officer Tomas and prepared for his return only six months away. I had already developed the consciousness inducing vapor and pre-programmed the chamber to depressurize and re-hydrate him. They also had possession of my 'Formula and Journals.'"

"What happened then, doctor?

"I imagine, at some point, they realized they no longer needed me."

"Why do you think they wanted to kill you?"

"I presume they saw me as unstable and made the decision to dispose of me permanently; he bound me with cordage, my wrists, and ankles. He secured a weight to the ankle rope, placed a hood on my head, and carried me outside, and from the unevenness of his gait, I believe he conveyed me across railroad ties. The next thing I sensed was plummeting through the air, striking the water, and sinking rapidly."

"How did you ever survive, tied up and weighted down?"

"Fear paralyzed me; however, the stress of the situation saved me. You see, when I first realized that he intended to do away with me, I began to hyperventilate from a panic attack. The point of fainting approached, but the process altered my blood gas levels, and my body contained an abnormally high content of oxygen. You know my best time for holding my breath was five minutes and fifty-two seconds.

"How long do you think you were underwater?"

"Well, Nicolaus, although I can't tell you the exact amount of time I was submerged, it felt like well over seven minutes. I sank and found the bottom cluttered, unlike the pristine rivers in Switzerland. Luck was with me, for the riverbed was full of discarded metal debris."

"How did you free yourself?"

"I maneuvered through the mud and scrap, enabling me to locate a serrated edge sharp enough to allow me to extricate myself from my bindings. Once loose, I went with the current and swam to the surface. When I broke through gasping for air, looking back through the darkness in the distance, I perceived what appeared to be a dark, ominous figure standing on a bridge stretching across the river."

Nick listened intently, mesmerized by the story as he continued to recount the night of horror, "I floated downriver, my mental condition started to regress, and I went 'in and out' of my mind, I can only recall the rest of the ordeal, in flashing segments.

"What do you recall while floating in the water?"

"I somehow made it to shore. The next thing I remember was becoming conscious lying on the floor of an empty boxcar. I had flashes of traveling a long way over mountains through dense forests. I had a flicker of being out of the train car, prostrate on the ground next to the tracks. That's when I suppose the Erie Police found me and delivered me to the psychiatric facility."

"Doctor, if we could find the lab, can we treat Sophia there, or can the machine be moved, say here to the hospital?"

"To discover the laboratory abandoned but in working order would be the optimum scenario for a positive outcome. However, if we are only able to locate the chamber itself, it could be transported."

"How big is it?"

"Although the name is grandiose, the actual dimensions are only the size of a small Italian sports car. The instrument is self-contained with all the necessary mechanisms built-in; the only external element we would need is an electrical power source."

"What like a two-twenty line or something?"

With a pragmatic expression, he responded, "More like two thousand volts alternating current."

"Two thousand volts! Nick said with amazement. "How did they secure that kind of voltage?"

"From the local provider, and the lab came equipped with an industrial electric turbine generator powered by natural gas. In fact, the night when Officer Tomas first arrived, I remember a massive storm with a power outage, and the generator ran most of the night."

After a moment, Nick declared, "Doc, we gotta find that lab, fast.

CHAPTER 64

N ICK RUSHED MAUER INTO THE hallway, and as they were leaving, he saw Gunny standing guard in front of Sophia's room. Nick advised him that they were going out to obtain the necessary medical equipment.

"I'll be stayin' here with them for the duration. They are my mission now," the Marine declared, as he stood stern-faced with his arms crossed.

A sense of relief came over Nick, knowing he was staying with Tommy. He stopped at a phone and contacted Detective Warner.

"Chuck, listen, you gotta do me a favor, in Tommy's case folder, the night he went missing, and the last guy who we figured saw Tommy was that PECO worker, I need you to read me his statement again."

"Hold on... I'll grab it."

He comes back to the phone and states, "Nicky, here it is, the guy's name is Robert Ackerman, he says, he's driving eastbound on Washington, he's coming to Broad Street."

"Go to the part where he says something to Tommy on the car stop."

"Yeah, here it is, 'I told the officer; the reason I was out that late is I just got relieved at work because of the storm. We had a lot of buildings without power.' "The detective asked him, 'What caused the blackouts?' He answers, 'A bolt struck a tree causing it to hit the main transformer supplying electric to just west Philly.'"

"Nothing else. What have you got, Nick?"

"Just a hunch for now. Chuck, do me another favor, call PECO, and grab a list of all properties in west Philly, where they supplied electrical power of more than two thousand volts on a steady basis for the last five years. Also, find out all the areas affected by the outage on December 20, 1986, then head down to Washington and Grays Ferry, and stand-by at that location. I'll call you on the air."

"You got it, Nicky."

After entering D-908, Nick asked, "Doc, I know you want to erase that night in the river out of your mind, but you have to think about it. You say when you got out of the bindings and surfaced, you drifted. Did you climb out on the right or left side of the current?"

The doctor ran his hands through his hair, trying to recall more details. After several minutes, he turned to Nick and declared, with a blank face, "It was the right side."

"Doc, now think again, when you got out. Where was the train?"

Mauer thought again, calming himself, unlocking his memories.

"It was stopped on a diagonal overpass that crossed the water."

More memories were flashing in his mind as he added, "A green space or park was down the road, and also I remember grasping onto a small concrete levy along the riverbank. The railroad bridge was elevated; I had to climb up an embankment to enter the rail car."

Nick considered these details and pulled out a city map from the glove compartment, unfolded it, and located the Schuylkill River, searching for that type of location. After a moment of study, he noticed something that matched that description.

"Buckle up, Doc," Nick instructed as he put the vehicle in gear and peeled out onto Civic Center Boulevard. He weaved his way through the streets of west Philadelphia, swerving in and out of traffic with lights and sirens until

309

they arrived at South Fifty-First Street, where he spotted a railroad trestle, crossing the river at an angle. Anxiously he drove down the street until he reached the underpass and stopped the vehicle. Mauer studied the area's features and announced, "Nicholas, this is the place I came ashore."

Nick reached for the mike and transmitted, "Dan-Nine-oh-eight to Radio."

"Dan-nine-oh-eight...proceed."

"Dan-nine-oh-eight... have an Eighteenth District car, and supervisor meet me out of service at South Fifty-First Street at the gate to Bartram's Garden under the railroad bridge, in reference to a further investigation."

"Dan-nine-oh-eight... Okay."

"Dan-nine-oh-eight...also I need a Marine Unit response at this same location."

"Dan-nine-oh-eight... Okay."

Nick reset the microphone, got out, and waited for the requested resources. Luckily, Marine-3 was near-by down-river when the call came out. They turned the vessel and headed north. The district units were all on the scene within several minutes. Upon their arrival, the detective advised them of the latest information and the urgency of finding the lab building.

Marine-3 floated up alongside, spotting the marked police vehicles. Officer Steve Sullivan was on board, part of the crew, and guided the boat to a small dock a hundred yards downstream where the vessel picked up the passengers. Once aboard, Nick explained the purpose of the investigation, and they slowly headed upriver. He instructed Doctor Mauer to point out anything he might recognize. Remembering Mauer's statement, he recalled him saying he was carried blindfolded, but the person's gait indicated he could be walking on rail tracks.

"Steve, what's the next railroad bridge upstream from this point?"

"That would be the one that crosses over at the Schuylkill Expressway and Rivers Field Drive, by the Pennypacker University baseball fields."

"Hit it!"

"Hold on tight," Sullivan replied as he throttled forward, causing the vessel's bow to rise and push water.

They arrived in less than five minutes, Marine-3 maneuvered to the west side embankment, where the passengers disembarked and made their way up onto Rivers Field Road.

Eighteenth District officers arrived with D-908 while Nick and Mauer continued to climb up to the track bed. The top revealed a clear view over the river to the east, and to the west sat a nondescript gray three-story triangular-shaped building.

On the hand-held radio, he transmitted, "Dan-nine-oh-eight to Radio."

"Dan-nine-oh-eight...proceed."

"Dan-nine-oh-eight...raise Dan-nine-oh-nine."

"Radio to Dan-nine-oh-nine."

"Dan-nine-oh-nine."

"Dan-nine-oh-eight...do you have that list?"

"Dan-nine-oh-nine... affirmative... I'm at the location...up on the tracks... I have a line of sight to you from here."

"Dan-nine-oh-eight to Dan-nine-oh-nine... secure from there and respond to River Fields Drive."

"Dan-nine-oh-nine...okay."

Warner arrived with a list and informed Nick, "I checked this out. Some university buildings had high usage, but their patterns peaked during business hours only and lowered after hours. Only one had a steady excessive feed of over two thousand volts, around the clock for the whole five-year period. The only address they could give me is River Fields Service Road number two, and check this out. This entire section was affected by the power outage on December 20, 1986."

The police activity in the area drew the attention of a couple of university police units who responded to the scene to offer their assistance. Nick asked one of the university officers where that location could be. He turned and pointed directly at the gray triangular-shaped building. The structure contained only two entrances, a standard windowless steel passageway, and an oversized loading dock door with railroad tracks running under the closed entry. Nick banged loudly; they heard nothing from the inside.

Due to the emergency circumstances, he ran to the trunk of D-908, retrieved a sledgehammer, and hurried back to the doorway entrance. On the run, he held the tool like a *Louisville Slugger* and swung, striking the lock tumbler dead-on. After four more swats, he shattered the deadbolt causing the door to swing open into the darkness.

The uniform officers rushed in with weapons drawn and searched the building for occupants. Nick escorted Doctor Mauer in, and upon stepping through the doorway, he blurted out, "This is the lab."

He ran towards a large rear section, entered, scanned the area, and then dropped to his knees and mumbled, "It's gone – it's gone." They scoured the interior and were unable to locate the hyperbolic chamber or the shipping container.

Nick and Chuck looked at one another, knowing time was running out for Sophia. They were suddenly exhausted not because it was late or because they worked an excessive number of hours, but worn out from the highs and lows of adrenaline rushing and receding through their systems. They shuffled throughout the building, struggling to detect a lead.

Standing together, Chuck remarked to Nick, "Yo, Nicky, so they got rid of the stuff; they didn't hold a yard sale. If I was them and I wanted to dump equipment like that, I'd want to do it quick and easy."

His wheels were turning, staring into the distance, when he responded, "Yeah, they would unload it in one shot if they could."

"Yeah, and they could! They had a twenty-foot shipping container."

"Where would they take it?"

"Not far."

They both look at one another as a mutual light bulb went off.

"Dan-nine-oh-eight to Marine Three."

"Marine Three...go."

"Dan-nine-oh-eight — are you equipped with side sonar?"

"Marine Three — affirmative."

Nick and Chuck grinned as they faced one another. They rushed out the door, heading on the rail tracks towards the Schuylkill River.

"Dan- nine-oh-eight to Marine Three — conduct a sweep under the bridge from one side of the river to the other — we're looking for a twenty-foot shipping container."

"Marine three — okay."

Working their way to the middle of the rusting span to watch the operation, Doctor Mauer shuddered as he walked, distressed at being at the place of his nightmares. After thirty tense minutes, Marine-3 lit up the radio.

"Marine Three to Dan-nine-oh-eight — we got a hit."

They all breathed a semi-sigh of relief, knowing they still must raise it from the river bed, open and inspect it. Police Divers entered into the murky waters while the Marine Unit recruited a local barge company with a derrick to retrieve the container, and the Police Garage contracted a flat-bed rig and tractor-trailer for transport and relocation. The crane raised the box onto the trailer, and the detectives opened it. As the water gushed out through the opened doors, the first thing detected were three bodies of deceased individuals, their throats slashed from ear to ear. Doctor Mauer identified them as Grimes's assistants, who provided security for the lab.

The chamber was located in the rear of the container and inspected by Doctor Mauer as he announced, "Thank God, it appears to be undamaged."

Although a homicide crime scene, Chuck fetched a camera from his vehicle, photographed the bodies in their found position, and directed the officers to relocate them to the ground to allow the hauler to transport the container immediately.

The investigators devised a plan to transport it to the basement of the Philadelphia Pediatric Hospital because the loading dock door could accommodate the container. The hospital equipped the building with a generator capable of supplying the necessary voltage to the chamber.

CHAPTER 65

THE HISSING SOUND OF THE air brakes reverberated through the loading dock bay of the hospital as the flat-bed tractor-trailer came to rest against the platform. Workers anxiously opened the twenty-foot container doors and found the chamber wedged at the far wall of the enclosure away from the entrance. They freed it, and the heavy equipment operators utilized a chain hoist to heave it onto a pallet. A forklift maneuvered the instrument out and over to an open area within the ground level.

The hospital staff cleared the space before the chamber's arrival, and the on-site electricians completed the installation of the industrial power line necessary to handle the extreme voltage required. The cable ran back to the massive generator inside the building.

Mauer visually inspected the machine while running his hands over every square inch. While under the device, he blurted out, "Oh no, Nicholas!"

"What is it, Doc? What's wrong?"

"One of the high-pressure conduits is damaged," the doctor frantically revealed.

"Can it be repaired?"

"I can't say with certainty. A specialized manufacturer constructed the instrument from exact specifications. I'm not sure if it could be mended on site."

"Show me," he ordered as he dropped down to his stomach and looked under the chamber.

He pointed out the damage as Nick felt the material, "It looks like some type of high caliber metallic alloy. It might be able to be welded."

"Nicholas, I just don't know.

As he stood, he rubbed the scar on his face and pondered his options. The tractor-trailer driver overheard the conversation and offered, "You need a welding job, call the Steamfitters. My cousin is one of them, and those guys can weld anything."

The detective and Mauer stared at one another when finally, Nick declared, "We gotta give it a shot."

Detective Avner reached out to the Union, explaining the dire circumstance.

"I'll have my best welder there within the hour," declared President Pat Morrissey from the Steamfitters Local 420.

In less than thirty minutes, a utility truck backed into the loading bay. Out of the cab stepped Matt Williams. His experience came from years of highly technical welding on many job sites and varied pipe fitting situations.

He shook hands with both men and inquired, "Where's the damage?"

"Under here," Mauer replied, showing him the line.

Williams produced a flashlight, got on his back, and proceeded to evaluate the situation. After several minutes he announced, "Yeah, this is 'Inconel.' I've worked on this alloy before."

"Inconel – what's that?" Nick asked.

"It's a super-alloy – we use it for environments of extreme heat or pressure," Matt replied.

"Yes, Inconel–that's correct." the doctor proclaimed, obviously impressed.

"What's the operating PSI for this line?" Williams inquired.

"Twenty-five hundred pounds per square inch," the doctor answered and then asked, "You can make the repair?"

"Doc, I've welded lines under pressure, rated as high as ten thousand pounds per square inch, and believe me, I know what's at stake here–I have a little girl of my own," he explained with a confident expression.

Both Nick and Doctor Mauer experienced a slight sense of relief with that answer.

The master welder went about retrieving various tools and pieces of equipment from the truck. He set up a stand-alone shield around the affected area, utilizing a "Tungsten Inert Gas" system to patch the defect. The preparations took longer than the actual procedure, but the professional wanted to be sure of his moves before striking up an arc.

He suited up with splatter resistant leather gloves and sleeves, his cap, and protective mask. He "arced-up," and in approximately six minutes, he finished, carefully removing any residual slag, a crusty by-product of the bonding process, and saw that the mend was perfect. It appeared to be a seamless row of dimes lying flat overlaying one another, fanned out along the seam. Matt isolated the repaired line and installed a calibrator to test the patch. He started the device, slowly building up the pressure to 2700 pounds per square inch, well over the required amount. He opened the valve, released the air, and removed the instrument, satisfied the task was complete.

Doctor Mauer inspected the repair and proclaimed, "Mr. Williams, you are a true craftsman. Your workmanship is magnificent."

Nick thanked him profusely, and everyone in the room shook his hand or slapped his back. After reloading his tools, he slid in behind the wheel of his truck and drove out.

The Doctor methodically prepared, making sure all the ancillary medical equipment was set up. He delicately inserted the "vial of life" into the dispensary implement and awaited Sophia's arrival.

While in her ICU hospital room, the pediatric staff carried out Doctor Maurer's instructions, preparing the patient and readying her for transfer to the chamber. Her parents were there, sobbing and holding her hand, not knowing what was to come. Rosie cried out, "We won't see her for five years — Tommy, what are we going to do?"

Upon entering the room and hearing her anguish, Mauer explained, "No, no, Mrs. Tabbozzi, your husband was gone that long because of greedy people. I need only one month to make her well."

He previously described the process to them, and although they didn't understand the science, they were broken with fear and down to their last sliver of hope.

The hospital staff proceeded to transport Sophia with her family and friends following. Upon their arrival, the scientist instructed the attending medical personnel to situate her into the chamber. He connected her intravenous lines to the internal instruments, turned away, and allowed the anguished parents to lean over and kiss her, just before he sealed the door.

Tears were streaming down Rosie's cheeks as Tommy faced him and pleaded, "Doc, you have to save our little girl, please tell me you can bring her back to us."

The Doctor looked intensely at the couple, reached out, grasped their hands. With a reassuring expression, he stated, "Officer Tomas, when I performed the process on you, I utilized all my knowledge and all my abilities to ensure you would return to your family."

As he turned his gaze to Sophia, lying in the chamber, he promised, "I vow to you this day, for your precious little child, I will double my efforts."

CHAPTER 66

THE SQUEAK OF THE DOOR opening caught Chuck's attention as the Vice Squad sergeant stuck his head into the room.

"Hey, they're gonna have to give you hazard pay if you stay in this dump much longer."

"Ain't that the truth," replied Detective Chuck Warner as he reached for the bottle of antacid tablets, raised it to his mouth, and shook in a couple of the chalky discs. His stomach was on fire from the stale coffee, cigarettes, and the perpetual electronic taste that hovered in the room from the wiretapping equipment. A voice recorder sat on the small desk in front of him in a one-story former Health Department building at Fourth Street and Girard Avenue.

"Hey, how did they ever pick this joint for your headquarters?" Chuck asked as he chewed on the Tums.

"We heard it was Councilman Hubbs' idea. He doesn't care much about a cop, and he's probably making a buck off of it somehow."

Chuck grinned at that answer, thinking of his present investigation.

"Yeah, last week, they even took some asbestos out of the basement," the sergeant added as he left the room.

Abandoned by the city, and then later condemned as unfit for human habitation due to various environmental conditions; nevertheless, the building became the headquarters of the Special Operations Division. The new division

319

would include Narcotics Special Investigations, City-Wide Vice, and Organized Crime Intelligence. They utilized wiretapping in the course of their investigations, so; they had the equipment and expertise. Other investigative units could use those resources, such as Major Crimes, thus bringing Detective Warner to that "condemned" building for hours on end, listening for information or evidence on the city hall corruption case. Wiretap assignments were dull; most conversations were the daily routine of persons interacting with one another. The target of that investigation was Mickey Frost, a License and Inspection Department Code Enforcement Inspector.On that particular day, he intercepted a call made from Frost's city-owned phone located in the Department's office to a private line tracked to the office of Councilman Ronald Hubbs.

After several rings, a male voice answered.

"Hello."

"Yeah, it's me."

"I told you, don't call me on this line."

"Listen, Ronald, I need that money, I owe some people, and they want it now."

"Did you make the last delivery on that night?"

"I took care of it, but I need that money."

"You'll be paid when I'm paid; it takes time. Now I have to get off the phone."

The call ended, and the line went dead. Chuck wrote down the timeline, the duration, and the possible identity of the callers in a notebook.

He thought to himself, *Hmm, that's interesting. Hubbs usually gets paid; he doesn't pay it out.*

He finished out his shift at the Fourth and Girard building, went back to his office to finish his reports, and then headed home for the day.

###

Chapter 66

Although Warner had been investigating Frost for a while, he wanted to learn more about his background. The next day in MCU headquarters, he asked other detectives if anyone knew a cop from Fishtown.

"Yeah, Charlie Spurgeon from Highway," offered Detective Lenny Woods, "I know he grew up in Fishtown, and I think his brother still lives there."

"Thanks, Len, I'll reach out to him."

He grabbed the phone, dialed Highway Patrol headquarters, and left a message for the officer to contact him as soon as he could. In forty minutes, the Highway cop stuck his head into the detective's office.

"Yo, Chuck. You wanted to see me?"

"Yeah, hey, Charlie, thanks for stopping."

"What do you need?"

"Charlie, you grew up in Fishtown, right? Did you ever run across Mickey Frost in the neighborhood?"

"Oh yeah, he wouldn't know me, but I knew about him. He was about ten years older than me, but he was a legend."

As Chuck handed Spurgeon a coffee mug he just poured, he asked, "What do you mean–how so?"

"He was one of the tough guys who was big for his age, and he liked to push people around. He would even smack Councilman Ronald around from time to time until Mickey's mother told him to stop."

"Yeah, I heard about that. Hubbs saved the kid brother and got Mickey as a prize."

The two cops grinned as they sat into chairs, and Chuck inquired, "Is he sharp or on the dumb side?"

"He's about average; if Ronald hadn't come along, he would have been your standard bouncer or maybe a goon collector for the bookies."

After Charlie Spurgeon took a sip of his coffee, he added, "Speaking of bookies, Mickey is a degenerate gambler. He always owes somebody money."

"It's a good thing Hubbs got him that 'shake-down' job at L and I," Warner said as he sat back in his chair with his hands interlocked behind his head.

Frost rode the political coattails of Councilman Hubbs, and as Ronald went up the ladder, he pulled Mickey along with him.

One of the "gopher" jobs that Hubbs assigned to Mickey was delivering a box of videotapes to a storage center in Maple Shade, New Jersey, on Route 73 every month. On December 25, 1991, Christmas day, he was to make a final delivery. On the way to make the drop-off, he decided to celebrate the holidays at his old neighborhood, Fishtown, at a little corner "tappy" at Shackamaxon Street and Girard Avenue. The place was packed, and he partied with some of his old pals until closing time at two a.m.

At about two-fifteen a.m., while driving the city-owned vehicle northbound on I-95, and as he approached the Bridge Street exit, the front tire struck a large pothole in the roadway. The fog and mist of the night made visibility difficult. He jerked the wheel to the right causing him to swerve off the ramp and into a roadside guardrail. The vehicle rode the barrier for about twenty feet until it came to a sudden stop. Mickey put the gearshift in park. He got out to inspect the damage, where he saw a long dent and scrape on the passenger side from the front quarter panel to the rear door.

"Damn," he cursed as he looked from the car up and down the roadway.

Because of the date and time, there was no traffic. Knowing he would have to make a report because it was damage to city property, he quickly devised a plan where he would claim that he parked the vehicle, and an unknown party struck it and left the scene.

He came around, got in, and proceeded to drive off. Mickey went on to make the usual delivery of the box of videotapes to Maple Shade. What he failed to realize, however, was that during the sudden stop at the time of the minor accident, one of the cassettes jolted from the open carton, tumbled to the floor, and slid under the driver's seat.

CHAPTER 67

LIEUTENANT DAVE TRICOSTE SCHEDULED A meeting at Major Crimes headquarters to review all the information and evidence regarding the case. Nick and Chuck attended and passed out summaries for reference.

"Alright, listen up. What have we got, so far?" the boss said, quieting down the chatter.

"Well, we know where the lab was located, and Doctor Mauer devised and conducted the process at the command of a local unknown investor" Nick explained and added, "Grimes was the security component along with those three dead associates, and no doubt the one who snatched Tommy."

"We're doing a background trace on the lab, but we're running into a maze of blind companies and corporations trying to determine the actual owner of the building. We're still 'up on the wire, 'and we're starting to pick up some interesting chatter between Frost and Councilman Hubbs. Can't really tie them together on this case, might just be talk about their regular shakedowns," Chuck interjected.

"Early on, I checked with the Pension Board, and determined 'Swarthmore Holdings' are the contracted chief financial investor for the fund with almost nine-hundred-million in capital," Nick continued with the summation.

"Yeah, and digging deeper, we find out our slimy little councilman was the sponsor of the bill to grant 'Swarthmore Holdings' the contract almost eight years ago. The only thing is, since the start, the investments have shown a consistent profit. The FBI Task Force wants their forensic accounting group to take a peek at the fund's accounts," Chuck added.

"Yeah, but if they do that, they'll have to subpoena their books through the courts. This will make that portion of the case public, and our little rats might take off before we can snatch them up," Lieutenant Tricoste remarked.

"So, where's the payoff for these guys? Who actually set the whole thing up?" Chuck wondered.

A thought snapped into Nick's mind at that question. *Follow the dollar trail to get to the real truth.*

He smiled slightly and answered, "Funny, you should mention that. I found out from Doctor Mauer that this process would be too expensive for the local investors to develop and market."

"Well, didn't they finance it?"

"Only the proof of concept. He told me, once they proved the process, only a mega multi-national corporation would have the resources and capital to purchase the formula from these guys, secure a patent, and bring it to market. He believes the local boys financed the venture on their own for about twenty-five to thirty million. They're goal was achieving a successful outcome, and sell everything to a corporation for big bucks after a series of due diligence investigations are completed."

"How much we talking about?" Tricoste asked.

"How's five-hundred million dollars sound?" Nick replied.

"Holy crap, a half a billion, yeah, but these people aren't going to put up twenty-five, thirty mil, set up the logistics, do the thing, and then shop around for a buyer. They had some company signed up before they started. One thing for sure, if I were going to pay out that kind of money in the end, these local guys would be doing things my way. I got the gold; I'm making the rules," the lieutenant stated.

"So the way I figure, this unknown corporation is just as complicit in the crime as any of them," Chuck observed.

The meeting adjourned with Chuck advising his group was securing a wire-tap warrant for the phones of Gifford

Bennett, the CEO of Swarthmore Holdings. Afterward, while sitting in his office, Nick was contemplating his next move when the thought struck him, Sullivan's statement about the patent attorney.

He reviewed the document, and as he came to the part about Mr. James J. Callahan with the law firm of 'Callahan, Latham, and Grimaldi, he pondered, *Hey, he might be worth a shot.*

Nick only had basic information about the man, so he decided to talk to someone who would be well acquainted with him. The phone was ringing on the other end as he hoped the guy he wanted was working that day.

"South Detectives."

The voice on the other end was one he recognized. "Larry — Nick Avner, how you doin'?"

"Nicky, how the hell are you? What's up — what do you need?" Larry responded in his usual gruff voice while smiling.

"Yo, Larr, I need some background info on a guy. You got time?"

"Yeah, I got time, and I could go for some crab legs too. How about I meet you at your office, we'll walk across to DiNardo's, and you can buy me some lunch and ask me anything you want."

"Sounds like a plan, thanks, Larry."

"Wait 'til you see the bill, and then thank me."

About thirty minutes later, the veteran detective entered the Major Crimes headquarters, and all the older investigators recognized him right away.

"Yo Larry, you still on the job? We figured you'd be retired by now," one of the detectives joked with a grin.

"Listen, I was makin' pinches when you were in kindergarten, and I'll still be making 'em long after you retire," the old-timer retorted, always primed for a ball busting match. They all shook hands, back-slapped, and laughed, asking each other about mutual friends from along the way. Upon hearing the commotion, Nick came out of his office, smiling, and asked, "You ready to go?"

"Yeah, let's go. I'm starvin'."

They walked across Race Street and on into DiNardo's Famous Seafood, which opened its door for business, in 1976 offering crabs Baltimore-style with sautéed-garlic as their main entrée. With a friendly atmosphere, it retained the ambiance and feel of a neighborhood establishment, although it was located in the downtown area. The hostess showed them to a table in the rear dining room, handed them menus, and after several minutes they ordered.

"So whatta you need?" Larry inquired.

"Larr, when you worked in the Homicide Unit, did you have the occasion to work with Mr. Callahan when he was with District Attorney's office?"

"Oh yeah, I had numerous cases where he was the prosecutor. He was one of the best, although he could be a pain in the ass sometimes because he was such a stickler for details. Stuff like, 'go grab another statement from that guy,' 'retake photos on this scene,' 'find that witness,' always making the case stronger. I'll tell you what, though, he got the convictions. He probably had a ninety-eight percent conviction rate. Defendants in court would groan when they found out Mr. Callahan was prosecuting; they knew they were goin' away."

"Why'd he leave the DA's office?"

"Got tired of all the political crap. You know, budget cuts, resources reduced, same old bullshit. He said one time, 'he wanted to work with people at their most creative instead of when they're at their most destructive,' that's why he went into patent law. I heard he would back some of the inventors if they were short of cash. This way, the inventor could move forward with his dream, and Callahan could make some money. He believed in the people, and he's a great guy too. He does a lot of 'Philly-tropic' work."

"Philanthropic?"

"Yeah, what I say? Well, anyway, he's a real gentleman; you know he posted fifty grand for any information in Tommy's case."

"I thought the FOP put up that reward."

"He gave them the money and wanted to remain anonymous."

"Larry, could you get me in to see him?"

"Yeah, sure, I'll make a call and set it up."

CHAPTER 68

T HE VIEW WAS MAGNIFICENT FROM the forty-eighth floor of One Liberty Place in the 1600 block
of Market Street. The fifty-eight story skyscraper was the
first building to tower above city hall. Before the construction, a "gentlemen's agreement" was in place not to build any
structure in Center City higher than the statue of William
Penn on top of Philadelphia City Hall. The builders tried to
honor the pact by placing a small statuette of "Old Willy" at
the new skyscraper's very peak to keep him watching over
his old town. Nick entered the reception area of 'Callahan,
Latham, and Grimaldi Law Firm' where he identified himself and took a seat. In about five minutes, a well-dressed
distinguished gentleman approached him, extended his
hand, and greeted him.

"Detective Avner, James Callahan."

"Mr. Callahan, it's an honor to meet you, sir. I wanted to
thank you for posting the reward on Officer Tabbozzi's case,"
Nick replied while standing and shaking his hand.

"How is his young daughter? I heard she's in the Pediatric
Hospital. I wish her all my best."

"There is hope; she's undergoing specialized treatment
as we speak."

"We'll pray for her recovery, now; how can I help you,
detective?" Callahan said while guiding him into his office.

Nick took a seat and recounted a summation of the case
from the beginning to the present.

The attorney sat with steepled hands contemplating, and after a moment, he proclaimed, "From what you described, the "process" utilizing a re-coded sequenced DNA falls within the category of a 'biological' patent."

"How's that different from a regular patent?"

"This is a utility patent; however, the 1970s marked the first time when scientists were granted patents for their methods on their biotechnological inventions with recombinant DNA."

"How would a company apply for a patent?"

"Many people become confused between patent inventorship and patent ownership. An individual can be an inventor, but not necessarily the owner of the rights, for example, where they assign them to a third-party entity. Also, a person or corporation may be the intellectual property developer, but not the inventor. It should be noted; a company can never be an inventor."

Nick further inquired, "If a corporation is aware of someone developing a formula for a new and unique DNA process, and the proof of concept has been established, I can imagine it could be very valuable to them. Is that right?"

"Definitely, proof of concept is expensive and risky. If that is achieved upfront, that would be the optimum scenario for a corporation, especially if another entity carried the burden of innovating and proving the hypothesis."

"Mr. Callahan, I believe local investors set up and funded Tommy's kidnapping to prove an advanced DNA based process. We think they did it with specific orders from a third-party organization. I think we can determine the identity of the local speculators and prosecute them, but this unknown firm is also criminally complicit in the crime."

"What is it you want me to do?"

"Sir, I want you to secure a patent before the corporation can. If we can beat them to it, I believe it'll flush them out due to the amount of money it would be worth to them."

"Well, several things would be needed to proceed. Number one, we're going to require an inventor. He'll be obliged to sign an affidavit affirming he is the true originator."

"Sir, we located him, presently he's a material witness in the case, but recently he's become a friend of mine. I'm not sure he'll be cooperative, but I can try."

"We're going to need a copy of the formula to prepare the application. A patent search is required; however, from what you described, I can tell you now this is unique. I don't expect to find anything similar covering this process, but I must say time is of the essence."

"Mr. Callahan, I'll work through the night and bring the papers as soon as possible."

"Detective Avner..."

"Nick, sir, please call me, Nick."

"Okay, Nick, I promise you this, if you deliver those documents to me by tomorrow, on the following day, I will submit the patent application at your request. Here is my business card. On the back is my home phone number. Call me anytime, remember the sooner, the better."

"Mr. Callahan, on behalf of Tommy and his family, and the entire police department, thank you."

In the lobby, he found a phone and called his headquarters. He spoke with Lieutenant Tricoste and advised him of the recent developments. He informed him, he'll be heading to the Greystone facility to retrieve the necessary documents. Tricoste assigned Chuck Warner to assist in the retrieval of the formula. It took about an hour to arrive at the location due to traffic. When he pulled onto the grounds, and into the parking lot, Chuck was already waiting, eating what appeared to be an oversized "hoagie" on the hood of D-909. As he exited D-908, he completed chewing a big chomp, swallowed, and mentioned, "Yo, I got you one, Italian, no onions. Right? In the front seat, there's coffee too."

Nick gave him a sideways glance as Chuck declared, "Hey, we're gonna be here all night, we gotta eat," as he proceeded to take another gnaw at the sandwich.

They enjoyed their meal outside, even though the weather was somewhat cold. The detectives finished and entered the building, meeting with the security manager to gain entrance to Doctor Mauer's living quarters. Nick knew he wouldn't be there because he was monitoring Sophia's treatment, twenty-four hours a day, at the hospital. They ventured into the suite and began to search for a possible specific journal that might contain the formula for the 'process.'

"Crap — look at all these whiteboards. How are we going to copy these?" Nick said with frustration.

Chuck studied them for a moment and stated, "We'll get the Crime Lab to come up and photograph them."

"Yeah, hey, you ain't bad to have around sometimes, you supply food, and every so often, you come up with a good idea. Nick said, busting them a little.

"Yo, screw you, Avner, next time, you buy the 'hoagies,'" Chuck commented with a grin.

They called the "Crime Lab," who responded to the location and photographed everything too oversized to be photocopied or carried, advising they will rush order the film development. The time was near midnight when he loaded the last of the boxes into the two police vehicles.

"Hey, you think Doc is gonna be pissed? We took his stuff." Chuck asked.

"I don't know, but I'll find out as soon as we drop this off at Mr. Callahan's. I'll stop at the hospital and see if he'll sign the 'Inventor's Affidavit.'"

Nick called Mr. Callahan from an inside phone, and they agreed to meet in his office in about an hour and a half to start the patent process.

"My legal assistants will type the forms and have the paperwork ready today."

He drove directly to the law office with Chuck stopping at the Photo Lab to pick up the photos. Upon arrival, he unloaded the car, entered the building, and rode the freight elevator up to the forty-eighth floor. The passenger elevator opened as he arrived at the glass entrance, and Mr. Callahan stepped into the hallway.

Upon seeing Nick standing in the hall, he expressed, "I hope you haven't been waiting long. I wanted to be here as soon as possible."

"No, I just arrived. I'm sorry I had to bring you out at such an hour."

"To be honest with you, I'm actually enjoying myself, kind of like working a case back in the DA's Homicide Unit. I'll stay here as long as you need me."

Nick couldn't believe that important man was so accommodating when a thought came to mind, *Why so surprised? That's the way everyone described him.*

He wheeled the boxes into the office, and Callahan, delved in right away, reviewing documents, making copious notes on a yellow legal-size pad. After asking about the paperwork needed for Doctor Mauer's signature, the lawyer retrieved from his legal assistant's desk several pages of the forms.

"I'll highlight where he needs to sign, and if he does, bring them back to me tonight."

"Alright, Mr. Callahan, wish me luck."

On the ride out to the hospital, he wondered if Doctor Mauer would be cooperative. He could be fearful for his life and believe whoever the corporation was; they could ultimately be the ones who ordered his murder. If he showed up publicly, such as a patent application, they might try to kill him again. He made a mental note to double the security detail on Mauer. The drive was relatively short as he drove across the Market Street Bridge, he gazed south downriver. Thinking to himself, *Tommy was there, so close all that time. I can't believe we didn't find him,* but another thought struck him.

What if we found him before the process was completed? We might have killed him by saving him. He shook these thoughts out of his mind as his head started to throb, trying to cover every angle.

At the loading dock of the hospital, he parked and entered the building where a security detail officer met him and escorted Nick into the storage area, where the chamber was located. They noticed Doctor Mauer, holding a clipboard, checking instruments, and making notations as they walked across the massive concrete floor. The clock was showing three a.m., but he was fully awake while he went about his duties.

The officer whispered to Nick.

"I don't know how he does it. He hasn't left her side since they brought her in. He does small catnaps, right beside the chamber, I can't figure him out,"

Nick called out as he approached, "Doctor Mauer, how's Sophia doing?"

The scientist glanced up at the sound of his voice and announced, "Ah, Nicholas, she is progressing according to the parameters of the 'process.'"

Nick walked towards the chamber and observed a small curved viewing window on the top.

"Wait, Nicholas, I must warn you before you examine the interior. I'm afraid you will not recognize her. You see, the procedure requires physiological modifications in her biological structure. It will be quite shocking to the untrained eye."

Nick hesitated for several moments, not knowing what to expect. He slowly moved toward the window, and with hesitation, he gazed down into the chamber. At first, his mind couldn't perceive what he was seeing. A figure the size of a little girl, but with the appearance of a mummified body with drawn-in skin and the consistency of leather emerged before him. He backed away, startled, and blurted out, "What in God's name did you do to her?"

"Nicholas, please do not be afraid; this is part of the process. Without becoming too technical, her DNA molecules have amalgamated with the mighty little Tardigrade. What you are witnessing is the 'tun' or the cryptobiotic state."

"But why does she look that way?

334

"The Tardigrada is an amazing creature. I discovered; they possess an adaptation proclivity, allowing them to live through the harshest conditions. They can enter a state of suspended animation, and that condition closely resembles death. Upon encountering environmental stresses, the animal curls up into a dry, lifeless ball called a 'tun,' reducing its metabolic activity to as low as .01 percent of normal levels."

"How — how is this possible?"

"To do so, they produce 'trehalose,' a special protective sugar which forms a gel-like medium, suspending and preserving the organelles and membranes within the cells. What you are seeing, Nicholas, are the animal's DNA molecules protecting her with adaptive abilities. When environmental conditions become hospitable again, the organism will return to its metabolic state of life, clear of all deficiencies prior to the cryptobiosis."

"What do you mean, doctor? I don't understand."

"When the cells are re-hydrated, and the pressure is lowered at a precise pace, she will come out of the 'tun,' and as the Tardigrade physically clears itself of all biological defects, so shall our little Sophia. If you have any further doubts, just observe her father, Officer Tomas."

Nick stood slack-jawed, amazed that anyone could devise such a process, but there he was in the presence of the genius who not only conceived that miracle but achieved it. That motivated him further to solve the case and bring those responsible to justice.

"Doctor Mauer, I have to speak with you concerning something of extreme importance."

"What is it, Nicholas?"

"We have to find out the identity of the corporation and make them accountable for Tommy's kidnapping. Would you agree?"

He studied Nick's face, then peered over to the chamber containing Sophia, and responded in a quiet voice, "Yes, we must."

"I have a plan."

Nick explained the strategy to file for a patent as soon as the next day. He produced the Inventors Affidavit for his signature, admitted to him how they retrieved the notes and journals from his suite, and transported them to the law office.

"Doc, I'm sorry I had to violate your personal space, but we don't have much time. We have to beat them to the punch."

The doctor glanced at him, and with a slight smile on his face, he said with a chuckle, "Well, alright, my dear friend Nicholas, we shall beat them to the punch. May I borrow your pen?"

Nick showed him where to sign the affidavit forms, and when he completed the signatures, he remarked with a sly grin, "Nicholas, I believe I can save you some time sorting through the notes taken from my suite. You must locate the leather-bound journal marked *Formeln verarbeiten.* That will contain all you need to file the patent application."

"Well, what are the other calculations and formulas?"

"It's my way of — how do you say it — doodling."

Nick grinned, shook his head, and started out the door. On the way out, he turned and said. "Hey, Doc."

"Yes, Nicholas?"

"Get some sleep."

CHAPTER 69

NICK HIT A PHONE, CALLED Mr. Callahan, and advised him to look for the leather-bound journal marked *Formeln verarbeiten;* he then drove to Callahan's office and dropped off the Inventors Affidavit. He was tired from working all night, and all the previous day, he needed to go home and get some sleep. On the ride home, the skies turned gray, misty, and cold.

Perfect sleeping weather, he thought to himself.

The house was empty; Abby was at work. He made himself a small sandwich and a glass of milk, finished half, was too tired, went to bed, and slept soundly. The metallic sound of a key in the lock awakened him. His wife was home; he got up, put on some old sweats, and met her as she was coming in the door.

"Oh, you're home. I was worried about you. You worked almost two days straight. How do you feel? Did you sleep?"

"I got about seven hours. How was work?"

"Not too bad, it's gotten slow lately."

"Yeah, why?"

"Well, for one thing, all the settlements with Swarthmore Holdings have dried up. We haven't had one with them for about five weeks now."

Hmm — interesting, he reflected as the wheels were turning in his head.

The next day, he entered headquarters, and on his desk was a message to contact Mr. Callahan. After dialing, on the third ring, he heard.

"Mr. Callahan's office may help you?"

"Is Mr. Callahan available? This is Detective Avner, returning his call."

"One moment, please."

In less than a minute, a male voice answered the phone.

"Nick, I received some good news. Yesterday we filed the Patent Application, which means they issued our Priority Date, which makes us first in. I would imagine whoever the corporation is, they'll become aware of this fact. These companies usually retain reviewers to check the applications at the U. S. Patent and Trademark Office."

"So, what's our next step?"

"Well, I listed myself as Attorney of Record, which means if anyone has any questions regarding the patent, they must call me. So, as soon as I receive any calls, I'll contact you."

Nick wanted to drive out to Philly Pediatric again and check in on Tommy and Rosie. Busy with the investigation for the last couple of days, he hadn't been able to stop by. Before leaving, he informed the lieutenant of the latest events.

They were on the fifth floor in a private, secure conference room provided by the hospital to rest during their vigil. The Highway Patrol team assigned to guard the family met Nick as he got off the elevator.

"Anything new on the case?" Highway Patrol Officer Charlie Spurgeon asked as he approached.

"We're making some progress. What did you hear, anything?"

"Nah, might be nothing, you know my older brother, he's a beer distributor, makes deliveries to all the local 'tappys' in Fishtown, he talks to all the bar owners. So, he was doin' a delivery last week, and he gets to talking with one of them. This one owner starts telling him about Mickey Frost from the neighborhood, says he's been layin' down some extra-large bets with the 'book.' So, he asks him, 'yo, Mickey, how you gonna pay them back?', and Frost tells him he's got a 'big payday' comin'. I ain't sure if it ties into what you're looking at, but I figured I tell you, the next time I saw you."

"Hey, thanks, Charlie, I appreciate it, do me a favor. When you guys are out on patrol, if you see this guy Frost, let me know what he was up to."

"You got it. I'll call you right away if we spot anything."

Nick walked down the hall to the secure room, tapped on the door, and entered. Inside, he noticed Gunny seated and speaking in a low voice to Rosie. Approaching, he hugged her and asked how she was holding up. The burly Marine stood and shook his hand. Tommy was by the window, sitting as he looked vacantly out. Nick turned to his friend, walked over, and took the chair next to him.

"Tommy?"

Not reacting, his eyes were blank, deep-set in a face drained of color sick with worry as he gazed into the distance. Nick spoke to him softly.

"Tommy, I want you to know, I'm still working hard on the case. I won't stop until I find out the truth."

An empty expression veiled his face as he continued his thousand-yard stare through the glass out across west Philadelphia. Nick sat at his side, quietly, for a time; finally, he rose and patted him on the shoulder.

As he approached Rosie and Gunny to say goodbye, she mentioned, "Nicky, for some reason, he blames himself for what happened to Sophia. I tried to tell him it wasn't his fault, but he just keeps beating himself up."

Not knowing what else to say, Nick professed as he stared at the floor, "If only I didn't take the Bus Detail that night, it might have been different."

Rosie reached out and stroked the back of his bowed head as she responded with a soft voice, "Oh Nicky, it's not your fault either — I told him about everything you did to find him over the five years. I told him how you looked out for Sophia and me. Believe me, Nicky; he knows what you've done for us."

With tears welling in his eyes, she hugged him, and as he shook Gunny's hand, the Marine declared, "I'll be here for the duration. I ain't leaving their side."

"Thanks, Gunny, they need you now," Nick expressed as he wiped his face and prepared to leave the room.

During the next week, he continued to make his daily visits. The wait was agonizing to all there.

###

On a Monday morning, while sitting at his desk, finishing up some reports, his phone rang. On the other end was Mr. Callahan.

"Nick, James Callahan, we got a nibble."

He perked up and replied, "What is it?"

"I received a call from a Mr. Wendell Renard, from the Law Offices of Attwood, Compton, and Harriman; he was calling from their New York office. This is a highly renowned law firm, specializing in negotiations for major companies and conglomerates."

"What exactly did he want?"

"He said his firm represents an international corporation, and they became aware of a patent, in which they may be interested in acquiring."

"What did you say?"

"I asked him, 'and what patent would that be'? At which time, he recited a Provisional Patent number, and he informed me I was the listed 'attorney of record.'"

He sat straight and leaned in as he asked, "So what happened?"

"I told him I handle many various clients, and I would have to refer to my files. So, I put him on hold for about five minutes, and after I had him hang on for a while, I got back on the line and said, I had found the file."

Nick was worried about scaring the person away as he commented, "Mr. Callahan, with all due respect, we don't want to lose this guy; he might be the only link back to the corporation."

"Trust me, Nick, we don't want to sound too anxious either. I've been doing this for a long time. There's a little dance we do before we get down to a deal."

Calming himself, he replied, "Okay, sir, I'm confident with your judgment completely. What's our next move?"

"I asked him the name of the company he represented, but he told me he was not at liberty to divulge that information. I told him I'm required to advise my client, the inventor of this inquiry, and I would inform him of the outcome. I'll let him stew for a couple of days, call him back, and take it to the next level."

Towards the end of the week, Nick arrived at his headquarters to find a message from Mr. Callahan with a request for him to stop by the law firm as soon as possible. Grabbing the car keys, out the door he went. Twenty minutes later, he stepped off the elevator on the forty-eighth floor and pulled open the glass door to the Law Offices of Callahan, Latham, and Grimaldi. The receptionist recognized him, picked up the intercom, spoke for a few seconds, and instructed, "You can go right in."

As he entered the office, the lawyer rose to greet him.

"Fresh coffee on the duvet, help yourself."

After pouring himself a cup, he took a seat in front of the expansive desk facing the attorney.

"Well, Nick, it appears we have a fish on the hook. Now we just have to reel him in."

"What happened, sir?"

"When we last spoke, I left it with me getting back to him. Well, he called me first thing this morning and informed me his client is motivated to acquire the patent with one contingency. They want access to the medical assessment of the test subject."

"Did they say how soon they wanted to do this?"

"He didn't say, but I believe, based on his phone conversation, they want to move fast. If it is indeed a fact, they were calling the shots with the local entrepreneurs, then I would say they have Doctor Maurer's formula from the lab. They, no doubt, compared it to the version outlined in the patent, and it matches, making them excited."

"So, if I can convince Doctor Mauer to sell, and we go through with this, we can discover the people who are ultimately responsible for these crimes, and we can prosecute?"

Mr. Callahan didn't reply; he studied the young detective, and after a moment, he spoke, "Nick, that's the reason why I asked you to stop by. You see, even if we do identify this corporation, to bring a prosecution against them would be like going after an octopus with a thousand tentacles. There wouldn't be just one person or persons a prosecutor could pin it on. They would play their legal games in the courts; tie up the case for years. They possess the money and resources to hold off even federal prosecutors, and besides, the evidence is circumstantial, at best. I'm afraid without solid direct proof, the top prosecutor in the country wouldn't take this on."

A dejected expression passed over his face as he responded, "So they just get away with it, they don't have to pay for what they did?"

"Oh, I didn't say they weren't going to pay. Believe me; they're going to pay."

With that latest setback, Nick suddenly felt tired, thinking the whole investigation was falling apart, sullenly he muttered, "So how do we proceed, Mr. Callahan?"

"I'll let him stew for a couple more days, I reached out to Doctor Mauer, and I explained everything to him and what could happen if we receive an offer. After all, the patent is his property. He's agreeable to assign his Patent Rights, and one more thing. He said he would leave all the details up to you, he advised me, 'he trusts you implicitly,' He also informed me; an innovation such as this should fetch somewhere in the area of five hundred million dollars."

Nick's mind was reeling; never in his wildest dreams could he envision himself being the assigned investigator on a case like that and then representing a world-renowned scientist in a half a billion-dollar transaction.

CHAPTER 70

ADMINISTRATIVE ASSISTANTS MOVED ABOUT THE room in the Law Offices of Callahan, Latham, and Grimaldi, preparing for the formal closing. The contracts sat on the conference table organized into seven identical portfolios. As per the contingency clause' in the Patent Purchase Agreement, Mr. Callahan previously delivered the test subject's medical assessments to the purchaser for their inspection and approval. They completed the examination and accepted those documents. The Assignment of Patent Rights proceeded forward, culminating in today's assembly allowing all parties to review, sign all forms, and disperse the agreed-upon funds.

The doctor refused to leave Sophia's side, so Mr. Callahan arranged for himself, a para-legal, and a notary public, to go to the hospital so that he could sign the paperwork.

Five buttoned-up attorneys, from the Law Firm of Attwood, Compton, and Harriman, attended, representing a still unknown purchaser. The closing went without a hitch. Wire transfers deposited the funds to a commercial bank, equipped to handle transactions of that nature. Once cleared, Callahan stood, presented the executed instruments, and shook the hands of each of the attorneys as they gathered their belongings and departed.

After they left, the lawyer turned to the young detective and declared, "Well, Nick, that's it, the undisclosed company is now the owner of the patent. What did you think of your first closing?"

"It went pretty quickly. I envisioned it being more complicated, what with the amount of money involved."

"Just like a good old fashion horse trade, they liked the pony, we agreed on a price, they put the cash on the barrel, and we handed them the reins."

He smiled and realized he just witnessed a five hundred and ninety million dollar horse trade. While gathering various documents and placing them in his briefcase, Callahan asked, "Nick, would you care to ride with me to the hospital? I prepared some papers for the Doctor, and I want to present them to him. We can go in my car, after which my driver will drop you off wherever you wish."

"Sure, I want to check in on the progress of Sophia's treatment."

The town-car was at the curb as they exited the building. While riding out onto the Market Street Bridge and across the Schuylkill River, Callahan turned to Nick and disclosed, "Doctor Mauer authorized me to reveal to you his intentions with the proceeds of the patent sale. In my briefcase are prepared papers establishing a scientific non-profit organization. He will donate his share as an endowment to this charitable foundation, providing scholarships and research funding specializing in the study and cure of childhood cancer."

"What?"

"He also advised me to tell you; he's been offered a position with the university, more specifically the Philadelphia Pediatric Hospital as Chief Cancer Researcher Emeritus; however, he realizes he's still a material witness in the on-going investigation, and he informs me he'll cooperate in any capacity that is needed."

"Work at the hospital? That means he'll be working around people. How's he going to handle that?"

"He's told me 'his eyes are open now'; he said being in the hospital observing the dying children has forced him to re-evaluate his scientific endeavors."

"I'm hoping and praying Sophia pulls through her treatment. God forbid, that will devastate him if she doesn't," Nick remarked while pondering the doctor's future.

"Nick, I know from dealing with inventors and creative people for a long time that all of them hold the utmost conviction and belief in their ideas and creations. When I speak to Doctor Mauer, I've never met anyone with more faith and confidence in their formulas and innovations than him."

Nick considered that statement as they continued the drive.

"One other thing, he directed me to draft an irrevocable trust for the Tabbozzi family. He will be the 'grantor,' and they will be the 'beneficiaries.' He's depositing enough money into it so that they will be financially secure for generations."

Nick was amazed at how far the Doctor had come since first meeting him in Erie. The car drove down East Service Drive and stopped before the loading dock entryway door. Mauer was busy at work, checking instruments, by the chamber. They approached, and he was so deep in thought he didn't notice. Callahan tapped him on the shoulder, and he turned to face them, breaking out into a wide smile.

"Nicholas, Mr. Callahan, how nice of you to stop by." With a turn of his head and a glint in his eye, he scanned Callahan's face.

"Everything went as planned; I take it?"

Smiling, the attorney replied, "It went flawlessly."

"I have those documents you requested. I'll present them to you at your convenience. I'll leave you two to talk. I must make an important phone call, excuse me for a moment or two," Callahan stated as he walked away.

Nick advised Mauer, who was still smiling.

"Doc, I'm sorry you had to sell your patent. I had hopes that by doing so, we could identify the corporation and bring them to justice. It's a shame these people own your process and will be able to reproduce it. For what? Money — greed?"

Doctor Mauer continued to smile broadly, and that started to make Nick nervous because he thought he might be having a psychotic episode. Still staring with a grin, he posed a question.

"Nicholas, my dear friend. Do you know how delicate a scientific formula can be?"

Not knowing where the conversation was going, he stayed silent.

"You know, Nicholas, a deviation of a decimal point in an equation. A plus or minus sign interchanged. A DNA genetic code letter transposed. These are but a few of the delicate machinations."

Nick was puzzled, trying to comprehend what the doctor was telling him when suddenly a light went on in his head.

"Doc, are you saying you sold them a phony patent?"

"Nicholas, I'm afraid, when that mysterious corporation attempts to re-create the process, the only commodity they are going to be able to produce will be the most expensive soup in the world," he stated with a chuckle.

Nick thought about that statement, and then asked, "But Doc, won't they spot the difference when they compare your journals from the lab to the patent formula?"

"They will match perfectly," he replied, with a grin on his face.

Standing there with his mouth slightly open, and pondering that he just participated in a five hundred and ninety million dollar scam when a thought came to him, he asked, "Doc, if neither the patent nor the lab copies are authentic, where's the real formula?"

The genius grinned at him with a twinkle in his eye, then raised his index finger, touching his right temple and, in a quiet voice, divulged, "Right here."

Several minutes passed, and he was still digesting the scenario when Mr. Callahan approached. He noticed him and the Doctor smiling at one another when Nick turned to the lawyer and grilled him, "You knew about this? You knew about this — this scam?"

He faced him, and with a slight frown, he declared, "Detective Avner, I have no knowledge of what you speak."

Nick stood there, contemplating, and then inquired, "Yeah, but aren't they going to sue when they find out?"

"Do you think they're going to want to get into a court-room with a lawsuit, in open court, where questions could be posed to them?" Callahan replied.

Nick stood wide-eyed and slack-jawed as he scanned back and forth between the two grinning men; he sighed, slowly shook his head, turned, and walked into the main hospital.

CHAPTER 71

THE HIGHWAY PATROL WAS A specialized and elite
part of the Philadelphia Police Department. They were
a special anti-crime task force and enforced traffic laws in
marked police vehicles and motorcycles throughout the city.

Officers assigned to that unit wore an exclusive shoulder
patch on their right arm embroidered with the distinctive "winged wheel" design surrounded by the words
"Philadelphia Highway Patrol" and the standard Philadelphia
Police Department emblem on their left sleeve.

In the winter months, the uniform of the day was a three-
quarter-length leather coat, including a full Sam Browne
gun belt with the cross strap. The outfit also consisted of
black knee-high cavalry boots, referred to as puttees, and
breeches, instead of regular trousers and shoes.

Topping off the uniform was a 50-Mission crushed hat, in
place of the eight-point police cap. They wore it low on the
forehead, with the visor almost touching their nose. When
off duty, most of the Highway Officers were gregarious and
humorous people, but in the performance of their duties,
they had no sense of humor whatsoever. It was about two
a.m. on Thursday morning, and Highway Patrol Officers
Charlie Spurgeon and John Pike were cruising northbound
on Girard Avenue operating H-28.

As they passed the Twenty-Sixth Police District headquarters at 615 East Girard Avenue, a dark brown Chrysler
with municipal license plates started swerving from one

lane to another. They activated their overhead lights, with Office Spurgeon focusing the spotlight on the driver's side-view mirror. The vehicle came to a stop at Susquehanna and Girard Avenues. H-28 pulled in behind it and stopped with the officers exiting the patrol car and proceeded toward the auto.

One white male in his late forties sat behind the wheel. As Spurgeon approached, the driver rolled down the window, and he asked him for his driver's license and vehicle's registration.

The driver reached into his back pocket, retrieving his wallet. The officer inquired after noticing the municipal tags on the rear of the car earlier, "Do you work for the city?"

"Yeah, I work at L&I. Don't you guys know me? I see youse at city hall all the time," answering with slurred speech, glazed eyes, and liquor breath.

The Highway Patrolman didn't answer but waited for him to produce his identification. After several minutes of fumbling with his wallet, he handed over the documents with the name of Michael Frost printed on the license.

"You been drinking tonight, Mr. Frost?"

"I had a couple of beers with my buddies."

Spurgeon's nostrils flared as a heavy whiff of alcohol hit his nose; he stepped back and instructed the occupant, "Sir, shut the engine down and step out of the vehicle."

"Why I gotta do that? I'm Mickey Frost. You guys know me. I'm an Inspector at L and I."

"Mr. Frost, I'm asking you to exit the vehicle."

With reluctance, he opened the driver's door. While swaying, he rolled out.

"Why the hell are you guys breaking my balls? Do you know who I work for? I work for Councilman Hubbs; you guys'll be walking a beat on the Walt Whitman Bridge if I make a call."

The officer sensing that Frost was becoming loud and boisterous, attempted to turn him by the arm and place his hands onto the car's roof. The driver shook off the officer's grasp, turned and faced him, and with a violent shove, he pushed Spurgeon, causing him to stumble back into the on-coming traffic lane. Dropping to the ground, he tumbled and came into a sitting position facing westbound on Girard Avenue, where he spotted a tractor-trailer approaching. The driver of the truck caught sight of the downed figure on the blacktop and immediately applied his brakes. In a cloud of smoke and the smell of rubber burning, the rear of the trailer fishtailed. The vehicle screeched to a stop within a foot of the seated officer who had his hands up, his head turned, and his eyes shut tight, waiting for the end.

The only way to describe Officer John Pike was massive, and for as huge as he was, he was twice as quiet. He let Spurgeon do all the talking during interactions with the public. If it weren't for his immense stature, a person wouldn't be aware he was in the room. In his early days, that giant was a professional wrestler competing at the old Arena in West Philadelphia, where he fought such notables as Bruno Sammartino.

Pike snapped his gaze towards Frost, and with a cat-like move, he pounced on the cowering man grabbing him by the collar with his enormous left hand. His right hand latched onto Mickey's belt buckle, and with one smooth and powerful thrust, he elevated him, straight above his head, keeping his body parallel to the ground.

Spurgeon, back on his feet, quickly approached his partner and yelled out, "Put him down, John. I'm okay. I'm okay."

Officer Pike realizing that his partner was uninjured, walked the elevated man around to the front of the vehicle and gently lowered him onto the hood. The officers placed him in handcuffs and stood him up. The drunk and dazed male swayed as a 26th District wagon arrived and transported him to East Detective Division to process the aggravated assault on police charge.

Officer Spurgeon started to feel a little light-headed, just realizing how close he came to becoming roadkill as he turned to his partner and expressed, "Thanks John, for grabbing that guy."

Due to his stature, Pike looked down at his partner and declared, "I thought you were dead."

"Yeah, me too."

After calming down, they began to investigate the vehicle. The engine was still running, and as Spurgeon reached in to shut down the ignition and retrieve the keys, he spotted on the floor sticking out from under the driver's side seat what appeared to be a VHS videocassette tape. Recovering the item, he took it out of the car to inspect it further in the light. On the outer surface was a sticker with the date of December 24, 1991. He wasn't exactly sure what he may have found, but he remembered his conversation with Nick out at the hospital. Before responding to East Detectives to process the arrest, they decided to stop by Major Crimes first.

Detective Warner was working late on reports when they entered the headquarters. After explaining the incident, they showed Chuck what they found. He led them into a squad-briefing room where a video cassette player and a TV sat on a wall shelf. Once the tape was in the machine, he hit the play button, and on the screen appeared the inside of a massive room containing multiple scientific instruments and equipment. One of which was the chamber that was now presently located at the Pediatric Hospital. The picture also included a marked police vehicle, with the numerals "178" painted on its side.

Inside was Officer Thomas Tabbozzi slumped unconscious behind the wheel. Standing next to the car were City Councilman Ronald Hubbs and Gifford Bennett, the CEO of Swarthmore Holdings. Bennett's left hand was on the vehicle's roof; he was hunching over slightly, looking in. The tape ended with four unidentified males, who appeared to be a security function for the lab, rolling the auto back into a twenty-foot shipping container.

"Holy shit, we got 'em," Chuck blurted out upon seeing the images on the screen.

"I gotta call Nick down here," he yelled while heading back to his office.

Abby and Nick were relaxing on the couch, watching a show, when a phone ringing broke the mood.

"Ah, crap, I wonder who that is," he mumbled as he rose and headed toward the kitchen to grab the wall phone. His hand grasped the receiver, and he answered, "Hello."

An excited and loud voice was on the other end, "Nick, you gotta get in here right away!"

"Chuck, what's going on?"

"Nicky, you ain't gonna friggin' believe this, we got 'em, we got 'em, Nicky."

After a moment, the detective calmed down and explained the circumstance of the arrest, and evidence recovery, describing how the tape showed Hubbs and Bennett in the lab with Tommy and the police car. Nick told him he was on his way and hung up.

"Nick, what is it? What's wrong?" Abby said as he ran up the stairs, changed clothes, and headed out the door.

"Abbs, we got it, we got the break in the case, I gotta go, I'll call you and explain everything, first chance I get," he proclaimed while he rushed out the door.

CHAPTER 72

TYPEWRITERS CLACKING, HALF-SMOKED CIGA-RETTES BURNING into the edges of the desks or dangling from the lips of men with a purpose were what met Nick at the door of MCU headquarters. The sergeant notified the lieutenant, who ordered all investigators to respond to the unit.

His heart was beating fast, and his senses were wide awake as Chuck guided him into the squad room to the tape player.

"We got 'em cold, Nicky, wait till you see this," he eagerly declared as he hit the play button.

While watching the playback, rage rose as he felt his temples pound. He thought to himself, *There was my friend, helpless, in the hands of multiple scum bags.*

From their facial expressions, he imagined they thought of Tommy and his fate as only a means to an end.

He calmed himself, knowing he had work to do. They decided to have Mickey Frost, transported from East Detective Division, directly to Major Crimes, for interview and interrogation.

Nick made a call to the Police Chemical Lab to determine the outcome of the comparison for the substance found on Bennett's pen and the roof of RPC-178.

A technician answered and stated, "We completed the analysis. Do you want me to send you the report?"

"Just tell me the results now, and I'll have an officer pick up the hard copy a little later."

"The substance detected on the submitted item was identified as 'microalga scenedesmus rubescens'...the same material recovered from RPC-178, a complete and positive match."

"Alright, thanks."

Lieutenant Tricoste arrived and started directing the investigation. Detectives pounded out reports and prepared affidavits on typewriters. Several FBI agents arrived, and the MCU supervisors briefed them on the evidence they would need to compose the federal court orders and subpoenas.

Mickey Frost arrived at Major Crimes by 2603-Wagon, and they placed him in an interview room. They began the interrogation by reading him his Miranda Warnings, at which time he indicated that he understood them and waived them. Nick started the questioning.

"Mickey, what do you know about the lab and the experiment?"

"I don't know nothing about nothing," he replied, slouched in the chair with folded arms staring down at the table.

"Hey Mickey, you do know that you're going to be arrested for the attempted murder of a police officer. We also got you on multiple shakedowns while working as an "L" and "I" inspector.

"Bullshit, you ain't got nothing."

"Oh yeah, we do Mickey, and we got you doin' it at the direction and in collusion with a city administrator...and that constitutes violations under the 'Rico Act.' And when we tack on the kidnapping, that means life."

He stared up from the desk, eyeballing the investigators with contempt as he answered, "Screw you."

"You're going away for life, Mickey, but that's okay; from what we hear, jail could be the safest place for you. Especially with all that big money you owe the mob. Well, at least for a little while — until somebody gets to you in there."

He remained silent, sitting with folded arms as he scowled at the officers. Frost refused to make any more statements, so they left the room, letting him think about it for a while. In twenty minutes, he began banging on the holding room door, calling out that he wanted to talk. The two detectives were standing outside the one-way glass, looking in as he started yelling.

Chuck turned to Nick and demanded, "Pay up."

Nick shook his head, pulled a ten-dollar bill from his pocket, and handed it to his partner, who took it with a smile and remarked, "I told you, he wasn't as stupid as he looks."

Mickey Frost provided a thirty-page deposition, outlining his involvement, along with Hubbs' and Bennett's connection in the case.

By eight a.m., the FBI Task Force secured subpoenas for the financial records of the City Pension Fund, as well as search warrants for the offices of Swarthmore Holdings and the home and office of Councilman Ronald Hubbs. Lieutenant Tricoste assigned Major Crimes detectives to accompany Special Agents of the FBI and assist in serving the various federal warrants.

Although the crime of 'Kidnapping' could fall under state law, the fact that a police officer was the victim, the Philadelphia Police Department and the FBI decided to pursue the charges and bring prosecution federally. The 'Task Force' supervisors assigned various Stakeout units to the warrant team to enter the locations and secure the scenes.

It was about nine a.m. on a Friday morning when one of the teams arrived at the office of Councilman Ronald Hubbs. He was not there; only his assistant and secretary were present at the time of the raid. The investigators seized numerous items and documents. At the same time, another team was searching his home in Roxborough. They discovered and confiscated a safe, along with various paperwork.

FBI agents from the 'Forensic Accounting Division' responded to the offices of the City Pension Fund. Although they had a court order, the administrators were very cooperative in producing any records or statements they requested. The agents entered the offices of Swarthmore Holdings, and they found CEO Gifford Bennett in a meeting with his attorney on a matter unrelated to the case. He was stunned that city detectives and FBI agents were in his office with a warrant. His lawyer immediately advised his client to remain quiet and not to interfere. Gifford Bennett sat at his desk fuming but silent. Documents and statements were confiscated and taken away. Officers were also at his townhouse on Pine Street, with his butler/valet acting as a witness to the search. After the detectives executed the warrants and finished, they transported all the evidence to their field office at 600 Arch Street for processing and evaluation.

By three p.m., the FBI secured a signed court order to freeze all the funds of Swarthmore Holdings, and the personal accounts of Gifford Bennett and Ronald Hubbs. That action affected Bennett immensely because, psychologically, he possessed no other identity other than his assets. With all the police and federal activity occurring within the city, the press got wind of it and responded in force. They swamped the PAB and the Federal Building with swarms of reporters.

At five-thirty p. m., the FBI Agent in Charge, along with Philadelphia Police investigators, held a news conference outside the Federal Building and made the following announcement,

"Today, members of the Federal Bureau of Investigation in conjunction with the Philadelphia Police Major Crimes Unit, conducted raids and executed search warrants at the home and office of City Councilman Ronald Hubbs, and the offices of Swarthmore Holdings LLC, as well as the home of its CEO Gifford Bennett, and the offices of the Philadelphia City Pension Fund. Evidence and documents were recovered and confiscated, and as of three p.m. this date, the court ordered all business and personal assets frozen on the two subjects, previously mentioned."

After the statement, the Agent in Charge fielded multiple questions from the press.

"What crimes are they suspected of committing?"

"Kidnapping of a Philadelphia Police Officer, as well as extensive financial offenses. We will be presenting evidence to a federal grand jury to seek indictments."

The story was the top headline throughout the country that evening. Every news outlet was covering the events. As word got out about the impending arrests for major financial crimes, numerous clients and investors with Swarthmore Holdings called the FBI regarding their investments. Later an FBI Forensic Accounting review discovered thirty-three million dollars embezzled from the City Pension Fund. They uncovered a "Ponzi" type investment scam conducted by Swarthmore Holdings involving hundreds of investors and millions of dollars.

At eight a. m., the following morning, Nick and Chuck were still at Major Crimes headquarters, completing various reports outlining the events of the day. The case had been long, tiring, and frustrating over the past five years, but tonight the finish line was within sight.

Running high on adrenaline, nicotine, and caffeine for the last forty-eight hours, they felt awake and alert. They were happy concluding a never-ending investigation with the same feeling a cop got on the final day of the midnight to eight shift. The end of another "Long Last Out."

CHAPTER 73

CITY COUNCILMAN RONALD HUBBS STAYED at his girlfriend's apartment, located at Eighteenth and Manning Streets, south of Rittenhouse Square, on Thursday night. She was on a business trip, so he had the place to himself. On Friday morning, he awoke late and leisurely prepared to go to City Hall, when the phone rang. His assistant informed him that the FBI was searching his office. Hubbs hung up and decided the best course of action would be to stay in place until he could gather further information. The TV media reported nothing regarding the raids. At about six p.m., a bulletin interrupted the program. The reporter presented a summary of the news conference held at the Federal Building earlier. Ronald turned white when he heard his name announced.

A bottle of thirty-year-old scotch was in his trembling hands as he poured himself a tumbler. The whiskey didn't help, as he talked to himself, trying to keep his head and think. No one was aware of his location, and he couldn't do anything at that time, so he laid low and stayed inside for the next two days. All the banks were closed and wouldn't be open until Monday morning. Just like when he was a kid, collecting soda bottles and redeeming them at the local candy store for pennies and nickels, Ronald learned young to stash some away behind the back shed for a rainy day, which was why he kept a safe deposit box, containing fifty thousand dollars, and a passport.

The weekend went by slow. Deep in thought and worry, he stayed in the study. In the early morning hours, after a restless night, he looked outside, and the weather was rainy, cold, and foggy. He decided to make his way on foot, wearing dark pants and jacket with a hood, pulled tight around his face, glasses to alter his appearance, and walked with his head down. The bank, located on the other side of the street at Eighteenth and Locust, was opening soon, and he wanted to be there when they unlocked the doors. Down in the lobby, he peered out the door as sheets of raindrops bounced off the sidewalk. Pulling the hood up, he stepped out of the building and proceeded into the storm, walking north on Eighteenth Street.

The store owners in Philadelphia said that they had a silent partner in their pocket up in City Council. Every time the politicians needed more money for some special interest project, they always seemed to bleed the small businessman. She was in the sandwich shop early that rainy Monday morning, as usual at five a.m., "running a rag over the counter" when she came upon a statement from the City of Philadelphia Department of License and Inspections. The bill was for the annual renewal of her business certificate, which was due that day.

"Madon, I forgot to send this in," she muttered, a little flustered.

She decided to drive up, pay in person, and pick up a receipt. Her Lou always told her to "get a receipt." So, she took five hundred and fifty-two dollars cash out of an old cigar box she kept hidden under the deli case, and slipped it into her pocketbook, pulled on her coat, and locked up. She wrote a small sign and taped it to the door window stating that the store would open late that day. In her car and working her way through South Philly's streets, she turned left onto northbound Eighteenth Street.

The wipers were not keeping up with the torrential downpour, and the visibility was poor. The windshield fogged, making her reach over and fumble for the defroster. She found the control; a blast of warm air blew out of the vents and circulated off the window and dashboard. Without warning, the air current dislodged the picture of her beloved husband Lou from its scotch-taped location midway on the dash and flew about the interior.

"Ah, madon, Lou, where you goin?" talking to the picture as she tried to grab it in mid-air and keep her eyes on the driving.

Unable to latch onto the photo, it settled down under the passenger seat. She leaned over to her right side, reaching, attempting to retrieve it. Her eyes diverted for a moment, from the road down to the floor. The car stayed straight, and she sensed a slight jolt and two rises of the auto, like going over a speed bump.

She recovered Lou's picture, held it up, kissed it, and commented, "Ming, wid all da taxes I pay, maybe dey could fix da potholes."

Nonie continued, unaware of the service she just rendered to society. She traveled with a slow and steady pace up the roadway until she got to Market Street, made a right turn, and proceeded towards City Hall.

The shifty councilman made it to the corner of Eighteenth and Rittenhouse Square, where he decided to cross over to the east side. He held his keyring tightly in his right hand, tucked inside his jacket pocket. Misjudging the curb's height caused him to reach out from his pocket to maintain his balance. The keyring containing his safe deposit box key abruptly flew from his hand and out to the street just past a parked car. Recovering his footing, he stooped to pick them up.

One of the last things that Ronald Hubbs experienced in the world was what could only be described as a "colossal kick in the ass." Now, if that particular "kick" were the only injury he had sustained, he would have survived because the vehicle that hit him was not traveling at high speed. Unfortunately for the councilman, when the car struck him, it knocked him forward onto his chest and stomach, and as he laid prostrate on the blacktop, the auto simply ran over him. The front driver's side tire first, then the rear. He no longer had to worry about the upcoming federal indictments; he faced more significant problems now, as his life-light faded away.

###

The gentleman walked everywhere, refusing to drive or take public transportation. He just liked walking. He was in his mid-seventies and magnificent physical shape for a man of his age. Impeccably dressed, in a black three-piece suit, fedora hat, and on that day, because of the weather, he wore a full length black "Burberrys" trench coat and an open umbrella. At first glance, he appeared to be one of the many "captains of industry" residing in the neighborhood.

Enrique Fernandez was the second son of a middle-class family in Spain. He was well-read and loved to cook, which led to his eventual employment as a butler and gourmet chef. During the past fifty years, he served the Bennett's from their suburban mansion in Chestnut Hill to the Pine Street townhouse owned by Gifford Bennett IV.

He was always punctual for his daily duties, and on that foul weather day, he allowed himself extra time to walk to his place of employment. At just about the time that Ronald Hubbs was "compressed into eternity," ten blocks west, and three north, Mr. Fernandez put the key into the lock of the magnificent townhouse located at 758 Pine Street. When he opened the door, a wave of heat met him immediately in the compact vestibule. The oversized stand-up cast iron radiator was hot to the touch as he tapped it with his index finger. He unlatched the interior door, and a foul odor made the refined gentleman turn his face in a contorted manner.

He was familiar with that particular stench, and he knew what he must do next. His on-the-job experience, in that type of situation, included finding the hanging body of Gifford Bennett III dangling from the library inside the expansive Chestnut Hill manor house many years ago. As he approached the ornate stairwell, he could first see the feet, toes pointing downward, one foot shoeless. As his eyes gradually moved up the body, he observed the familiar sight of the tongue slightly protruding from the blackened face of another Bennett family member.

CHAPTER 74

THE SNOWS OF WINTER MELTED, the flowers of spring bloomed, and the sunshine of summer shone. Nick and Abby were happy, with windows open and radio blasting, enjoying the drive down the shore. They listened to the "oldies" and sang along with most of the songs. As they rolled south on the Atlantic City Expressway, they approached the exit for the Garden State Parkway south, when one of the all-time shore favorites of "Under the Boardwalk" came over the radio. They were harmonizing and laughing together as they attempted to hold the high notes and change pitch throughout the song.

The weather was perfect, sunny with intermittent lofty clouds, the kind that formed pictures in the sky. The tune played out as they approached the Somers Point/Ocean City exit. Nick bore the vehicle right onto the ramp and on down to a small toll booth. As he dropped the coins into the basket, they entered Somers Point, a friendly well-kept residential community of ranch-style houses. As they passed the circle right before what most locals refer to as the Ninth Street Bridge, the light turned green, and they proceeded up onto the roadway. The span was about two miles long and crossed the Great Egg Harbor. The footings were on various small islands in the bay, and as they got nearer to the bay shore of Ocean City, they passed Cow Pens Island, a landmark telling them they were almost across.

They were now on Ninth Street when Abby asked, "Do they know we're coming?"

"Yeah, I called. They said for us to meet them on the beach," Nick answered.

Their excitement increased in anticipation of seeing the ocean again as they made their way through town to Twenty-Ninth Street. He was able to find a parking spot adjoining the entrance. They exited the car, with Nick going directly to the trunk, gathering two folding chairs, a bulky collapsible umbrella, towels, and a cooler. They walked the half a block, crossing through the dune, and out onto the hot sand. The beach was warm and sunny, with a slight breeze blowing. Sounds of the waves crashing performed the melody, and the caws of the gulls sang the lyrics of the seashore.

They trudged through the white sand dragging their gear, and in the distance, they could make out three people down by the ocean's edge sitting and digging with colorful plastic shovels and buckets. As they moved closer, a larger male person noticed them, stood, turned, and approached the couple.

Tommy appeared older, not physically aged, just somehow wiser, more reflective. As he trod through the sand, Nick set up the two chairs, and they stood waiting for him to arrive. Abby hugged him and kissed his cheek, and he shook Nick's hand.

She sensed they might want to talk and declared, "I'm going to see what they made," as she strolled off down towards the surf.

They sat in the chairs, staring down toward the two people laboring in the sand.

After several minutes of taking in the sights and sounds, Nick said while looking down at the castle builders, "You're a lucky man — Tommy Tabbs."

With squinting eyes and a smile, he studied his family and nodded in agreement. He reflected, and after a moment, glanced towards Nick, and expressed, "I'm sorry I wasn't there for you when you got shot."

He faced his friend, looking him straight in his eyes, and replied. "Hey, Tommy — you were there — for the whole five years. I remembered everything you taught me from day one."

After studying Nick's face, he stared out to the horizon, and with a contented grin, he considered those words.

"Daddy, come help us build the castle, daddy." A little girl's voice beckoned from down by the water's edge.

"I'll be right there, baby," Tommy called out as he stood from the chair.

He took two steps towards the little girl, stopped, pivoted back, and with a slight hesitation, he professed,

"I'm proud of you — son."

They silently stared at one another for a moment. Tommy then turned, trotted away, and yelled out, "I'm on my way, baby — I'm on my way."

Nick studied his friend as he hurried to his family. From somewhere down the beach, the voice of Dionne Warwick singing "That's What Friends Are For" floated through the air, intermingling with the muffled thunder of the waves and the seabird's call. Listening to the song's lyrics and reflecting on Tommy's words, Nick gazed out to sea with a contented smile and a feeling of tranquility. The world was spinning right again.

The End

CPSIA information can be obtained
at www.ICGtesting.com
Printed in the USA
BVHW070809230321
603188BV00001B/59